Praise

Sailing Toward

"Ride with British Naval Captain Joseph Duncan as he sails the Atlantic in search of enemy French ships while battling treacherous waters, mercurial weather, and ever-shifting winds. Set in 1795, this nautical tale is filled with fierce sea conflicts, military intrigue, and even a bit of romance."

–Katrina Thomas

Sailing Toward the Tempest

Sailing Toward the Tempest

Kent M. Schwendy

Black Rose Writing | Texas

The author grants the final approval for this literary material.

First printing

This is a work of fiction. Names, characters, businesses, places, events, and incidents are either the products of the author's imagination or used in a fictitious manner. Any resemblance to actual persons, living or dead, or actual events is purely coincidental.

ISBN: 978-1-68513-567-6
LIBRARY OF CONGRESS CONTROL NUMBER: 2024946850
PUBLISHED BY BLACK ROSE WRITING
www.blackrosewriting.com

Printed in the United States of America
Suggested Retail Price (SRP) $24.95

Sailing Toward the Tempest is printed in Book Antiqua

*As a planet-friendly publisher, Black Rose Writing does its best to eliminate unnecessary waste to reduce paper usage and energy costs, while never compromising the reading experience. As a result, the final word count vs. page count may not meet common expectations.

Chapter One

Lieutenant Joseph Duncan paused in his pacing along the windward side of the quarterdeck as he came to the rail at its forward limit. A sudden gust of wind caused the ship to heel more sharply at the same moment her nose was passing over a swell. The bow plunged into the sea and shouldered a fountain of spray and spindrift across the larboard side of the ship. Several crew members up forward were drenched and looked at each other, laughing and smiling in camaraderie.

HMS Fidelity was racing along with the wind on her aft larboard quarter. The last cast of the log had revealed her speed to be 9 ½ knots - and that without stud sails or scrapers set. The sea was a glittering expanse of small, choppy whitecaps as far as the eye could see. The air was clear after a brief rainstorm during the night and with the sun behind her, the horizon ahead was a crisp line separating the slightly darker blue of the sea from that of the sky.

Duncan felt the spray as a cool mist against his face, and he couldn't suppress a small smile. This was sailing the way it was meant to be, and he loved it. Perhaps some, maybe most, British officers were stoic or unmoved by these simple pleasures of being at sea, but in his more than ten years in the Navy, Duncan had learned to appreciate these gentler moments - just as he had learned to respect the power of a storm. The sea could be a fickle companion, and you needed to learn to read her moods. Something in the air today portended a change in mood, but it wasn't clear what that would mean.

Glancing forward along the deck, it was hard to argue that the French didn't build beautiful ships. *Fidelity*, then known as *La Fidelité*, had been built at Paimboeuf and was launched by the French and captured by the British within months of the war beginning. She was beautiful and fast, but like most French ships, she was of lighter construction and had less room for stores than a similar British ship. Duncan had heard the gunner, Wendt, and the carpenter, Carson, discussing whether her scantlings were large enough to withstand the repeated recoil from her 24-pounder cannons. Wendt predicted that they would be replaced with 18-pounders within a year and Carson doubted they could wait that long - he reasoned that although French 24-pounders were heavier and threw a larger ball than the British guns, British powder was more powerful. Still, for now, she was fast, powerful, and new. Duncan felt very lucky to be aboard her.

As he looked out at the expanse of empty sea before him, his musings were interrupted by the appearance of the surgeon, Mr. Whitehall, at the forward ladder. He was dressed in his normal all black suit with the bright white neck stock almost blinding in the sunlight. He walked without looking left or right, or up at Duncan, as he passed almost directly under him to enter the captain's cabin below his feet.

Mr. Whitehall was not a close friend, but having spent the last nine months with him as a fellow member of the wardroom made Duncan think he could have at least recognized his existence with a glance or a nod. Pondering this, he was again interrupted, this time by the sound of the ship's bell as five bells in the forenoon watch was struck. Only an hour and a half left in his watch and his mind wandered to what he might do during his brief time off duty. With the first lieutenant sick and second lieutenant off in a prize, Duncan and Lieutenant Williams had been standing watch and watch for the past six days and time off was precious, and often spent asleep.

"Nine knots!" Midshipman Harvey called out from aft as he reeled the string back in from the latest cast.

Duncan looked around at Harvey and in doing so caught the eye of the helmsman, who called out, "West Nor'west and steady, sir."

"Thank you, Jenkins. Keep her thus," Duncan responded, although he didn't really care at that particular moment. With the sea empty in all directions and with no idea where the enemy might be, any direction seemed as good as any other. He sighed and resumed his pacing along the windward railing. Other than the small sloop captured last week, the past three months had been a rather boring cruise. Especially when compared to the phenomenal successes of their previous cruise.

"Permission to mount the quarterdeck, sir?" called out William Christian, the captain's clerk, from a step or two below the deck.

Duncan looked around and called back, "Please do, Mr. Christian." He tried to cover the questioning in his voice. It was unusual for the clerk to be on the quarterdeck, especially when the captain was below.

"Sir, Captain Blackwell's compliments and might you join him in his cabin at your earliest convenience, sir," Mr. Christian stated as he drew near to Duncan. He said it in a voice that was not a whisper, but also not quite what one might consider loud given the sounds of the wind in the rigging. It was almost as if he didn't want to be overheard, but not quite like he was being secretive. This was also odd when passing along a simple message from the captain. Christian had also served him a "sir sandwich", beginning and ending his statement with "sir". For some reason, that bothered Duncan - it always had.

"I shall attend immediately. Mr. Jones, you have the deck until my return."

The master, Mr. Jones, responded from near the log slate where he was inspecting Midshipman Harvey's entries, barely looking up, "Aye, aye, sir. I have the deck."

Duncan walked briskly forward, down the ladder, and back under the quarterdeck toward the captain's cabin. Luckily, he knew the way well because the contrast of the gloom below the deck was impenetrable after the glare of the sun off the wave crests. Christian was following closely behind him without saying anything or walking too closely, almost as a shadow. He slowed as he approached the marine sentry at the door to the captain's cabin.

"Morning, Private Smyth."

"Good morning, sir," the marine responded quietly, before he slammed the butt of his musket against the deck and yelled, "Lieutenant Duncan and the captain's clerk, sir!"

"Enter," came Blackwell's immediate response from within the cabin.

Duncan opened the thin door to the cabin and ducked his head as he walked in, taking his hat off and tucking it under his arm in one motion. If it had been too dark outside and too bright on the deck, the lighting in the cabin was almost perfect. The venetian blinds on the transom windows were adjusted to let in just the right amount of light, and the glare one might have expected was muted by light linen curtains pulled completely across.

The captain's cabins were tastefully, if not elegantly, appointed. The furniture was of obviously high quality, but was rather understated in appearance. It had been selected to withstand the rigors of life at sea and frequent removal to the hold when the decks were cleared for action and this room ceased to exist.

"Have a seat Mr. Duncan. Would you be interested in something to drink? Stanley has almost succeeded in chilling a hock, or you could have a brandy like Mr. Whitehall."

"Thank you, sir. Perhaps just a lemonade if it's not too much trouble. It's quite warm on deck for this early in the day, sir," Duncan responded, as he gently lowered himself into the proffered chair. He glanced at Whitehall and nodded to him as he sat down. Whitehall responded with a thin smile and a tip of his glass as he took a sip of brandy.

"No trouble at all, is it Stanley?" Blackwell said cheerfully as his steward slipped into the pantry and returned with a carafe of lemonade he had already prepared. He poured a glass for Duncan and then placed the carafe on the sideboard alongside a decanter of brandy and an open bottle of wine wrapped in a wet towel to keep it cool. "That will be all for now. I'll call if I need you."

Stanley bowed slightly without saying anything and slipped out the door, quietly closing it behind him.

"Any changes in the weather?" Blackwell questioned.

"No sir, the wind hasn't shifted more than a point since yesterday. It's still occasionally gusty, but not dangerously so. The master says it will likely stay this way until at least tomorrow. After that, he's being rather non-committal."

"Yes, well, Mr. Jones doesn't like to risk his perfect record by making long-range predictions." Blackwell took a sip of his wine and then looked directly at Duncan. "I suppose you know that I didn't ask you down to discuss the weather, so I might as well get on with it."

"Since you've stood more of his watches in the last six months than he has himself, you are well aware of Lieutenant Miller's illness. Mr. Whitehall has informed me that he may not survive the latest bout of the ague and even if he does, he won't be fit for duty for weeks…if not months."

"I cannot expect my ship to perform at its best with the First Lieutenant stuck in the sick bay for heaven knows how long. Lieutenant Henry, you, and Lieutenant Williams have been doing an excellent job, but it's not fair to you or the crew to leave everything up in the air."

"Mr. Whitehall has certified Lieutenant Miller as unfit for duty and I have decided that as of tomorrow, I will relieve him from his position. Lieutenant Henry will assume the position of first lieutenant and you will move up to second with Williams as third."

"Since Henry is off in a prize, you will be acting first lieutenant until his return. Which, come to think of it, you've been doing unofficially, anyway. However, as such, I would ask that you nominate a midshipman for temporary assignment as an acting lieutenant." Blackwell paused and waited for Duncan to respond.

"I would recommend Mr. Cole, sir. He's the senior, and he's earned it," Duncan responded immediately. He had never thought about it before, but Cole seemed to be the natural choice.

Blackwell nodded and continued, "I concur. More important than being senior, Mr. Cole is deserving." He looked past Duncan and spoke a bit louder, "Will, write up a fair copy of orders for Mr. Cole as acting lieutenant, same effective date, etc. That will be all for now."

"Aye, aye, sir," Christian responded, as he stood, gathered up his papers, and headed out of the cabin. Duncan had forgotten he was even in the room until the exchange.

"So, a toast to new opportunities," Blackwell said as he raised his glass.

"Joy to you on your promotion, Joseph," Whitehall added as he, too, raised his glass.

"Thank you, sir. Thank you, Alfred," Duncan said, before they all took a drink.

Whitehall drained his brandy and stood up. "If you'll excuse me, sir, I really should get back to my duties."

Blackwell nodded, and Whitehall patted Duncan on the shoulder as he walked past, deposited his empty glass on the sideboard, and left the cabin.

"I should be getting back to the deck, too, sir, if you'll excuse me. And thank you again, sir."

Duncan started to get up, but Blackwell stopped him by raising his hand and saying, "One more moment, if you don't mind, Joseph."

He couldn't recall the captain ever using his Christian name and immediately sat back down.

Blackwell finished his wine and put the glass down gently before speaking. "When I sent George Henry off in the prize, I included a recommendation with my report to the admiral requesting that he be promoted to commander and given the sloop. I have every expectation that the admiral will honor my request."

Duncan's mind began to race as Blackwell paused for a moment. This would mean that only he and Rupert Williams would remain and there would be two new lieutenants. Duncan didn't particularly like Henry and had barely gotten to know Miller, but who knew what it would be like with new officers in the wardroom. He realized Blackwell had continued talking and quickly focused his attention again.

"I'll not ask for a new First. I'd like you to take that position and I've also informed the admiral of that in my report."

Duncan was stunned for a moment and then managed to stammer, "Thank you, sir."

Blackwell chuckled. "You're quite capable and well deserving of it, Joseph. You've been doing the job lately, anyway. The least I can do is make it official."

"Thank you, sir. I don't really know what to say."

"You don't need to say anything. I'd like you and Lieutenant Williams to join me for dinner tonight. I'm sure Mr. Jones will be willing to stand watch with our new Lieutenant Cole to allow the two of you time for a leisurely meal."

"That sounds lovely, sir. Thank you, again."

Blackwell stood to indicate the meeting was over and offered his hand to Duncan. Shaking his hand, Blackwell said, "I'll make the announcement at noon sights, when it becomes official. Perhaps you could tell Rupert before then, so he's not taken by surprise…of course, I'll not mention that part about George, just yet, so let's keep that between us, for now, eh?" Blackwell winked and Duncan smiled and nodded, before leaving the cabin.

•   •   •

On any day clear enough to make out the sun, noon was anticipated by all the midshipmen, several petty officers, the master, and most of the officers standing with sextants by the quarterdeck rail. As the hour approached, they would all watch anxiously through their sextants for the exact moment when the sun reached its highest point in the sky - local solar noon. At this point, they would lock the angle above the horizon and write it down on a slate or piece of paper. A few calculations later and they would have the latitude of the ship. The time difference between noon on the ship and noon at the Royal Observatory in England provided the basis for calculating the longitude. For this reason, the ship's clock and the sextants were treated with great care and respect.

Noon was also significant on a Royal Navy ship because, by long tradition (and naval regulations) the new day began at noon, rather than at midnight. More than one drunken fight had begun between navy and army officers over the navy being twelve hours behind on the start of every day - and the many reasons that could be offered to explain why.

Besides the obvious issues related to correctly calculating the math, the angle was measured from a pitching and rolling deck against an often-fuzzy horizon. Despite this, they often were very close in their calculations and in case of disagreement, the master was considered to have the correct answer. For the officers, it was a point of pride in seamanship to get the correct answer as quickly as possible and besides bragging rights, there were sometimes small side wagers unofficially riding on the outcome. For the midshipmen, it was part of their training.

Today, there was no side bet between Joseph and Rupert Williams. Both were too tired from their duties and too excited about the announcement the captain would be making soon, to do anything more than make their calculations and quietly compare the results. The midshipmen and master's mates, however, were scribbling nervously and hoping they would at least be close.

As usual, the master finished first and stood waiting for a few minutes before choosing his target and firing his first shot. "So, Mr. Webb, are we still somewhere in the Baltic Sea, as you predicted yesterday?"

"Umm...no, sir. We seem to have moved west by a most prodigious amount," Midshipman Webb responded.

"Cheeky little snot, isn't he?" Rupert said quietly to Duncan as they stood a few feet away, pretending not to watch and listen.

"Aye, but the master will have him kissing the gunner's daughter if he pushes too far."

Williams chuckled, "I seem to remember several occasions having my backside tenderized with a cane while I hugged a cannon. How about you? You were probably Mr. Perfect Midshipman, never punished for anything, eh?"

This brought an outright laugh from Duncan, but no other response. Meanwhile, the master was checking Webb's calculations and looking at the young man. With a huge smile, he slapped him on the shoulder.

"Congratulations Mr. Webb, we have made it all the way to the Pacific Ocean. I suppose if we average your last two estimates, they'd at least put us near here."

Webb hung his head, but mostly to hide a smirk that would likely be pushing a bit too far, and mercifully, the master moved on. "Mr. O'Toole, for the honor of all Ireland, is there a chance you might know where we are?"

And so it went. A minor variation on the drama that played out every day as the master tried, with varying success, to drill the art and science of navigation into the sometimes thick skulls of the future leaders of the King's Navy. *God save us all*, Duncan thought, *Was I like that myself?*

"Capt'n comin', sir," Jenkins quietly warned the two lieutenants who had still been watching the master torment the midshipmen.

As it was now officially Williams' watch, he turned to greet the captain while Duncan moved to the lee side of the quarterdeck and out of the area reserved for the captain alone whenever on deck. Passing the wheel, Duncan thanked Jenkins for the warning. It was a sign of a happy ship that the crew willingly helped the officers.

Blackwell nodded to Williams and Duncan as he mounted the quarterdeck and then asked in a loud voice, "Mr. Jones, how has Mr. Cole done today?"

"Extremely well, as usual, sir. Mr. Cole is diligent in his calculations and, in my opinion, shall be an excellent navigator," the master replied in a somewhat stilted tone that made Duncan think this had been rehearsed.

Blackwell smiled and said, "Lieutenant Williams, be so kind as to have the crew assemble aft, so I may address them."

The word was passed, and the crew quickly crowded below the quarterdeck. Some climbed partway up the shrouds or stood atop cannons for a better view.

"I won't keep you from your grog for long," Blackwell began. There were some polite chuckles from the crew, but the joke may have had too much truth to be amusing. "As you are all no doubt aware, Lieutenant Miller has been ill for some time now. Effective immediately, I have removed him from his position on this ship. He will return to Antigua with us as supernumerary." Blackwell paused for a moment while a murmur went through the assembled crew. None of them had really gotten to know the first lieutenant, but a King's Officer being removed from a posting was serious business.

"Therefore, also effective immediately, Lieutenant Henry will assume the position of first lieutenant, Lieutenant Duncan will be second, and Lieutenant Williams will be third." Blackwell paused again, as there was more murmuring. Many captains would have enforced silence while he spoke, but Blackwell felt that the crew should be given some latitude to react to the news.

"That leaves us with the position of fourth lieutenant open. Mr. Cole is hereby appointed acting lieutenant, until such time as we receive a replacement fourth, or he passes his exam and is confirmed." Cole was generally liked by the crew, so there was another bit of murmuring and quite a few smiles from men in his division.

Cole was too stunned to smile and stood with his mouth open, staring at the captain. Midshipman Webb was standing next to him and said, "You might want to close your mouth before you catch a fly, or the captain rethinks his decision…sir." Webb and Cole had been close friends, but this would be the last time Webb could poke fun at him. "Congratulations, sir." He held out his hand to Cole, who shook it as his face finally split into a huge grin.

Blackwell held his hand up to stop the discussions among the crew. "As a celebration is in order, we shall splice the mainstay." This was met with a hearty cheer from the crew, as it meant the captain had just ordered a double measure of rum for them. "Dismiss the crew and pipe up spirits!"

•   •   •

Duncan stood in front of a small mirror, adjusting his neck stock as Williams opened the thin deal partition to his cabin and stepped into the common area of the wardroom. "You look to be a rather shabby acting first lieutenant, if you ask me."

"I don't recall asking you, and you're not all that spiffy yourself. Were you sleeping in your uniform again?"

"Ah, but for a fortnight in date of rank, I'd be over you."

"Yet more proof that God is just, Rupert," Duncan said as he stopped fiddling with his neck stock. He turned, smiling at his friend, wishing he could tell him about the likelihood of Henry being promoted out of the ship. Still, it might not happen, so better to keep his mouth shut - otherwise, Williams would never let him live it down.

"We really should see about new uniforms back in port. Between the sun fading the fabric and the salt dulling the gold, we don't look nearly as dapper as we should for the next ball at the Governor's."

Duncan laughed. "What makes you think you'll get an invitation?"

"No need to be nasty, Joseph," Williams jokingly chided. "Speaking of invitations, I believe we should head up to dinner so as not to be late. I suppose you get to enter first, Your High and Mightiness, so I have a better chance of being late. Is anyone else going to be there, or am I to give the toast to the King? It's been a while since I've been the junior at a gathering."

As they started out of the wardroom, with Duncan leading the way, he asked, "Is there ever a time that you don't complain?" But in fairness, it seemed like no one he knew could roll with the punches the way Rupert did. He often complained, but always in a joking manner, and Duncan couldn't recall him ever being in a truly bad mood.

It was just the three of them for dinner and Blackwell was a perfect host, keeping the conversation moving along by asking questions and telling stories in equal measure, so everyone had a chance to eat and listen, as well as speak. To signal the end of an enjoyable dinner, he said, "Well, again, I must apologize for the fare this evening. This late in a cruise, I'm afraid my supplies are rather low and there's little more to work with than standard rations."

"It was quite delicious, sir, and the company made it thus," Williams said with a perfectly straight face while Duncan tried to suppress a smile. The ingredients were only part of the problem. Stanley might be a good servant, but he was a fairly terrible cook.

"Thank you, Rupert, but I would prefer you not lie to me. Now, I believe you have the next watch, so perhaps you should go relieve Lieutenant Cole and I'll just have a quick word with Joseph."

Williams smiled, wiped his face, and stood to leave. "I really did enjoy the company, sir."

Blackwell chuckled, "So did I, Rupert. So did I."

After Williams had left, Blackwell asked, "How do we stand for supplies?"

Duncan guessed that Blackwell already knew the answer, and that this was probably a test. "We're fairly well set for water and firewood, having resupplied at the island. However, we're down to about three weeks' rations of meat and perhaps four of biscuit and peas. The cheese is all but gone and the purser will likely be talking to you about substitutions for the next banyan day."

"Yes, as I thought. No doubt the men won't mind having meat instead of cheese, but that means it won't last even three weeks." The captain paused and drank the last of his port wine. "I suppose it's time to end this cruise. We're already into hurricane season so we shouldn't look forward to another anytime soon. It's unlikely there'll be any convoys this late, anyway. If we don't sight anything by noon tomorrow, we'll start back to Antigua, Joseph."

"Aye, aye, sir," Duncan responded with the standard naval answer. It usually worked well when you weren't sure what to say.

"I'll see you in the morning, then. Call me if I'm needed."

"Aye, sir. Goodnight." Duncan put his wineglass on the table, stood, and left. Closing the door behind him, he caught a glimpse of Stanley entering from the pantry to clean up. *I hope he's a better servant than a cook*, he thought.

●   ●   ●

Williams had the watch the next morning, but Duncan was still on deck after completing the ritual of changing the officer of the watch when the captain came up. It was not quite light yet.

"Good morning, gentlemen," Blackwell said as he approached. "Have the men go to quarters and send the lookouts aloft."

"Aye, aye, sir," Williams responded. Every day at war, the ship greeted the dawn ready to fight in case the receding darkness revealed an enemy. Cannons were loaded and rumbled across the deck into position in a well-trained, almost monotonous fashion. At night, the lookouts stood on deck since the added height of the masts did little in the darkness to help them see anything, and made it easier for them to sleep without being caught.

A few minutes later, the darkness turned gray and continued to brighten as the stars dimmed and disappeared. Suddenly, it was bright enough to see clearly. They were still alone on the great expanse of ocean.

"Sir," the master addressed Blackwell, "on this heading we may raise Isla Mona or Isla Saona off Hispaniola today - presuming the wind holds."

"Perhaps we'll bump into our Spanish allies then," Blackwell responded.

The master snorted, "I'd not trust the Dagos further than I can spit into the wind, Captain."

Blackwell smiled, "Come now, Mr. Jones. I called them our allies. I never said I trusted them. I'm going down for my breakfast. Perhaps you and Lieutenant Duncan might join me, and we can discuss our course."

"That would be my pleasure, sir."

"Good, then let's head down. Lieutenant Duncan, will you be joining us?"

"Aye, sir. I'd especially relish a cup of coffee."

"I suppose we might even send a cup up for Lieutenant Williams, as his duties will keep him from joining us," Blackwell commented as they walked toward the ladder leading down from the quarterdeck.

"That would be most kind, sir," Williams said, happy to have not been forgotten.

•   •   •

Later that morning, Duncan was on deck - although again it was not his watch. The master was there, as well, and they were standing near each other on the leeward side of the quarterdeck along with Acting Lieutenant Cole, who had the watch. The captain was pacing the weather side of the quarterdeck, apparently deep in thought.

The master looked at his watch, snapped it shut and said, "Weather's goin' to turn on us tonight - tomorrow morning at the latest. The glass has already started to drop and there's something strange about the air."

"So, we'll have the wind in our teeth as we head back to Antigua," Cole half asked and half commented.

"Aye, it'll be in our teeth if we can stand it, or we may have to run a bit before we can make our way," the master responded.

"Well, if it doesn't turn until tomorrow, we'll at least be closer. How long do you expect the blow to last, Mr. Jones?" Duncan asked as he continued to look out at the sea; except perhaps for a bit of a swell, it looked pretty much as it had yesterday. *Yes*, he thought to himself, *the ship definitely feels like she's riding more of a swell than yesterday.*

"Oh, I wouldn't expect it to last very long. Aside from hurricanes, squalls in the tropics tend to come and go quickly," Blackwell said, as he approached them. None of them had noticed him crossing the deck, and they were somewhat startled. "May I join you?"

"Of course, sir," Duncan said. "It is, after all, your ship."

Blackwell smiled as Cole and the master moved apart enough to let the captain step against the rail between them. "So, Mr. Jones, you feel the storm approaching as well?"

"Aye, sir, I feel it in my bones."

"And you're sure that's not just rheumatism?" the captain said in a playful tone.

The master chuckled, "It might be a bit of that, as well, sir, but I'd bet my grog there's a storm coming."

"Yes, I feel it. Do you think our hunting luck will change, as well? Perhaps we should turn about now and start back before the wind freshens more," Blackwell said, addressing the group at large.

"There's little worry of a lee shore unless the winds come around from the south. Seems we might as well press on a bit more and perhaps see our friends the Dons," Duncan said, partially to get a rise out of the master.

"I've no interest in seeing the Spanish, but I agree with the lieutenant. We might as well continue on," he grumbled.

"And what say you, Lieutenant Cole?" Blackwell asked.

"I'm inclined to agree with the master and Lieutenant Duncan, sir. To be honest, a bit more with the master, sir."

Blackwell laughed, "It seems there is little love aboard this ship for our Spanish brothers-in-arms. It's decided, then. We'll carry on until noon."

Just as he finished speaking, a gust of wind hit the ship, causing her to roll to leeward. Duncan grabbed the rail to steady himself as he heard a crack from above, like the firing of a musket, as a line parted from the strain. The ship was still heeling over as the sounds of a sail violently flapping loose followed the crack and mixed with the twang of other lines stretching to their breaking point.

Something flew near Lieutenant Cole's head and he instinctively ducked, although it had already missed him. There was a sickening thud as a wooden block crashed into the captain's head and he crumpled to the ground. Lieutenant Cole quickly kneeled at his side as Duncan and the master began to yell out commands.

"Helmsman, put her before the wind. Hands aloft to take in the mizzen. Afterguard - braces, bring that yard back around. Mr. Jones, have a relieving tackle rigged," Duncan directed as *Fidelity* righted herself and began to respond to the change in rudder and move before the wind. The sail was still flapping, but already men were moving into position to wrestle it back into control.

Duncan looked down and saw that Cole was next to the captain, easing him into a more natural position on the deck. There was blood coming from the captain's nose and a small pool of blood was forming on the deck next to his head, where the wooden pulley had struck him. In an emergency, the ship was more important than any man aboard - even the captain. At sea, a delay in reaction could turn an emergency into a crisis. The crew was responding fantastically, and amid the apparent chaos, there was, in fact, order and structure as each man moved quickly to perform his role and to restore control and repair the damage to the rigging. There was little more Duncan could do for the ship now that it was in the hands of the petty officers who knew their duties. He called out, "Mr. Webb, my compliments to the surgeon, and he is to attend the captain on the quarterdeck immediately."

"I'm here," Whitehall announced as he stepped onto the deck, followed by Midshipman O'Toole.

Cole said, "I sent for him, sir." He stood as Whitehall kneeled beside Blackwell and lifted one eyelid and then the other. He felt for a pulse in the captain's neck and put his ear over his lips to check his breathing. He then gently probed the wound on his head and pushed aside some of the hair matted with blood.

Whitehall looked up at Duncan. "Get some men to take him down to the orlap. His skull is fractured, but I can't tell how badly until I get him cleaned up. I may have to operate to relieve the pressure. I'll send word if he regains consciousness, but I wouldn't expect that for a while, at least. It's best in these situations if he doesn't, since I can do my work more easily."

"Thank you, Mr. Whitehall. I know he's in good hands." Duncan said this a bit louder than necessary, hoping it would help to reassure the crew. Then softer, he added, "Take good care of him, Alfred. Mr. O'Toole, accompany Mr. Whitehall and bring me any updates he provides."

"Aye, aye, sir," O'Toole responded, as several crewmen gently lifted the captain and started forward with his limp body.

The lookout yelled down from his perch atop the mainmast, "Deck there! Sail ho. Fine on the starboard bow. Looks to be a warship by the topsails."

Chapter Two

"Mr. Cole, take a glass up and get a closer look." Until his promotion to acting lieutenant, Cole had been the midshipman in charge of signals. As a result, he was experienced with focusing on distant ships with a telescope and picking out details. It would be no easy task in the maintop, with the mast rotating through dizzying circles.

Cole calmly selected a telescope from the rack by the binnacle, slung it over his shoulder, stepped up to the railing, and pulled himself onto the shrouds on the windward side of the ship. He adjusted the sling and started to climb. Without thinking, he grabbed the shrouds while stepping on the ratlines. He had learned through years at sea and thousands of times climbing that on the windward side, you were pressed against the shrouds rather than having the wind trying to tug you off. The ratlines were horizontal lines between the shrouds and were convenient to step on, but being thinner, were more likely to break. Hanging onto the shrouds provided a measure of safety in case a foot suddenly had no support.

All of this was second nature now - just like not choosing the signal telescope before climbing. Although it was by far the strongest and best telescope on the ship, it was too long and had too narrow a field of view to be used in these conditions from the maintop - some hundred feet above the deck.

Cole made it to the point where the shrouds went under the top to attach to the mast at the step where the lower and middle sections of the mast joined together. He waited for the right motion of the ship and reached backwards and up to grasp the next set of shrouds, where they were held out by the top. For an agonizing second, his feet hung in midair as he pulled himself to the next level and started climbing again.

The process was repeated as he reached the point where the middle section joined the top section of the mast. Pulling himself up, he noticed the lookout shift aside to make room. Cole was a bit out of breath from the climb, and he nodded to the lookout as he unslung the telescope from his left shoulder.

"Welcome to the best view in the ship, sir," the lookout said. He pointed with a calloused finger to a white smudge on the horizon and said, "There she be, sir, and I'm thinking there might just be another sail beyond."

Cole nodded again and slid the telescope open and lifted it to his eye. With his arm wrapped around the shrouds, he fought to control his breathing as he tried to find the distant ship. Finally, it swam into view, and he adjusted the telescope to bring it into focus. They had gained on it quite a bit while he had climbed, and it was clearly a warship. There were definitely more sails beyond.

He spoke for the first time while still looking through the glass, "Good eyes, Carlson." He didn't see the broad smile split the lookout's face in reaction to both the compliment and having an officer call him by name. Cole wasn't thinking about that, either. Captain Blackwell expected his officers to maintain discipline, but also expected the crew to be treated as humans. It's what Cole had learned, and he did it without thinking. That's what training does. It makes you act and react in predicable ways without having to think. Cole was lucky to have received the training he had - but of course, he wasn't thinking about that, either.

He studied the ships for a few more minutes. Accuracy was important now, speed less so. They were miles away downwind and wouldn't be within range of the cannons for a long time. *Fidelity* had the wind gauge and could control the encounter, so the information he provided would be used to make decisions that affected everyone on the ship - in what could result in life or death. Accuracy is what mattered. This he also did without thinking.

•   •   •

A hundred feet below on the quarterdeck, Lieutenant Duncan waited with an affected air of patience for Cole to report. He knew that Cole needed time to gather meaningful information to report. Calling to him and rushing him would not help and would just make Duncan look nervous in front of the crew. However, Duncan was thinking about it . . . because with the captain below, he was going to be making the decisions.

Cole could afford to react according to training. Duncan was in a different place now. He was expected to think and make decisions that affected hundreds of lives. Duncan was thinking about this too, when Cole's voice finally called down after what seemed like hours.

"Deck there! It's a large frigate and there are at least three more sail beyond. They look to be on roughly the same tack and heading as we are - perhaps a point or two more off the wind. We're gaining on them by at least three or four knots. The frigate has her sails reefed and the sails beyond look full."

Duncan thought quickly about the direction of the wind, the best sailing points for *Fidelity,* and the information he had just received. He pictured the courses and the potential outcomes based on the unknowns - which were still numerous and came quickly to a decision.

"Helmsman, put her another point to windward. Mr. Jones, all hands to make sail. Get every stitch of canvas up that you think she can carry in these winds," he ordered, as he took out his watch and noted the time. The bosun calls alerted both watches of the crew to come on deck and report to sail stations. Then he cupped his hands to his mouth and called much louder aloft, "Mr. Cole, stay until you think you have a more complete understanding and then report to me on deck."

"Aye, aye, sir," came the distant response as topmen streamed up the shrouds and out onto the yards to set more sail.

Several minutes later, Duncan was pacing along the windward side of the deck, trying desperately to look calm and in charge while resisting the urge to climb up and look for himself. The first sail was visible from deck now but was barely hull up and even with a scope kept disappearing below the waves and swell. He had taken a quick look with his telescope, but then decided that pacing might look more officer-like to the crew while Cole was still aloft.

Williams was on the leeward side staring at the ship through a telescope - seemingly unconcerned about how it might look to the crew. Of course, Williams wasn't in charge, so perhaps he had more latitude in these matters. Duncan forced himself to stop thinking about such trivial things and focus on what to do next. There had been no word on the captain yet, so he was left to make the decisions that needed to be made. *First things first,* he thought, *you can't keep trying to think what the captain would do. Do what you think is right and the captain will agree - or perhaps not, but you must think for yourself, not guess what he would do.*

It was not that Duncan lacked experience, training, or qualifications for command. Rather, it was his huge respect for Captain Blackwell - the best commander he had ever had - that was making him feel the way he did. He was worried less about failing than about disappointing Blackwell. He knew he could command the ship and make the decisions . . . but what would the captain think? He had demonstrated his trust by telling him of his decision to request Duncan as the new first lieutenant. That trust must be based on something and with this realization, Duncan felt empowered and ready, just as Lieutenant Cole's feet hit the deck after he slid down the backstay.

Lieutenant Cole walked over to Duncan, and Williams wandered over from his spot by the lee rail. Duncan stopped his pacing and waited as they both approached. Once they both arrived in easy earshot, he said, "Well, Mr. Cole, what have you to report? I trust you weren't napping up there."

Cole smiled and responded, "No sir, no napping. Beyond the frigate are a couple of smaller warships, perhaps sloops, or light frigates - corvettes, I think the French call them. By the lines and the cut of sails, I'm fairly sure they're French, but I didn't actually see any colors. In addition, there are at least five sail of what appear to be supply or merchant ships. There are perhaps two more sail beyond that, but they're still too far away to be sure . . . might be another warship downwind of the mules."

Williams looked at Duncan. Something was different there. A few hours ago, they were close friends who were the same effective rank, with only days separating them in seniority. Now, suddenly, there was an air of authority in Duncan's eyes and even the way he stood. It was nothing in particular, but somehow Williams felt he was standing with his leader - not just his friend. He was pondering that as Duncan spoke.

"So that's what you saw, Mr. Cole. Now, tell me what you think it means."

Cole thought for a moment and then said, "It looks like a French supply convoy. On that heading, they could be bound for Saint-Domingue . . . but . . ."

"Yes, Mr. Cole," Duncan prodded.

"Well, sir, it just seems like a lot of protection for such a small convoy."

"Then we'll just have to go ask them to explain," Duncan said. "You can return to your normal duties and check on your division. I intend to beat to quarters and clear for action, as we get a bit closer."

"Mr. Webb," Duncan called to the midshipman standing near the helm, "get down to the orlop and bring me an update on the captain. If he's awake, my respects and alert him that we've spotted a French convoy and we're closing to investigate."

"Aye, aye, sir. Your respects to the captain and we've spotted a French convoy and we're closing, sir." He repeated the message both to commit it to memory and to demonstrate he had heard it correctly and was off at a brisk walk to complete his mission.

Duncan turned to Williams, who had been standing quietly observing his friend transformed into the acting commander of the ship. "Well, Rupert, looks like we may have some hot work ahead."

"Nine or ten to one doesn't seem quite fair, sir. Perhaps we should only man every other cannon to give them more of a chance," he quipped.

Duncan smiled a bit, revealing to Williams that his friend was still in there somewhere under this new mantle of authority. "Just what I was thinking, but instead, we'll use all the guns but put you in charge of both batteries. They really can't ask for better than that."

"Shall I aim each gun as well?"

Duncan pretended to ponder that for a moment and then responded, "No, I really don't think we can justify wasting the King's powder and shot on such folly. Let's just leave you in charge and let the gun captains do the aiming. I'd hate to return the ship to the captain with the paint all messed up."

The mood changed and Duncan was serious again, the look in his eyes shifting to the authority of leadership. "Let's get ready, shall we? Beat to quarters and clear for action."

"Aye, aye, sir!" Williams turned and shouted the order that would transform the *Fidelity* from a beautiful sailing ship to a deadly weapon of war in the matter of ten minutes or less. "Clear for action and sound general quarters!"

The relative silence was shattered by the marine drummer beating a quick staccato tune. Bosun calls whistled, and orders were shouted throughout the ship. In reality, everyone was expecting and anticipating the order and they moved quickly and efficiently to their tasks. Partitions were swung up out of the way or taken down. The captain's furniture was carried to the hold. Breach tackle was removed, and guns were run in from their traveling positions snugged up tight against the bulkheads. Shot, wadding, and loading tools were placed in exact locations next to each. Flintlocks were brought up from the armory and carefully attached to the cannons while the decks were sluiced with water and sand was spread to make it less slippery. Tubs of water were placed by each cannon with lit slow match smoldering over each - to be used in case the flint failed. These and hundreds of other little tasks were completed by the crew in a finely rehearsed orchestra of movements that, to an outsider, might have appeared to be complete chaos.

Williams returned to Duncan less than nine minutes later to report, "The ship is cleared and ready for action, sir."

Duncan nodded but did not respond as he noticed Midshipman Webb returning at the same time. Webb approached cautiously and nervously said, "Sir, the captain is not yet awake, and Mr. Whitehall says, um . . . he says . . . um . . ."

"Well, spit it out, Mr. Webb. What exactly did Mr. Whitehall say?"

"Um . . . well, exactly, sir? He said that he bloody well told you that he'd send word if the captain regained consciousness and he'd appreciate it if you would leave him to do his job unless you think you can do better . . . sir."

Midshipman Webb hung his head, not sure what would happen next, but guessing it was not going to end well for him. He was surprised, perhaps even shocked, to hear Duncan start laughing. "And he's quite right, of course. Thank you for reminding me of our previous agreement. Carry on Mr. Webb."

Webb said, "Aye, aye, sir," touched his hat in quick salute and left the quarterdeck to head to his position on the foredeck with the carronades. He was relieved to have gotten away. For once, nobody killed the messenger.

•   •   •

Duncan looked at his watch - again - and thought to himself that he had probably already made a mistake. It would take hours to overtake the French convoy (if indeed they were even French). He should not have cleared for action so early. There was still plenty of time. Of course, it was better to be ready early in case something unexpected happened to delay the process. Still, it seemed he had moved too quickly and since everything went normally, the crew was now facing a long wait with little to distract them.

•   •   •

Down in the waist, Able Seaman Carlson was sitting with his back against the larboard side by number nine gun, in what little shade there was from the gangway. He had been relieved from his spell at lookout and this was his duty position for general quarters, serving as part of the gun crew for the cannon they called "Nellie". He watched one of his closest friends, the gun captain, Edwards, fiddling with the flintlock and testing the spark.

"We're in for a fair bit of waitin' even if the Frenchies want to fight," he stated, as he closed his eyes and leaned his head back against the bulwark. "They's most of four leagues off to wind'ard and likely running for all they's worth."

"Doesn't mean we shouldn't be ready," Edwards replied gruffly. "I'm not sure I like the look of this flint. Mayhaps I should change it out while we wait."

"Do what you like and let me know if you're wantin' any help. Else I'll be saving up my energy for what's coming."

Edwards eased his not inconsiderable bulk down next to Carlson and leaned back. Carlson was taller, perhaps what one would call average height, but thin and rangy. Edwards was below average height but powerfully built with a great barrel chest and massive arms. "Might be as well to leave good enough alone. Spark seems strong enough, and what else does a flint need to be about anyhow?"

Carlson produced a ship's biscuit from somewhere and offered it to Edwards without opening his eyes. "Care for a bit of something to gnaw on?"

"Thankee kindly," Edwards responded as he took the square biscuit and rapped it against the deck to knock any weevils loose. He rapped the stone-hard biscuit against the deck again and then examined it. "Not even any bargemen along for the ride. Where'd you have this hidden?"

"Special stock, my friend. Ain't no softer, though, so mind your teeth."

After this, they lapsed into silence to wait in the quiet way they had learned in their years of service. Catch a nap and save your energy while you can. There is always something coming that will make you hurry later. Hurry and wait - that was the way of the Royal Navy.

"Deck there!" They heard the new lookout yelling down to the officers on the quarterdeck. "The frigate is shortening sail, shifted two points toward the wind, and has raised colors . . . French colors."

"Well now, that will shorten the wait a bit, I'm thinkin'," Carlson said, but still he did not open his eyes or move.

•   •   •

It did shorten the wait, but almost an hour and a half later, they were still more than two miles apart on slowly converging paths. Duncan stood along the lee rail with a telescope to his eye to absorb every detail he could of the enemy. The two corvettes (and corvettes they certainly were) had continued with the five bulkier supply ships and were at least three miles beyond the big frigate. Just beyond the furthest supply ship, another frigate eased along with its sails triple reefed to match the lumbering speed of the supply ships with all their sails set.

There had been a series of flag hoists, mostly between the two frigates. Without a codebook, it was impossible to know what they were communicating, but it seemed clear that the closer frigate was issuing orders to the rest and had the most to say to the furthest frigate.

They were still a bit too far away to make out the name on the transom of their foe, but a broad pennant flying from the foremast indicated that the commodore of the convoy was aboard. Duncan considered that it made sense that the commodore would have more to signal to the other frigate, as its captain was likely the next highest-ranking officer.

Still, it was curious that one of the hoists had been repeated three times, even though it should have been clearly visible to the other frigate and had appeared to be acknowledged each time. Duncan could tell this even though he didn't know what the signals meant. He had ordered the new signals midshipman, Connor, to carefully record each hoist, the time, and any responses. Perhaps it would be useful later.

The big frigate they would be meeting first would have been rated a 38-gun, fifth rate, in the Royal Navy. It was likely mounting 18-pounders with a secondary battery of 8-pounders. It was a big frigate, but *Fidelity* was bigger - although also rated at 38 guns, she was carrying 24-pounders in the main battery and 32-pound carronades and two 9-pounder long guns on the foredeck. *Fidelity* had almost twice the broadside weight of metal and was likely more strongly built, so the effective difference would be magnified if they fought side-to-side trading broadsides.

Duncan wondered if the French commodore realized the difference. There were only a handful of 24-pounder frigates on the British navy list, but surely he could see the number of gunports. If he did recognize *Fidelity's* power, was he really intending a single ship to ship action when he had the advantage of numbers? The corvettes were no match for *Fidelity* and would have been rated sloops, or perhaps post ships, in the British system. However, if they could maneuver to rake her while the frigates were engaged, they could do a lot of damage with their 8-pounders. Was there some trick here that Duncan was too inexperienced to recognize? Could it be that the Commodore was arrogant enough to think he could match *Fidelity* even with the difference in fire power?

There were other possibilities, too, of course. Might the convoy be so important that the commodore was risking one frigate to slow *Fidelity* enough that the others could get away? Or might the corvettes turn at the last moment and move to rake *Fidelity*? If this were the French strategy, they were certainly a long way off. The frigates would have quite a while to knock it out, side to side, before the corvettes could come about and beat back into the wind to gain position.

Duncan made his decision, closed the telescope, and motioned to Williams to come up from the waist. He might not be able to guess what the French were thinking, but he could make his own plans. He thought of the age-old toast, "Confusion to our enemies!" and smiled.

"You beckoned, sir?" Williams asked as he mounted the quarterdeck and approached Duncan, who was still within a few feet of the starboard ladder from the waist.

"Have the main battery - both sides - double shotted, with grape atop, for good measure," Duncan instructed. "Same for the chase guns, but load the carronades with grape and canister."

"Aye, aye, sir. It might hearten the crew to take some early ranging shots with the chasers," Williams offered. He was not sure if he was allowed to offer advice in the current circumstances, but with no one else nearby, he felt he could risk it. "Shall I keep the chase guns single shotted?"

"No, double shot and grape for all the long guns - chase guns included," Duncan smiled as he responded, clearly not offended by the suggestion. "Long-range shots are not in keeping with my current plan, Rupert. Load the cannons as I've directed, but don't run them out just yet."

"So, it's to be a close-range slugging match, then, eh? Aye, aye, sir." Rupert touched his hat in salute and climbed back to the main deck to distribute the orders.

As Duncan passed near the wheel on his way to resuming his pacing along the weather rail, he ordered the quartermaster, "Put her another half point with the wind, but mind your luff."

"Aye, aye, sir!"

The course change would leave the two frigates on converging courses, but on an even narrower angle of approach. *Fidelity* would still remain to windward, but unless the French frigate shifted its course, they would not be able to make their broadside bare on *Fidelity* until the last moment.

"Deck there!" the lookout yelled down. "There's movement on the deck of the frigate. Looks like they're shifting a cannon aft."

"Mr. Connor, take a glass up and see if there's anything else you can puzzle out about our Frenchmen."

Connor responded, selected a telescope, swung out onto the shrouds, and started up. Duncan walked to the lee rail where his view was less obstructed by the sails and raised his glass. They were closing quickly now and were just over a mile apart. He still could not make out the name, but could tell that it was in gold letters on a dark red transom board. He could see sunlight glittering off other details picked out in gold leaf across the ornate gallery of the frigate. The captain, or the commodore, must have put some of his own money into that - unusual in the revolutionary French Navy, but the letters were too bright to be left over from before.

There was little Duncan could see from this angle, but there was definitely a lot of activity on the quarterdeck. He could see officers and crew moving about and saw two men standing next to each other, looking back at him through telescopes. Although he couldn't be sure of the rank at this distance, he could tell they were officers and guessed it was the captain and the commodore, or - if there was no flag captain - perhaps the commodore and first lieutenant.

Duncan thought for a moment. He was not sure that the French used the same system as the British, with its two ranks of commodore: one with a captain, and one without. The pennant of a British commodore would have told him, by having a black ball to signify a commodore - first class, who rated a flag captain, versus a plain pennant for a commodore without a captain. Of course, it didn't really matter, and Duncan chided himself for daydreaming again and willed himself to focus.

Connor came sliding down the backstay and landed lightly on the deck with the telescope slung over his shoulder. He glanced around for Duncan and then made his way over to give his report. "Sir, they appear to be in the process of shifting two of the main battery 18-pounders from the starboard side to use as chase guns. They've had to shift two of the quarterdeck long guns, one on each side, farther forward to make room. There appear to be ports available, but I don't think it will be comfortable working those guns so close together."

"How long do you estimate before they're ready to fire?"

"They had the larboard gun in place and were working on setting up the tackle when I came down, sir. The truck is there on the starboard side, but they still need to sway up the cannon. Must be tricky business in these seas."

"Excellent report, Mr. Connor. I shall mention it to the captain when he returns to the deck. Carry on." Duncan turned back to look at the French warship while Connor walked, smiling, to his duty location near the signal locker. There was little likelihood of him needing to send signals since they were the only British ship in sight, but still, it was his duty location, unless called upon to be elsewhere.

Two decks below, Midshipman O'Toole was not smiling. He stood at the bottom of the ladder outside the orlap and tried to control his tears. He had been there for several minutes, hesitant to go on deck in such a state but having trouble regaining his composure. He took a deep breath, and it caught in his throat and turned into gasps. He fought down the emotion and breathed out slowly. He had a duty to fulfill, and he better be about it. He took another breath and began to climb the ladder.

Duncan watched the French gun crew working on the larboard chase gun. He saw them finish loading and then watched as the ugly black muzzle poked out from the taffrail. They shifted and adjusted the aim, while he hoped they would miss. They likely would on this shot. The ships were still almost three quarters of a mile apart - within range, but not close enough for dependable accuracy. He pondered the added difficulties of firing from the stern, where they had to deal with the roll, rise, and swell so differently than when firing from the side, as they normally practiced.

He saw a puff of smoke instantly whipped away by the wind, and a flash from where the cannon used to be. It had recoiled back out of view through the railing. He saw a white plume of water shoot up about 200 yards in front of *Fidelity* at about the same time he heard the distant boom of the cannon. For a split second, he thought it was a miss until he heard the splintering crash up forward where the cannonball struck *Fidelity* after ricocheting off the water.

O'Toole was gaining confidence as he climbed. Just as his head went above the deck, he heard a sound like distant thunder, followed almost immediately by a crash and buzzing sounds as splinters of oak scythed through the air. One struck him in the forehead above his left eye and rotated around his head, laying his scalp wide open to somewhere above his ear. He crumpled back down the ladder and lay in an untidy heap on the deck below.

"Mr. Connor!" Duncan called out.

"Here, sir," the midshipman responded instantly as he walked toward the lieutenant.

"Go down to my cabin and open my chest. You'll find my pistols in a case near the top. Bring them to me, along with my sword."

"Aye, aye, sir," Connor replied as he walked forward and down from the quarterdeck. He turned under the quarterdeck and headed to the ladder that would take him down just forward of the wardroom door.

·   ·   ·

Jenkins was at the cannon nearest on the starboard side and spoke to Connor as he passed. "Beggin' your pardon, sir. Are you retrieving the lieutenant's sword and such?"

Connor paused and looked suspiciously at Jenkins. "Aye, I am. What business is it of yours?"

"Only that I thought to offer to help you load his pistols, sir . . . thinking it might go quicker with two loading, is all, sir."

Connor glanced up, realizing that Jenkins must have overheard them through the grating above his head. They must have been standing right next to it when Lieutenant Duncan ordered him below. He was not sure what to make of it, but he decided there was little harm that could be done in accepting the offer and it would go quicker. "Right then, come along, Jenkins. I'll have him back before he's needed to serve the gun, Mitchell," he said to the gun captain.

Mitchell nodded, and Jenkins fell in behind Connor. After they had disappeared, Mitchell turned to the rest of his crew. "Good thought by Jenkins. I've seen Mr. Connor try to load a musket, and he'd probably get the lieutenant killed by forgetting the powder or something." The gun crew chuckled and then went back to waiting.

Down in the wardroom, Connor found Duncan's sword hanging from the deal partition and opened the worn sea chest. Nestled atop some neatly folded silk shirts was a polished wooden box. He lifted it and opened it to reveal two rather plain, but very nicely made, pistols. He suddenly realized that he would probably not have even remembered to load them, and he was not sure how much powder to use. He handed the box to Jenkins.

Jenkins took them and immediately checked the flints and took out the powder flask. He quickly but carefully worked to load the pistols as Lieutenant Williams entered the wardroom and looked questioningly at the unexpected pair standing before him.

Connor responded to the look. "Sorry to intrude, sir. Lieutenant Duncan sent me to get his sword and pistols and Jenkins is helping me load them, sir."

Williams nodded and said, "While you're at it, take his Indian tomahawks along, too. They're fastened inside the top of his chest." He reached into his cabin, grabbed his own sword, and headed back to the main deck.

"Aye, aye, sir," Connor said, relieved that he was not in trouble for being in the wardroom and allowing Jenkins to enter as well.

Connor found the tomahawks. They were odd looking and nothing like the standard issue ones in the arms chest. These were lighter and smaller, but also sharper and well balanced. He had no idea how one might use them, but then he was not yet very good with any weapon. He was focusing on learning to use the cutlass, but he did not seem to have much natural ability when it came to such things. He was much better at learning navigation and sail handling.

Jenkins finished loading the second pistol and handed both to Connor. Connor walked out of the wardroom and headed for the quarterdeck. On the main deck, he paused and said, "Thank you, Jenkins."

Jenkins nodded and retook his place by the cannon, just as another shot was fired from the French ship. This one missed narrowly, passing within feet of the figurehead.

Connor was surprised to hear another cannon shot as he stepped onto the quarterdeck and realized that the French must have both chase guns ready now since they could not have reloaded that quickly.

•   •   •

Duncan was standing along the starboard rail watching the French load and fire. So far, there had been little effect after the first shot. The second gun was in place, but the first shot seemed to demonstrate that it could not be traversed far enough to bear on the *Fidelity* as its first shot fell yards behind. The French seemed to have given up on the starboard gun and were focusing on loading the larboard gun. They were moving quickly and efficiently. Duncan had heard that French ships sometimes carried artillery soldiers to serve the guns, and he wondered if this crew included any.

The muzzle of the cannon came slowly through the gunport, and Duncan looked at his watch. By British standards, they were quite slow. While he was looking at his watch, he heard the shot and almost simultaneously the whizzing of the shot overhead and a popping and tearing sound as it passed through a sail and the wind split it in two. He glanced up, but there was no need to give any orders. The crew was already moving to repair the damage.

Duncan paced forward to the rail and called down, "Lieutenant Williams, might I have a moment of your time, if you can spare it?"

Williams moved lightly across the deck to the ladder and came bounding onto the quarterdeck, and touched his hat in salute. Duncan moved his head to indicate Williams should follow and walked over to the quartermaster at the helm, where the master was also standing. "We'll be engaging soon, so here's what I have in mind…"

Chapter Three

Connor had waited a short distance from the group as they had talked. He was too far away to hear what was said, but it was clear that Duncan had been giving the master and Lieutenant Williams instructions. There had been some questions and discussion, but it all seemed rather routine from the body language. Duncan said something that ended the discussion and beckoned for Connor to approach as the master walked to the helm.

Duncan reached for his sword and pistols, then spotted the tomahawks and frowned at Connor. "What's all this, then? I don't recall asking for my tomahawks."

A look of panic crossed Connor's face, but Williams spoke up immediately. "I'm sorry, sir, that was my idea. Mr. Connor was just following my orders." Duncan turned his gaze to Williams, but did not say anything further.

Duncan fitted the belt around his waist and adjusted the frog supporting the sword in its thin, black leather sheath. He tucked a pistol into the belt on each side and then crossed the tomahawks through the belt in the small of his back. All this made the belt feel a bit tight, and he loosened it as he spoke.

"Thank you, Mr. Connor. That is all. You may return to your post."

"You've made me look more like a bloody pirate than a king's officer, Rupert," Duncan said quietly.

"Aye, sir, but if you'll allow me the liberty, I don't think I can take all the credit (if that's the appropriate word) for how you look. Besides, I'd rather you be a live pirate than a dead acting first lieutenant." Duncan laughed out loud, and Williams added, "Not that I'm getting sentimental, mind you. It's a purely practical consideration as you owe me money. Otherwise, I might welcome the chance for my own advancement."

Duncan laughed again and clapped Williams on the shoulder. "Thank you, in spite of your motives." He debated whether he should go on, but could not stop himself. "I suppose you think I'm daft for what I'm planning. I appreciate you not saying anything in front of the master…although I suspect he agrees with you."

Williams spoke very quietly, "Joseph, I expect that you're right about the master agreeing with me, but not in thinking you're daft. I think your plan is uncommonly brave and perhaps brilliant. Captain Blackwell would certainly approve. You know as well as I, that the Admiralty doesn't always value innovative thinking, but if we're successful, they won't complain." Having reached his limit for serious discussion, he then added, "And of course, if it all goes horribly wrong, you're unlikely to be alive to answer their complaints, and I'm out the money you owe me. May I return to my post, sir?"

Duncan laughed again and shook William's hand. "Thank you and good luck Rupert." Williams winked, nodded, and saluted before turning and walking away.

The helmsmen had watched the exchange and, although they could not hear the discussions, had heard the laughter and seen the easy manner of the two officers talking. One turned to the other and said, "Ain't he a cool one, our Lieutenant Duncan?

You'd think he'd done this every day and hadn't a care in the world."

"Silence there and stand ready!" the master bellowed from behind the helmsmen.

"Aye, Mr. Jones."

•   •   •

Duncan had returned to a spot near the front edge of the quarterdeck along the starboard side. He stood there with his feet spread to balance himself against the pitch and roll as *Fidelity* surged forward toward the French ship. The name of their adversary, *La Tempête*, was clearly legible on the transom board now, even without a telescope.

They were very close and had begun to take in sail to slow down and not shoot past as they approached. *La Tempête* had continued to fire the single chase gun, but to surprisingly little effect. It was clear that the gun crew, no matter how skilled, was struggling to adjust to the unusual movement from the stern of the ship. Some shots went wildly high while others flew somewhere behind *Fidelity,* with only a few striking or cutting through the rigging and sails.

Duncan realized that they were getting close enough that he should start pacing so as to not present too easy a target for sharpshooters. The quarterdeck was often a very dangerous place to be in battle. Not only did the officers gathering there present prime targets, there was little protection beyond firmly rolled canvas hammocks stuffed into nets along the rails. They might stop a musket ball or a few splinters, but beyond that, they offered little comfort.

Fidelity was slowly overtaking *La Tempête*. Both ships were prepared for battle with their fore and main sails partially brailed up to keep them from catching fire once the cannons started spitting long tongues of flame and smoldering wadding.

Duncan turned around as he reached the front of the quarterdeck and tried to gauge how much closer they would be by the time he paced back to the same spot. Timing was critical to his plan, as was the coordination of various actions by the crew. It suddenly occurred to him that his plan was not quite so simple as it had seemed when he first thought of it. What he was asking of the ship was fairly simple, but the actions required of the crew and the timing left quite a bit of room for error.

As he reached the rear of the quarterdeck, he realized that the moment had come to make the final decision. He could give the order now to try his somewhat unorthodox plan, or he could let *Fidelity* continue forward and end up side by side with *La Tempête*, exchanging a close range cannonade with the enemy ship. Reaching the front of the quarterdeck again, he stopped, drew his sword, and raising it above his head, ordered, "Run out the starboard battery. Helm two points into the wind." As he said the second part, he looked to the master standing by the helm and nodded slowly.

In response to the first command, the covers on the starboard gunports were opened and gun crews worked the tackles to move the cannons into firing position. The rumbling of the guns across the deck was almost instantly greeted by the larboard gunports of *La Tempête* opening and the black muzzles of cannons appearing to answer the challenge.

The master moved to the helm and replaced one of the helmsmen by gripping the spokes of the wheel and starting to turn slowly with the wind, which would allow the entire broadside of cannons to bear on their target. Crewmen moved into the rigging and stood ready to brace lines as if they would be trimming sail in response to the change in course.

Duncan could see the commodore and captain of the *Le Tempête* watching from their quarterdeck and shouting orders to the crew. He saw the French helmsmen starting to turn the wheel to match *Fidelity*'s change in course, which would allow them to avoid exposing their stern to raking fire and to maintain a parallel course. Duncan smiled a bit as he realized the first part of his plan was working. He turned to the master and yelled, as he sliced his sword through the air until it was against his leg and pointed at the deck, "Now! Larboard the helm and run out the larboard battery. Fire as you bear!"

The master and helmsman quickly spun the wheel back in the opposite direction and *Fidelity* immediately started to turn to starboard as the French ship continued to turn slowly the other way. Crewmen adjusted the sails while the gun crews from the starboard side rushed to the larboard side to help run out the guns and prepare to fire.

Duncan looked back to see his enemies on their quarterdeck. He expected the French to realize what was happening and try to turn back, but hoped to have a chance to rake their stern as they passed. It would leave him downwind of the French - ceding them the weather gauge but hopefully inflicting significant damage in exchange for the loss of position.

A moment of fear passed over him as he watched events unfold as little more than a spectator. The French ship was not turning back. The helm was hard over, and the ship was turning even faster off the wind. The commodore knew what Duncan was attempting and was trying to turn fast enough to protect the stern of his ship by turning back through the wind. *Fidelity* would travel well past the French ship and leave it to windward, controlling the next move in the encounter. Duncan had not anticipated that response.

Of more immediate concern, however, was the very real possibility that he had waited a bit too late to start the maneuver and the bowsprit might strike the stern of the enemy. He jumped as the starboard chase gun fired. He had not really expected any of the starboard guns to fire, as most could not be brought to bear on the enemy ship. If they could not make the turn without running afoul of *La Tempete*, it might ironically be the only gun they could fire. Duncan made a mental note to compliment Midshipman Webb, who was in command of the guns on the foredeck.

Duncan could not see if there was any visible damage from the shot. His view was blocked by the bowsprit sail . . . and he realized, by the bowsprit itself. They were moving past, and with a huge sense of relief, he knew they would not run aboard the enemy as the other 9-pounder chase gun barked out. Duncan moved to the other side of the deck to try to see what was happening up front and got there just as the first 32-pound carronade on the foredeck roared and belched out fire and smoke.

Almost immediately, the first of fourteen 24-pound cannons of the larboard main battery added its deep throated thunder to the growing din of battle. Through momentary clear pockets in the smoke, Duncan could see large holes in the stern gallery windows as the firing was rippling down the side of the ship in a rolling broadside, with each cannon firing as it passed in turn along the stern of the *La Tempête*. She had not turned fast enough to save herself from a murderous hail of iron flying the length of her decks.

•   •   •

Edwards stood with the lanyard to the flintlock loosely in his hand as he peered along the barrel at the empty sea. He started to take up the slack in the line and hold it taut as he waited for the edge of the enemy ship to come into view through the gunport. He could see the forward part of the ship just as the gun next to his fired. His orders were to fire into the stern, and he stood poised and ready.

The stern of the ship began to pass, and he waited a moment longer to aim for the exact center. There were no gallery windows remaining, just a gaping hole exposing the dark interior of the ship where the solid cannon balls and egg-shaped grape shot must be creating unthinkable horror for the enemy gunners who could not return fire. He pulled the lanyard, and nothing happened. The flint had broken in two, flying from the lock without creating a sufficient spark to ignite the powder in the touch hole and quill.

Edwards cursed loudly as he reached for the linstock holding a length of smoldering slow match. In one smooth motion, he raised it to his lips and blew on it until it glowed orange in the smoky gloom while he moved to the side and placed the slow match to the touch hole on the cannon. He arched his back to get out of the way as the cannon leaped off the deck and roared back until the breech tackle stopped it and returned it to the deck with a thump that could be felt more than heard. Starting to call out the commands to reload, he glanced out the gunport, wondering if he had even hit the enemy ship or if they were already past it when he fired. Carlson would never let him live it down if he had missed from this range.

•   •   •

Duncan had shifted his position again to be sure he was clear of the crews serving the seven carronades on the larboard side of the quarterdeck. The gunfire had been almost as consistent as a carefully timed salute, and he realized as he got to the helm and turned back toward the action that there had been a pause in the pattern. Just as he wondered why, he heard two of the great guns fire almost simultaneously, followed quickly by the forward most carronade right in front of him.

Although Edwards did not know it, he had missed the stern of the ship. In fact, he had practically missed the entire ship. One of the cannon balls had struck the starboard quarter galley and shattered it into a cloud of splinters. This had done little to affect the fighting capabilities of La Tempête, although the commodore had lost his washroom. The grapeshot had caused even less damage by scoring the side of the hull and falling into the water after glancing off. However, the other round shot had traveled along almost the length of the ship before scything through the lanyards and lower shrouds immediately above the forechains.

The commodore was still standing by the rear rail of his quarterdeck, and Duncan could see him glaring across the narrow gap of water between the ships. It was with an odd mixture of horror, awe, and sense of accomplishment that Duncan surveyed the utter destruction of the stern of *La Tempête* as the carronades continued to fire into the ship directly below the commodore's feet.

Duncan's ears were ringing from the cannonade, but in the distance, he could hear the popping of muskets and the louder bang of the swivel guns in the fighting tops. He felt a thump near his left foot and looked down to see the deck raised into splinters where a musket ball had struck within an inch of his boot. He remembered the need to keep pacing and instinctively looked back at the commodore, who continued to stand with his hands held behind his back. *Was he too angry, too brave, or too stupid to move?* As he watched, two enemy officers started to approach the commodore. There was another distant bang, and both officers crumpled into messy heaps as they were cut down by dozens of musket balls in the canister shot from a swivel gun - and still the commodore stood unmoving.

The orderly sequence of firing was replaced by what amounted to a ragged half-broadside as the final cannons and carronades blasted their deadly loads into the shattered stern of the French frigate. A high shot from one of the carronades swept away the helmsman, a junior officer, and most of the wheel itself. The rudder hung precariously from a single, partially severed pintle hook. As if in slow motion, the mizzenmast, cut through below decks by a round shot, twisted and fell across the quarterdeck in a heap of rigging and sails. The commodore disappeared under the canvas and Duncan felt a sense of relief to finally have the glaring, seemingly unblinking enemy removed from view.

The main mast of the frigate was also clearly damaged and, although still standing, was listing to leeward. Crewmen were working feverishly to rig additional tackle and keep the mast from snapping. With the mizzen shot away and most of the sails on the mainmast furled to relieve strain, the French ship was slowing down quickly as the broken and unresponsive rudder kept it turning toward the wind. The crew was forced to remove sail from the forward mast to counteract the loss of mizzen sails. Topmen were swarming along the yards of the foremast as the ship pointed directly into the wind and came to almost a complete stop.

For a moment, it seemed that *La Tempête* would remain suspended there, unable to move. Then, her nose passed slowly through the wind and the pressure on the remaining sails switched to the other side. It was at this moment, as the starboard shrouds began to take the strain, that Edwards' mistimed shot became important. The damaged shrouds and forechains were unable to withstand the tension and gave way. The foremast snapped off a few feet above deck and plunged into the sea, taking dozens of crewmen with it.

In less than fifteen minutes, the beautiful French ship had been turned into a shattered jumble of broken spars, masts, and ripped canvas. Miles of rigging was mixed into the tangle and most of the visible crewmen were busy hacking feverishly with axes to cut away the wreckage. Dark stains running down from the scuppers gave the appearance that the ship itself was bleeding. The slaughter that must have occurred on the gun deck was almost unthinkable. The gun crews would have been standing, unable to return fire, while wave after wave of iron shot swept the length of the ship, ricocheting off cannons, and creating deadly clouds of splinters from strikes on wood.

Duncan's plan had been to cut across the stern of the ship and move to the leeward side. He had expected the French ship to turn and face *Fidelity* side to side. Although he hoped to do some damage as they crossed the stern, his real goal was to get between the French frigate and the rest of the convoy so he could continue to work downwind toward the rest of the enemy while fighting *La Tempête*. He looked at the shattered remains of his adversary and was faced with another difficult decision. "Mr. Jones, set a course to intercept the forward most ship in the convoy, and set all plain sail." Duncan took one last look back at *La Tempête*, wallowing helplessly in *Fidelity's* wake, and paced back to the front of the quarterdeck. His decision was made.

Duncan took a telescope from the rack by the binnacle and moved to the leeward side of the deck. He stepped up onto a carronade slide and put his arm through the rigging to steady himself. He quickly located the enemy convoy. The corvettes were perhaps seven or eight miles away, with the other frigate and the rest of the convoy spread out another mile or two beyond. He could see signal flags breaking out on the various ships as orders were exchanged. Clearly, the captain of the second frigate was taking command. "Mr. Connor, are you still recording the signals?"

"Aye, sir, I am. There weren't any while we were firing, but I kept watch, just in case, sir."

"Excellent. However, I'd like you to take a break now and signal 'acknowledged'."

"Um…aye, aye, sir. Signal 'acknowledged'," Connor stammered, and then added, "Who am I signaling, sir, and what am I acknowledging?"

"You are responding to our superior, who is still beyond the site of our foe with the rest of the fleet, of course."

Connor looked back into the wind and only saw the wrecked French frigate getting smaller and smaller as they pulled away.

Duncan spoke again, "There aren't any, Mr. Connor, but the French don't know that. Please make the signal."

Connor still didn't fully understand, but an order was an order. "Aye, aye, sir."

Just then, Williams climbed onto the quarterdeck and moved toward Duncan. "All set up forward, sir. What's your next brilliant plan? We certainly made quick work of that first frigate. The odds are getting better, eh?"

Duncan smiled and responded. "Well, I'll admit the first encounter went a bit better than I had anticipated, but she was broken, not beaten. If they can get sails back on her, they've still got all the guns and they're upwind now."

Williams understood the concern and the choice Duncan had made. "Bird in the hand versus two in the bush and all that? We'd be likely to lose the convoy if we stayed to take control of the frigate. Your plan is working - just not quite how you envisioned it. You can never trust the French to play along, you know?"

Duncan laughed and lifted the telescope back to his eye to study the enemy convoy again. "I'll keep that in mind." Then, louder, he added, "Mr. Connor, signal 'seven, two, five'."

Williams retrieved a telescope from the rack and stood next to Duncan, looking at the French ships. Adjusting the focus, he asked, "So, what's next?"

"That depends on our untrustworthy foes," Duncan responded. "It looks like the second frigate is standing to, waiting for the corvettes to catch up while the convoy sails on. The question is whether they'll slow down to fight us or stay with the convoy and make us chase them down."

"I'll bet you a case of wine they come back to fight us. We just smashed their flagship in one pass. They've got to be looking for some revenge and trying to keep us away from their little flock."

Duncan kept studying the enemy while he responded, "Good wine, a claret perhaps, not that swill you bought for the wardroom mess." He paused and then added, "I'm trying to convince them we're the eyes of a fleet that's beyond the horizon from them. I want them to run. I want a chance to hit the supply ships, and they're not fast enough to outrun us before dark. Besides, the more distance we put between us and *La Tempête*, the less likely she can rejoin the action."

"Ah, so you're cheating. Well, I still stand by my bet. You've always been lousy at bluffing. Even the French won't fall for it."

Duncan lowered the telescope, looked at his friend, and held his hand out to make the bet official. "Then I accept the wager and look forward to enjoying the wine." Williams shook his outstretched hand and smiled.

•   •   •

It did not take long to confirm that Duncan was going to win the bet. Once the corvettes caught up with the second frigate, they sailed on together, keeping pace with the gaggle of supply ships. The wind continued to freshen, and the convoy was clearly trying to outrun the British ship. However, even with all sail set the supply ships could not manage more than five or six knots. Ironically, as the wind grew stronger, they would have to reduce sail or increase the risk of losing a spar or mast and becoming easy prey. Meanwhile, *Fidelity* was skipping across the sea at more than eight knots.

Although it took almost three hours to close the distance, the time went quickly for the British, as they were busy with minor repairs and preparation for the next engagement.

Connor had continued to send meaningless signals to imaginary allies. There was no way of knowing if it was affecting the French tactics, or if they were even paying attention. However, it did not hurt to try, and it kept Connor occupied, rather than thinking about the coming action.

After the first few signals, Duncan had left it to Connor to decide what signals to send and when to acknowledge orders or make responses. Connor had made it into a bit of a game by imagining what he might have been ordering if he commanded the fleet, and then acting out the signals. It helped to distract him from wondering what it would be like in a battle. The encounter with *La Tempête* had been too quick and one-sided to be considered a real battle. With the odds stacked against them as they approached the enemy convoy, it was likely that the next engagement would be very different. Connor wondered how he would react if called upon to lead sailors onto the decks of an enemy ship for hand-to-hand combat or to repel boarders to save *Fidelity* from capture.

Nearby, Duncan was pacing along the weather side of the quarterdeck, contemplating similar thoughts. He stepped over ringbolts and other obstacles without having to actually see them and wondered how the crew would perform and for how many this might be their first, or last, sea fight. *Fidelity* had captured several enemy ships during her cruises, but none of them had really fought back and all had surrendered without the need to board under fire.

Williams stepped back onto the quarterdeck, and Duncan was grateful for the distraction. "Is everything ready and have all the men had something to eat?"

"Aye, sir," Williams responded. "Cheese, biscuit, and a tot of rum. They're as ready as can be without lighting the galley fire. That little dust up with *La Tempête* has put them in high spirits - although it's likely the grog helped that, too. Have you ever wondered if the average jack tar would fight better with less rum, or if it helps?"

"I suppose it's a bit of both. Some might be sharper with less, but some could use more to bolster their courage and handle what comes."

Williams paused, and then asked, "You were with Lord Howe last year at Ushant, weren't you?"

"Yes, I was. I was third lieutenant in *Defense* serving under James Gambier. They're calling it the Glorious First of June now, but it didn't seem so wonderful at the time."

"Admiral James Gambier? Hasn't he been appointed as a Lord of the Admiralty?"

"Aye, he was Captain Gambier when I knew him, but he's a rear-admiral, now. He's a good man. I learned a bit from him, even though I didn't serve with him for long. He was quite serious most of the time. His nickname was Dismal Jimmy."

"*Defense* was the first ship through the French line, wasn't it? You were right in the thick of it, eh?"

"We outran *Queen Charlotte* and broke the line between *Mucius* and *Tourville,* ending up engaged with both - then *Gasparin* and *Convention* joined in. Not everyone responded to Lord Howe's orders with the same vigor and enthusiasm, and we were getting knocked about pretty badly until *Marlborough* got there and tangled up with *Impétureux*. We ended up completely dismasted and holed in several places. I was transferred to *Fidelity* while *Defense* was being repaired."

"Were you still on *Defense* when King George visited Spithead?"

"Yes, I was there, but I doubt King George, or any of the royalty, remembers me. It was quite a party, though. I received my orders for *Fidelity* right after that and ended up stuck with you in Portsmouth. Talk about highs to lows." Duncan smiled as he spoke and tried to shake off the memories of fleet action that saw thousands of sailors die.

Williams realized from his friend's tone that the subject should be changed and decided to focus back on the present. "I don't think the French are going to line up for us this time. What are your plans?"

"I thought we'd smash our way through as many of the French as we can, capture and damage the most possible, and harry the rest until dark. Do you suppose I'm overthinking it?"

"I've never noticed that you have a sarcastic side. If possible, I believe it makes you even less likable," Williams responded while laughing.

Duncan laughed with him. "I wish that were just sarcasm, but I really don't know what to do other than attack. I'm not sure how to best engage a frigate and two corvettes, and a lot will depend on how they react. I'll try to maneuver to keep them from raking us, but three to one means we've got more enemies than broadsides. I suggest you keep the crews firing at anything they see and be prepared to repel boarders if it goes poorly."

"Well, then, it sounds like we've got a good, solid plan and I should get back to the main deck. Best of luck to you, sir." With a quick salute and a final smile, Williams left the quarterdeck, and Duncan lifted the telescope back to his eye and studied his enemy more closely.

Despite Williams' comment, it did in fact appear as if the French were sailing roughly in line. The two corvettes were out in front, but all were close enough now for Duncan to make out their names through the telescope. The furthest from *Fidelity* was called *Le Furet*, and she was slightly leeward of the frigate. Next came *Le Carcajou*, which was slightly windward of the frigate called *L'Enchanté*.

All three ships had the clean lines and slightly raked masts that made French ships look fast and beautiful. Although they showed signs of having been at sea for a while, they were well-kept and looked fit for battle. The two corvettes were virtually identical and were likely to have been built at the same yard. Duncan assumed they would be carrying a main armament of 8-pounder cannons - the French equivalent of the British 9-pounder long guns. If he was right, they were what the French called *Corvettes de 20 x 8*. In British service, they might be rated as post ships, under the command of post captains, or sloops-of-war, with commanders in charge.

L'Enchanté, on the other hand, was a proper frigate of 36 guns and very likely carried a main battery of 18-pounder long guns. A few French ships carried howitzers on their foredecks and quarterdecks, but most carried long guns. A ship of *L'Enchanté*'s size would likely have twelve or fourteen 6-pounder cannons and perhaps a pair of 8-pounder chase guns, in addition to the 26 great guns of the main battery. Duncan did some quick calculations in his head and came to the conclusion that the enemy would have a weight of broadside of somewhat less than 300 pounds versus the almost 600 pounds of *Fidelity*.

Accuracy and rate of fire ultimately meant more than weight of broadside, and Duncan had confidence in his crew to match or better the French in these aspects, as well. In a single ship to ship action, there would be little reason to doubt the British would be victorious, but the presence of the corvettes complicated matters considerably. He looked back over the stern and searched for *La Tempête*. They had sailed her under the horizon, as he had expected, and she was no longer visible.

Still contemplating the best engagement strategy, Duncan walked forward from the quarterdeck along the leeward gangway to the foredeck and approached the chase guns. After returning the salute from the midshipman in charge, he said, "Mr. Webb, congratulations to you and your crew on striking the first blow against our last adversary. It seems you'll have the honor again. You may open fire at your convenience at whatever target you choose."

Webb beamed and responded, "Aye, aye, sir…and thank you sir." Then he added to the gun crew, "Right then, lads, let's be about it and see if we can bloody the Frenchies' noses, or bring down a spar, or two." The crew gave a cheer and ran out the starboard 9-pounder while the gun captain, Anderson, called orders to adjust the elevation and windage. When all was ready, the crew stood back and the gun captain held his fist in the air and looked back to Webb, who nodded and called out, "Fire!"

Anderson waited a moment for the movement of the ship to match the lay of the gun and then yanked the lanyard. The 9-pounder barked out and the smoke was immediately whipped away by the wind. "Huzzah! A hit!" the crew yelled as splinters and dust rose amidships of *Le Carcajou's* side and a small rust-ringed, black hole was left where the shot struck a few feet above the waterline.

"Very good then. Nice shot. Carry on," Duncan said, as he smiled and started to walk back to the quarterdeck.

When he was about halfway along the gangway, the lookout called down from the maintop, "Deck there! The convoy is signaling and changing course. New heading has the wind two points on the larboard quarter." Duncan wanted to speed up, but his training forced him to remain outwardly calm as he continued at the same pace. That heading would bring the convoy onto a course converging more quickly with *Fidelity* rather than moving away on a roughly parallel course. *What would make the convoy change course now, and why would they be making the change and signaling the frigate rather than the other way around*? He wondered.

The master met him at the edge of the quarterdeck just as the lookout called down with the answer to Duncan's question, "Land ho! One point forward of the starboard beam."

"That will be Isla Mona, if I'm not mistaken, sir," Jones commented. "Which means we're heading directly for Isla Saona, about 40 miles off. The French have cut it too closely or made a mistake in navigation. They'll need to work south to avoid a lee shore on Hispaniola or Isla Beata." He clapped and rubbed his hands together. "I think we've got them, sir. They'll be hard pressed to avoid a fight, now."

"Aye, Mr. Jones. When the frigate changes course, I'd like you to match them point by point. However, you're to continue the turn until the leeward guns will bear on the corvette in the middle of the formation. Understood?"

The master smiled, "Aye, sir, I understand. You're looking to even up the odds with the first strike, eh, sir?"

Duncan returned the smile. "Let's hope so." Then, he turned and called down to the main deck, "Mr. Williams, run out the starboard battery and elevate the guns for the first corvette." Since he knew the whole crew was listening, he added, "We'll slap one of the little terriers before we go for the hound."

L'Enchanté ran out her larboard battery and began her turn within a few minutes, with *Fidelity* matching her movement perfectly. With the courses remaining roughly parallel and *Fidelity* 500 feet astern of *L'Enchanté*, neither ship could make their broadside bear on the other. However, once the French completed their turn, *Fidelity* kept turning.

The French had to make a quick decision. They could turn further to be in a position to return fire, or they could continue on their new course and take a broadside without responding. The downside for *Fidelity* was that she would lose speed and position by turning so far and would have to turn back and regain speed to close with the French. There would only be time for one broadside.

The French frigate captain knew all of this as well, and held his course, expecting to be the target. He waited as the British ship's broadside faced his stern quarter and then saw the ship continuing beyond. He glanced over his shoulder at *Le Carcajou* and realized they were also in range. He scowled and turned to watch what would happen. He had accepted some time before that a battle was inevitable, but this was not the way he had intended it to begin.

Williams was leaning over so he could see out through a gunport, and he watched as the frigate crossed his field of vision and waited for the corvette to come into view. "Hold, men. Remember, it's the little one we want. There'll only be time for one shot, so gun captains make your aim true." A few moments later, he stood up and made sure he was well out of the way before he yelled, "Fire!"

Fidelity shook violently and was pushed sideways in the water as all the guns of the starboard battery fired in a thunderous explosion. The wind whipped the smoke away from them, but the yellowish gray cloud obscured their view of the target. The crews were busy reloading, having been trained to continue their work without looking for the effect of the previous shot. Although Williams was trying to see, he could not from his vantage point.

Webb's little battery on the foredeck could only make their single starboard carronade bear on the target, but even from his higher position, the smoke was blowing forward and away from the ship, thus making it impossible to see what was happening.

Duncan's view from the quarterdeck was much better, although far from perfect. His ears were ringing, and the tremendous concussion of broadside made him feel as if he had been struck in the chest. He knew the corvette was at the extreme range of the carronades, but the long guns could easily reach it.

He realized he was holding his breath and exhaled as the sea around *Le Carcajou* looked as if it was boiling from the fall of shot. He could see dust and splinters rising in clouds in several locations and watched as sails split and yards hung precariously or fell into the netting below. He stepped toward the side for a better view as he ordered, "Mr. Jones, put us back on a course matching the French."

The smoke was beginning to thin and clear. The gun crews had completed reloading and were now free to look and see the result of their handiwork. A cheer erupted as the maintopmast slowly broke and fell to the deck, followed by the foretopmast.

The captain of the French frigate watched from his quarterdeck and knew at once that things had just changed dramatically. *Le Carcajou* was already slowing down and would not be able to make repairs quickly enough to keep away from the British. It was time to stop running, and he gave orders to signal his new intent to the captain of *Le Furet*.

Duncan was still focused on the corvette when he realized *L'Enchanté* was turning again. He quickly adjusted to the changing situation and called out, "Belay that order, Master, maintain course. Mr. Williams, prepare to engage the frigate. Hold the first round until I give the order, then fire as fast and hard as you can." He was conscious that his orders were perhaps not the classical, cool-headed type he would have wished, but the excitement was too much to contain. The battle was about to begin in earnest.

Chapter Four

It was the French who fired first. *Fidelity* had started to turn as the larboard side of *L'Enchanté* disappeared behind a thick cloud of smoke with bright jets of flame stabbing through. The whizzing and whining of chain shot and langridge tearing through the sails and rigging overhead was almost simultaneous with the cannon blasts.

Duncan took a quick look aloft and scanned for damage. Nothing critical had been hit and all the spars and masts were intact. Top men were already moving to splice ropes, control ripped sails, and fix other minor damage. It was a typical French tactic to fire the first broadside into the rigging in hopes of disabling or slowing their opponent.

It was another variation in approach based on the pursuit of different strategic goals. French ships were lighter and had less room for supplies because they were not designed to constantly patrol the seas like the British. The French were not trying to command the sea. Their ships and fleets left port with specific strategic goals, which were more important than tactical ship to ship actions, and captains were instructed to avoid combat to pursue those greater goals. Where a British commander might face court martial for cowardice if they failed to engage an enemy, a French commander might be commended for avoiding a delay in their mission.

Of course, that did not mean the French could not or would not fight, it simply meant they might try to avoid it within reasonable limits. If forced to engage in close combat, they would switch to round shot and fire into the hull of an opponent, just as the British would. Once engaged, national strategies meant very little, as actions became an immediate issue of life or death. For most of the crew, the world would shrink to a small group of trusted mates for whom they would fight, kill, or die. The nation, the government, even the ship, were difficult to consider in the heat of battle.

Duncan was not surprised by the first broadside being aimed high, but seeing that it had done little damage, he expected the next to be aimed lower. There was little chance the French could escape now, and *Fidelity* was too strong an opponent to toy with. *Fidelity* had continued to turn and now her broadside was targeting *L'Enchanté* across about four hundred feet of water. Duncan turned to find Williams standing below in the waist of the ship and called out to him, "Fire!"

Williams relayed the order and again the starboard battery roared out in a tremendous broadside. With the wind blowing through the ship and almost directly at their opponent, the gun crews had the advantage of being able to reload without the smoke obscuring their vision and stinging their eyes. The French were not so fortunate, and the smoke from their cannons would be blown back into their faces and fill the deck where they would be forced to toil on in a stinking haze.

"Mr. Jones, keep her thus," Duncan ordered as he looked for damage on the French frigate while also making a mental note of the locations, headings, and movement of the two corvettes. Virtually every shot had struck the hull of the enemy, but for all that, there was little apparent damage. The muzzles of the French cannons began poking out through gunports as he was watching. Their captain had decided on another complete broadside and was waiting until all the guns were ready. It did not take long before the French ship temporarily disappeared behind a wall of smoke and flame again, but almost immediately, the faster reloading British carronades began to reply.

Fidelity and *L'Enchanté* continued to exchange a fierce cannonade as they sailed along on almost parallel courses. After their second broadside, the French had begun firing individual cannons as quickly as they could be reloaded. The British were doing the same, and the result was like constant thunder rolling back and forth between the ships. Duncan had stuffed cotton and beeswax in his ears, but the noise was still painfully loud. He had to yell as loud as he could to be heard by those standing within a few feet.

Rather than just pacing back and forth on the quarterdeck, he was moving to various locations to see what was happening and try to keep track of the two corvettes. There was little he needed to do concerning *L'Enchanté* at this time. The gun crews knew to keep firing, and the master knew to keep them in range. Both crews were slowing down as fatigue began to take its toll, but the British were still firing faster than the French.

Duncan glanced back over at *L'Enchanté* and could see real damage now. Two gunports had been smashed into a single opening, and the lack of movement indicated that the guns had been dismounted or overturned. The rail was missing in large sections, and there were numerous shot holes in the hull. Here and there, yards hung at odd angles and rigging hung with frayed ends. Several sails were pockmarked with shot holes. Then he turned his attention to *Fidelity* and quickly surveyed the damage.

•   •   •

Jenkins was doing his duty, serving one of the starboard guns. In addition to hauling on tackle to move the huge iron beast into position to fire, it was his job to swab out the barrel each time they fired. It was a critical task, since one missed smoldering ember could prematurely ignite the powder charge when it was placed into the cannon. Mitchell fired the cannon again - how many times they had fired, nobody could remember. The gun hit the deck, and Mitchell started calling out the commands to reload. At this point, few could hear his hoarse yells, but they all knew the steps and just kept going through the monotonous motions as quickly as their tired, aching muscles would allow.

Jenkins dipped the swab in a large tub of sea water and then shoved it into the black barrel of the cannon as soon as another crew member had removed the worm. The swab sizzled and steamed from the heat of the iron, and he rammed it in and out while turning it as best he could with his sore hands. He could feel blisters forming, even through his rough and calloused skin. He pulled the swab out and moved out of the way for the next step in reloading.

Suddenly, there was a crashing sound mixed with buzzing and whining as the air was filled with wooden splinters. Jenkins was thrown to the deck and onto his hands and knees. He reached up and touched his head where something had struck him. He looked at the blood on his fingers and decided it could not be too bad a wound based on the amount and color of the blood. He was dazed and trying to orient himself when he felt strong hands grabbing him by the arm and shoulder, lifting him to his feet and tossing him to the side of the ship. He was able to maintain his balance as he landed against the side of the ship and struck the back of his head. Somehow, the pain helped him to focus again, and he looked to see what was happening.

An enemy cannonball had come through the side of the ship where the tackle was mounted to hold the cannon in place. With the ropes severed, the cannon had nothing to hold it and it was beginning to roll around with the movement of the ship. Mitchell had been the one to move Jenkins before the cannon could strike him. He was yelling orders to the rest of the gun crew to try to regain control of the cannon.

With his mind clearing, Jenkins looked around and grabbed one of the stout pieces of wood used to adjust the aim of the cannons. The cannon had to be tripped onto its side so it would stop rolling on the wooden wheels of its truck.

Up forward, Williams was moving back and forth to keep the crews firing as quickly as they could. He saw the commotion under the quarterdeck and realized immediately what was happening. A loose cannon was one of the more dangerous things you could encounter on a ship. The iron barrel of a 24-pounder was nine and half feet long and, together with the wooden truck, weighed almost three tons. It could easily crush people or even smash right through the side of the ship. He started to yell orders to help the gun crew control the weapon.

On the quarterdeck, Duncan could tell that something was happening below the quarterdeck. He had felt the impact of a shot followed by screams of pain and now excited yelling, but he could not make out the words. His first thought was fire - every sailor's worst nightmare, but he quickly ruled this out since no one was forming a bucket brigade. He looked down at Williams and saw him pointing toward the stern of the ship and yelling something, but again, Duncan could not make out the words. There was a black blur as a cannonball flew past and Williams' hand disappeared in a puff of pink mist. Williams looked blankly at the empty end of his sleeve and slumped to the deck.

Duncan felt a lump in his throat but forced himself to look away and find something else to focus on. He looked for the two corvettes and could make out the masts and sails of *Le Carcajou*, still being masked by *L'Enchanté*. The damaged corvette had fallen back at first, but as the frigates slowed to fight each other, *Le Carcajou* could keep up and was sailing roughly parallel to *L'Enchanté* about a quarter of a mile off her leeward beam. In that location, she was effectively out of the fight - for now.

Le Furet had been slowly working her way to windward and trying to position herself off *Fidelity*'s larboard front quarter. Although she could turn and fire on the British at any time from her current position, she would likely continue to work herself into a better position to be able to make her broadside bear without becoming a target. Properly positioned, she could stand off and fire into *Fidelity*'s relatively unprotected and weak bow without getting in the way of *L'Enchanté*.

With neither corvette presenting an immediate danger, Duncan was about to continue ignoring them and focus on *L'Enchanté*, when an idea occurred to him. He decided instantly to pursue this new idea. He looked back into the waist where Williams had fallen. Williams was no longer there, likely having been taken to the surgeon in the orlap. Lieutenant Cole had taken over command of the gundeck, and Duncan called to him. "Mr. Cole, run out the larboard battery and prepare to engage the corvette." Turning to the helm, he added, "Larboard your helm and run us alongside the frigate." Finally, to the men of the afterguard, he ordered, "Prepare grapples."

Under the direct supervision of the master, the two helmsmen began quickly turning the wheel to starboard, thus moving the tiller to larboard. This, in turn moved the rudder and the ship to starboard. The extra drag of the rudder would significantly slow the ship. In fact, the master was counting on it. He would turn sharply toward the French and then back to a parallel course. If he timed it right, they would glide alongside and grapples would be thrown to keep the two ships together. If he timed it wrong, they would either crash into the French or end up very close to the enemy cannons, but unable to silence them by boarding.

Very few British ships carried enough crew members to fully man both batteries at the same time, so it was common for members of gun crews on the unengaged side to supplement the crews of the other. So it was that Edwards and Carlson were helping serve a gun on the starboard side, opposite their normal location. When the cannon directly astern of their position came loose and started to roll about the deck, they both leaped into action. Along with Jenkins and several others, they were using crows to try to block the wheels and stop the motion long enough to lever the cannon onto its side.

Mitchell was directing the work and calling out commands. It seemed the gun was relatively stable, and he stepped forward to help a young sailor struggling with the weight. Lieutenant Cole was yelling for the larboard crews to return to their guns, but Edwards and Carlson could not let go of their hold on the cannon. Suddenly, the ship began to turn and heal over. The cannon shifted again and twisted sideways, crushing Mitchell and the other sailor as it fell onto its side. Mitchell was killed instantly, but the young sailor screamed in pain as his legs were pinned under the weight.

Carlson started toward the injured man, but Edwards stopped him. "His mates will help him as much as he can be helped. We've got to get to Nellie." Carlson took one more look at the young sailor and Mitchell's crushed body and moved back to the larboard side. Jenkins was organizing what was left of the gun crew to try to free the trapped man. Everyone had their duty and must play their part.

Fidelity's sharp turn toward *L'Enchanté* suddenly shifted the battle in two significant ways. First, *Fidelity's* larboard cannons could now bear on *Le Furet*. However, this meant that not only could the starboard cannons not continue to fire at *L'Enchanté*, but the French frigate could now fire into the bow of the British ship. Duncan had decided to take this risk - hoping that the French would not be ready to take full advantage of the situation and calculating that the angle would not allow the French an opportunity to truly rake the ship. His luck held, and both hopes were realized.

Duncan was about to command Cole to fire as the guns began to bear but changed his mind. Instead, he raised his sword and made sure Cole was watching for his command to fire. Although it seemed logical that each gun fired individually would do the same total damage as if they were all fired together in a broadside, the psychological effect of a complete broadside, and the sudden devastation it could cause, made it a valuable tactic. So Duncan waited.

Finally, he swung the sword down to his side and yelled, "Fire! By broadside! Fire!"

Cole and the gun captains were ready, and all the long guns and carronades of the larboard battery roared out in unison. Even after the nearly constant din of the cannonade with *L'Enchanté*, this sound was bone-jarringly loud. Almost immediately, the master commanded the helmsman to begin the turn back to come alongside the French. *L'Enchanté* had only managed to fire a single cannon during this time and her crews were now beginning to line the side, preparing to repel boarders - or perhaps cross to the deck of *Fidelity* when they touched.

Duncan looked toward *Le Furet* as he ordered, "Man the starboard guns and fire by broadside." The corvette was a complete ruin. All three masts had toppled and what remained was a heap of sails, rigging, and broken spars.

Fidelity completed the turn back parallel to *L'Enchanté* just before they struck. French crewman had already begun to climb onto the rails and now stood waiting as the ships moved within twenty feet of each other. The British cannons and carronades fired for one last time before the ships touched with many of the 24-pound shot punching right through both sides of the ship, leaving deadly splinters and severed bodies in their wake. Not all the guns were ready, so it was not a full broadside, but the damage was severe, nonetheless.

Along the British rails and from their fighting tops, the swivel guns sprayed the French deck with canister shot. The defenseless Frenchmen waiting along the rails were mowed down like wheat before a scythe. A few left standing were targets for the sharpshooters. One man struck in the chest by a musket ball looked down in confusion at the hole and spreading bloom of blood on his shirt before teetering forward and splashing headfirst into the sea between the two ships.

On *Fidelity's* opposite side, the gun crews had finished reloading and poured another broadside into the hapless corvette that now lay in ruin, totally dismasted and unable to maneuver out of the way. Too late, Duncan realized that he had failed to order them to stop firing on the helpless ship., He yelled as the last cannon fired, "Secure the guns and prepare to board!"

The bosun was walking along behind the crews to relay the message to those whose hearing was too damaged by the cannonade to hear the shouts. He lifted his whistle to his mouth and sounded the command to prepare to board just as a French musket ball struck him in the back of the neck. He fell to his knees with the whistle still in his lips and then fell forward, face first, onto the deck.

The hulls of the two ships came grinding together. Duncan could feel the shuddering through the deck, and even with his dulled hearing could make out the sounds of creaking as the ships pushed against one another. "Grapples away!" he ordered as he moved toward the side and used the rigging to pull himself onto the rail. He was about to give the order to board the French ship when he realized that his crew were already swarming across and leaping onto the enemy rigging while screaming and yelling. The first across were hacking their way through boarding nets and French sailors to make way for their comrades to follow.

Duncan drew his sword, timed the movements of the ships, and leaped across, aiming for a hole in the boarding nets near the front of the French quarterdeck. He grabbed a secure rope with one hand and swung down from the rail onto the enemy deck. Suddenly, the rush and excitement that came with anticipating hand to hand combat left him, and he felt the calmness and sense of purpose that he always did in these situations. The noise and chaos of battle seemed to fade, and he experienced his surroundings with a sharp clarity, as if time had slowed down.

Two French marines were moving toward him. The closest was charging toward him from slightly to his right with a bayonet mounted on his musket, while the second had a cutlass and was coming straight toward him. He deflected the bayonet with the blade of his sword, then parried the cutlass and, with a flick of his wrist, slashed across the second man's throat. At almost the same time, he raised his right knee and struck the first Frenchman hard in the stomach as the momentum of his charge carried him past. The marine fell forward, still clutching his musket, and Duncan struck the back of his head with a powerful blow using the hilt of his sword. There was a crunch, and the Frenchman went limp and crumpled to the deck.

The second marine had dropped his cutlass and had both hands to his neck, trying in vain to stop the bright red blood squirting between his fingers from his wound. Duncan stepped past him, knowing he was no longer a threat.

Another French seaman with a cutlass was directly in front of him. He parried the first blow and drew a pistol from his belt with his left hand. The Frenchman lunged forward, and Duncan dodged left, causing the blade to just miss. They both regained their balance and this time, Duncan struck first, with a slicing attack from right to left. His adversary deflected the sword down and Duncan extended the blade and struck the man in the ribs. At the same time, he raised the pistol and fired it directly into the man's chest.

The Frenchman fell forward and to Duncan's right, twisting his sword from his hand as he went down. Duncan dropped the first pistol, drew the second from his belt, and fired it at a large man with a boarding axe who was rushing toward him. The shot was too quick and poorly aimed with the ball grazing the man's right arm, but doing nothing to stop him, or even slow him down.

As this latest assailant swung his axe, Duncan dropped to the deck while pulling both tomahawks from the back of his belt. The axe arced over his head, and he spun to his left as the man stepped almost past him. With two quick strikes, he severed the man's left hamstring and slashed his right calf. Duncan stood back up, completing his spin, and brought a tomahawk down hard into the man's back. The man fell to his knees and tumbled forward.

Withdrawing the thin blade of the tomahawk, Duncan turned toward the rear of the quarterdeck and came face to face with a French lieutenant holding an elegantly decorated sword. The lieutenant's wide eyes flashed from both tomahawks to Duncan's face, and he dropped the sword and put his hands up as he yelled, "*Je me rends, je me rends! S'il vous plaît, ne me tuez pas!*"

Duncan responded in English while still holding the tomahawks in a threatening position, "Do you speak English? Are your surrendering yourself, or the ship?"

The scared Frenchman glanced toward a midshipman near the mast and nodded his head while saying, "*Oui! Oui!* I surrender the ship. We yield!" As he spoke, the midshipman cut the halyards and the French flag blew fluttering into the sea. Within a few moments, the rest of the French crew noticed and started dropping their weapons. Some, unfortunately, did not notice in time to avoid being wounded or killed as the melee slowly ground to a halt.

Duncan spoke to the lieutenant again, "Where is your captain?"

"He has fallen and was taken below. I am Jean-Pierre Bernier, third lieutenant of *L'Enchanté*, and ranking officer still alive, or fit for duty." He slowly bent down and picked his sword up from the deck, being careful to hold it by the blade with the hilt extended toward Duncan. "I surrender the ship to you, *monsieur*."

Duncan finally lowered his hands. "You may keep the sword, so long as you give your parole. You and your crew fought bravely. I am Lieutenant Joseph Duncan, in temporary command of His Majesty's Ship, *Fidelity*. Please instruct your crew to assemble forward."

Bernier nodded, mumbled that he accepted parole, and with a shaky voice called out commands to the crew in French while Duncan wiped the blood from his tomahawks and slid them back into his belt. He glanced about, making a quick survey of the situation and personnel available. Looking back to *Fidelity*'s quarterdeck, he cupped his hands and called out, "Mr. Connor, take the launch and a prize crew to secure the corvette, *Le Furet*." Turning back to the deck of the captured French frigate, he searched for the red uniforms of the marines and spotted two midshipmen standing nearby. "Mr. Rogers, take a file of marines and search below decks. Get all the prisoners up on deck together. Mr. Powell, organize a search of the French for weapons and gather them forward under guard with marines manning the pivot guns to cover them."

"Aye, aye, sir," they both responded, almost in unison, as they quickly went about their tasks.

Lieutenant Cole was in the waist of the ship talking to Edwards, the quarter gunner. He turned and called to Duncan, "Excuse me, sir. It appears that the starboard battery is loaded and could be brought to bear on the corvette, yonder." He pointed out to *Le Carcajou*, sailing along on a parallel course slightly forward of amidships.

Duncan glanced at the corvette and smiled. "Excellent observation, Mr. Cole. Be so kind as to serve them a load of their own iron, if you would, please. Fire at your convenience."

Cole turned to Edwards and soon two guns were manned, run out, and prepared to fire. With *L'Enchanté* and *Fidelity* still tied together with the grapples, the motion of the ship was somewhat odd. However, when Edwards judged the moment to be right, he yanked the lanyard of the forward gun. The other gun fired almost simultaneously. Before the smoke had cleared, the French flag aboard *Le Carcajou* was hauled down. Duncan was not sure if either gun had hit the target, but with the French surrendering, it really did not matter.

"Good work, Mr. Cole. Please send a prize crew to take possession - perhaps a master's mate to command. We seem to be running low on midshipmen and I'd like you back aboard *Fidelity*, making preparations to get underway as soon as we secure the prizes. I still have a mind to run down those transports."

"Aye, aye, sir," Cole smiled back as the crew secured the guns.

Duncan turned as he heard a voice say, "Sir, I think you may have dropped these." Jenkins was standing there holding Duncan's sword and one of his pistols. He automatically felt for the other pistol and found it back in his belt. He did not remember putting that one back and only vaguely remembered dropping the other. The sword had been cleaned.

Reaching out for the sword and pistol, he thanked Jenkins, who knuckled his forehead and walked away to his other duties.

The defeated French crew were being herded forward into a sullen mass with heads hanging low while being closely watched by marines and seaman. Mates and crew were slowly organizing things about the deck, and some were headed back to *Fidelity* to set things right there as well. There was considerable damage to both ships, with rigging, sails, and yards hanging in unnatural positions. However, both were in generally good sailing condition and there was no immediate danger. A few hours would see most of the minor damage repaired and the ships fully functional, even if not pretty.

Duncan was studying the damage to *Fidelity* and judging how long it might take to get her underway in pursuit of the convoy, which was now some five miles away. He was also considering how many men he should leave to man each prize. Even without accounting for casualties, *Fidelity* would be very shorthanded. He glanced back east, wondering about *La Tempête* and considering whether it was foolhardy to chase after the convoy and risk the current prizes being retaken. There would not be sufficient crew aboard any ship to fight off an attack. He could barely spare enough men to sail the ships and guard the prisoners.

"Pardon me, sir," Midshipman Rogers spoke from behind.

Duncan turned around and saw the young man standing with a British officer he did not recognize. In answer to his questioning look, Rogers spoke. "Sir, we found some British prisoners locked up in the hold."

The officer stepped past Rogers and spoke for himself as he offered his hand, "Lieutenant Alan Cahill, previously in command of *HM Brig Swallow*, at your service, sir."

Duncan shook the man's hand, noticing the smiling but obviously tired face and the disheveled uniform. "Pleased to meet you, sir. I'm Joseph Duncan, lieutenant in acting command of *HMS Fidelity*." He nodded toward the ship. "The frigate alongside. Might I enquire as to how you came to take passage on a French national ship?"

Cahill was a little taken aback by the form of the question, but responded, "At sunrise three days ago, we found ourselves surrounded by French warships at first light. We must have sailed among them in the dark. We had no hope of outrunning them, and being so outgunned, I saw no choice but to surrender the crew and try to save their lives." He had been looking down while he said this, but then looked Duncan in the eye, and concluded, "So, I set fire to *Swallow* and put the crew in the boats. The French got us, but they didn't get the *Swallow*, sir."

Duncan's mind was racing again. "Very good. I'm pleased to make your acquaintance. Why were you below with the men? Did the French not offer you parole?"

"Oh, they offered, sir, but I refused, so they locked me below."

"How many men do you have fit for duty, Lieutenant?" Duncan inquired.

"A few minor cuts, bruises, and burns, but they're all fit for duty, sir. I'm the only officer and I have 58 men and 15 marines."

Duncan thought quickly about the best way to use these unexpected reinforcements. "Excellent! If you and your crew would be so kind as to take control of this ship and get her fixed up, I'll take my crew and see if we can't catch the rest of the convoy. I'll leave a few extra marines to help with the prisoners until we can figure out something more permanent."

Cahill looked conflicted as he spoke. "Um…sir…I should remind you, I lost my command and must face court martial for my actions."

Duncan frowned, "Yes, quite, but the needs of the service take precedent, and all that. If you'd like, I can leave one of my marine lieutenants onboard with you and you can consider yourself under open arrest pending your court martial when we get to Antigua. Or perhaps I should say, 'if' we get to Antigua. There's still another frigate out there, *Le Tempête*. We knocked her about a bit, but I'm not sanguine that she's down for the count. If she comes back, we'll need everyone we've got. I'm desperately short of officers. So, unless you have further objections, please carry on."

Cahill's relief was palpable as he responded, "Aye, aye, sir!"

●   ●   ●

Forty-five minutes later, Duncan was back aboard *Fidelity*, which had been cut loose from *L'Enchanté* and was under sail.

There was still damage apparent almost anywhere you looked - missing sections of railing, raised furrows of oak splinters in the deck, a dismounted cannon lashed to the side, splices in rigging, patches in sails, and bloodstains. However, the masts and spars had been mostly spared any significant damage and sails were blossoming in the wind and being sheeted home.

Duncan, Lieutenant Cole, and the master were all standing on the quarterdeck. "Mr. Jones, do you judge she'll carry any more sail in her current condition?"

The master took a whistling breath through his clenched teeth and responded, "I'd not recommend more, sir. Everything seems to be holding together, but there might be more damage than we can see, and most of the rigging is dependent on temporary splices and bends. If anything, I'd say we're tempting fate a bit, as it is."

"I concur. I'd like to put on more sail, but it will do us little good if we spring a yard or lose a mast," Duncan commented.

Several minutes passed. The crew was still working on various repairs and trimming sails. Recovering from the battle sounds, emotions, and memories, they were working in silence. They all knew that they were among the lucky ones to still be alive, and even luckier to not be down in the orlap waiting for their turn with the surgeon. Some of those unfortunate souls might rather be dead than to suffer what was before them.

Duncan studied what was left of the convoy through his telescope. The swell was getting even larger, and it was hard to focus on individual ships as they popped up and down. Through the corner of his eye, he could see the master making observations with his sextant for the third time since they had cut loose from the French frigate. Duncan was curious about one of the ships in the convoy. Four were clearly large merchant ships, but the fifth looked different. He called out to Cole, who was also studying the convoy through a telescope, "Mr. Cole, what do you observe about the lead ship in the convoy?"

Cole lowered his telescope and turned to face Duncan. "Sir, for all the life of me, it looks to be a warship. It's hard to make out clearly, but it seems to be a small frigate. I could be wrong, though."

Duncan nodded, "That's what I thought, too. It looks like we might still have a fight left today. Please be sure the guns and crew are ready. See if the carpenter can remount the cannon in the starboard battery."

"Aye, aye, sir." Cole saluted and headed to the waist of the ship.

The master wandered over to Duncan, holding his sextant and a slate with some calculations. "Sir, we're head reaching the convoy by over four knots. At this rate, we'll be in range in just over an hour."

"Thank you, Mr. Jones. At least we'll know soon what we're up against." Then, in a much louder voice, Duncan called out, "Mr. Webb, take a glass and head aloft. I'd like you to observe the convoy, the individual movements of the ships, and especially the large one in the lead. Do you have a watch?"

Webb reached for a telescope from the rack and responded, "Yes, sir, I have a watch, but it doesn't have a second hand, sir."

"Very well, that will do. I want you back down here to report in 30 minutes. Understood?"

"Aye, aye, sir," the midshipman responded. He turned and scampered up the shrouds with the telescope bouncing on a sling over his shoulder.

•   •   •

It seemed odd for time to pass without hearing the ubiquitous ship's bell. However, at some point in the previous battle, the bell had been cleanly shot away and was nowhere to be found. Duncan found himself repeatedly looking at his watch to keep track of time.

Repairs were continuing all over the ship - some makeshift and expedient, others careful and complete. Where time and materials permitted, there was a sense of doing it once rather than having to come back again. However, as *Fidelity* sailed toward another potential battle, there simply was not time to correct everything to the normal, high standard of the British Navy.

The dismounted gun from the starboard battery had been reattached to its truck, and the carpenter had installed new fittings in the side of the ship. A crew of men were swarming around it now, reconnecting the tackle and testing everything. The deck they were working on was stained with blood, as it would remain until there was time to scrub it clean and let the sun bleach it out.

Duncan looked at his watch again. Sunset would be in less than two hours. He glanced forward at the remainder of the convoy and then back at the group of damaged warships they had left in their wake. He lifted his telescope and slid it open to the mark on the barrel that best focused it for his eye. Through it, he looked at the damaged ships bobbing up and down on the increasing swell and tried to judge their condition. He strained intently at the horizon beyond for any sign of *La Tempête,* but saw nothing.

Shifting his attention back, he could see that preparations were being made to have *L'Enchanté* take *Le Furet* under tow. It appeared that a line had been passed between the two, and crews working from boats were pulling back and forth. *Le Carcajou* was standing to and seemed ready to get under way as soon as *L'Enchanté* was ready. Duncan's orders had been for the three ships to sail toward *Fidelity* as soon as they were ready. The sails started to fall and be sheeted home on *L'Enchanté* as they started to get underway.

Duncan heard footsteps behind him and turned to find Midshipman Webb ready to report. "Well then, Mr. Webb, what have you learned?"

"Sir. There are four fat supply ships that are clearly struggling to carry as much sail as possible, but they're straining in the freshening wind and their bows are slamming through the waves instead of riding the swell. I think it unlikely they can maintain even their current speed for much longer."

Webb paused to swallow and suck in a quick breath, then continued, "And then, sir, there's a fifth ship. She's forward and leeward of the others and has maintained that position. However, she's sailing rather easily, given the conditions, and has her sails brailed up. Even then, she tends to start to outrun the others and then shorten sail to fall back into position. Sir, I think it's a frigate, but she seems lightly manned…from what I could see, sir."

Duncan nodded at the report and asked, "If you were commanding a warship escorting merchant ships, what advantage could be gained by staying to leeward while an enemy came down with the wind?"

Webb looked puzzled and a bit nervous being asked a question which confused him. "Um…I don't know, sir. I can't think of any reason."

"Exactly what I was thinking, Mr. Webb. I suppose we'll only find out by sailing over and asking them nicely to explain." Duncan smiled. "Excellent report and good observations. Off you go then, get yourself back forward and prepare the long nines to begin the questioning."

Webb knuckled his head and responded before walking briskly away, "Aye, aye, sir!"

Duncan turned to the helm and spoke in a louder voice, "Mr. Jones, did you hear Mr. Webb's report?"

Jones lowered the sextant from his eye, scribbled something quickly on his slate and then responded. "Aye, sir. Matches what I've been seeing myself and it just don't signify. I can't puzzle out what they're about. But I suspect we'll know soon enough." He glanced at the slate. "I judge us to be in range of random shot now for the chase guns."

Duncan turned back to look forward at the convoy lumbering along and ordered, "Lieutenant Cole, send word forward instructing Mr. Webb to fire at will and to continue until told otherwise."

Cole responded quickly, "Aye, aye, sir."

"One more thing, Mr. Cole," Duncan added in a lower voice, "you're the only other officer fit for duty. You're to stay with me on the quarterdeck. When we engage, I'd like you to have Midshipman Webb command the main batteries, with Midshipman Hyde rotated forward."

Cole swallowed hard. He felt a long way from the midshipman in charge of signals just a day and a half ago. He had always dreamed of promotion, but the reality was much more frightening than he had imagined. "Aye, aye, sir!" He hoped it sounded more convincing than he felt.

Ten minutes later, the starboard chase gun barked out and the faint, acrid smell of burned powder swirled about the ship despite the strong wind. Almost immediately, the entire convoy cut loose their sails, hauled down their colors, and sat wallowing on the sea in total submission.

In a manner of minutes, *Fidelity* was hove to within a cable with her full starboard battery run out and ready for any duplicity while Midshipmen Webb and Hyde led boarding parties. Duncan was on the quarterdeck with Cole, watching the boats pulling through the swell with the sailors and marines being soaked by spindrift.

The master approached them and spoke to Duncan, "Sir, the French prizes - that is, the first batch - will be here in about fifteen minutes at their current rate."

Duncan spun around as he responded, "Ah, excellent. I had rather lost track of them. Do we have anyone left who could bend on a signal and instruct them to heave to while remaining to windward of us?"

Jones smiled at the lighthearted nature of the *command* and replied, "Aye, sir. I'm thinking Jenkins could be spared from the wheel, as we're not moving at the moment."

"Thank you, Mr. Jones. After they acknowledge, have him prepare a general hoist of 'captain repair aboard' and have it ready once our crews have secured this current flock of prizes."

Whitehall appeared at the top of the ladder. He had removed the apron he wore during surgery, but his clothes were spotted with blood and the rolled-up cuffs of his sleeves were a dark crimson, slowly drying to a ruddy brown. His face was drawn and strained, and his eyes were tired and bloodshot from working in the darkness below deck with only the light from smoky lanthorns.

He approached Duncan and asked, "Would now be a good time to make my report on casualties, sir?"

"There's never a good time to hear about those that have fallen, but now is as good a time as any. I sincerely hope there will be no more lost today. First, though, how is the captain?"

Whitehall looked shocked and confused and then gathered himself. "Did you not receive my message from Midshipman O'Toole?"

"I haven't seen Mr. O'Toole since he accompanied you to the orlap. The last I heard was your rather curt update via Mr. Webb."

The confusion left Whitehall's face, and he responded, "Ah, I believe I understand. First, sir, I must regret to inform you that Captain Blackwell succumbed to his wounds before the first battle this morning."

Now it was Duncan who stood stunned while Whitehall continued, "I sent O'Toole with the message while I finished cleaning up. Before I had a chance to come up myself, I started to receive wounded as the battle began. Among the first was O'Toole, but I assumed he had delivered his message before falling, as I sent him a quarter hour, or more, before I heard the first shots. He has a nasty head wound and has been unconscious. It will leave a horrible scar, but I'm hopeful he'll pull through."

Duncan's mind was racing, but at the same time, there was a fog making it hard for him to keep up with what he was hearing. All he could force himself to ask was a needless question. "The captain is dead?"

A look of compassion replaced the exhaustion as Whitehall responded quietly, "Yes, and I'm very sorry to have told you in this manner. Perhaps my report can wait until later, sir."

To say that Duncan began to recover would be a stretch, but he was able to begin to control his emotions and think more clearly. "That's quite alright, Alfred. You had no reason to think I didn't already know. Please do continue with your full report."

"Thank you, sir. We've suffered seven dead…that would be in addition to the captain. Among them was the bosun, but no other warrants or officers. There are twenty-eight wounded still in the sickbay, among them Lieutenant Williams and Midshipman O'Toole. Twelve, I judge serious enough that I fear they won't survive, but I'm hopeful for the rest - which would include the Lieutenant and Midshipman. However, I must caution you to remember that wounds are not always fully apparent and there remains the possibility of corruption of the remaining flesh, or loss to fever. We'll know more in twenty-four hours, sir."

"What of Rupert? What is his condition? I saw him fall, but I wasn't sure of the extent of his injuries. He lost his hand. Was there more?"

"An odd case, to be sure. A cannon ball amputated his left hand as cleanly, if not better, than I could have done myself. Of course, I had to do a little to clean it up and provide for sufficient skin to cover the stump, but really the French did most of the hard work. He lost a lot of blood, but I can find no other sign of injury. Barring fever or corruption, I expect he'll be fine."

"Thank you, Alfred."

"I'm just doing my duty, sir. Here is a full list of the wounded," Whitehall responded, as he offered a piece of paper. Duncan took it, noting silently that it was smudged with the blood of some unknown sailor.

Chapter Five

The sun was just beginning to set as Duncan assembled the senior leaders left under what was now his command. It felt odd to be in the great cabin knowing that the captain was gone, but it was the only place in the ship big enough to hold the group, and even then, they were sitting and standing shoulder to shoulder, as Duncan addressed them.

There had been no further trouble in securing the French prizes, and there was no sign of *La Tempête*. Duncan knew the big frigate was out there somewhere and still presented a significant threat. *Fidelity* had been repositioned slightly windward of the cluster of prize ships, in the best position to protect them from attack or recapture. The ships were all hove to and bobbing and rolling on the increasingly troubled sea, casting long shadows in the dying light.

"As most of you are no doubt already aware, Captain Blackwell was among those who have been taken from us. While we will have time to mourn our losses and say our goodbyes, those that remain must toil on. The enemy is still out there, and the storm Mr. Jones has predicted is about to make for a messy night."

Duncan glanced about the group, measuring the mood and noting reactions as he continued, "I'd like to introduce Lieutenant Cahill, who was a prisoner, along with his crew, aboard the frigate *L'Enchanté*."

"Thank you, sir. I appreciate you coming along when you did and look forward to helping in any way I can," Cahill announced. There was a general, if somewhat subdued, welcome from those present, and a few sitting close by offered their hands in welcome while those further away nodded or mumbled their regards.

Duncan understood that the awkwardness was not just caused by having a stranger among them, but also a result of that "stranger" outranking virtually all of them. He decided to press on and let things settle themselves later. "Lieutenant Cahill, you will keep most of your crew from *Swallow* and take command of *L'Enchanté*. You are to select from your men a prize crew to man the supply ship, *Adelelmus*."

"Aye, aye, sir," came the standard response from Cahill.

Duncan looked from Cahill to the rest of the group. "We will be desperately short of men to man all the prizes. The other three supply ships, *Ebontius*, *Petit Mulet*, and *Émeraude* will be manned by *Fidelity* crewman. All of the French prisoners, except the officers, will be placed aboard *Le Furet* and guarded by marines under the command of Marine Lieutenant Hobbs. Mr. Powell will command six seamen, who will stay aboard to monitor the tow line to *L'Enchanté* and control the helm. Lieutenant Cole will tell off the list of crewmen for each ship.

"The French officers have all given their parole and will be brought aboard *Fidelity*, with the exception of the recent captain of *L'Enchanté*, whom Mr. Whitehall has informed me is in too delicate a state to move at this time, due to his injuries." Duncan turned to address Cahill directly. "I presume you have no objection to keeping your former captor as your guest while he recovers."

Cahill smiled. "No objection at all, sir. I only have a surgeon's mate among my crew, but we'll take care of Captain Bouchard.

I only met him on one occasion, and I would enjoy the opportunity to speak to him again with the tables turned."

Duncan returned the smile and continued, "In the event that we meet with the enemy and engage in battle, you will cut loose from the tow and fight to the best of your ability. Lieutenant Cole, you will command *Le Carcajou*. You'll have a limited crew, but as many as we can spare. Along with *L'Enchanté*, and of course, *Fidelity*, *Le Carcajou* is the only other ship in condition to fight. If called upon to do so, you will engage with the enemy and fight to protect the rest of the convoy.

"Mr. Webb will take command of *Le Zephyr*." As it turned out, the suspected small frigate traveling with the supply ships had, in fact, been a very old 8-pounder, 26-gun frigate traveling en flute, with almost all her cannons removed. "Since she is unarmed, you will have a minimal crew to sail her and will travel with the supply ships."

Duncan continued describing the assignment and expectations of the prize captains and crews. After answering questions, he concluded, "So, to recap, we will make course for Antigua and travel together, remaining in close formation to allow for easy signaling and for protection. At night we will have taffrail lanthorns lit at all times. In the event of distress or spotting the enemy at night, the general alarm will be two red rockets. If separated from the rest of the group, you are each charged with making your way to Antigua and reporting there to the commander-in-chief. You will all be provided with written orders by Mr. Christian. If there are no further questions, please return to your ships and prepare to get underway. It's likely to be a rough night, but I have full confidence in you and all the crew. Godspeed."

•   •   •

The first squall struck the flotilla about two hours after dark. Sheets of driving rain were accompanied by brilliant flashes of lightning and a combination of deep growls of rolling thunder and sharp crashes that shook the ships. The gusting winds made the rigging hum in varying tones while the masts and spars creaked and groaned. The ships had reduced sail to the minimum needed to maintain steerage and continued to beat almost futilely against the wind.

Duncan stood on the quarterdeck near the helm with a safety line lashed about his waist. The wind was ripping at his oilskin tarpaulin coat, and under it his uniform was thoroughly soaked. His leather boots squished when he moved, and he shivered uncontrollably. The storm had come too suddenly to allow time to turn the ships to run before the wind. If they could hold their own against the wind, they at least would not be pushed further from Antigua, even if they were not getting any closer. So far, all the ships seemed to be managing and it would be far too dangerous risking being rolled on their sides to try to turn off the wind now.

Another flash of lightning lit up the night, temporarily illuminating the surrounding ships in ghostly silhouettes. At the front of the pack was L'Enchanté, with Le Furet still in tow. The balance of speed versus risk to sail and rigging was greatest for L'Enchanté, as she needed to keep constant strain on the towline. Failure to do so could allow a collision, or a slack line suddenly strained again, might snap. Le Furet had no chance if cut loose - without even a stump of a mast left standing, there was no way to carry sail and provide the necessary headway to allow the rudder to bite and steer the ship. If the towline parted, it would only be a matter of time until she rolled and foundered.

Not for the first time this evening, Duncan questioned his decisions. Lieutenant Cahill and Midshipman Powell were facing daunting challenges, and Duncan's orders had forced them into the situation. He had no way of knowing Cahill's capabilities, and he had chosen Powell because he was the most junior, and to be perfectly frank with himself, the most expendable midshipman. He may have sentenced them both to death, but short of abandoning *Le Furet*, someone had to face the challenge.

As he thought of that option, he wondered why he hadn't considered abandoning, or burning, the damaged corvette. It had immediately struck him as a convenient and relatively secure way to transport the French prisoners. After that, he had directed all his thoughts to implementing the idea. He had ordered the cannons cast overboard to provide more room, decrease the weight, and remove them from use in any potential uprising by the prisoners. He had provided marines to guard the prisoners so fewer sailors were needed. Should he have given more thought to not trying to keep the prize? He promised himself he would consider all options in the future, but for now, the die was cast and the fate of both crews and prisoners would be decided by powers and further decisions that were outside his control.

He kept reviewing in his mind the assignment of prize crew and command for each vessel. Again and again, he questioned whether he had made the correct decisions on the number of crew needed to control each ship and the balance of experience between the commander and the chosen crewmen. With so few officers available, he was relying on midshipmen, master's mates, and even one quartermaster's mate. Had he kept too many crew members aboard *Fidelity* in an attempt to preserve some ability to fight *La Tempête*, or another enemy? Or had he not kept enough - would the big frigate descend upon them after the storm and recapture the weakened ships one at a time? *Fidelity* had captured them all, so there was no reason to think *La Tempête* could not do the same.

The questions and doubts kept swirling around his head. He became aware of someone yelling to him and turned to see the master. Jones was yelling through cupped hands, but still Duncan could not hear him over the din of the storm. He tried again to yell something and then pointed past Duncan off the larboard side. This, at least, Duncan understood, and he turned his head to look in that direction.

There was little Duncan could see in the blackness of the night until the next stroke of lightning lit up the sky and sea. That moment of light revealed the supply ship, *Petit Mulet*, facing a dire emergency. What little sail she had carried was blowing loose and whipping in the wind. Without the force of the wind providing forward thrust, she would soon lose her ability to steer. The flash captured several sailors on the yards trying to control the wild canvas. As the lightning faded, the view went back to black.

Moments later, another flash provided the next snapshot of what was transpiring. Duncan watched in horror as each new flash showed the progress of the unfolding disaster. *Petit Mulet* was beginning to be turned by the wind and soon would be beam on to both the wind and running sea. The utter helplessness of watching caused both a lump in Duncan's throat and a rising anger in his chest. He was riveted to the scene but appalled by what he was seeing.

Another flash and this time *Petit Mulet* was heeling over as a wave towered over her. Duncan suspected this was the end...but then another flash, and she had righted herself - perhaps there was still hope. Darkness followed for what seemed an eternity and, for the first time, Duncan found himself wishing for more lightning. Some dim flashes in the distance provided an unclear picture of what was happening, but it looked as if *Petit Mulet* had turned about and was running before the wind. More time passed and then another flash confirmed this - although the stricken ship was now two or three cables behind *Fidelity* and heading in a completely different direction. If they could hold that course and get control of the sails, there was a good chance they might yet survive.

As if to torment Duncan, the lightning abruptly stopped. He realized it was just his foul mood overwhelming his reason in wishing for more lightning, so he could see what had happened. He also realized that he could now hear the master. The wind, although still gusting, was dropping from gale force.

Jones was shouting a question. "Do you think she'll make it, sir? I thought sure she was lost but somehow she turned and might just make it if she isn't pooped. It's too bloody dark to see anymore, but unless I'm imagining it, I think I may have caught the twinkling of her taffrail lamps between the waves. On that course, she'll be miles away soon enough."

Duncan tried to respond, but had to clear his throat and try again after he produced little more than a croak. "Let's hope she made it and can get some canvas back on. What of the rest of the ships? Could you see anything?"

Jones shook his head and Duncan noticed the wind had once more become significantly gentler. "I couldn't keep track of them all, sir. Everything else I saw looked like they were holding their own. But I wouldn't say that I could see them all."

The storm left almost as suddenly as it started, but the cloudy sky obscured any moon or starlight. There were some taffrail lights visible, but the continuing swell made it hard to count the number of ships still traveling with *Fidelity*. Several more times during the night, squalls struck the ships, but nothing as dangerous or violent as the first. Each cell of the storm seemed a bit weaker than the previous.

The wind had died down to a level that allowed more easy conversation when Stanley appeared on deck with a wooden mug and approached Duncan. "Sir, I couldn't make anything hot, what with the ship bouncing about like an apple in a bucket, but I've brought you a little something to wet your mouth."

Duncan was suddenly aware of how thirsty he was, and he took it gratefully. "Thank you, Stanley. The rest of me is plenty wet, but I could use something to drink." He raised the cup and took first a sip and then a gulp. It was lime juice and water with more than a hint of brandy. The lime juice stung his swollen tongue, and the brandy burned his throat, but the combination of quenching his thirst and warming his stomach was worth the discomfort. He drained the cup and handed it back as he felt the warmth spreading through his body. "Thank you, again."

Stanley took the cup and asked, "Would you like me to bring you another?"

Duncan thought for a moment and then responded, "Yes, please, but this time without brandy. One was good, but two might be too much tonight. Oh, and if you wouldn't mind, please bring one, brandy and all, for the master."

Stanley's face broke into a wide smile. "Aye, aye, sir. I'll be back in a jiffy."

•   •   •

The master snapped the cover shut on his watch and then said, "Sir, it's almost sunrise. I don't expect we'll see much sun, but there should be enough light to see."

"Aye, Mr. Jones. Then we'll see what's left of our little fleet. What do you predict for the weather today?"

"Well, sir, I haven't had a chance to check the glass, but I'd say it feels like it will clear. I'd say a cloudy morning and strong swell continuing for several days, but otherwise, I think we're in for a bit o' sun."

"I'd relish a chance to dry out, not to mention some calm weather to put things to right," Duncan commented. "At least it's unlikely *La Tempête* will be able to find us. To be honest, I've very little idea where we are. What are your thoughts on our position?"

"No idea, sir, and I don't mind admitting it. The way we bounced around last night, I'd be lucky to guess within 50 miles. Not much to even dead reckon with, as we couldn't cast a log and I can't read me own writing on the slate for the headings. Maybe it will clear by noon and we can take sights. If not, I don't think we can go far amiss by continuing southeast until we can get a fix. My gut tells me we didn't lose much easting, but the leeway to the south is anyone's guess."

"What about currents in this area?"

"Nothing much to speak of, sir. It's the wind what did for us."

Duncan realized the sky was starting to brighten in the east and resisted the urge to cross his fingers for what he would soon see. Slowly, much more slowly than normal in the West Indies, the sunrise finally turned night into day. The sky was still filled with dark, angry clouds scudding quickly, so low that it looked as if you might reach them from the upper masthead.

The lookout called out, "Sail, ho. Multiple sail."

Duncan and the master used telescopes to quickly scan the horizon in all directions.

Duncan finally spoke. "I count six sail. What do you see?"

The master lowered his glass. "Aye, sir, I get six as well."

The lookout called down again, "Six sail. Two sail three points off the starboard bow, one sail on the starboard beam, one sail off the starboard aft quarter, one sail a point forward of the larboard beam, and one sail a point starboard of directly astern."

The master smiled and said, "Not a bad start after such a night. Let's hope the others are just a bit further off."

"Aye, Mr. Jones. Let's hope. Fire a gun and send up a blue flare," Duncan ordered. He had been tempted to use the night signal for "close on flag" during the night, after the storm, to try to keep the group together but was concerned about the potential for collisions in the dark. Even with daylight, it was still too dark to expect the others to see a flag hoist, so the night signal seemed like a good compromise. "As our friends are spread about, let's heave to and let them come to us."

It took several hours for four of the ships to close on *Fidelity*. *L'Enchanté* and *Le Furet* were several miles downwind and could not easily return without coming completely about. They had clearly tried to slow, but with *Fidelity* standing to, they were actually getting slowly further away.

While waiting for the other ships, Duncan went down to his cabin. The wardroom was strangely empty and quiet. The door to Williams' cabin was unlatched and swinging with the roll of the ship. Duncan walked over and closed it. He thought again about Whitehall's latest report concerning his friend. Williams was unconscious and had developed a fever overnight. There was nothing they could do but wait. Whitehall had explained that normally for a fever, he might try bleeding the patient, but Williams had lost too much blood already.

Duncan opened the door to his cabin and looked longingly at his bed, swinging gently from the eyehooks in the deck beams. His eyes felt like they had sand in them and every muscle and joint in his body ached. The cabin was so tiny and dark he was concerned that if he went in, he might not have the will to resist sleep, so he dragged his chest into the wardroom and sat in a chair by the table to remove his soggy boots.

After tugging and pulling to little effect, he gave up and, using a penknife, slit the side of each leather boot in order to get his swollen feet out. It was a shame to destroy a serviceable pair of boots, but he was too tired and sore to care right now. Even removing his soaked shirt took almost more effort than he could muster. Finally, he finished undressing and left the wet clothes draped over chairs and hanging from hooks on the beams. Normally, he would have been appalled to see such a mess, but right now, it did not matter.

After standing shivering and naked for a few moments to let his skin dry, he reached into his sea chest and started to dress in the best uniform he had left. Finally, he forced his feet into his shoes - there was no chance of getting his other pair of boots on. He closed the chest and thought about putting it away in his cabin, but instead left it where it was and walked slowly out of the wardroom.

His next stop was the captain's cabin, to find the book of prayers he would need for the burial service. Duncan sat down at the captain's desk and started to open the small doors and drawers. Only one drawer had a lock, and Duncan didn't think the book would be there. In any event, he had the key, as Whitehall had given it to him, along with a key to the arms chest. The captain had normally worn them both on a thin chain around his neck, and now Duncan had put it around his own.

He opened a drawer on the left side of the desk and immediately recognized the small book bound in worn, black leather. The cover was embossed in faded gold and said simply, "Book of Prayer". He picked it up and opened it. On the first page, the full title was printed, "Abridgement of the Book of Common Prayer (1773), by Benjamin Franklin & Sir Francis Dashwood".

Duncan leafed through to find the correct page and found that it was already marked. He glanced through the text to refresh his memory on the service. Although he had heard it read more times than he cared to remember, this would be the first time he was the one to read it. He looked at his watch, put the desk back in order, and then stood, walked out, and climbed to the quarterdeck.

It was just before noon, and the flotilla had caught up with *L'Enchanté* and *Le Furet*. All seven ships were sailing easily within a couple of cables of each other. The sky was still blanketed in thick dark clouds and a strong breeze was blowing. No other sails had been sighted. *Petit Mulet* and *Le Zephyr* were missing.

"Hoist a general signal to heave to," Duncan ordered. "Then, run up the 'church' signal and call all hands for burial services." The signal went up and the ships quickly complied and sat, rolling and pitching in the swell. The crews of the other ships were all turned out and stood lining the rails or watching from perches in the rigging.

On Duncan's signal, the senior bosun's mate, as the acting bosun, signaled for all hands on deck and the crew slowly shuffled into place. It seemed like a small number with so many off in prizes, or still on the sick list. There were a few who had gotten permission from the surgeon to attend the services, and stood, or sat in chairs, with their bright white bandages conspicuous in the crowd.

Duncan waited until the movements had stopped and then stepped to the front of the quarterdeck and looked down at the twelve bodies lying under sailcloth in a neat row in the waist of the ship. Four more had not survived the night. Each was sown into his own hammock, usually by a surviving friend, with the final stitch being superstitiously sown through the nose of the victim to ensure they were dead. At their feet were two cannonballs to make sure the bodies did not float.

Duncan cleared his throat, opened the book of prayers to the well-worn page marked with a thin, faded blue ribbon, and blinked to clear his eyes. He looked up at the assembled crew and ordered, "Off hats." After a pause, he began the service.

"I am the resurrection and the life, saith the Lord: he that believeth in me, though he were dead, yet shall he live.

"We brought nothing into this world, and it is certain we can carry nothing out. The Lord gave, and the Lord hath taken away; blessed be the Name of the Lord."

He flipped the page to the Psalm he had chosen and continued,

"Before ever the earth and the world were made: thou art God everlasting, and without end. For a thousand years in thy sight are but as yesterday. We consume away in thy displeasure: and are afraid. The days of our age are but threescore years and ten; and though men be so strong, that they come to fourscore years: yet is their strength then but labor and sorrow; So teach us to number our days: that we may apply our hearts unto wisdom. Amen."

He paused again and blinked to clear his eyes as he turned back to the burial rites.

"O death, where is thy sting? O grave, where is thy victory? The sting of death is sin. Thanks be to God, which giveth us the victory, through Jesus Christ. Therefore, my beloved, be ye stedfast, unmoveable, always abounding in the work of the Lord, forasmuch as ye know that your labor is not in vain."

Duncan paused and looked at the men standing near the end of each plank upon which rested a body. At this signal, they stepped solemnly forward. A few were weeping quietly. Lieutenant Cole was standing at the nearest plank where the body of Captain Blackwell was waiting in the stillness of death. Cole was not crying, but was staring out to sea with a deeply sorrowful expression. Duncan had to clear his throat to continue,

"Man hath but a short time to live, and is full of misery. He cometh up, and is cut down like a flower; he fleeth as it were a shadow, and never continueth in one stay.

"Yet, O Lord God most holy, O Lord most mighty, O holy and most merciful Savior, deliver us not into eternal death.

"Thou knowest, Lord, the secrets of our hearts: suffer us not at our last hour, for any pains of death, to fall from thee."

Duncan nodded to the men at the planks and they each reached down and slowly lifted the end of the planks to let the bodies slip from beneath the sailcloth and slide off into the sea, one at a time, beginning with Cole sending Captain Blackwell's body on its last journey. Duncan read in a strong voice,

"Forasmuch as it hath pleased Almighty God, to take unto him the souls of our dear brothers here departed, we commit their bodies to the sea."

Duncan waited until the last body splashed into the water and then said, "Blessed are the dead which die in the Lord: even so, saith the Spirit; for they rest from their labors."

"Lord, have mercy upon us."

Most of the crew had been through this service many times before and did not require prompting to begin to pray the Lord's Prayer together. When they had finished, Duncan waited a moment, listening to the sobs of some that had lost close friends, before he concluded,

"The grace of our Lord Jesus Christ, and the love of God, be with us all evermore. Amen."

Duncan slowly and carefully closed the book and adjusted the ribbon to lie flat, marking the correct page for the next time it would be needed. Sadly, there was little chance it would not be needed again, and probably quite soon. He thought about saying a few words, but decided to let each man deal with the losses in his own way. "Dismiss the crew and make preparations to get underway." He turned and walked toward the captain's cabin to return the prayer book as Lieutenant Cole gave orders to ready the ship and signal the rest of the flotilla to make sail.

Just as he reached the top of the ladder, Duncan froze in his tracks as he heard the lookout call down, "Deck there! Sail ho! Two points to starboard off the stern!"

With everyone on deck, there was a moment of confusion as those on watch rushed to their sail making duty stations, while those off watch tried to find locations with a view of the unknown ship. Of course, they could not see anything from the deck yet, and milled about, waiting to see what might happen. Just then, there was a break in the clouds and sunlight poured suddenly onto *Fidelity* and the surrounding ships.

Duncan slipped the book into his pocket and moved back near the taffrail where he instructed the master's mate, currently in charge of signals, "General signal to make sail in line ahead." Then, turning back and walking to the helm, "All hands to make sail and come about." He turned to Mr. Jones and added, "Let's go find out who our new guest is, shall we?"

Freed to run with the wind again, *Fidelity* surged forward, dancing over the swell and charging with a bone in her in teeth toward the new sail. They were not quite at the ship's best point of sail but were as close as they could come to provide the course Duncan wanted to close with the strange sail. If it were friendly, he wanted to be in a position relative to the wind and other vessels to allow signals to be easily seen and answered. If it were an enemy, he would protect the advantage of approaching from upwind.

Within an hour, the mysterious sail had been identified by hoisting her number and responding properly to the challenge hoist from *Fidelity*. It was *Petit Mulet* and their next signal, "rejoining the fleet," was greeted with cheers from the crew.

Duncan stood beaming on the quarterdeck and ordered, "Acknowledge and prepare to come about. Then, signal *L'Enchanté* 'sail is friendly' followed by 'heave to' and 'repair to flag'. Let's hope Lieutenant Cahill makes out that I'd like the convoy to wait for us before heading to Antigua."

The helmsmen and others on deck chuckled lightly.

Chapter Six

Eight days later, Admiral Lord Edmund Fairhurst, Commander-in-Chief of the West Indies Windward Fleet, was sitting in his cabin at his big mahogany desk, reviewing various boring documents when his flag lieutenant, Richard Strickland, entered and said, "Excuse me, M'Lord. The shore lookout has signaled eight sail approaching. Seven are flying the ensign over French colors and the eighth appears to be *Fidelity*."

Admiral Fairhurst dropped his papers and slammed his fist on the desk. "Ha! He found them! I knew I could count on Blackwell. How far out are they?"

"They appear to be on a tack to weather the headland and the winds are favorable for them to enter the harbor. I expect they'll be at anchor within three hours, M'Lord."

"Excellent! Excellent! Send a messenger alerting Mr. Hirschhorn and requesting he repair aboard immediately. I presume Captain Tankersley is already aware of this news?"

"Aye, M'Lord, he was on deck when the signal was received."

"So yet again, I'm the last to know, eh, Flags?" the Admiral jokingly chided, with a mischievous glimmer in his eyes.

.   .   .

Duncan stood on the quarterdeck, feeling a combination of relief and apprehension. With the entrance to English Harbour clearly visible, he was quite sure now that he would succeed in bringing his flotilla of prizes home. However, he would be facing the admiral, and there was no way of knowing what would follow. He might be promoted out of the ship, perhaps even to a command of his own, or he might serve under the new captain appointed to *Fidelity*. Would he still be considered for first lieutenant, or did that possibility die with Captain Blackwell? Perhaps the admiral never even received the recommendation.

He thought about the two thick stacks of paper sealed in oilskin and tied with twine that were locked in the captain's desk. One was the report that Duncan had written and rewritten, again and again, trying to accurately portray what had transpired. He had labored over it almost every day as they sailed back. Each time he thought it was complete, a sleepless night would leave him with a thought to note the actions of another crewmember or a way to better describe the events.

The other package was made up of Captain Blackwell's notes, logs, and unfinished reports. Duncan had felt guilty reading them, but it was important to make sure he knew all he could about the command he had temporarily assumed. In the end, he learned very little he had not already known and felt it proper to provide them all to the admiral for consideration.

After *Petit Mulet* had rejoined the group, there was not much to report. Three more crewmembers had died from their injuries and a topman in the prize crew aboard *Le Carcajou* had fallen and broken his leg while making repairs to the rigging. Six of the other injured crewmembers had recovered enough to return to at least light duty. The others were stable and recovering, except Lieutenant Williams, who was still in a fevered sleep. Hopefully, more could be done for him at the naval hospital on Antigua.

Even Midshipman O'Toole had recovered enough to sit up and eat. He was plagued by headaches, and his head was still bandaged to cover the gash from forehead to ear. His biggest concern was that half his head had been shaved by the surgeon and his queue was now lopsided. Whitehall assured him that it would grow back, and they had daily arguments about when he could return to duty.

O'Toole didn't have any memory of what had happened after beginning to climb the ladder up to the deck. How he had been found and taken back to the orlap and how long he had been laying there before he was found was a mystery lost in the fog of war. Perhaps the one that found him was one of the later casualties. It seemed that they would never know.

As the master had predicted, the swell lasted for three days after the storm, but the weather was clear and the fresh wind allowed them to make a quick passage of long board tacks - which was no doubt appreciated by the under-manned crews of the prize ships. Duncan had even allowed the ships to wear away from the wind, instead of tacking through it, in an effort to reduce the demands on the crews and strain on the riggings.

He did not feel these measures were soft, but rather were the responsible choice given the conditions. He did, however, wonder if it might come back to haunt him, or perhaps help him, later with the crew, if he were appointed as first lieutenant. He consoled himself with the knowledge that he did not make the decision based on any consideration of what would be thought of him either way by the crew or officers. It had been his decision; he had made it, and he was comfortable with it.

He had also made a decision concerning how they would enter the harbor. He was somewhat less comfortable with that, but still felt it was right. It was customary that the ships bringing prizes into port would lead the way. He had decided to hold *Fidelity* back to enter last. It was not a decision based on show, as much as a concern that if anything happened at the last moment, he wanted *Fidelity* in a position to offer assistance. Mostly, he was concerned about *L'Enchanté* still towing *Le Furet*. After making it this far, he did not want to be helplessly downwind, or even anchored, if they needed assistance.

He watched the group of ships sailing in almost perfect line formation with two cable lengths between each one and was suddenly filled with pride. They had done it. *L'Enchanté* had already sailed into the bay. They had cast loose the tow and allowed *Le Furet* to anchor and then had sailed to their own anchorage as directed by the harbor pilot boat. The pilot boats were having a busy time of it as *Émeraude*, *Petit Mulet*, *Adelelmus*, and *Ebontius* sailed into their anchorages.

Le Carcajou was next and was dutifully following the pilot boat. Another pilot boat was signaling *Fidelity* to follow as they glided slowly through the entrance to English Harbour. Able Seaman Carlson dropped lightly onto the deck and approached Duncan while knuckling his head and said, "I had a good view of the anchorage, sir. There's no sign of anything that looks to be *Le Zephyr*."

Duncan sighed and responded, "Thank you, Carlson. You may return to duty."

Carlson knuckled his head again and loped off along the catwalk and climbed back into the riggings to help bring in sail when they anchored. Duncan had sent him to the crosstrees to search the anchorage for the missing frigate. They had doubled the lookout each day on their sail back to Antigua and having never spotted her, he had hoped that she had made it back ahead of the rest.

Even lightly manned as she was, the frigate should have been able to easily outsail the flotilla, which was limited by the speed of the lumbering supply ships. Duncan was forced to accept that

Le Zephyr had been lost, either to the sea or perhaps recaptured by the French. For the hundredth time in the last week, Duncan wondered about the fate of Midshipman Webb and the prize crew.

He turned back and ordered, "Mr. Wendt, please begin the salute to the flag."

Wendt was ready and almost instantly the first gun banged out, followed in perfect rhythm by the rest until the last gun of the salute. The echoing of the last cannon rebounded around the bay as the first gun of the return salute from the mighty first-rate flagship could be heard. There were a few minutes of silence as *Fidelity* approached her anchorage, came gently about, and dropped anchor. In a sudden motion that was a true credit to the crew, the sails disappeared at once, and *Fidelity* snubbed to her anchor.

Just as the anchor had hit the water, a signal broke out from the flagship. It was "captain repair aboard" as he had expected, and Duncan had started to the captain's cabin to retrieve the reports before the signal had been officially relayed. He called back to the signalman as he started down the ladder, "Acknowledge."

Everyone was expecting the summons and by the time Duncan had returned to the deck, the barge was alongside and manned by the captain's boat crew. The captain's coxswain had been one of the crewmen injured in the battle who had not yet returned to duty. Sitting instead in at the tiller was Jenkins. Duncan saluted the deck and descended the side. He timed his last step to the movements of the boat and ship and dropped lightly into the boat and made his way to the sternsheets. He moved his sword out of the way and sat down, then ordered, "Cast off and make way."

Jenkins complied without hesitation and released the stern painter, "Bowman, push off. Out oars. Make way all and put your backs into it, lads, the admiral is watchin'."

Admiral Fairhurst was not, in fact, watching. However, Flag Captain George Tankersley, and Flag Lieutenant Richard Strickland, were standing next to each other on the deck of the flagship, and they *were* watching. They both wore a look of concern and, almost in unison, they raised telescopes to their eyes. Lowering his telescope, Tankersley said, "You better inform the admiral."

"Aye, aye, sir," Strickland responded and walked off at a brisk pace.

A few moments later, he entered the admiral's cabin, approached the desk and waited until the admiral finished what he was doing, looked up with a smile and asked, "Ah, is Blackwell on his way over?"

"M'Lord, I'm afraid there may be bad news. *Fidelity* came to anchor with her yards all acockbill and there is a lieutenant in the sternsheets of the approaching boat. I couldn't make out the face from this distance, but from their build, I'm quite certain that it is not Lieutenant Miller. Commander Henry is in port, as you are aware. That leaves Lieutenants Duncan and Williams, but it could be either."

The admiral's face fell instantly, and the mirthful spark left his eyes. "Bring whoever it is down as soon as they're aboard and find Mr. Hirschhorn and get him down here, now."

"Aye, M'Lord."

There was a gentle breeze blowing to keep it from being oppressively hot, but the direct sun on his dark uniform was making Duncan sweat. He could feel the sweat running down his back, and any movement was uncomfortable because his shirt was plastered to his skin. He sat up as straight as he could and stared forward. He knew there were many eyes upon him, not just from the flagship, but from all the naval ships in harbor and probably from land, as well.

It was, of course, impossible to sail in unnoticed considering the need to fire a salute, and by now everyone would be abuzz about the prizes and the condition of *Fidelity*. Normally, a ship's crew would pride themselves on the appearance of their ship in port. Sails would be carefully gathered and gaskets placed to make a neat and even appearance. Each yard would be carefully turned to the same angle and leveled to be perfectly perpendicular to the mast or parallel to the sea. There was one exception to this custom. If the captain of the ship was dead, the yards would be purposefully left at odd, conflicting angles.

Fidelity had returned home and was mourning the loss of her captain. Everyone could plainly see this, and word was spreading through the town and through the fleet. Duncan knew everyone was watching the boat pull toward the flagship with a lieutenant rather than the captain, and everyone wanted to know what had happened. This was always the case, but even more so when the captain was a popular and well-known commander, such as Elijah Blackwell.

As the boat approached the flagship, a sentry on deck called out, "Boat, ahoy!"

Jenkins was ready and responded, "Aye, aye," holding up one finger to alert the side party that an officer was aboard and that he was a lieutenant. In that way, they would know what honors to provide as he mounted the deck. For a lieutenant, this did not amount to very much, but Duncan was used to it. Jenkins gave the final commands to the boat crew as he pushed the tiller hard over to bring the boat alongside. "Toss your oars. Bowman hook on." They glided to a stop with a hook in the main chains and two ropes dropped from above to secure the boat.

Duncan stood up and moved to the side of the boat. "Jenkins, you may lay off, I don't know how long I shall be." Jenkins responded with the customary confirmation of the order and Duncan adjusted his sword, timed his step, and then clamored up the side of the flagship, pulling himself up the manropes and through the entry port.

As he stepped through the entry port, he turned to salute the quarterdeck and found himself face to face, or perhaps more accurately, face to chest, with a great bear of a man - a captain, and in fact, the flag captain. Although surprised to be greeted by such a high-ranking individual, he maintained his composure and announced, "Lieutenant Joseph Duncan, in temporary command of his majesty's frigate *Fidelity*, reporting to the flag, as ordered, sir."

Captain Tankersley returned the salute and asked, "So it's true, then? Captain Blackwell is dead?"

"Aye, sir. I'm sorry to have to bear such news." He became aware of the flag lieutenant standing next to the captain.

The lieutenant stepped forward and offered his hand. "Welcome aboard, sir. I'm Lieutenant Richard Strickland, the admiral's aide-de-camp. The admiral will see you now. Please follow us."

The flag captain recovered a bit, and also offered his hand to Duncan, "I'm terribly sorry, please forgive my impoliteness. I'm Tankersley, flag captain. Welcome aboard *Glory*."

They walked in a file following the flag captain and entered the admiral's cabin without being announced. Captain Tankersley walked to the right of the huge desk and sat down in a chair. The two lieutenants approached the desk and stood before it. "Sir, may I present Lieutenant Joseph Duncan, in acting command of *Fidelity*."

Duncan had seen the admiral from a distance at several events, but had never met him, or even been this close to him. He was a man of an indeterminate age - and likely older than he actually looked. He was of medium height and had the appearance of someone who probably had a strong build when he was younger. Unlike many in high station, he appeared to have remained very fit, and although his physical strength and size may have been somewhat diminished with age, he was far from looking feeble, or even old. Only his hair, almost completely white and close cropped to somewhat disguise the thinning across the crown of his head, betrayed his age.

The admiral's face was dominated by a somewhat bulbous nose and shockingly bright blue eyes that gave the impression of being made of ice. His face was weathered and wrinkled from a life spent at sea, but his skin color was relatively light - at this point in his career, he spent more of his time in his cabin with paperwork than out exposed to the elements. The overall effect radiated strength, and his somewhat intimidating expression made him seem far from pleased.

He looked at Duncan, scanned him slowly from face to foot and back to face, as if taking his measure, before speaking. "What's become of Captain Blackwell?"

Duncan had, of course, expected there to be questions about Blackwell's death, but so far, this was not quite how he had envisioned the interview and giving his report. However, he had been taught to respond when questioned and to endeavor to be succinct, accurate, and complete in his answers. "M'Lord, I regret to inform you that a gusting wind caused a line to part and Captain Blackwell was struck in the head by a falling block on June 15th, early in the forenoon watch. He died about three hours later."

"A parting line and a falling block? So, he wasn't killed during the capture of the convoy? Had the line been damaged in the fighting?" The admiral's expression had seemed to soften a little.

Duncan quickly composed his thoughts to be sure and answer all three questions. "The line had not been damaged in battle, M'Lord. We had not yet spotted the convoy when the accident occurred. The line had shown no signs of excessive wear or damage prior to breaking, M'Lord."

The admiral's expression suddenly hardened again. "Captain Blackwell died before the capture of the convoy."

"Yes, M'Lord. He was struck just prior to the lookout's call at the sighting of the first sail and died just before we engaged the French."

"So, Lieutenant Miller had assumed command and ordered the attack? What has become of him? Is he wounded or dead?"

"Lieutenant Miller had been certified unfit for duty due to illness and removed from his post, M'Lord. I was in command of *Fidelity* and ordered the attack."

The admiral's expression hardened again, and his tone was almost menacing. "This is a bit to take in. The captain was dead, the first lieutenant incapacitated, the second lieutenant away in a prize, and you, as a junior lieutenant, acting on your own initiative, engaged and captured a convoy of seven French ships? Is that what you're telling me?"

Duncan was not sure where this line of questioning was heading, but it did not look to be a good place. Still, there was little he could do but respond, as demanded. "Yes, M'Lord, except there were nine French ships. A second large frigate was engaged, but not captured, and a light frigate traveling en flute was captured but disappeared in a squall during the sail back to Antigua."

The admiral stared at Duncan for a moment. Duncan was not sure if he was supposed to say something more or wait. He decided to wait and forced himself to continue to look the admiral in the eye, despite the icy glare. Finally, the admiral broke the silence. "I presume you have this all detailed in your report. I think it might be better that I read it before we continue."

Duncan had almost forgotten about the reports, but he quickly produced them. "Aye, M'Lord. I have my report, as well as the unfinished report and notes from Captain Blackwell and the master's log." He held them out to the admiral.

The admiral took the reports without looking away from Duncan and placed them on the corner of his desk before dismissing him. "That will be all for now, Lieutenant. You may return to *Fidelity*."

Duncan saluted and responded, "Thank you, M'Lord," before turning and leaving the cabin. Lieutenant Strickland followed him in silence until they had returned to the entry port. The officer of the watch had already signaled for the boat to return, and it was just gliding into place, bumping gently against the flagship as it did so.

Just after he saluted the quarterdeck and turned to go over the side, Strickland stepped close and spoke, "Please understand, sir, the admiral and Captain Blackwell were quite close friends, and his loss has come as something of a shock to all of us. We are at war and good men die. Although it's unreasonable, there are some that you don't think capable of dying. Captain Blackwell was such a man, and the loss is all that much more poignant because of it."

Duncan replied, "Thank you." He wasn't sure what else to say and was a little confused by what had transpired in the admiral's cabin.

"*Fidelity* will, of course, need supplies and repairs. The dockyard will take care of that. Is there anything else with which I might be of assistance?" Strickland offered.

Duncan thought for a moment, considering all he had expected to say and discuss with the admiral, and two thoughts came to mind. "Very kind of you to offer, sir. I've several wounded, including Lieutenant Williams, who is my particular friend. If there is a way to expedite his transfer to the shore hospital, I would be much obliged." Strickland nodded and Duncan added, "I've also a midshipman aboard who was promoted to acting lieutenant by Captain Blackwell. If there is to be an examination, soon, is there a way to get him on the list?"

Strickland replied, "There is one scheduled for tomorrow, and the list has already been prepared. However, if you give me his name, I'll have him added. Instructions will be delivered to

Fidelity this afternoon. He'll need all his certificates and logs. I trust he can get them prepared in time?"

Duncan smiled and offered his hand. "Thank you very much! His name is David Cole and I'm sure he'll be strongly motivated to be prepared. Thank you again, and good day."

Duncan descended the side feeling a bit better but still upset by his brief interview with the admiral. Jenkins sensed the mood and wondered how it could have gone so quickly, but tried to act normally, as he greeted the lieutenant, "Welcome back, sir. Back to *Fidelity*?"

Duncan sat down and responded, "Aye." The crossing was made in silence except for the necessary commands to the boat crew. They approached *Fidelity* and Duncan ordered, "Pull slowly once around. I've not had an opportunity to survey the damage and repairs from this viewpoint."

After circling the ship, they pulled to the entry port and Duncan went aboard. He responded flatly to the welcomes and headed directly to the orlap, both to check on Williams and to avoid the questioning looks.

•   •   •

Williams' condition was unchanged. He was still unconscious and in a restless, fevered state. Duncan had taken the time to talk to the other wounded and provided encouragement for a speedy recovery or condolences and kind words for those who would never truly recover. It was sad that some of these men, who had fought so bravely for King and Country, would now be cast aside, discarded as broken and useless, without any further support from the navy that had been their life.

Barely an hour later, Duncan returned to the quarterdeck to find a boat coming alongside to transport the wounded to the hospital. Lieutenant Strickland was certainly someone upon whose word you could depend. Duncan suddenly remembered the news for Cole and felt guilty for not telling him immediately. He turned to the master's mate in charge of the harbor watch and ordered, "Send word for Lieutenant Cole and Mr. Christian. My compliments and they're to report to me in the captain's cabin at their earliest convenience."

Duncan went down to the cabin as calls began to pass through the ship. Within a few minutes, first Christian, and then Cole, arrived. Duncan greeted them and led them to the table in the coach. "Have a seat, gentlemen. Mr. Cole, you'll be examined for lieutenant tomorrow. Orders and instructions will arrive this afternoon. You'll need to have all your paperwork in order. Mr. Christian, I would appreciate it if you would lend a hand to Mr. Cole. Once you have your paperwork together, the master and I would be happy to help you prepare for the examination."

Cole sat stunned for a moment. He had worked for years hoping for a chance at examination and promotion to lieutenant. However, things were happening so quickly, and he felt totally unprepared. He thought about his logs and paperwork. They were in pretty good shape, but he had always expected to have weeks of warning to make final preparations. Still, this was his chance, and he could not waste it. "Thank you, sir! I'll be ready and make the ship proud." Then, turning to the former captain's clerk, he said, "Mr. Christian, I could very much use your help if you're willing."

Christian looked as if it were the most natural thing in the world. "But, of course, I should be happy to assist you in any way I can. Perhaps we should start by reviewing your papers. I once assisted Captain Blackwell when he sat as an examiner. I've some idea of what they will want to see and how it might best be presented."

A huge smile split Cole's face and Duncan stood up and said, "Then I'll leave the two of you to the paperwork while I attend to the ship's needs. You are both relieved from any other duties until your preparations are complete. You may use this space for your work, and I will alert the sentry to allow you access without further need for me to be here. Good luck." With that, he left the cabin and headed back to the quarterdeck.

The afternoon went quickly with supply lighters and boats from the dockyards coming and going constantly as *Fidelity* was assessed and plans were made to get her back into full readiness. Duncan spent the day directing the operations and barely took a break for a light meal at lunch. Just before the newly installed bell sounded the first dog watch, a messenger arrived with a package addressed to "Cole, David - acting lieutenant aboard *HMS Fidelity*".

Duncan signed for the letter and took it down himself to Cole. He found Cole and Christian at the captain's dining table, surrounded by papers, notes, and logbooks. He handed the letter to Cole and waited as he slit it open and quickly read it before passing it to Christian to read the specific requirements. He smiled and spoke to Duncan, "Noon tomorrow aboard *Saturn*, sir. Thank you, again!"

Duncan smiled and headed back to the deck. Cole still had a lot of preparations to make. Hopefully, he would be ready in time. It was unlikely he would get much sleep tonight, so he might as well be studying and preparing. Duncan thought back to his own examination for lieutenant. It had been just four and a half years ago, though it seemed like a lifetime. He had just returned with Lieutenant King from New South Wales, and soon after passing the examination, he had left with Captain Vancouver to return to the Pacific Ocean, only this time exploring to the north. Although there were slow days at times, overall, eleven years in the navy had gone by in a blur.

Midway through the first dog watch, Duncan was alerted to a boat coming from the flagship., He could see Lieutenant Cahill seated in the back as it approached. A few minutes later, Cahill stepped through the entry port and after the formal welcome, he said to Duncan, "I just wanted to stop by to thank you in person for demonstrating trust in me and allowing me to sail *L'Enchanté* back. She's a beautiful ship. I'd love to see what she could do in a strong wind without a corvette dragging behind."

Duncan returned the smile and said, "I was quite happy to have the help. What happens now? You've just come from the flag, eh?"

The smile left Cahill's face. "I'll face a court martial, as expected. There are plenty of post captains in port, so it shouldn't take long to assemble. I've been ordered ashore under open house arrest until the details are completed. After that, it depends on the outcome, I suppose."

Duncan thought back to his short discussion with the admiral that morning. He had intended to talk about Cahill's actions and support and put in a good word for him. Although he had not had a chance to do that, he was satisfied that it was at least detailed in his report. He hoped his description of the events would help in some way. "I'm sure everything will work out."

"Well," Cahill concluded, "I'd better say goodbye and be off. I had to get special permission to stop here on my way ashore. I told them I had to retrieve my personal belongings, though I don't actually have anything to retrieve. It all went up in flames with my dear *Swallow*."

Duncan thought about the sad condition of his remaining uniforms and wished there was something he could offer to help. Even if he had something worth offering, Cahill was a fair bit taller and of thinner build than Duncan.

He noticed the sword at Cahill's side and realized that it was a poor-quality French sword he must have found. "If you'd like to borrow my sword, you could at least have good British steel to present to the court," he offered.

Cahill smiled again. "I'd be honored, if you really wouldn't mind. I've barely enough means to get a new uniform run up in time until my affairs can be settled, and I can draw on a local bank."

Duncan considered that he could offer a loan, as well, but he did not know Cahill well enough, and it might cause offense. He decided to leave it at the sword, which he quickly retrieved from his cabin in the wardroom and handed it to Cahill, who thanked him again and left for shore.

Duncan was on the quarterdeck early the next morning, sipping a hot cup of coffee Stanley had provided. He and the master had spent almost the whole night quizzing and instructing Cole in everything they could think of that might come up in the examination. It was well into the morning watch when Cole took his leave to go prepare his uniform and study more on his own.

Duncan noticed a boat working its way through the anchored ships and realized it was pulling for *Fidelity*. He put the mug down on the rail and retrieved a telescope from the rack by the binnacle to take a closer look. Sitting in the sternsheets was an officer wearing the uniform of a commander. It was George Henry. Duncan picked up his coffee and took another sip before ordering, "Prepare a side party. It appears Commander Henry is coming to pay us a visit, and likely retrieve his chest. Best rig a whip to lower it over the side."

"Aye, aye, sir," responded the duty officer, as he relayed the orders and made the preparations.

Fifteen minutes later, to the sound of pipes, Commander Henry of His Majesty's Sloop *Charger*, came aboard. Duncan was there to greet him. "Welcome aboard, sir, and joy on your promotion."

Henry smiled and responded, "Thank you, Duncan. Just a quick trip to grab my dunnage. I trust it's still in my cabin. Dreadful shame about Blackwell. He was a good man, a bit soft on the crew perhaps, but a good man, just the same."

Duncan bristled at the slight against a dead man, not to mention a great captain, and instantly remembered how little he thought of Henry. However, he was now Duncan's superior, so Duncan controlled his temper and hoped he was able to hide his true feelings. "Your things are just as you left them, sir. I've two crewmen ready to assist you at your convenience."

"Very thoughtful of you, Duncan." Henry smiled without warmth. "I hear Miller got the boot and Williams lost a hand. Ha! Quite a combination."

Duncan was at a loss to respond, but Henry did not notice and continued, "Quite a flock of prizes you've brought back. The fleet is buzzing. Have you any idea the prize money you'll see from this?"

Again, Duncan had no response - he had not really considered the prize money. But again, Henry did not notice and rattled on. "I'll grab my things and be off. I've still much to do to get *Charger* ready for sea. Stinking French don't know how to properly care for a ship. A right mess they left it in. I'll set it to rights and then show them what she's capable of."

With that, Henry stomped off to the wardroom and mercifully left with his belongings about a half an hour later with only a final, "Best of luck to you, Duncan."

Throughout the day, the rest of the *Fidelity* crew returned from the various prizes as replacement crews were provided. The last to return were Midshipman Powell, Lieutenant Hobbs, and the sailors and marines from *Le Furet*. The day went quickly, and *Fidelity* seemed crowded and noisy with the extra dockyard hands coming and going while the crew worked virtually everywhere on repairs and resupply.

Late in the afternoon, watch a boat returned from *Saturn* carrying Cole. His beaming face in the sternsheets made it no surprise when he burst through the entry port and exploded, "I passed, sir! I passed for lieutenant!"

"Congratulations, Lieutenant Cole. It is quite well deserved."

Cole could not stop smiling. "Thank you so much, sir. Thank you for giving me the chance. Thank you for helping me prepare, and thank you, especially, for believing in me." Then, turning to Christian, he added, "And thank you, William. The captain in charge commented that I had the best organized and well-documented file he had ever seen. I couldn't have possibly been ready without you." Then he was off to the master. "Thank you, Mr. Jones. Your lessons on navigation and the ideas about a lee shore were almost exactly one of the questions they asked."

Duncan noted that the word spread quickly through the ship and the crew were eager to offer their congratulations and were proud of Lieutenant Cole. No doubt he would make a good officer. The crew respected him and would accept him as a leader.

Just before sunset in the last dog watch, Duncan visited the shore hospital and was surprised, but happy to find Williams awake, although far from alert. He was being fed soup by an attendant and barely had the strength to hold his head up. His face was almost as white as the sheets, and he was terribly thin, with his eyes sunken deep into dark holes in his face. Still, he smiled at Duncan and croaked a barely audible "hello". Duncan did not stay long, but he was in quite a happy mood as he was rowed back to *Fidelity*.

The next day started much like the previous, with the crew and additional workers from the dockyard swarming about the ship working everywhere at once. Duncan had to take a trip to the dockyard to argue for a replacement spar that the dockyard carpenters insisted could be glued and fished instead. On his way back, he stopped to check on Williams and found him to already be looking somewhat better.

Things were just winding down for the day. The sun hung low in the sky, barely visible above the hillside, when a boat approached from shore carrying a lieutenant. The stranger climbed through the entry port and saluted the quarterdeck.

Duncan stepped forward, but before he could say anything, the man offered his hand and said, "Ah, you must be Lieutenant Duncan. Well met, sir. The world is simply abuzz with your exploits. I'm Gideon Maxwell, come aboard as the new first lieutenant. I wanted to arrive tonight to be sure to be onboard when the new captain arrives tomorrow. I've not met Captain Zimmermann, and I'm sure we all want to make a good impression."

Duncan was surprised and felt a sudden loss. He had expected a new captain to be assigned, but had hoped he would be named the new first lieutenant. Even more than the battle with the French or the storm that followed, the repair work over the past few days had made him feel a closeness with *Fidelity* that made her seem like his. He tried to cover his emotion, which was made easier by the instant liking he had taken to this new officer. "Welcome aboard, sir. May I show you to your cabin and have your dunnage brought aboard?"

Chapter Seven

When Duncan stepped onto the deck the next day, Lieutenant Maxwell was already there, talking to the master and assigning various duties to the crew. Duncan approached them. "Good morning, sir."

Maxwell turned and smiled. "And a very good morning to you, Lieutenant Duncan. You're just full of surprises, aren't you?"

Duncan looked confused, and the master pointed toward a ship anchored further out in the bay. "Look who has joined the party. It would appear Mr. Webb's navigational skills were better than I gave him credit for."

There was *Le Zephyr*, gently tugging at her single anchor cable. The mizzen mast was jury-rigged and there were several splices in the standing rigging, but otherwise she looked no worse for the wear.

Maxwell said, "So, are you done now, or do you have more prizes up your sleeve?"

Duncan smiled and felt a huge sense of relief to have the prize crew back safely. "I'm quite done, sir...at least for now," he added in jest.

The rest of the morning went quickly, with the work continuing and some priorities shifting in order to prepare for the arrival of the new captain. Duncan had seen Webb being pulled back to *Le Zephyr* from the flagship in a boat and had waved his hat in salute. Webb had returned the gesture but was too far off to communicate otherwise. The prize crew had not returned to *Fidelity* yet, and were probably dealing with the dockyard surveyors and awaiting a relief crew to be assigned.

Just after noon, a boat was spotted leaving the shore with a captain and several other officers aboard. Maxwell and Duncan walked onto the quarterdeck together and took a closer look through telescopes.

"Do you suppose that's the new owner, sir?" Duncan asked. He had already grown to like Maxwell and was comfortable with him. Maxwell had several years seniority over Duncan and had an easy manner and firm but fair hand with the crew. Duncan felt they would get along well and was beginning to look forward to getting to know him better.

"I don't know Captain Zimmermann, but from the descriptions I've been given, I dare say it is," Maxwell responded. "That is quite a herd of midshipmen, and at least two lieutenants with him."

Duncan continued to look, "Aye, they'll be elbow to elbow in the midshipmen's berth. He must have quite a few friends who needed favors."

"Let's hope they're not all totally useless…like we were when we were young, eh?"

"Aye, sir. I forget sometimes that we all started like that. It's amazing the navy can keep ships afloat."

Maxwell closed his telescope and said, "Well, we best get spiffed up a bit. If that is the new owner, he'll be here in a quarter hour expecting to see his officers, not deckhands."

Duncan put his telescope back in the rack and looked down at his clothes. He was dressed in standard issue slops and covered in tar. It was hard to keep clean when working the ship the way they had been for the last few days. He had given up on wearing a uniform as soon as he returned from the flagship, and had been in slops since then, like the crew. They all knew him, and since Maxwell had done the same when he joined the ship, Duncan did not feel it was an issue. However, a new captain might see the matter differently.

A few minutes later, he was in his cabin, pulling on his uniform. He looked at his tar-stained hands and decided there was little he could do about them now. Picking up his jacket, he felt something in the pocket and pulled out Captain Blackwell's book of prayers. He thought for a moment and then placed it in his chest. Nobody should miss it and it would be a nice reminder of the captain.

When he reached for his sword, he remembered having loaned it to Cahill. He went down to Williams' cabin and borrowed his, making a mental note to ask him for permission the next time he visited the hospital. Then he realized that the new officers would likely be using this cabin. He quickly loaded everything into the sea chest and dragged it into his cabin. There really was not room for it, but he managed to push it in sideways. He closed the door to his cabin just as Maxwell emerged from his own and they headed topside together, with Duncan following, as was befitting their respective ranks.

The boat with the captain and assorted junior offices was still approaching, as was a second boat bearing a single midshipman in the stern sheets. The boat with the midshipman slowed and backed water to allow the captain's boat to reach *Fidelity* first. The boat approached, and the sentry challenged, "Boat ahoy!"

"Aye, aye!" came back the instant reply, with four fingers raised by the coxswain. This was expected. A captain of a ship would be identified by the name of his command, but a captain without a ship would just be an officer. If this were the new captain, he would not officially be the captain until he had read himself in on the deck.

Just as the captain's head lifted above the entry port, the bosun's pipes trilled and the marines stomped to attention. A stern-faced man stepped onto the deck, and after saluting the quarterdeck, announced, "Captain Stephen Zimmermann, come aboard to take command." There was no question anymore - *Fidelity*'s new captain had arrived.

Maxwell stepped forward. "Welcome aboard, sir. I have the honor of being your first lieutenant, Gideon Maxwell, and this is Lieutenant Joseph Duncan." Duncan realized with a start that he did not know what his position would be among the lieutenants. It would all come down to date of rank and he might well be junior and end up fourth lieutenant.

"Excellent! Well met, Lieutenant Maxwell," Zimmermann said in a light tone that did not match his original stern look. He seemed more at ease now as he shook Maxwell's hand. "We'll save the other introductions until I've read myself in. I've the rest of the officers with me. Have our dunnage swayed aboard and then assemble the crew." Then, turning to Duncan, he added, "So this is the famous Lieutenant Duncan? I must say I'm surprised you're still aboard, but it is a pleasure to meet you. I didn't really expect you to be a mere mortal from the way you're being talked about in town." He offered his hand.

Duncan shook his hand and, although a little confused, tried to keep the puzzlement from his voice as he replied, "Thank you, sir. It's very nice to meet you as well. Welcome aboard."

The rest of the officers and boat crew came over the side, and after the sea chests and bags were hoisted aboard, the boat was led to the back of the ship by a painter so the waiting boat with the midshipman could come into position under the entry port. The crew was gathering, and Captain Zimmermann was preparing to read himself in when the midshipman stepped onto the deck almost unnoticed and announced, "Message from the Flag! Lieutenant Joseph Duncan to repair to Flag, instanter!"

Zimmermann glanced over as if it did not really concern him and said, "Off you go then, Duncan. There's no need for you to be here for this."

Duncan replied, "Aye, aye," and stepped forward to identify himself to the midshipman. They were over the side and pulling toward the flagship as Captain Zimmermann started to read his commission aloud to the crew.

The row across the smooth bay to *Glory* was silent and uneventful. Once they had hooked on, Duncan exited first and found Lieutenant Strickland there to greet him. "Welcome back, sir. The admiral will see you immediately. I believe you know the way."

Duncan replied, "Thank you. And thank you for your help with Williams and Cole."

Strickland smiled, "My pleasure, sir. I understand Cole passed and is only wanting a commission and assignment to assume his new rank. I'm glad I could be of some small assistance."

Duncan made his way to the admiral's cabin and announced himself to the marine sentry. The marine slammed the butt of his musket against the deck and called out in a loud voice, "Lieutenant Joseph Duncan!"

There was a short pause and then a voice from within called back, "Enter." Duncan opened the door and stepped past the sentry. He removed his hat as he ducked in. He realized that the deck was high enough here that he did not need to duck between beams, as he had become accustomed to doing in frigates.

He approached the desk where the admiral was seated, as he had been last time. Captain Tankersley was seated in his previous location as well. Approaching the desk, Duncan noticed several piles of papers neatly arranged on the desk. One he recognized as his report, and another as Captain Blackwell's notes. He stopped in front of the desk and saluted, "Lieutenant Duncan, reporting as ordered, M'Lord."

"Welcome, Lieutenant," the admiral responded, as he returned the salute. "Please take a seat."

Duncan adjusted his borrowed sword and sat in the chair before the desk.

The admiral leaned forward and rested his arms on the desk. "I have read your report and found it quite interesting. I have several questions for you."

"Yes, M'Lord," Duncan responded, but then was not sure that he should have. After his last experience in this cabin, he was not sure what to expect or what was expected of him.

"I shall try to take things in order so as to make it easier for both of us. Let us begin with Captain Blackwell being struck by the block and taken to the orlap by the surgeon…" He paused to look at one of the papers, "…Mr. Whitehall. It was at about that time that the lookout spotted a sail. Is this correct?"

"Aye, M'Lord."

"It took some time to work downwind toward the strange sail and during that time you determined there were as many as seven or eight sail, possibly more. Is this correct?"

"Aye, M'Lord."

"You state in your report that you received an update on the condition of Captain Blackwell indicating that he was still unconscious. If I recall correctly, that report was from Midshipman Webb, who I met this morning when he brought in *Le Zephyr*. Is this as you recall it?"

"Aye, M'Lord."

The admiral looked at Duncan for a moment and then said, "Lieutenant, please feel free to expand beyond saying 'yes' if there are things you think important to add."

"Aye, M'Lord," Duncan responded and then added, "I will, M'Lord."

The admiral looked back at the papers and continued, "So, you were fairly certain that this was a French convoy, including several warships, and you continued toward them to investigate?"

"Aye, M'Lord. I couldn't be certain they were French, but I felt it my duty to investigate."

"Once you determined that they were in fact French, you decided to engage and that was your decision and your responsibility alone?"

"Aye, M'Lord. With Captain Blackwell incapacitated, it was my duty and responsibility to make the decision to engage."

"*La Tempête* slowed to meet *Fidelity*, and you gave up the advantage of the wind and moved to leeward. Although the French ship was disabled by your first broadside, you failed to secure her. Instead, you chose to descend upon a fleet of eight ships, including at least three you had clearly identified as additional warships. Why were you so intent on attacking the convoy?"

"I considered anything the French wished to protect so badly must necessarily be something we should want to destroy, M'Lord."

The Admiral stared at Duncan for a few moments. "You had no thoughts of prize money or glory?"

"No, M'Lord. I felt it my duty to attack, and I was confident in the crew of the *Fidelity* to acquit themselves well. So few supply ships with such a heavy escort indicated to me that the target was important enough to justify the risk."

"Even the very real risk of losing *Fidelity*?"

"Yes, M'Lord. That was my judgement and considered decision at the time, based on the information available to me."

"Had Captain Blackwell told you of any special orders for your cruise?"

Duncan was thrown by this sudden change of direction. "No, M'Lord."

"What were your mission and orders, and by 'your' I am referring to those for *Fidelity* as you understood them?"

"We were to cruise the area within a triangle bounded roughly by Saint Thomas, Saint Croix, and Hispaniola. We were to take, burn, or destroy any enemy ships encountered, to the best of our abilities and consistent with the best traditions of the British Navy, M'Lord."

"And that is all Blackwell told you?"

"Aye, M'Lord, it is what Captain Blackwell instructed me and the other officers, and it is what I read in our written orders after the captain's death."

"Let's move on. You captured the French frigate *L'Enchanté* by boarding her and you found a British officer aboard who informed you that he had lost his command, the brig, *Swallow*, to the French. You chose to not only leave him free, while knowing he must face court martial, but actually gave him command of the prize. What made you feel justified in that course of action?"

Duncan did not feel that this was going much better than the first meeting with the admiral. However, he had no choice other than to continue responding. "As I stated in my report, I felt it in the best interest of the Service to fully utilize all available resources to prosecute the attack against the enemy. Without Lieutenant Cahill and his crew, *Fidelity* would have been weakened and dangerously under-manned and would not have been able to pursue and capture the rest of the convoy, M'Lord."

"And what gave you the impression that you could determine the 'best interest of the Service', Lieutenant?"

Duncan forced himself to stay calm. "M'Lord, as the ranking officer in the action, it was my duty to make that determination."

"How did you know if you outranked Lieutenant Cahill?"

Duncan froze. He had never considered that. They had not discussed dates of rank. Did it matter that Cahill had lost his ship? Cahill had been in command of a brig. It was quite likely he did outrank Duncan. Why had he not thought to ask? Even on the voyage back, it had not come up. Finally, he said in a low voice, "I don't know, M'Lord. It didn't occur to me to ask."

The admiral sat back in his chair and put his hands together on his stomach.

"On the sail back to Antigua, you personally visited each prize and instructed the prize commanders to prepare a detailed list of everything found on board. Is this correct?"

Duncan was still deflated by the issue of who was the ranking officer in the engagement. "Aye, M'Lord."

"Were you aware of a lockbox hidden in the transom bench aboard *L'Enchanté*?"

Duncan was surprised by this question as well. "No, M'Lord."

"Did Lieutenant Cahill mention its existence or contents when you were aboard?"

"No M'Lord."

"Do you recall the contents of *Émeraude*?"

Duncan thought hard and went through the lists in his mind. "I believe she was carrying cannons, M'Lord."

"What do you know about the cannons? What type, size, etc.?"

"I recall they were mostly small bore - 6-pounders and smaller. I don't recall any further details, M'Lord."

"What of the cargo on the other ships?"

"Mostly ships' equipment and stores, M'Lord. Cordage, powder, shot, general naval supplies. I don't recall more detail."

"Just a few more questions, Lieutenant. This isn't in your report. I'd like your opinions now that you've had more time to consider things. First, do these supplies really justify the size of the escort, and second, what would you guess the French intended to do with them?"

Duncan thought for a moment. At this point, he did not feel like he had much to lose. "Well, M'Lord, as to the first question, no, I don't think the supplies we captured justified the escort. Based on the small sizes of cannon and amounts of other supplies, I would think it most likely they were arming small vessels, likely as privateers."

"Excellent, Lieutenant. Now, last question. What else would they need that they couldn't acquire in the West Indies?"

Duncan thought about this for a moment, suddenly understood, and guessed what was in the hidden lock box aboard *L'Enchanté*. "Gold, M'Lord. They would need gold to buy ships and hire crews."

The admiral smiled for the first time that Duncan had ever seen. "Quite right. There are no foundries in the West Indies to produce cannons. Powder supplies are limited. Ships and men are available, but they come at a cost. The lockbox contained assorted specie worth more than 100,000 guineas. It seems you're going to be quite a rich man. Especially if I am correct in presuming the prize court will rule that you will get the captain's share as the acting commander of *Fidelity*, since Captain Blackwell died before the battle began. Coincidentally, you've made me a rich man, as well."

Duncan was stunned. He did not really need the money, but it would be nice to be less dependent on his family.

"I've learned from the former captain of *L'Enchanté*, Marcel Bouchard, the Marquis de Lormay, that *La Tempête* was carrying even more gold. That's probably why they made no attempt to recapture the other ships. In addition to the storm, they may have decided to cut their losses and go lick their wounds."

The admiral continued, "You are aware that I have placed Captain Zimmermann in command of *Fidelity* and provided replacement officers. The surveyors have completed their preliminary assessments of the ships you captured. There is no question as to their status as legitimate prizes. Therefore, I intend to buy in the corvettes and rate them as sloops. Do you know Lieutenant Cary, the first in *Saturn*?"

"I believe I have met him, M'Lord, but I don't know him well."

"No matter. I will promote him to commander and give him *Le Carcajou*, probably with a new name. I don't really care for that."

"As for *Le Furet*, she will need extensive repairs before I put her in commission. I've someone on my staff in mind for her, but I'll make the decision later."

Duncan sat listening, surprised by the change in the tone and how much the admiral was sharing with him.

"I've no use for the supply ships, so I'll have them sold at auction. Same for the latecomer, *Le Zephyr*. She's a pretty little ship, but she's too old and small for my purposes. She should fetch a good price at auction."

The admiral leaned forward on the desk again and looked at Duncan. "That leaves *L'Enchanté*. Quite a lovely frigate. Well-built, with good lines, and although knocked about a bit by you and *Fidelity*, still very sound. I intend to promote you to post captain and give her to you."

Duncan sat stunned. He was not sure he had heard correctly. The admiral was smiling broadly and so was Captain Tankersley, who spoke for the first time during the meeting. "Congratulations, Captain Duncan. Joy to you on your promotion."

It started to sink in, and Duncan smiled. "Thank you, M'Lord." And then to Tankersley, "Thank you, sir."

The admiral was still smiling broadly. "It will, of course, be subject to confirmation by the Admiralty, but they would have to be fools not to agree. You're already a hero here and when word gets back to London, you'll be the talk of the town. The war has not been going so well lately. You can count on the administration playing this up as the greatest naval feat since the Glorious First of June."

"I have a few more things to discuss. Do you have a good tailor in town? I'll give you the name of my man. You'll need some new uniforms run up. The governor is away, but I've received word that he'll want to hold a reception in your honor in a month or so. You should look sharp. Your orders have been drawn up. I've given you two weeks' shore leave before you read yourself in. The dockyard still needs some time with *L'Enchanté*."

Duncan was trying to keep up as the admiral charged on, "Have you any requests for officers?"

There certainly had not been time to think about that. "Well, sir, a previous midshipman from *Fidelity* passed for lieutenant yesterday."

"Ah, yes, Cole, the one Blackwell had made acting lieutenant. If you want him, he's yours. What about a first, someone with some experience?"

"What's to become of Lieutenant Cahill, M'Lord?"

"Cahill? He'll face court martial. As the senior officer on station, it would be inappropriate for me to give an opinion as to how the court may rule. However, if your question is whether he'll be given another command, the answer is 'no'."

"If he is acquitted, I'd like him as first, M'Lord."

"Very well. If not, I will assign someone else. If you have no other names in mind, I'll assign another to serve as second as well."

"That would be fine, M'Lord, thank you."

"Now, there's the matter of several midshipmen still aboard *Fidelity*. You know captains agree to take on midshipmen for a variety of reasons. Captain Zimmermann has a full complement of his own that he'll take with him. Those already aboard *Fidelity* will have to find somewhere to go, or they'll end up on the shore."

"I'll gladly take them all, M'Lord. They are a good bunch and I know them all already."

The admiral nodded. "Fine, fine. I had hoped you would. As to a crew, Captain Zimmermann has agreed to let you take 20 or 30 volunteers from *Fidelity*. You can work that out with him when you go to get your chest. The rest we'll provide, at least to get you minimally manned. Beyond that, you'll have to do some recruiting if you want to get to your full complement. I doubt you'll have much trouble. Sailing in with that many prizes, men will be lining up to have a shot with the lucky, new captain."

"Thank you, M'Lord."

"I asked Cahill the same question about why you both assumed you outranked him," the admiral stated, then asked rhetorically, "Do you know what he said?"

"No, M'Lord."

"He said you acted like you were and he never thought to check. That's one of the reasons I want to promote you. You're willing to take charge. You never hesitated against almost overwhelming odds, and you did it only because you thought it was the right thing to do. What was it you said? If they wanted to protect it that badly, you thought you should take it? We need that type of initiative."

"Thank you, M'Lord."

"You did outrank him, by the way. It did not matter, but you had him by a couple of months."

After celebrating with a glass of wine, the meeting ended, and Duncan walked out on to the deck of the flagship and looked across the bay at *L'Enchanté*. He could hardly believe it, but she was his.

Chapter Eight

In later years, when Duncan reflected on the two weeks following his second meeting with the admiral, he could only remember a blur of activity and a few flashes of seemingly random events. How they fit together and what happened in between was beyond his recollection.

Somehow, he retrieved his trunk and dunnage from *Fidelity* and acquired a room on the second floor at one of the more upscale boarding houses, known as "The Brown Pelican". He had ended up with Williams' trunk, as well, but he was never quite sure how that had happened.

One clear memory was that every morning he would begin his day by removing the crisp piece of parchment from his pocket, slowly reading his commission, and then carefully folding and replacing it in his pocket. He repeated this ritual to remind himself that he was not dreaming. He was not naïve enough to not consider that the Admiralty Board might refuse to confirm his commission. However, not even accounting for how long it might take the Board to make a decision, it would take months just for the request to travel to England and a reply to make its way back to Antigua. He was going to make the best of the time he had.

It was a typically hot and sunny morning when he visited the tailor recommended by the admiral. He was not sure if he would need to mention the admiral in order to be accepted as a client, but as soon as he announced himself, the man practically fell over himself to take his order and measurements, confirm the times for delivery, and, of course, accept the down payment for the new uniforms. He had agreed to an extra charge to have the first uniform ready in just two days. Until then, he would have to make do with his worn lieutenant's uniform or civilian clothes.

He visited another tailor to expand on his options for civilian attire, as well as a cobbler to replace his ruined boots. He ended up ordering two pairs with one intended for service wear and the other, made of beautifully supple and smooth leather, intended for dress occasions ashore.

As his funds were starting to run low by this point, he visited a bank to make a draw on his account. After that, he visited several other shops, thinking and planning what he would need to purchase to furnish his cabins and assemble the stores needed for sea. It occurred to him that he was going to need help. Passing an armorer's shop, he considered the need to have a dress sword, but he was unable to find anything to his liking. In the end, he decided his current sword was of high quality, and although not in any way fancy, it looked good enough and was perfectly acceptable.

By midafternoon, Duncan was ready to take a break and find a shady place to enjoy something light to eat and something cool to drink. He met up with several officers he knew vaguely and had met at various events. Thus came the first of many invitations to eat or drink with people he often barely knew who wanted to hear the story of the great battle against the French and how he had come to sail in with all those prizes.

The sheer number of meals, faces, and bottles of wine that he encountered over that fortnight contributed in no small way to his blurred memory of events. There were times when one dinner seemed to run into another and still there were those he had to disappoint by declining their invitations due to prior commitments.

One afternoon as he was strolling back to The Brown Pelican from some errand, he chanced upon Captain Blackwell's servant, Stanley. He realized that he did not know if Stanley was his Christian name or his surname - he had always just been, "Stanley".

"Ahoy, Stanley! Well met and how do you do?" he called out as he approached.

Stanley had been looking the other way and evidently had not noticed Duncan; nor had he expected to be addressed. He visibly jumped, and it took a moment for the shock to leave his face and be replaced by a broad smile of recognition. He knuckled his forehead and responded with sincerity, "Nice to see you, Lieut...I mean to say, Captain Duncan. It's nice to see a familiar face. I don't know many ashore, it seems, sir."

"Are you ashore for leave alone?" From what Duncan could remember of past times in port, Stanley had several friends aboard *Fidelity* with whom he had always traveled as a pack when taking time away from the ship.

Stanley's face fell, and he looked down at his shoes as he responded. "Ah, well, sir, I've been put ashore. The new captain didn't need me as a servant and I'm not fit for other duties, what with my hernia and all. Mr. Christian got sent ashore as well. I heard he was looking for work along this street somewhere with a barrister and I was hoping I'd recognize the name and check on him. He was always kind to me, and I didn't get a chance to say goodbye...proper-like, sir."

Duncan responded, perhaps without giving it as much thought as he should have, "Well, if you're in need of berth, you're welcome to join *Enchanté*. I suppose Captain Zimmerman already had full staff, including a clerk."

Stanley's face lit up again. "Oh, thank you, sir! It would be my pleasure to serve you aboard your new ship, sir."

"I'll not be joining for a few more days, but Lieutenant Cole is aboard organizing things and working with the dockyard to put her back together. If you need a place to stay, you can go aboard anytime and tell Lieutenant Cole I sent you. If you'd rather have some time off, I won't need you there until next week, or later, so you can join when you like."

"I've nowhere else to go, sir, so if it's all the same to you, I'll get myself out to *Enchanté*."

Duncan was still thinking about needing a clerk more than a servant and said, "That's fine. What were you saying about Mr. Christian taking work along this street?"

"Aye, sir. He was looking to see if some distant relative or friend of the family, who is a local barrister, might have work for him. He said the name, but it didn't stick, sir, since it were no one I knew. The street name, though I recall, because my mates and I used to come to a…well, a business…along this street, sir."

Duncan thought for a moment, wondering, but not wanting to ask what type of business Stanley and his friends had been frequenting. There were several somewhat seedy taverns and at least two brothels at the far end of the street, and it was likely one of those. More importantly, he was thinking of how to find William Christian, when the problem answered itself by the very same man walking around a corner and heading towards them.

"Good afternoon, sir, and hello, Stanley. What happy luck I should see you both," Christian said as he approached.

"Good afternoon, Mr. Christian. We were just this moment not only talking about you but planning a search to find you - and now here you are. Quite fortuitous, I should think," Duncan responded.

"Looking for me, sir? Whatever may I do for you?" Christian enquired.

"I find myself in not insignificant need of the services of a good clerk, and I was hoping you might be persuaded to accept the position."

"Would it be a temporary position, sir, or a chance to join you on your new ship? To be clear, I accept either, but I'm hoping for something permanent," Christian immediately responded.

"It would be a permanent position, in so far as the word applies to military matters, as my ship's clerk, and you could begin immediately or as soon as convenient for you, as there are absolute mountains of paperwork required to put a ship into active service."

"I should be quite happy to begin, sir. I was just coming from a search for gainful employment and not only has that been unsuccessful so far, but I should much prefer to be at sea. I am quite honored to have you ask me to join you, sir."

"Excellent!" Duncan exclaimed. "Are you familiar with the Brown Pelican?" Christian nodded. "Ah, good. That's where I'm staying until *Enchanté* is ready to enter commission. Please come by tomorrow morning, at eight bells, and we'll get started. How are you for writing supplies?"

"I'm sorry to say that I have very little available, sir. A couple of decent quills and a half of a small bottle of ink, sir. No paper to speak of. I left everything else aboard *Fidelity* as it belonged to the ship, not to me."

"Not to worry. You can begin today then by purchasing what we might need for, say, a six-month cruise, and you can resupply before we go aboard, if necessary." Duncan smiled as he handed Christian several coins. "Here, you can use this."

Christian accepted the money and said, "Thank you, sir. I would be happy to do so and will write a note of hand indicating expenditures."

"That won't be necessary, Mr. Christian. If I didn't think I could trust you entirely, I wouldn't have offered you the position. Buy what you need and let me know if you need more."

"Aye, aye, sir…thank you for the job and the trust."

Stanley had stood quietly listening to the discussion but as it seemed to be coming to an end, he spoke, "Well, Mr. Christian, it seems I won't be needing to say goodbye, what was my intention in looking for you. I wanted to tell you that I enjoyed serving with you on *Fidelity* and wished you well wherever you might be heading. Now, it seems we'll be shipmates, again, so instead of goodbye I'll say welcome. And mighty happy it makes me, too! Thank you, Lieut…Captain."

With this and some final pleasantries, the impromptu meeting ended and the three each went their own way, with feelings of happiness and relief for what had been decided. Christian and Stanley had jobs and positions with an officer they knew and respected, while Duncan had a trusted clerk and…Stanley, whatever his talents might be.

•   •   •

The next morning, as Duncan had finished his breakfast and was sipping a final cup of coffee in the dining area of The Brown Pelican, Christian walked in carrying a parcel of quills and paper. Duncan waved him to come over and greeted him warmly. "Good morning, Mr. Christian. You're right on time."

"Good morning, sir. I must say it is a bit harder having to look at a watch rather than listen for bells. I think I was able to get everything we'll need, sir, but if necessary, I found a shop nearby that might supply any additional wants."

"Splendid! Would you care for a bite to eat or some coffee before we begin?" Duncan offered.

"Thank you, no, sir. I've already eaten. I'm quite ready when you are."

Duncan dabbed his mouth and placed the napkin on the table. "Well, then let's have at it. I've a number of official letters which will need to be copied for entry in my log or otherwise kept for records. I've almost completed the draft of the Standing Orders for *Enchanté*, but I thought of a few changes last night. Perhaps you could start working on the fair copies of the letters while I finish my edits. Then, you may work here, or take the orders with you and work wherever you like. I fear you've several hours of writing to copy those. Let's see, we'll need one for the log, one for the ship's book, and one for each officer...we'll carry a normal complement for a frigate of just three lieutenants, rather than the four we had on *Fidelity*. Then one for the master, one for the wardroom, and one for the gunroom. The midshipmen and others can make their own copies from those. So, what's that then?"

"Eight, sir," Christian responded.

"Good, eight should do it, then. Before we get started, I've a question for you. Do you know Stanley's full name?"

"Aye, sir. He is Alexander Stanley, but he doesn't care for Alexander, so everyone just calls him Stanley."

"Ah, thank you. Let's get to work, then."

The rest of the morning was spent listening to the scratching of each other's quills, sharing a couple of pots of tea, and Duncan getting smudges of ink on his fingers. There seemed to be papers and sand everywhere on his side of the table, despite how careful he thought he had been. Christian's side of the table, and his fingers, were completely clean and his paperwork was in neat stacks. At least Duncan could be happy with his own neat copperplate writing. His mother had insisted he learn to write and spell properly and today it was coming in handy. Still, Christian's font was crisper, and he wrote nearly twice as fast as Duncan. Each profession has its skills, he supposed, as he sat back and stretched his shoulders.

"I believe I've had as much enjoyment from writing as I can endure for one day," Duncan said. "Please carry on, while I take care of some other pressing matters."

"Certainly, sir," Christian said as he finished the sentence he was writing, sanded the page, and then looked up. "If you won't need me here, further, I shall retire to my own residence to complete the copies."

"By all means. Please do. I won't be available the rest of today, or tomorrow, so let's say we meet here again the next morning at eight bells. Do you think that will give you sufficient time to complete these copies?" Duncan asked.

"Aye, sir. I can have them sooner if you like."

"No, thank you. That will be soon enough and I'm likely to have more to do by then. Sometimes I think ships must float on paper, not water."

Duncan went back to his room to get his hat while Christian began to organize and pack up his work. When Duncan returned a few minutes later, Christian was gone, and Duncan headed out the door to be blinded by the bright sunlight.

•　　•　　•

Admiral Fairhurst was sitting comfortably in a rattan chair enjoying the sea breeze, a cool drink, and the view from the second-floor balcony of a residence owned by Ebenezer Hirschhorn, the senior representative of the Foreign Service in the West Indies. The spacious and well-appointed home sat just below the top of a hill on the east side of the harbor with commanding views of the entrance lanes as well as the anchored ships and bustling activities along the west side of English Harbour.

Hirschhorn stepped out of the adjacent room where he had been talking with one of his staff and reviewing some paperwork. He paused a few steps to the side of Fairhurst's chair and looked out at the harbor, scanning it from north to south. A servant approached with a glass on a silver tray. After taking the glass, Hirschhorn sat down in a chair a few feet from Fairhurst and took a sip.

While still gazing out at the water, he posed a question to the admiral, "So you think this young Duncan can be a replacement for Blackwell?"

Fairhurst put his glass down on a small table next to his chair and looked at Hirschhorn. "He's a very intelligent officer who demonstrates initiative and good judgement. Properly positioned, he could be a valuable asset."

"That may be true, but that may also be true of many officers in the fleet. What makes you think this is the one? Positioning, as you name it, requires resources, time, and great effort."

"I feel it, and sometimes you have to trust your gut and what your feelings are telling you. Duncan may not be the right candidate, but I think he is, and we won't truly know unless we commit to a path and try."

Hirschhorn was still watching the harbor and not looking at Fairhurst, as he responded, "I prefer to have more to go on than a feeling. True, sometimes that is all we have, but usually there is information available to help test our feelings and guide our judgement. We can use our minds as well as our guts…perhaps sometimes even our hearts. You were quite close to Blackwell. Are you sure your judgement is not clouded by that loss? It would be natural to favor one about whom he spoke favorably. Blackwell sought Duncan's promotion, but made no mention of anything beyond that."

"Blackwell would never have committed such thoughts to writing, and you well know it. Perhaps he would have said more in confidence if he had survived to return. In any event, it's not just Blackwell's opinion that affects my view. I have interviewed Duncan about his actions and read his reports - as you have. I see within him a potential, not just because of what he does, but because of why he does it."

"What do you know of Joseph Duncan beyond your interactions over the past few days?"

Fairhurst had anticipated this discussion and was ready to answer. "He entered service as a midshipman when he was 14, a bit older than most, but he excelled and overcame the late start. His first service was almost three years here in the West Indies, just following the end of the war with the American colonies. Still, as a mid, he served with Arthur Phillip on a trip to New South Wales and returned to England with Lieutenant King after the loss of *Sirius*. He passed for lieutenant and almost immediately sailed again - back to the Pacific, with Vancouver. He made it back just after the beginning of the war with France and served with Gambier at the First of June. Then, he came here with Blackwell. He's been in active service all but a few weeks since he first joined in '84 and has an exemplary record."

Hirschhorn waited a moment and then said, "If you want to know what the honey is made from, you don't watch the hive - you watch the bees in the field."

This was the part Fairhurst had been dreading. Hirschhorn always knew more than he first admitted - that was his job. However, it was annoying to be asked questions and then be told the answers. Furthermore, Hirschhorn's quaint, sometimes tangential, if not downright perplexing, sayings were also annoying. Fairhurst suppressed a sigh as Hirschhorn continued.

"Do you know his family situation?"

Apparently, it still was not time for Hirschhorn to share what he knew. "His father is a retired army officer, and they live somewhere south of London, I believe. Can we skip all this and get to the part where you tell me what you know and stop asking questions to prove what I don't know?"

Hirschhorn smiled and looked at Fairhurst for the first time in the conversation. "If you like, but it really takes a lot of the fun out of it. His father is a retired army officer, a major, but there's more to it than that. His father quite successfully led a group of skirmishers in bush-fighting during the Seven Years' War. He was well known for his effectiveness and unconventional tactics. I suspect that's where Duncan gets his interesting melee style.

"His mother is French and how his parents ended up together, when they should have been enemies, is something I still haven't discovered. He was born in the Massachusetts Bay Colony before the family moved north when the unrest began in the lower colonies. Now, here's the best part: they went to live with his uncle, the Sixth Earl of Edgemond, for several years until they moved to England."

Fairhurst returned the smile. "So maybe the 'positioning' won't be quite so hard, after all. You agree then that he might make a good replacement for Blackwell?"

Hirschhorn leaned back in his chair and gazed back out at the harbor. "Oh, I don't know about him being a replacement, so much as an 'alternative'. Blackwell was a fine man and very useful on our team. Duncan has different talents and capabilities. I suspect he will also be very useful, but not just a replacement for Blackwell."

"Again, you surprise me with your ability to see the correct move based on instinct without knowing all the facts. Your gut seems to have gotten this one right.

"None of us know how long this war might last. We need to consider our own replacements, as well, and be sure they are ready when their time comes. Let's see how he does, but perhaps we should set lofty goals."

The admiral leaned back in his chair and relaxed now, too. "You make me feel old. I'm not quite done yet and I dare say neither are you. However, what you say is true. We must train the next generation and pray they're not needed because this vile war comes quickly to an end."

"My friend," Hirschhorn said softly, "we are getting old, and people like us are not only needed during times of war, but to avoid future wars."

"Well, I have given him a ship. It's up to you and your people to get him in the right position."

Hirschhorn spoke more loudly again, "True. We must begin with further investigation, testing, and training…and I think I know just how to start."

•   •   •

Duncan was sitting in the great cabin of *HMS Saturn,* wearing one of his new uniforms. This was his first official public event dressed as a captain, and he wished it could have been for some other reason.

There were rows of chairs arranged facing the stern of the ship with an aisle left open down the middle from the door to the cabin to a single empty chair facing a long table set up across the width of the ship just in front of the transom windows. Behind the table, facing the others assembled in chairs, were five post captains looking very grave and official.

As befitted Duncan's new rank, he had been given a seat in the front row. It was very strange to see his sword laying across the table in front of the captains, but he consoled himself with the knowledge that it was not there to represent him, but rather Lieutenant Cahill, to whom he had loaned it. He glanced to his right, where Alan Cahill was sitting nervously a few seats away.

Along each side of the room, three marines stood at attention, holding their Brown Bess sea service pattern muskets. Other than the scarlet shakos of the marines, the room was filled with blue uniforms.

The captain at the center of the table surveyed the room and then spoke, "I am Captain Elliot Graham, in command of *HMS Saturn* and ranking member of this tribunal. I call to order this court martial regarding Lieutenant Alan Cahill, previously of His Majesty's Brig *Swallow* who is charged with the loss of said ship, on or about Friday, the 29th day of May, in the Year of Our Lord, 1795."

He paused and nodded to someone at the back of the room. After a short delay a cannon fired from the poop deck above them. Duncan knew that at the same time the cannon fired, a signal would have been raised, so the whole fleet would know what was happening aboard *Saturn*.

Graham glanced to his right and continued, "I ask now that the rest of the members of the court identify themselves for the record and for the convenience of those assembled." He nodded to the man at the end of the table, who turned to look at the clerk sitting at a small table to the side, feverishly taking notes.

"I am Captain Theodore Larson, of *HMS Active*."

The next spoke immediately, "Captain Francis Milliken, *Heroine*."

Captain Graham turned to his left, and the next to introduce himself was at least a familiar face. "I'm Captain George Tankersley, Flag Captain and in command of *HMS Glory*."

That left one man to introduce himself and he spoke in a booming voice, "Captain Timothy Ribacoff, of *HMS Crescent*."

Captain Graham turned back towards the onlookers and scanned the crowd as he spoke, "Many of you present are here because you received orders to appear before this court as witnesses to the events or to establish the character and state of mind of Lieutenant Cahill. As the facts concerning the events do not seem to be in question based on the logs and written testimony previously submitted to and reviewed in detail by the members of the court, I will dispense with the normal practice of clearing the room of witnesses before we proceed. You are each welcome, therefore, to remain here until called to testify, or go out on deck, where we will send for you. It's a warm day, and it's likely to get rather warmer in here. However, you will only be allowed to stand, leave, or enter when a witness is not on the stand. If you choose to stay, you shall remain seated and silent at all times during testimony and questioning."

"As a further warning, you are reminded that, as stated in your orders to appear, you are forbidden from discussing the case, your opinions, or facts and circumstances, that might be part of your testimony, or that of others. Anyone violating this rule will be punished severely."

There was some fidgeting, but there was absolute silence in the room while Graham paused to underscore the severity of his words. Satisfied, he continued, "Once you complete your testimony and questioning by the court, you will be released. At that time, you will be free to leave the ship, or if you prefer, you may stay for the remainder of the proceedings. We have a fairly large number of witnesses and, as the case concerns the most serious matter of losing a ship from His Majesty's Navy, we will take whatever time is warranted and required to determine the truth and come to a fair and just decision. If necessary, we will adjourn for meals and continue for multiple days. You will be given further instructions as needed, but you are not to leave the ship without permission until your testimony is complete and you are expressly released by the court."

After another pause and some more fidgeting in the crowd, he stated, "Anyone who would like to leave the room, please do so instanter. We are about to begin."

Duncan considered the options, unsure what would be best. He thought it might be awkward to get up from his seat in the front row to walk out - especially considering he would have to walk in front of Cahill on his way. It was getting warm in the room, and although there would be sun to deal with on deck, there would likely be a breeze and perhaps some shade from a tarp. He noticed that very few people seemed to be taking the opportunity to leave, and he decided to stay. He could always leave between witnesses if it became too uncomfortable in the room.

It was not long before Duncan was satisfied with his decision. He had never attended a court martial, and he found himself quite interested in both the process and the testimony. Cahill was called first and was questioned by all the captains, with the exception of Larson, who hardly spoke after introducing himself.

The most interesting part to Duncan was the apparent attitudes of the different members of the court. Almost immediately, from the tone of their voices and structure of their questions, it seemed that Tankersley was somewhat sympathetic to, or at least understanding of, Cahill's position, while Milliken and Ribacoff were negative, if not openly hostile. Larson was difficult to judge as he continued to say almost nothing, asked no questions, and kept a blank, but interested, expression on his face. Graham was clearly trying to look and sound impartial, and although he was doing a good job on the whole, an occasional nod or fleeting reaction seemed to put him more in agreement with Tankersley.

This situation surprised Duncan. He had expected this to be a mostly perfunctory exercise, leading to a quick acquittal of Cahill. Of course, he did not know all the details and had not read the reports submitted to the court, but from his knowledge of what had happened, it seemed Cahill had acted in a wholly appropriate and reasonable manner. That he might actually be found guilty of a crime and punished had seemed an extremely remote possibility, but now seemed more possible.

The questions were unexpected in both their breadth and depth, delving into details concerning the setting of the watch and lookouts, the preparation of the great guns and powder stores, setting of course headings, weather for the preceding days, and even what Cahill had eaten for dinner and drank with it the night before. It was almost two hours of constant questions, answers, follow-up questions, and further responses before Cahill was told he could leave the stand.

The next several witnesses were dealt with much more quickly and with less detailed questions, which mostly focused on confirming statements made by Cahill and providing additional perspectives of events based on the points of view of various other members of the *Swallow* crew. Milliken seemed disinterested in the testimony of the crew, and the value he placed on the comments seemed more closely correlated with their rank than their knowledge of events. Even without having met him, Duncan was starting to dislike this man.

Ribacoff continued his aggressive questioning, including going to great lengths to explore the record of one of the lookouts and how many times he had been punished for even the most common types of occasional offenses. It was revealed that three years prior, or thereabouts, as the poor sailor could not recall the exact date no matter how many times Ribacoff asked, he had been punished for falling asleep while on night watch. His punishment, as was quite common for a first offense of this type, had been to have a bucket of cold seawater poured over his head in front of the rest of the crew. This embarrassment had been enough, according to his further testimony in response to a kindly worded question from Tankersley, to keep him from ever repeating the offense. He left the stand with his head hanging low after being reminded of this previously forgotten shame. Duncan now disliked Ribacoff even more than Milliken.

The treatment of the lookout seemed to set a low point for the morning so far, and Graham declared a 15-minute recess, which was welcomed by everyone present. Out on deck there was a stiff breeze blowing and Duncan took deep breaths of the fresh air, realizing just how stuffy the cabin had become. The members of the court stayed close together while everyone else milled about slowly, hesitant to speak to each other for fear of saying something they should not and being overheard.

As the participants began shuffling back into the great cabin, several decided to stay on deck. Although Duncan was enjoying the fresh air and dreading the stuffy cabin and sticky chair that awaited him, he was very interested in the proceedings now and did not hesitate to walk back in.

Once everyone was settled back in their seats, Graham spoke to the recording clerk, "Mr. Baker, is your hand rested and are you ready for us to continue?"

"Aye, sir," came the immediate response.

Graham glanced at a list in front of him and then said, "Captain Joseph Duncan, please take your place in the witness chair. You're next."

Twenty minutes later, Duncan was dismissed. Although he could have left, he moved back to his original chair, determined to see this to the end. He left the witness chair with an even more well-formed dislike of both Milliken and Ribacoff.

Duncan's testimony had been interrupted almost immediately by Captain Milliken objecting that there could be nothing relevant added by someone who had not even met Cahill until after the loss of *Swallow*. Tankersley had taken the contrary position that it was important to understand the man in order to put his actions into perspective. Surprisingly, Larson spoke up and sided with Tankersley. After a bit more discussion, Graham ruled that Duncan's testimony would proceed.

Milliken abstained from asking any questions in some form of silent protest and rolled his eyes several times as Larson seemed to finally come alive to ask Duncan questions about the engagement with the French fleet and the role Cahill had played. Ribacoff asked several infuriating questions, including one worded in such a way as to imply that perhaps Cahill had not actually been being held as a 'prisoner' aboard *L'Enchanté*.

The witnesses who followed Duncan were treated very much the same. Larson had continued to ask questions after finally finding his voice and certainly seemed to be leaning towards acquittal, along with Tankersley. Perhaps sensing that the tide was turning against them, the tone of Milliken and Ribacoff's questions became even more harsh and both were reprimanded by Captain Graham, who required them to rephrase questions on more than one occasion.

There was a second break, this time for 30 minutes, late in the afternoon, followed by three more witnesses. Finally, everyone on the list had been called and Graham addressed the accused. "We have now heard the testimony and are prepared to deliberate to make our judgement as to your fate. Lieutenant Cahill, do you have anything further to say to the court?"

Cahill responded after a short pause, "No, sir."

Tankersley grinned slightly and Larson turned to glance at Milliken, who was sneering and looking at Ribacoff at the other end of the table. Graham ignored the rest of the members of the court and spoke to those still assembled in the room. "Clear the cabin! Mr. Baker, you are to remain in case we need to review something in the record of the testimony. Everyone else out - including you, marines…everyone."

The room was filled with the sounds of chairs sliding across the deck and boots walking towards the door. Relatively few people had stayed until this point and there were less than a dozen (not counting the marines) to shuffle out onto the deck.

The sun was getting low, and Duncan walked to the rail and looked out across the harbor at the various ships at anchor. Only warships and a messenger packet were here in English Harbour. The privately owned merchant ships were less than a mile away at Falmouth Harbor, but the hills separating the two inlets blocked his view of those. Close to shore, near the dockyards, he could see *Enchanté* riding high in the water. She would have been stripped and emptied by now so the surveyors could sound her hull, completely inspect her, and take down measurements to record and add her to the British Navy list.

He sensed someone approaching and turned just as a lieutenant spoke to him, "Excuse me, sir. May I have a moment of your time?"

Duncan nodded his consent, thinking the man looked somewhat familiar but being unable to put a name with the face.

"Thank you, sir. I'm Jonathan Cary, first lieutenant of *Saturn* and soon to be commander of *Wolverine*. I just wanted to thank you, sir. But for your valor in engaging and defeating the French convoy, I would not be getting this chance for command."

Duncan smiled, a bit embarrassed to have had to be reminded of the name, and responded sincerely, "Ah, yes, *Le Carcajou* - a fine ship. Joy to you on your promotion and best of luck in your command."

"And the very same to you, sir," Cary replied.

"I apologize for not recognizing you. You caught me daydreaming while I was looking at my future command. Now that I think about it, that must be your ship next to *Enchanté* at anchor."

"Aye, sir. That is indeed *Wolverine*. I can hardly wait until she is ready, and the surveyors are done. Well, sir, I'm sorry to have bothered you and thank you again." With that, he saluted and walked away.

Duncan smiled to himself and then, remembering why he was on *Saturn,* he frowned and pulled out his watch to check the time. He did not know how long the deliberations might take, and he had not eaten since breakfast. His stomach was rumbling, but he was determined to stay until the end.

It was almost an hour later when Baker came on deck and announced that the court had reached a decision and Lieutenant Cahill - and any interested parties - could return. The marines marched in first, moving to their previous positions along the sides of the cabin. Cahill walked in next, holding his head high, but looking somewhat white with worry. Duncan was right behind Cahill and let out a sigh of relief when he saw his sword on the table with the hilt turned toward the witness chair.

As soon as everyone was back in the cabin and the door was shut, Graham confirmed what had been signaled by the position of the sword. "Lieutenant Cahill, this court has found that you acted honorably and in keeping with the best traditions of an officer in service to His Majesty's Navy during the unfortunate events that led to the destruction and loss of *HMS Swallow*. You are hereby acquitted of all charges and released with no further censure."

Cahill was beaming as he exclaimed, "Thank you, sir!"

Graham stood and said, "This court is dismissed." He shook Cahill's hand and walked out of the cabin, followed by Tankersley, who shook Cahill's hand as well. Milliken and Ribacoff left without even looking towards Cahill. The last of the court members to leave was Captain Larson, who shook Cahill's hand with a broad smile on his face, and then nodded an acknowledgement to Duncan.

Duncan was the highest-ranking person left in the room, and he paused to speak to Cahill as he prepared to take his turn to leave. "Congratulations, Lieutenant. Justice has indeed been served today."

"Thank you, sir. It seems I've many things for which to thank you. I appreciate you coming to speak on my behalf and also for staying the whole day. And, of course, thank you for letting me borrow your sword for the…occasion, sir." Cahill held out the sword to return it and Duncan took it from him.

"You're most welcome. I would say 'anytime,' but you really shouldn't make a habit of being placed on trial."

Cahill smiled easily and replied, "Aye, sir. I think I've had enough for now - hopefully forever. Until I can find another commission, I'll be hard pressed to get into this much trouble, and I doubt I'll ever be in command of a vessel again."

Duncan smiled and patted Cahill on the shoulder as he walked towards the door. "I doubt you'll have to wait too long for a new job, Mr. Cahill. There's a war on and we need good officers. Good day to you. I'm sure I'll see you again soon. Falmouth is a small town, after all."

•   •   •

When the day finally arrived for Duncan to join his new ship and officially take command, he was practically overcome with excitement. He rose early, before the sun had risen, since he had not been able to sleep, anyway. It had a been a fitful night, as he was tormented by equal parts of nervous apprehension and excitement. In the brief moments he did sleep, his dreams were also split between glorious visions of sailing in command and nightmares of losing the ship in various ways.

He pulled back the curtain and looked out the window. The glass was spattered with rain and, as the sun rose, it did little more than add a dim glow to the low, scudding, dark clouds. The wind was gusting and changing direction frequently. On the muddy street below, people scurried quickly from building to building or huddled under the overhang of buildings.

A few days earlier, he had sent a note to alert his officers that he would join the ship early in the afternoon watch and now he wondered what he would do for the intervening hours. He was not particularly hungry, but he could go down to the dining room for some tea or coffee and perhaps force himself to eat something to pass the time.

He had laid out his uniform the night before and he glanced at it before deciding to wait until later to wash and put it on. Instead, he grabbed the civilian attire he had been wearing the evening before when he spent a quiet night, alone for a change, dining by himself and then retiring to the room at the inn that they called the library. There were not a lot of books in the library, but he had stayed there until after midnight reading one of his own.

He strode into the dining room and took a quick glance around. There were only a few other people up at this hour - a couple sitting at a side table and an older man sitting alone at one end of the large communal table at the center of the room. Duncan had taken his breakfast at the main table most mornings while staying at the Brown Pelican. It was a nice way to meet people and engage in enjoyable, even if often meaningless, conversation.

This morning, he decided to sit at one of the small tables that lined the wall. He chose one of the smallest, which had only two chairs. A servant followed him and as soon as he was seated asked, "May I get you something, sir?"

Normally, Duncan was a coffee drinker, but his stomach was so unsettled from the night of tossing and turning that this morning he responded, "Tea, please. I shall peruse the sideboard on my own when I'm ready to eat."

He ended up spending about half an hour slowly sipping tea and eating a dry scone. Finally, he could not justify sitting there any longer and he got up and wandered into the main room. Before heading to the stairs, he walked to the window and was pleased to see that the wind was not as gusty as it had been earlier, and the rain had all but stopped. Happy for the opportunity this provided, he walked out the front door of the inn and took a long walk around Falmouth and even up into the hills to the west of the little town.

Late morning, he was back at the inn to wash and dress in his uniform. Just before noon, he had his chest and other belongings loaded into a cart and taken to a boat waiting at the waterfront. He had hired a boat to take him out, rather than arranging for a ship's boat to come and get him. Once he was settled in the boat, the boatman smiled at him and said, "Well, Capt'n, I suspect you be heading for the pretty little French frigate over yonder, unless I miss my mark."

In a town this small and with the excitement that Duncan's return with the flotilla of prizes had caused two weeks earlier, it was no surprise that everyone knew his business. He simply smiled, and responded, "Yes, if you please."

The boatman accepted his payment and pushed off from the dock. With a smooth and practiced stroke, he rowed the boat directly toward *Enchanté*. He spoke to Duncan, again, in a low voice, as they approached the ship, "You've not read yerself in, yet, have ye Capt'n?"

Duncan knew why he was asking and responded, "No, not yet."

The boatmen nodded and winked just as the challenge was called out from the ship, "Ahoy, the boat!"

In a booming voice, the boatman called back, "Aye, aye!" and paused in rowing long enough to hold up four fingers. This would be the last time Duncan would be announced as a generic officer until his command ended. From today, he would be "*Enchanté*" and his identity would be inexorably linked to the ship. He was about to step across the great divide that separated the rest of the officers and crew from the one in command.

As the boat bumped against the side and the side boys held out the hand ropes, Duncan tipped the boatman, thanked him, and climbed up and over the tumblehome. The bosun piped Duncan aboard just as the feather on his brand-new hat rose above the deck. He stepped through the opening in the railing and saluted the ship.

Lieutenant Cahill stepped forward with a huge smile splitting his face and said, "Welcome aboard, sir!"

Duncan was trying to look the part of a captain, but could not completely contain a smile in return. Despite the gravity of the situation, he could not resist jesting, "I'm glad to see you were able to find quick employment and hope it is to your satisfaction." He did not expect or wait for a reply and added, "Assemble the crew, Mr. Cahill. I shall read myself in and then you can introduce me to the other officers and warrants before we take a little tour."

The crew assembled quickly, and it was clear by the number that the ship was not yet fully manned. This did not surprise

Duncan, and he walked to the front edge of the quarterdeck and withdrew the parchment from inside his coat. He cleared his throat and began reading in a strong, steady voice.

"By the Commander-in-Chief of the West Indies Windward Fleet, under authority granted by the Commissioners for executing the Office of the Lord High Admiral of Great Britain and Ireland."

"To Captain Joseph Duncan, hereby appointed Captain of His Majesty's Ship the *Enchanté*."

"By Virtue of the Power and Authority to us given, We do hereby constitute and appoint you Captain of His Majesty's Ship the *Enchanté* willing and requiring you forthwith to go on board and take upon you the Charge and Command of Captain in her accordingly. Strictly Charging and Commanding all the Officers and Company belonging to the said ship subordinate to you to behave themselves jointly and severally in their respective Employments with all the Respect and Obedience unto you their said Captain; And you likewise to observe and execute as well the General printed Instructions as what Orders and Directions you shall from time to time receive from your Admiral or any other your superior Officers for His Majesty's service. Hereof nor you nor any of you may fail, as you will answer the contrary at your peril. And for so doing, this shall be your Warrant. Given under our hands and the Seal of the Fleet this 14th day of June, 1795 in the 36th Year of His Majesty's Reign."

"By Admiral Lord Edmund Fairhurst, Third Viscount of Hemington, Knight Companion Order of the Bath, Commander-in-Chief of the West Indies Windward Fleet."

As Duncan finished, the commissioning pennant was raised and fluttered out in the wind. *HMS Enchanté* was now part of the fleet, and Duncan was in command.

Chapter Nine

Duncan walked into the hospital ward and spotted Williams sitting on his bed, propped up against several pillows with a sheet across his legs. Pleased at the improvement in his friend's condition, Duncan crossed the room and sat in a chair next to the bed. "Good morning. You seem to be getting stronger. Are you annoying the staff yet?"

Williams smiled. "Many happy returns of the day and congratulations on your ascension, Captain."

Duncan chuckled and responded, "Thank you, Rupert."

"You realize that you can be totally incompetent now - like usual - and it won't make a bit of difference. All you have to do is survive and eventually, you'll be an admiral. I shudder to think of it, but there's no place for merit now, just longevity. I never really thought about how flawed the system is. Scandalous, I say."

Duncan laughed again. "Have you given any thought to your plans for after you recover?"

Williams looked down at the bandaged stump at the end of his arm. "I suppose I should appreciate the fact that they shot off my left hand rather than my right. Still, you know the old saying, 'one hand for the ship and one hand for the King.' One of them doesn't get a hand now, so there's no place for me in the Navy. No one wants a one-handed lieutenant."

Duncan sat in silence, wishing he could think of something encouraging to say. Unfortunately, Rupert was correct. As a captain, or certainly as an admiral, there might still be a commission, but for a lieutenant, there was little hope. Williams broke the awkward silence.

"Well, as I see it, I have two choices. I can either get a hook and become a pirate, or I can go back to London and face my father and admit he was right about the dangers of joining the Navy."

"They hang pirates."

"Aye, but you don't know my father."

"That's true. I don't know him, and I don't recall you ever talking much about him. Is there a family business for you to join? If not, perhaps you could become a barrister. You're quite good at talking while saying nothing of importance."

Williams dropped his gaze to his own lap and any cheerful expressions left his face. After a moment, he responded. "My father didn't want me to join the Navy because I'm the eldest son and stand to inherit the family title. As such, I was supposed to stay home and do nothing while my brothers served the crown or worked for the family."

Duncan was shocked and not entirely sure Williams was serious. Before he could think of anything to say, Williams continued.

"It's not a big deal, just a baronetcy - not a peerage. As for a family business, well, that's a bit embarrassing in polite society. You see, my father wasn't satisfied just owning ships like a proper gentleman. No, he had to get more directly involved and many see him as little more than a merchant. God forbid a baronet might actually do something to earn a living rather than just collecting for what others do."

Williams finally looked back up at Duncan as he concluded. "On the plus side, I used his unconventional views against him, which is how I convinced him to let me join the Navy. I've never made anything of the family connections. Some would resent me for being the son of a baronet and others would make fun of my father being 'in the trade'. There was really no advantage in letting anyone know - even friends. So, now I'll go back and be a merchant and someday become a one-handed baronet. Not so different from being a pirate, really." He ended with a tentative smile.

Duncan still was not sure he was serious, but from the look in Williams' eye, he thought he was probably telling the truth. "Wow. I didn't see that one coming. All this time I thought you were a nobody, and here you are being practically famous - with family secrets and everything."

Williams laughed, clearly relieved to finally tell his friend the truth. Duncan asked, "So, does your father own his own ships? Where do they sail?"

"He owns about a score of his own bottoms and then leases more, depending on the season and the need. As for where, anywhere there's cargo to be moved, but mostly timber, tar, and the like from the Baltic and several routes here in the West Indies. There are two of his ships in port here now. I plan to take one back to England when they sail." Williams seemed completely open now and talking easily about the situation.

"So, you stand to be something of an admiral of your own private fleet someday. That doesn't sound any more just or deserved than my situation and you're much less likely to be shot...again, that is."

This time, they both laughed. The next hour was spent chatting and joking about very little of importance. Finally, Duncan decided it was time for him to go and said, "I suppose I should get back to my duties. You're right about not needing to be competent - for the most part, but they could take my ship and leave me ashore on half pay. There's one last thing I'd like you to consider. Once you're back in London, I'll need someone to act as my agent for a variety of things, including the use and disposition of prize money. Might you be willing to do that for me? I'd feel much more at ease knowing it was in the hands of someone I really trust."

Williams responded immediately, "I would be honored and won't waste it any more than I do my own money. However, I should point out that it will be in a single good hand, not hands. Nevertheless, you can certainly trust me, my friend." They shook hands and Duncan departed.

•   •   •

In the two weeks since Duncan had assumed command of *Enchanté*, there had been significant progress towards getting her ready for sea. Stores and cannons had come aboard, and most importantly to Duncan, the crew was filling out. They were still more than four score short of their authorized complement of 274 souls and they were also still missing their second lieutenant, but the ship was beginning to feel less empty. There were some familiar faces, too, since 34 crewmen had been allowed to join from *Fidelity*.

Between the efforts of the crew and the dockyard workers, almost all the damage from the battle with *Fidelity* had been repaired. Even parts not showing obvious damage were removed, inspected, and then either put back or replaced. This included the masts, which in the end were all certified as acceptable, even though they did not meet the standard dimensions and sizes preferred by the British. Several yards had been replaced and all the standing and running rigging had been completely replaced with new ropes and cables.

Enchanté smelled "new". Wherever you went in the ship, the overwhelming aromas were of fresh oak, pine, paint, and tar. On deck, the smell of paint mixed with the peculiar, somewhat musty scent of rope. What was missing was the normal funk of humans who had been packed together with little chance to wash off the sweat that came from almost constant labor in the hot Caribbean sun. That would replace the smell of newness soon enough, and Duncan was glad of the temporary reprieve.

Even deep in the hold, *Enchanté* did not stink like a normal ship. Her ballast had all been removed to allow proper sounding of the hull and the dockyard had been considerate enough to wash everything down with vinegar before replacing the ballast. Duncan had never been in a sweeter smelling ship.

The pleasant scents might not last long, but the other work done on the ship would benefit her in more important ways. She had been taken to the careenage and her bottom had not only been inspected and her copper repaired, but it had been scraped and burned clean of weeds and barnacles. Duncan was anxious to get her out to sea in a stiff breeze to see what she was capable of in such pristine condition. Within weeks, the bottom would begin to be fouled again and she would slowly lose speed until the next time she could be careened.

Although *Enchanté* had been rated as a 38-gun ship while flying French colors, she would be listed in the British Navy as a 36-gun, fifth rate frigate. Her main battery had been replaced with twenty-six 18-pounder cannons. On her quarterdeck she now carried eight 6-pounder long guns and six 32-pound carronades. On her forecastle, she had two brass 9-pounder chase guns and two 32-pound carronades. She carried fewer long guns than she had in French service, but at close range her weight of broadside had been increased dramatically by the inclusion of the massive carronades. The carronades, or smashers as they were more commonly called, required a smaller gun crew and took less time to reload as well, but the tradeoffs were shorter range and decreased accuracy.

Duncan was sitting at the desk in his cabin reviewing the latest reports on stores that had been brought aboard. He was vaguely aware of the noise on deck as boats came to and from the side bearing equipment, stores, dockyard workers, and, occasionally, new crew members. It was a nearly constant flow of material and manpower during the daylight hours. Casks of beef and pork had already been brought aboard, but they were still well below standard rations of cheese, biscuit, and water. None of this mattered much while in port, since fresh food and water was brought aboard each day to feed the crew. However, it was a glaring reminder that *Enchanté* was not ready for sea, and it bothered Duncan.

Over the background noise of men working, he heard a musket butt strike the deck outside his door and the marine sentry call out, "First Lieutenant, sir."

Duncan sat back and rubbed his eyes as he called back, "Enter."

Lieutenant Cahill removed his hat and walked in followed by Lieutenant Strickland, who also removed his hat and then walked forward to Duncan's desk, handed him a folded piece of paper, and announced, "Lieutenant Richard Strickland, reporting for duty, sir."

Duncan opened the paper and scanned it. He was a little surprised, but clearly this was Strickland's assignment to the *Enchanté* where he would serve as second lieutenant. He laid the document aside for a more thorough reading later and said, "Welcome aboard, Lieutenant. Have a seat. Mr. Cahill, please do sit down as well."

As Cahill sat down, he reached out with another piece of paper, this one sealed with wax and the admiral's personal seal. "This was also delivered for you, sir."

Duncan took it, broke the seal, and quickly read the short note inviting him to join the admiral for dinner the next day. He laid that aside as well and looked back at Strickland. "We have been expecting a second lieutenant to join, but I must admit that I'm surprised that it's you. I'm not displeased, mind you, just…surprised."

It seemed that Strickland had anticipated this reaction, and he replied, "Yes, sir. I can understand that. I've been on the admiral's staff for just under two years and he feels it is important for me to get more active service, sailing time, and leadership experience."

"I see. Well, Lieutenant Cahill will certainly be happy to have another officer aboard. Commissioning a ship is a dreadful amount of work in both labor and paperwork. Have you any experience with commissioning?"

Strickland replied easily, "Aye, sir. I was Fourth in *Glory*, under Captain Tankersley, when she was commissioned for the West Indies. I was transferred to the admiral's staff after we arrived here in Antigua. I also was aboard *Veteran*, as a mid when she was commissioned, sir."

"*Veteran*? She's a 64, isn't she?"

"Yes, sir. The last to be built, if I'm not mistaken, sir."

"What other ships have you served on?"

"*Resolution* was my first ship, sir. Then, *Zealous*, *Veteran*, and *Monarch*, before I joined *Glory*."

Duncan thought for a moment and then asked, "So you've spent your entire career on ships of the line, Lieutenant?"

"Aye, sir." For the first time, Strickland looked a little nervous and unsure of himself.

"Well, you'll find we have quite a bit less room on a frigate, but we tend to have more fun, I think." Duncan smiled and Strickland relaxed and smiled back quickly.

The next forty-five minutes were spent in an enjoyable conversation between the three officers, sharing stories of ships they had known and other officers they had served with. The focus was mostly on Strickland, but Cahill and Duncan had said enough to keep it from seeming like an interrogation. All three felt that they knew each other better when the discussion finally drew to a close, with Duncan saying, "Well, I suppose we all need to get back to work."

He looked around the cabin as he continued, "Now that we've got all the officers aboard, I should dine you in…but given that I don't yet have a dining table or a cook, perhaps I'll find a place ashore, instead. Be on the lookout for an invitation."

The two lieutenants rose to leave, and Duncan offered his hand and said sincerely, "Welcome aboard, Mr. Strickland."

"Thank you, sir."

"Mr. Cahill, please pass the word for the three of you lieutenants, the master, bosun, gunner, carpenter, and purser to all assemble here at the end of the second dog watch. I've a meeting with the admiral tomorrow, so I'll want to know the latest details concerning the status and timeline for having *Enchanté* ready for sea."

"Aye, aye, sir," was Cahill's response as he ducked out the door and placed his hat back on his head.

"One last thing, Mr. Cahill. Please pass the word for Jenkins."

"Aye, sir. Will that be all?" Cahill stood smiling and holding the door open.

Duncan returned the smile. "Yes, I think that will do for now, but don't go far. I might think of something else."

A few minutes later, the marine sentry called out, "Able Seaman Jenkins, sir!"

Duncan put down the papers he was reading, called out, "Enter," and sat back in his chair.

Jenkins walked in, knuckled his forehead, and half-stated and half-asked, "You sent for me, sir?"

"Yes, please have a seat."

Jenkins walked over to the desk and sat gingerly on the front of the chair without leaning back or relaxing. Duncan continued, "I'm in need of a coxswain and if you're willing, I would like you to take the position. However, before you answer me, I'd like to make sure you understand the choice you'd be making.

"Being the captain's coxswain would leave you with one foot firmly on each side of a fence. You'll still have your normal duties and mess with the crew, but you'll also spend time here in my cabin and be trusted with things you might be told or overhear. You'll not be able to share that information with your crewmates, and although I would never expect you to violate any confidences among your mates, I may ask you to help me understand the mood and feelings on the gun deck. So, you'll be both a part of the crew and somewhat apart from the crew - neither fish nor fowl, so to speak.

"If you have any questions, you may ask them now and if you would like to some time to consider your decision, you may have until tomorrow."

Jenkins responded immediately, "Thank you, sir, and I don't need no time to think it over. I accept, and I'd be honored to be your coxswain, sir. I can keep my trap shut when I need to. I ain't no snitch, but I reckon I can tell you how folks are getting along, sir."

"Excellent. If anyone is here in the cabin with me, I'll expect you to be announced before entering, but if I'm alone, or not here and you need to enter, I'll instruct the marines to let you come and go, as you please. Once I have a cook, there might be times that there is extra food prepared and you may have a share in that, if you like."

"Thankee, Cap'tn."

"You may select the boat crew and provide a list to the first officer. I'll be heading over to *Glory* tomorrow morning, so please have them ready."

"Aye, sir." Jenkins hesitated and then added, "Might this be one of those times I could mention something about the feelings on the lower deck, sir?"

"Please do. I think you probably know from our time together on *Fidelity* that I try to be fair and steady, even if I don't shy from using the cat if necessary to maintain discipline and efficiency. I'm not interested in being popular, but I do think that a happy ship performs better."

"That signifies, sir. What I was thinking was that being part of the captain's boat crew is a special thing, and the lads would like to look good and have something to show who they are. Something like a special shirt or outfit, maybe like."

Duncan considered for a moment, and then said, "That sounds like a good idea. I shall speak to the Purser and have him work out the details with you."

"Thankee, sir. There mightn't be time by tomorrow for that, but I'll make sure they're scrubbed, shaved, and turned out proper, sir."

"Thank you, Jenkins. Unless you have any further questions…or 'feelings' to share, you can return to your duties."

Jenkins stood, knuckled his head, and walked out of the cabin.

The rest of the afternoon was spent reading reports and writing requests to the dockyard for various things they still needed. He took the time to reread the commission appointing Lieutenant Strickland to the ship, as well as the invitation from the admiral. An invitation and order were really the same thing in this instance, and there was no need to send a response.

He picked up the last piece of paper on his review pile and found that it was the latest watch list prepared by Cahill. Balancing the capabilities of the two watches and organizing them to maximize efficiency was as much art as science. Men not only needed to work well and know their duty, but also had to work well together. That was difficult enough once you knew the crew and was mostly guesswork with a new group of men assembled from other ships or time ashore.

Duncan was pleased to see that Cahill had distributed the former members of *Fidelity* and *Swallow* in such ways that their familiarity with each other might help them, while not allowing them to form too strong a group that might alienate others. All in all, Cahill had done a very good job on the watch list - as he seemed to do with all his duties. Duncan certainly had not known him well when he requested him as his first lieutenant and if he was to be honest with himself, he was not really sure why he made the request. In any event, it was looking like a good decision.

His eye traveled down the page to the list of "idlers", those who did not serve as part of a watch, but rather worked during the day and for the most part had the nights off. Among them were the boatswain, Philip Murray, the carpenter, Joshua Greene, and the gunner, Jonas Chapman. Along with the master, Nathaniel Ellis, they would be the standing officers of the ship, and once assigned, would stay with it as long as it was in service. Duncan had not known any of them before their appointments to *Enchanté* and was very happy they all seemed like experienced and professional seamen.

He put the watch list in a drawer in his desk, wiped his quill clean, and stood up to stretch. His back ached from sitting so long and he rolled his head from side to side to relieve the pain in his neck. He had lost track of the bells sounding in the distance and pulled out his watch to check the time. He had about half an hour before supper, so he headed on deck and spent the time walking on the quarterdeck to clear his head.

Supper consisted of cold chicken and potatoes left over from dinner, along with a small salad of fresh greens, some not too stale bread, and practically melted butter. Since he did not have a table yet, he ate at his desk. After finishing his meal and watching Stanley whisk the dirty dishes and some breadcrumbs away, he realized a fresh pile of paper to review had mysteriously appeared and sighed heavily. He left the pile where it was and went back on deck for more pacing on the quarterdeck until sunset.

Duncan spent the following two hours dealing with the review pile (which had grown yet again while he was on deck) and reading a book by the lanthorn on his desk. The master was the first to arrive for the meeting and Duncan welcomed him, "Ah, Mr. Ellis, please do come in and make yourself as comfortable as you can."

Ellis looked around the room and said in his normal, cheery voice, "Aye, Cap'tn, we'll be standing then by the looks of it."

Duncan smiled back. He was still getting to know the master, but he liked him. He was a somewhat short man of medium build with a balding head. He seemed to have given up on having hair, and what little grew was shaved to not much more than stubble. His face was weather-beaten and darkened by the sun, standing in contrast to his bright eyes. He was a jovial man and wrinkles around his eyes seemed to be as much from laughing as from age or squinting at the weather.

Everyone else began to arrive and soon the cabin was full., The meeting was held standing up, as the master had predicted, and was quick and efficient. In about twenty minutes, Duncan had a good understanding of what was left to do and how long it was expected to take. With that, he dismissed the group by saying, "Thank you. That will be all for now. Mr. Lloyd, please be so kind as to stay for a moment. To the rest of you, good night."

After the others had shuffled out, Duncan returned to the chair at his desk and signaled Lloyd to be seated in one of the two chairs in front of the desk. Once he was seated, Duncan began, "Mr. Lloyd, I've been meaning to have a word with you. I understand that you have had to pledge hundreds, if not thousands, of pounds of your own funds in order to get your warrant as a purser. I also understand that you will need to make a profit. I would not stand between any man and the money he justifiably earns to support himself and whatever family he might have.

"I am not one who thinks that all pursers are evil or crooked. I'm quite sure there are many good men who take up the profession and unless given reason to think otherwise, I shall assume that you are among the most honest and good in your profession."

"However, I would be remiss in not making clear that I will not tolerate any advantage being taken of the crew. You may make your honest profit, and they will be treated fairly. Are we in agreement about this?"

Jason Lloyd was a small man who normally wore a coarse brown wool jacket and pants. He was timid by nature and more comfortable with numbers than people. He swallowed hard and responded, "Yes, sir."

Duncan sat back and said, "Good. Then, let's never have to speak of that again. In addition to the ship's regular accounts, I should like you to manage an account that I shall personally fund. This account will be used for items, as I direct, which are beyond, or in addition to, the standards allowed by the Boards. For example, additional powder for gunnery practice beyond the standard allotment, food and drink for my cabin and guests, etc. I will ask you to keep account of these items and charges, and for this you may add your customary profit, as if it were on standard account. Is that acceptable?"

Lloyd was beginning to relax a little, and this sounded like a potentially profitable venture. "Yes, sir. That sounds fine."

Duncan continued, "Excellent. I shall expect a monthly accounting, including remuneration of the charges you have added. We can schedule a time to review it along with the ship's books. One further thing is that I should like this to remain between us - no one else should know or care whether something is to be paid for by me or the Navy. Agreed?"

"Yes, sir. I can keep a separate book, but only you and I will know what goes in either, sir."

"Very well. I have your first items for this account, then. Would you please work with my coxswain, Jenkins, to outfit the boat crew in something uniform and pleasing, but not gaudy? Just something nicer than standard slops. I don't want the crew to have to pay for the privilege, and it's fine if they think it's standard issue."

"Yes, sir, I think I know what you mean, and I have some ideas."

Duncan nodded and as he glanced around the cabin, he added, "And one more thing. Please be so kind as to find furniture for the cabin. I haven't had time and wouldn't know where to look, anyway."

Lloyd smiled and responded, "I'd be happy to, sir. You can count on me."

•   •   •

Duncan stepped back to see more of himself reflected in the small mirror hanging from the bulkhead. He could not really distinguish much from this distance in such a small mirror, but he could make out the single gold epaulet on his right shoulder identifying him as a captain. This, along with the rest of his uniform, was in the newly approved style.

Stanley helped him to buckle on his belt and sword and handed him his hat. The hat, too, was of the new style and was to be worn forward and back, rather the side to side on his head. He would certainly be much better dressed for this meeting with the admiral than he was the last time he visited *Glory*. He glanced down at his boots, which looked nice but were not quite comfortable yet, as he had not had time to properly break them in.

With one more glance at the mirror, he headed for the door and out into the bright, late morning sunshine. The time of his departure had been known since the day before, so everything was ready. The side party was gathered by the entry port, and Jenkins sat below in the rear of the captain's gig. The four oarsmen were each seated in their own row with their single oar on alternating sides of the gig raised - currently straight up, so as to not hit the side of the ship or create a tripping hazard within the boat.

Cahill, Strickland, and Cole were all standing near the entry port and came to attention as Duncan approached. He spoke to them as he went over the side and started down to the gig, "Please keep her in one piece and redouble your efforts to get her ready for sea. I hope the admiral will give us a chance to take her out soon."

"Aye, aye, sir!" Cahill responded for all of them.

Duncan timed his step from the ship to the gunwale of the boat to match the swell and made his way to the back. He positioned his sword and sat down in the stern sheets. Jenkins looked at him and he gave a quick single nod.

Jenkins looked forward at the stroke oarsman just in front of him, pulled the tiller over, and yelled, "Cast off, forward and back! Ship your oars…and stroke!" The gig surged forward and once it was moving enough for the tiller to bite, Jenkins began to ease it back to bring the boat around the bow of *Enchanté* and head toward the huge first rate moored closer to the entrance of the bay.

It was a short ride across the bay. The lack of much wind was both a blessing and a curse for Duncan. It provided very little relief from the hot sun beating down on the dark blue uniform, but also meant there was very little spindrift or splash from the oars, so he did not need to cover himself with a tarp or boat cloak. He noticed the crew were all clean-shaven and wearing their best clothes, with their queues freshly plaited. Even more importantly, they were pulling in unison and had similar enough power in their strokes that the gig was traveling easily in a straight line with very little tiller adjustment needed by Jenkins.

As the gig approached *Glory*, the sentry called out the challenge, "Boat ahoy!"

Jenkins held up four fingers and replied, "*Enchanté!*"

Two ropes, known as painters, were dropped over the side to secure the front and back of the boat and Duncan could see the side boys at the railing, ready to man the side ropes and hold them out away from the side of the ship so he could use them to climb up the curved side. Jenkins put the tiller hard over and yelled, "Boat your oars! Bowman hook on forward." The oarsman in the front seat pulled a pole with a hook on the end from where it had been stored and used it to hook onto the chains and pull the boat gently to the side. The two painters were secured. Duncan stood and instructed Jenkins, "You may return to *Enchanté* and be back in two hours to pick me up."

He heard Jenkins respond, "Aye, aye, sir!" as he clambered up the side and onto the deck of the flagship.

Tankersley was waiting to greet him and held out his hand with a broad smile splitting his face. "Welcome back aboard, Captain Duncan. It's good to see you again."

Duncan's hand felt lost in the flag captain's massive grip. "Good to see you, too, sir, and thank you!"

"How's Strickland settling in?" Tankersley asked as he motioned towards the admiral's cabin and started to walk that way.

Duncan fell in beside him and responded, "Main, well. I understand he served under you before joining the flag staff."

"Aye, he did and a very good, although a somewhat green and inexperienced officer, he was. I hope you don't mind, but it was me who put the bug in the admiral's ear to transfer him to your command. A good young officer with potential needs a chance to hone his craft, and a frigate is the best place to do it."

Duncan replied honestly, "I thank you for it and consider myself to be in your debt. I'm quite pleased to have him. Although I was a bit surprised the admiral was willing to give him up. I understand a little better now."

"We've not long left on this commission and there's no way of knowing what awaits us all back in England. I saw an opportunity for Strickland and I helped it along. You don't owe me anything for doing my duty by a fellow officer."

They had reached the admiral's door and, after being announced by the marine sentry and invited in, they entered the cabin.

The admiral was standing with his hands clasped behind his back near a man Duncan did not recognize and he spoke as they came in. "Captain Duncan, welcome. Allow me to introduce Mr. Ebenezer Hirschhorn, of the Foreign Office." Then, turning his head to Hirschhorn, he added, "Captain Joseph Duncan of His Majesty's frigate, *Enchanté*."

Hirschhorn offered his hand and smiled in a way that did not quite reach his eyes. "A pleasure to meet you, Captain. I've heard of your exploits and look forward to getting to know you."

"Thank you, sir. It's a pleasure to meet you, as well," Duncan replied.

The admiral began to speak again as one of his cabin servants appeared with a small silver tray bearing four wine glasses of a cool, white wine and offered one to each of the men. "Mr. Hirschhorn is the senior representative of the Foreign Office in the West Indies. As such, he acts sometimes in an advisory capacity to me, as well as to the governor. I asked him to join us based on the nature of part of the discussion we shall have before dinner. I intend to make sure you all earn your meals." The admiral smiled and took a sip of wine before continuing, "How go the preparations and when will *Enchanté* be ready for sea, Captain Duncan?"

This was a line of questioning Duncan was well prepared for. "The ship is in good shape and if necessary, we could sail within two days, but I'm sorry to report we would still be short of some provisions and equipment. To be fully ready for an extended cruise will take six to seven days, M'Lord."

Tankersley interjected, "Given the damage she sustained, you must have been riding the dockyard pretty hard to have her ready in so short a time."

"I'm sure the captain is anxious to get back to sea," Hirschhorn noted.

The admiral pondered for a moment and then said, "I've never met an officer worth his salt that wasn't anxious to be at sea when stuck in port with his admiral. You've done a fine job getting her ready so quickly. As she's just entering service, we'll try some short trips and sea trials to check her trim before any long cruises."

"Thank you, M'Lord," Duncan responded. "I would welcome a chance to test the new riggings and trim, as well as exercise the new crew. They're a good bunch of lads, but not used to working together yet, and are still getting to know each other."

"Yes, that's to be expected. You've a pretty young set of officers, as well. Cahill and Cole were your choices, and Tankersley convinced me to add Strickland. Perhaps I should have found someone with more sea time, given that Cole just passed for his commission," Fairhurst reflected.

"I'm quite pleased with them, M'Lord, and I thank you."

The conversation drifted along for several more minutes in a discussion of the specific shortages and condition of the ship. Hirschhorn seemed little interested and had nothing in particular to add, so he stood silently sipping his wine and listening.

The admiral moved toward some chairs and said, "Well, on to other business, please do all take a seat." After they had all sat down, he continued by addressing Duncan specifically, "Mr. Hirschhorn and Captain Tankersley are already aware of this, so I'll just make the situation clear to you. What we are about to discuss is not to leave this room or be talked about beyond the four of us. Is that clear, Captain?"

"Aye, M'Lord," Duncan responded. He was both intrigued and surprised by this sudden change in the mood of the conversation.

"Good. Do you recall any specifics concerning the cannons being carried by the French convoy you intercepted? I'm referring specifically to those carried in the holds. I'm sure you have some vivid memories of the ones on deck."

Duncan smiled, "Not really, no, M'Lord. I remember they were mostly small weight cannons, but nothing more specific."

Tankersley asked Duncan, "Did you look at them, or did you just see the listing on the inventories prepared by the prize commanders?"

Duncan was not sure where all this was going but did not feel he had done anything wrong, so he simply answered honestly and openly, "I saw them briefly from the hatchway in the light of a lanthorn, but not close enough to count them or see any detail, sir. I just glanced into the holds when I visited each prize."

"Well," said the admiral, "the thing is, they're British cannons - current Blomefield pattern. What's more, they are all new, never fired, not even bearing a proving mark from the foundry or Ordinance Board."

Duncan was working through the implications of those statements as the admiral sat back and continued, "You'll likely recall that I asked you about your orders when sailing with Captain Blackwell and you only knew of a general cruise in a certain area. I had given Blackwell more specific secret orders. Mr. Hirschhorn, would you please explain?"

Hirschhorn nodded slowly and then began, "The Foreign Office had…become aware of certain information indicating that the French were intending to send a small convoy with supplies and money to outfit privateers to harry British merchant ships. We only had a vague idea of the timing, potential route, and size of the convoy. I shared what we knew with Lord Fairhurst, and he saw fit to send *Fidelity* to try to intercept the convoy, which in the end you accomplished, without knowing it was the true reason for your cruise."

After a short pause, Hirschhorn continued, "However, nothing in our information would have led us to expect to find such a large number of British cannons. Perhaps a few captured or stolen could have been expected, but these would have been few in number and would have shown signs of prior use."

The admiral went on from there. "So, you not only captured the convoy, but in doing so, you uncovered a mystery. As far as I, or Mr. Hirschhorn, have been able to ascertain from our sources without directly revealing what we've found, there is only one logical way so many new British cannons could have ended up on French national ships. Treason, Captain Duncan. One of the foundries must have directly supplied the enemy."

Tankersley was watching and listening closely and after a moment he said, "You look like you have a question, Captain Duncan. No need to be shy here."

Duncan swallowed and tried to think of a better way to phrase his question, but finally just asked, "Why are you telling me?"

Tankersley smiled and sat back. "Good question!"

The admiral glanced at Tankersley and then looked back at Duncan as he spoke. "We need more information, and *La Tempête* is still out there, along with Commodore De La Fountain. We've spoken to Captain Bouchard, the previous commander of *Enchanté*, and I'm convinced he doesn't know the origin of the cannons. He and De La Fountain didn't get along very well. I intend to send you to try to find *La Tempête,* and I needed you to understand why."

Before Duncan could say anything, Hirschhorn spoke, "Until we know more and are sure of the situation, we can't let others know - both because it could be very damaging and because it might give those responsible time to hide. I think we can all agree that if, in fact, so heinous a crime has been committed, we want to see those responsible brought to justice."

"Yes, quite," the admiral responded. "We'll also need more information on where to send you looking for *La Tempête*. It's a big ocean out there. So, in the meantime, we'll get you ready for sea and have you make sure *Enchanté* is prepared when the time comes. You're not to tell your officers, or anyone else, about the reasons behind the mission. To begin with, I think a short sail to Saint Kitts in, say, a week to ten days would be a good first test."

The admiral motioned to a servant standing near his desk and said, "We can't have you go too far. I almost forgot to give you the invitation. Drake, bring me the invitation from the governor for Captain Duncan."

The servant brought a wax sealed envelope to the admiral, who handed it to Duncan. "The governor is to host a ball in three weeks' time to honor you. It would be bad form, indeed, if I were to have you out at sea during the ball."

He stood and started toward the dining area, and motioned for the others to follow. "I do believe it's time for dinner. Do you happen to have a cook yet, Duncan?"

"Erm, no M'Lord. I've not yet found one."

"Perhaps you could do me a favor, then. A good friend of mine recently passed away rather suddenly. He was a botanist, who spent the last several years sailing aboard his private yacht, visiting various places, studying plants and whatnot. He was a Frenchman, but a loyalist, and a good man. He died on Nevis and his yacht is stuck in Basseterre, on Saint Kitts, until the probate can rule on his will. His cook is quite a talented man but finds himself unemployed and facing limited prospects as a Frenchman on a British island during wartime. I would appreciate if you would consider him."

Duncan responded, "I'd be happy to, M'Lord."

"Good. Thank you. I'm not saying you have to take him. I'm just asking you give him a try and see what you think. I've eaten a few meals prepared by him and although it might not suit all British palates, if you like more worldly fare, you might find he fits the bill. His name is Étienne Thibeault and I shall include a letter of introduction with your orders to sail to Saint Kitts. Beyond that, it's up to you."

Chapter Ten

The morning after his dinner with the admiral, Duncan was sitting at his desk reviewing various reports and papers when the marine sentry at the cabin door announced, "The pusser, sir!"

Duncan smiled to himself, wondering what the purser thought of this common mispronunciation. "Enter."

Jason Lloyd came in, looking a little annoyed but quickly brightening with a smile. "I'm sorry to bother you, sir, but I was wondering when a convenient time would be to have your cabin furniture brought in."

"Furniture? You've already found something?"

"Yes, sir. I've found a lovely table with matching chairs, a hutch, side table, wine cabinet, two bookcases, and I hope you don't mind but I also took the liberty of acquiring a different desk and chairs - something more appropriate to your position, sir."

"Well, I look forward to seeing it all. You may have it brought aboard whenever is convenient."

Lloyd shifted nervously. "Ah, perhaps I wasn't clear, sir. The furniture is on the deck already and we can bring it in and set it up whenever it would not inconvenience you or disturb your work."

Duncan smiled and stood up. "Now is fine, Mr. Lloyd. I can hardly wait. Would it be best for me to go on deck to be out of the way, or would you like me here to help decide where to place things?"

"If you would indulge me, sir, I should very much like to set everything up for full effect before you see it. Of course, we can always shift things any way you like later, but I have a certain arrangement in mind and had such as I picked out the pieces."

"I shall gladly go for a turn or several around the quarterdeck then, and you may have free rein of the cabin to work your magic. Thank you, Mr. Lloyd." With that, Duncan walked out onto the deck, up the ladderway, and onto the quarterdeck to enjoy the beautiful day and stretch his legs.

The furniture was piled on the deck between the cannons. It was all wrapped in tarps and cloth, so he could not see more than rough shapes. He paced the deck a few times and then took a telescope from the rack and had a look about the bay and the surrounding hills. After that, he returned to pacing the deck and was soon lost in thought about the preparations to ready the ship for sea.

Lloyd stopped short of stepping onto the quarterdeck and called to Duncan from near the top of the gangway ladder, "Sir, we are prepared, and the cabin awaits inspection at your convenience."

Duncan could tell that Lloyd was excited to show off his purchases and Duncan was anxious to see them. "I shall attend instanter," he said, as he walked forward and down the gangway. Lloyd fell in behind him as he reached the door of the coach, which he opened to reveal a large dark mahogany desk with three side chairs, made of a similar color wood and rich brown leather seats. The chair behind the desk was similar to the side chairs, with the addition of leather-upholstered arms. It looked very comfortable.

A matching bookcase with three shelves was nestled against the side of the ship, next to one of the cannons, which now had a cover made of old sailcloth.

Duncan walked over to the desk and ran his hand across the shiny surface. There was a small hutch of shelves and compartments sitting on the right side of the desk against the partition for his bedchamber, and the desk itself had a large center drawer with a key protruding from the keyhole as well as drawers down both sides.

"It's quite lovely," he said honestly, as he slid the drawer open and closed.

Lloyd smiled broadly and said, "I'm glad you like it, sir. We slid your old desk into your bed chamber temporarily. We can remove it after you've had a chance to transfer your papers and such. Shall we review the great cabin, now, sir?"

Duncan had been pleased with the new furniture in the coach, but the transformation of the great cabin was truly astonishing. The floor was covered from wall to wall with sailcloth painted in a checkerboard pattern of black and white, to give the illusion of tile. In front of the transom windows, was a long table surrounded by ten chairs. Two large upholstered chairs of dark leather were sitting, one at each end of the transom, with small brass-topped side tables next to each.

On one side, next to the cannon (which, like the one in the coach, now had a sailcloth cover) was a wine cabinet. In the same location on the other side was a tall, five-shelf bookcase. On the wall, between the doors to the coach and bed chamber, stood a large hutch. A side table was on the other side of the coach door, and a large dresser and wardrobe cabinet filled the similar spot by the bedchamber door.

The wood, light colored cherry, all matched perfectly; as did the dark brass fixtures, hinges, and draw pulls. It looked elegant without being fancy or delicately constructed. It actually looked like it might survive life at sea. Of course, ringbolts would have to be added to secure the table to the deck, and the other items would have to be secured as well. The carpenter could see to that.

"I must say, Mr. Lloyd, I am quite impressed. That you could find such a set of furniture and on such short notice truly astounds me. Thank you," Duncan said, as he looked around the cabin. Perhaps soon, he would have a cook and could dine in his officers in style.

•   •   •

Duncan was sitting at his new desk, enjoying the comfort of his new chair, and disliking the task of reading and checking provision reports. He had told Cahill about the potential trip to Saint Christopher Island, better known as Saint Kitts, once they were ready in all respects for sea, and all the lieutenants had been pushing the crew to their limits ever since. It had been four days since he had met with the admiral, and almost everything was ready. All they lacked was powder for the guns, which, for safety reasons, was always the last thing brought aboard a newly commissioned ship.

"First Lieutenant, sir!" came the call from the sentry.

Duncan kept working on the list he was reviewing so as to not lose his place, and called back, "Come on in."

Cahill ducked in and removed his hat. "Sorry to interrupt you, sir, but I thought you might want to know that the powder hoy is being warped over and should be alongside in fifteen minutes, there or near."

Duncan finished the column he was checking and looked up with a smile. "I'll be right up. Thank you for letting me know."

•   •   •

The land breeze that was typical at night was still blowing softly as Duncan left his cabin and made his way to the quarterdeck in the early morning light. Cahill, Strickland, and Cole were all there waiting for him, along with the master and the bosun.

"Good morning, gentlemen," Duncan greeted them. "It seems like a nice day for a sail. Please make your report, Lieutenant Cahill."

"Good morning, sir," Cahill responded with a smile tugging at the edges of his mouth. "The ship and crew are ready for sea in all respects."

Duncan clasped his hands behind his back, partially to conceal his excitement, and walked slowly to the weather side rail. "Signal the flag that we are ready to sail."

"Mr. O'Toole, make *Glory*'s number and signal 'request permission to leave the fleet'!" Cahill relayed to the signal midshipman standing at the flag locker.

Duncan noted that O'Toole already had the appropriate flags laid out and ready to bend on the signal halyards. Within moments, the brightly colored flags were fluttering in the wind. Along with the commissioning pennant, they gave a good indication of the wind direction and speed at the top of the masts. The winds were fair for departing from English Harbour.

He tried to avoid looking in the direction of the flagship as he paced along the railing and was relieved when, in just a few minutes, Midshipman O'Toole called out, "Signal from the Flag, sir. Acknowledged and Godspeed."

That sounded more like Tankersley than the admiral, Duncan thought to himself, as he walked to the front of the quarterdeck and took a long, critical look down at the main deck and up into the riggings. He knew the new rope of the topsail halyards had been repeatedly stretched and exercised to avoid the risk of it becoming cable-laid and kinking when needed. In addition to these halyards, he could see that the braces, lifts, tacks, and sheets were coiled down and free for running with dry stoppers conveniently placed for belaying them.

Aloft, the chaffing gear had been prepared and placed to reduce wear on the rigging. The top-gallant masts had been slushed, and the covers were off the sails. Grab lines and Jacob's ladders had been rigged in the mizzen channels and the lifebuoy was ready. In case something needed to be cut or cleared away, the junk-axes had been sharpened and were hanging in their beckets by the masts. All was ready.

Finally, after what was only a few seconds but seemed like an eternity to everyone aboard, he turned back to Cahill and the others and said, "Mr. Cahill, I shall certainly give you the honor next time, but seeing as this will be our first time weighing, I shall take her out myself."

Cahill was not surprised, and although a little disappointed, he did not let it show, as he responded, "Of course, sir."

Duncan moved to a position just to the side of the ship's wheel and stood with his legs wide and his hands clasped behind his back as he gave his first orders, "Man the capstan! Prepare to weigh anchor. Helmsman, test the rudder!"

The quartermaster mate at the wheel turned it clockwise until it stopped and then turned it all the way back before returning it to a center position and calling out, "Rudder is free and the tiller rope runs smoothly, sir."

Down on the deck, men had removed the storage drawers from the capstan, placed the bars in the openings, and were in position to begin turning. A fiddler hopped up on the capstan and stood with his bow poised, ready to help encourage the men with a tune. Once the men were in place, a rope was run around in a circle connecting the ends of all the bars in case one slipped out or broke.

The bosun called out, "Messenger fitted and shipped, nippers ready, capstan manned, and ready to weigh!"

"Turn!" Duncan called out, and the men put their chests against the bars and began to apply pressure.

"Put your backs into it, lads! Turn, now! Altogether...heave...heave...that's right, step off and heave together!" As the boson provided encouragement and instruction, the fiddler started playing and the capstan slowly began to turn, and the pawls clicked in a steady rhythm.

Duncan glanced around again to make sure everything was ready and in its proper place. From upfront he heard, "Long stay!" and he knew the anchor cable was taut and running out at a shallow angle.

He waited a moment, and then called out, "Topmen aloft and out! Man the upper yards!" Instantly, the waiting sailors swarmed up the shrouds and made their way out along the upper yards, leaning on the top of the yard while shuffling their feet along the man ropes strung below.

Just as the topmen were in place, another call came from forward, "Short stay!"

Duncan looked up and cupped his hands at his mouth to better direct his voice. "Release gaskets."

Things were happening quickly now, as the capstan crew found their rhythm and were marching around easily, drawing the cable in faster with a steady clicking of the pawls. "Up and down!" came the call from forward.

"Let fall the topsails! Sheet home!" Duncan called out, and immediately the sails fluttered down from the yards, at first blowing out with the wind and then being pulled tight by the crew on the deck as they walked back the halyards. "Man the main yards and release the gaskets!"

The call from forward could barely be heard over the sounds of sails snapping into place, blocks squealing, and men stomping across the deck, "Anchor aweigh!"

Duncan could feel the difference in motion as *Enchanté* released her grip on the land and was free. The steady breeze was filling the topsails and starting to push her forward. The wind was not quite a landsman's breeze, directly from astern, and the bow wandered back and forth a little as they accelerated. After a few moments, the helmsman called out, "Helm is answering."

Duncan had not realized how tense he had been until he felt himself relax. With the ship moving forward under sail fast enough for the rudder to bite, the most dangerous part of leaving port was behind them. England Harbor was a small bay, so they did not have far to go to the entrance and the open sea beyond. Now that they had captured the wind and could steer the ship, the chances of running afoul of another ship at anchor or being pushed by the wind onto the shore were greatly diminished.

As they approached the entrance to the bay, he ordered, "Let fall the main sails! Sheet home! Helmsman, bring her two points starboard."

The ship turned gracefully until they were sailing with the wind fine on the quarter and they had reached the open sea. Duncan turned to find Cahill with a broad smile splitting his face. "You have the conn, Mr. Cahill. Let's hold this course for a while and see how she does." With that, he walked to the weather side railing and began pacing forward and back while Cahill gave the orders to tidy up the deck and riggings now that they were underway.

Duncan had decided to sail away from Antigua, broad-reaching before the prevailing winds, staying north of Montserrat and south of Redonda Island. They would turn toward St. Kitts later and beat their way back against the wind if necessary. He wanted to see how the ship performed and find her best points of sail. He also wanted to work the crew through multiple sail evolutions, both for practice and to get them used to the workings of a new ship. His orders allowed him up to eight days for a voyage of only about 100 nautical miles round trip. The return journey would take longer than the trip out because of the prevailing wind direction, but even so, there should be plenty of time.

He walked over to Cahill, who was talking to the master near the wheel, and spoke, "So, how does she feel to you? You're the only one who's sailed her before."

Cahill chuckled and responded, "She might as well be a different ship. I've never sailed her without another in tow. She certainly seems to be a light dancer compared to that, sir."

The master added, "She seems to like the wind on the quarter at these moderate speeds and light sail, sir."

Duncan smiled. "Are you hinting that we should add some canvas and let her run, Mr. Ellis?"

"Aye, sir, and I'm glad of your powers of perception." The master flashed one of his huge smiles with twinkling eyes.

Cahill looked at Duncan, anticipating an order. Duncan waited a moment and then relented, "Oh, very well. Mr. Cahill put as much sail on as she'll handle, right up to the royals and skysail. Put studs on her if the master thinks she can carry them. Let's make her fly, gentlemen!"

The boson whistled for all hands to make sail, and for the next half an hour they set more sail, sent up the scrapers, and constantly tweaked and adjusted. They did try to run out stud sails, but as the wind was beginning to freshen, they had to abandon that effort.

Soon, *Enchanté* was skipping across the white-capped ocean with the riggings humming, and spindrift creating a mist along both sides. It was as if she were floating on a cloud and skimming the surface of the sea.

The master came up onto the quarterdeck, leading the two youngest midshipmen, Rogers and Powell. They walked along the lee side of the deck carrying the chip log, reel, and small sand glass used for timing the log. Duncan watched from the weather side rail where he had been enjoying the motion of the ship and scanning the empty horizon. He could not hear the master over the sounds of the ship and wind, but he could tell that he was giving the midshipmen guidance and instruction and double checking how tight the brindle lines were attached to the chip.

As the ship's bell sounded, Rogers cast the log over the rail and watched the line start to wind off the reel. The first knot in the line came off the reel he called, "Turn!" and Powell started the small sand glass and watched intently as the sand flowed down.

Exactly 28 seconds later, Powell called out, "Stop!"

Rogers' voice broke as he called out, "Fourteen! Fourteen knots!" The master was smiling as he said something, and Rogers quickly grabbed the log line. He gave it a quick tug to release the plugs in the brindle lines and began reeling in the more than 400 feet of line that had run out from the reel.

Enchanté was certainly a fast ship.

The rest of the day was spent testing the ship and crew. At times they hove to, stopping their motion by balancing the forward and backwards thrust against the sails by turning them at angles to push in both directions equally. At other times, they reduced sail and even brought down the topgallant masts, topgallant yards, and even the royal yards. They stripped the sails back as if they were readying for a storm and then hauled everything back up again and spread sail to let her run before the wind. They never topped the fourteen knots of the first run of the day, but they equaled it twice more.

As the sun had sunk to just above the horizon, the men were exhausted, and Duncan was well satisfied. They had more to learn and needed additional practice, but the ship and crew were coming together. For today, it would be enough. "Dismiss the men not on watch. Mr. Ellis, might you join me in the chart room to discuss our course for this evening?"

"Aye, aye, sir!" the master responded cheerily, as usual.

"May I join you, sir?" Cahill requested.

"Of course, Mr. Cahill, you are most welcome."

The three assembled around the chart in the small chartroom and lit a lanthorn hanging from a beam above the table. The master produced a small bit of paper and a stub of a pencil from a pocket and referred to some scribbles and notes that would have been indecipherable to anyone else. He took a set of dividers from the rack on the table, along with the straightedge and compass. After a few minutes, he drew a small "x" on the chart and said, "This is our approximate position, to the best of my reckoning, sirs."

Duncan picked up the dividers and measured from the location. Then, while tapping the dividers absentmindedly against the table he asked, "So, if we were to turn south by west and continue at about our current pace until two bells in the first watch, we could turn north northeast and shape a course, close-hauled, directly for Basseterre Bay? If we made about four knots after the turn, we should arrive well after sunrise...perhaps around two bells in the forenoon watch?"

The master motioned toward the dividers and asked, "May I, sir?"

"Oh, of course, yes." Duncan stopped tapping and handed the device to Ellis.

After a few measurements and some scribbling on his scrap, the master announced, "Aye, sir. I concur with your calculations, presuming we hold at eight knots before the wind and can make four beating back, and the wind doesn't shift."

"Well, that's the plan, then, Mr. Cahill. Any questions?" Duncan asked.

"Aye, sir. Just one. How did you do that in your head?"

Duncan smiled and winked at him. "I guessed and knew Mr. Ellis would correct me if I was wrong." With that, he turned and left the chart room. Cahill looked at the master, who shrugged his shoulders, and then they both followed their captain out.

Everything went according to plan until they turned north-northeast during the night. Duncan was on deck for the maneuver, and the change of course went smoothly, but with the yards turned and sails adjusted, *Enchanté* fell away from the wind. "Helmsman, mind your luff!" Lieutenant Cole bellowed as the bow of the ship slid back toward northeast by north.

"I'm trying, sir, but she's griping and fighting me, sir," the helmsman said, as he leaned into the wheel to force the bow back to north northeast. With a jerk and skip, she turned back of her own accord and the master stepped to the wheel to assist.

After another attempt to turn her back to north northeast, the master spoke, "It's no use, sir, she won't hold so close to the wind. She's still griping and we might need to give her another half point."

Duncan frowned, but there was nothing to do at the moment other than face the facts. "Put her another half point off the wind and we'll do a series of short board tacks to make Basseterre Bay. Tack at the beginning of the next watch while both watches are still on deck, so at least the crew can get a little sleep. We'll do four hours on the starboard weather side tack and two hours on the leeward larboard. That should put us just south of Nevis by around noon. It's going to be a long night. Call me if anything changes." With that, he stomped off the quarterdeck and headed to his cabin.

Cahill looked at the master and raised his eyebrows in question. Ellis responded quietly, "I'll double check the math." And headed to the chart room.

By midnight, it no longer mattered if Duncan had been correct in his calculations, and the situation was considerably more frustrating. The wind had shifted two points northward, which made it even more difficult to sail towards St. Kitts. Light rain and gusty squalls had accompanied the shift in the wind.

Duncan was in the chartroom again with Cahill and Ellis. The lanthorn was swinging in ever-changing elliptical orbits from the deck beam, and they had shifted the chart towards one end of the table to make room for a bucket to catch the water dripping from a leak at the other end. It was stuffy and warm in the chartroom.

"Well, gentlemen, I'm open to suggestions," Duncan stated, as they all stared down at the chart and the latest small "x" the master had placed in their supposed position.

Ellis spoke first. "We can't make her sail closer than seven points to the wind and even there she gripes something fierce. I've never seen the wind so far north at this time of year."

Cahill picked up from there, completing the restatement of what they all knew. "So we have a choice between traveling north and increasing our westerly distance from Basseterre, or making up some easting while continuing to go further south." He paused, and then added, "If we believe the wind will shift back to a more seasonal direction, we'd be better off heading south."

"And if the wind shifts further, we'll run aground in Guadeloupe before we can turn back north," the master grumbled. "Still, sir, I agree with the lieutenant. We might as well make it farther east than west, while we can."

Duncan let out a sigh. "Agreed. Set a course for southeast by south…or as close to that as you can hold her. I'll be in my cabin. Have the duty officer call me at the end of the middle watch, or sooner if the wind shifts again. Who has the next watch?"

Cahill stifled a yawn and excused himself. "Sorry, sir. Strickland is next up."

"Good. I want the two of you to try to get some sleep as well. Strickland can handle things, unless the weather worsens, and he knows to call us."

"Aye, sir," they both responded.

Duncan felt like he had just closed his eyes when he heard a voice calling, "Sir! Captain, sir!"

He cleared his throat and responded, "Yes, Mr. Hyde. What is it?"

"Lieutenant Strickland's respects, sir, and the wind is shifting again, and we can't hold course, sir," Hyde said.

"My compliments to Mr. Strickland and I'll be on deck shortly."

"Aye, aye, sir."

With that, Hyde left the cabin and Duncan put his legs over the side of his hanging cot, slid off, and stood unsteadily for a moment while he shook off the sleep. He scrunched his eyes to help himself focus, reached for his jacket, and headed out of the cabin while pulling it on.

As soon as he was on deck, he could tell the wind was shifting back toward the east. He instinctively looked up to see the commissioning pendant, but it was too dark to make out. The master stumbled out of the chartroom and followed Duncan up the ladder to the quarterdeck. With his customary smile back on his face, he said, "Good morning, sir. I hope you slept well."

"Hrumph," was Duncan's only response.

Strickland walked over from the binnacle to meet them as they mounted the deck. "Sorry to have to bother you, sir, but the wind has shifted more than a point back easterly and seems to be continuing. We're barely able to hold south southeast at the moment, and we're drifting toward south by east."

"You were right to call me. Thank you," Duncan said, and then asked the master, "Mr. Ellis, what do your charts tell you?"

Ellis wiped his bald head with a handkerchief and responded, "If the wind continues and ends up coming from due east, I think we can make straight for St. Kitt's, close hauled, north by east, sir."

Seven bells rang out as Duncan ordered, "Call all hands and tack to north by east, Mr. Strickland. We'll get there, yet."

The wind did, in fact, continue to shift until it was coming from almost due east - perhaps even a few degrees south of east. The master's calculations were accurate enough that early in the first dog watch, *Enchanté* and her tired crew sailed slowly into Basseterre Bay across the glittering water in full sunshine.

One of the leadsmen in the chains called out, "No bottom. No bottom this lead." And then began hauling in the line, as the other leadsman cast his out.

"By the deep nineteen," came the next call.

"By the mark seventeen," from the first leadsman on his next cast.

The chant continued, with the depth steadily decreasing. When the call was "and a half five" Duncan started paying closer attention, and Cahill began giving orders.

"Furl topgallants and royals! Stow the flying jib! Helm a lee!" The helmsman spun the wheel, and the ship turned gracefully into the wind while Cahill continued to bark directions. "Man topsail clewlines! Haul taut! Let go topsail sheets, clew up! Down jib. Haul out the spanker! Settle away topsail halliards! Square away! Stream the buoy! Let go the anchor!"

Just as the ship stopped moving forward, the anchor splashed into the water. The wind started to push the ship backwards and Cahill ordered the helmsman, "Midships." The cable slid out of the hawsehole as the ship floated backwards until the angle was right and the cable stopped. The anchor dug in and *Enchanté* snubbed to a stop, tied to the land again. The rest of the sails quickly disappeared, and the crew was ready to lower the boats over the side.

"A very credible job, Mr. Cahill," Duncan complimented his first lieutenant, "As soon as things are tidied up, I'd like to see you and the master in my cabin."

"Aye, aye, sir," Cahill responded.

About half an hour later, the ship looked as if she had been at anchor for a month. Cahill and Ellis walked into the captain's coach after being announced by the sentry and invited by Duncan. Duncan spoke to them as they entered, "Gentlemen, have a seat. I'd like to discuss our problems sailing close to the wind and consider options for improvement. Would either of you care for something to drink?"

Cahill declined the drink offer, but the master responded, "Don't mind if I do, sir," and Stanley brought him a glass of red wine.

Duncan started the discussion, "So, we have to try to find a way to get her to sail closer to the wind. What are your thoughts?"

Cahill responded while Ellis took a sip of wine. "The main thing that I notice, sir, that seems changed from when she flew French colors, is that the masts are not raked as far astern as they were. Might this be the issue?"

"As much as I hate to ever disagree with an officer," Ellis began, "it seems to me that further raking the fore-mast would make matters worse, as the bow would lift even more. If anything, the fore-mast could be stay-forward to increase the down pressure. However, the shrouds would move forward as well, and that would prevent the yards from being braced up as sharply. Besides, it would almost certainly make her want to pitch more."

Cahill considered this briefly and then said, "All three masts were raked more than they are now. How did the French sail her like that?"

"Oh, I don't suppose the rake signifies much for how she performs versus how she looks, Lieutenant," Ellis responded. "I think she's just too high in the water at the bow and out of trim."

"The bow rides no higher than she did before, by my memory," Cahill stated.

Ellis took another sip of wine and then asked, "Aye, and didn't you say you'd never sailed her without another ship in tow?"

Cahill realized he had just lost the argument. Of course, with a ship in tow, the stern would be depressed and give the feeling of a higher bow than her actual trim would have allowed. He accepted defeat graciously. "You make a good point, Mr. Ellis. Would not the dockyard surveyors have measured the trim before they began work and put her back accordingly?"

"Well, this part I'm only guessing, sirs. I wasn't there when they surveyed and unloaded her. *Enchanté* is a French frigate, and she came in with quite a bit of damage. She's not so pointed at the nose as most French ships. I think the dockyard didn't take her draught into proper account and treated her more French than she really is." Ellis finished his wine and then finished his thought, "So, I think they loaded her with what the shipbuilders call 'the center of cavity' too far astern, and her nose blows off the wind because of it."

Duncan considered this for a moment and then said, "That's easy enough to test, Mr. Ellis. We shift some weight forward and go for another sail."

Cahill added, "We're fully provisioned and just out of port, sir. There's not much room in the hold. Shuffling things around will require bringing things up on deck to make room before putting them back. We'll be guessing about how much change we're making until we finish. It might take several tries."

"True," Duncan said, "but we have plenty of weight on deck where we can see it. If we roll a couple of cannons from the stern to the bow, we'll shift more than you could move in the hold in several days. We'd be short a few cannons if we happen across an enemy, but for a short test cruise, it seems like an acceptable chance to take. Would that work, Mr. Ellis?"

"Aye, sir, I don't see why not. In so far as buoyancy and the center of cavity go, it doesn't matter what deck the weight is on. Stability and roll are different issues, but if we keep the guns outboard, I don't see a problem."

"Would one gun on each side be sufficient?" Cahill asked.

The master scratched his chin and answered, "To be sure, sir, I don't really know, but it's a good start to the test. We can move just two cannons at first and see how she does. We can move them back and forward to find the best trim and use a second pair if we need to...with the captain's permission, of course. I don't want to leave us defenseless."

Duncan was warming to the idea and added, "Since we know the weight of the guns and we can measure their location when we find the best trim, we could calculate the shift of weight needed in the hold. Even easier, we can come back to the sheltered bay here and measure her height to the rail forward and back. That way, we'll be able to make sure we've got it right before we sail again."

"That sounds about right, sir," Ellis agreed.

"Excellent! Let's make preparations and get the guns shifted tonight, so if the weather is good, we can sail tomorrow to see if it works," Duncan said excitedly. "Mr. Cahill, I've a note I'd like taken ashore. Please assign a mid to deliver it. They may take my gig."

"Aye, aye, sir," Cahill responded, and with that, the meeting ended, and he and Ellis left the cabin.

Immediately following breakfast the next morning, Duncan gave the order to weigh anchor. He had worked out a plan for their route the night before with Cahill and Ellis. In case the experiment failed, they did not want to get caught trying to beat their way back again. Additionally, none of them could wait to try the new trim by sailing away with the wind before turning back. So, the decision had been made to sail south around Nevis, as tight to the land as they could weather and immediately tack as close as they could hold her to north northeast.

The plan was not without potential problems. As the master pointed out, the biggest problem with the West Indies was that there was always an island in the way. In this case, there were two - Barbuda to the north and Antigua to the south. Neither really presented a danger, as they could come about and sail away with the wind, but it was a little annoying that they might not be able to conduct their experiments without some additional course changes to avoid running aground.

Cahill ducked his head into Duncan's cabin and said, "Sir, we've made it around Nevis and the master feels it is safe to begin."

Duncan practically leaped up from his desk. "Excellent. I shall join you on the deck."

They walked out together and up the gangway to the quarterdeck, where both Lieutenants Cole and Strickland were standing near the wheel with the master. They all turned and acknowledged Duncan. "Good morning, sir."

"Good morning," Duncan replied. "How shall we conduct the tests, then, Mr. Ellis?"

"The first test should be pretty simple, sir. We've placed the deuce cannons amidships and secured them well. All we have to do is see how far she'll point into the wind with them in that position. Then, sir, we'll move them a little forward and try again. If she's better, we move them a little further, and so on, until she stops improving. If she's still griping, we'll keep moving them about forward and back until we find the sweet spot, sir."

Duncan raised an eyebrow and asked, "Did you say 'deuce cannons', Mr. Ellis?"

"Erm...," Ellis started.

Strickland rescued him by interjecting, "Aye, sir. That was my idea. We certainly don't want them to become loose cannons and there are two being used for the test, so..." He trailed off when he saw the look on Duncan's face.

Duncan slowly smiled and shook his head. "Fine, if the deuce cannons are in place, let's turn her towards the wind. It's nice to know my officers have a sense of humor...even if not a very good one." He laughed after saying this and the others joined in.

After about four hours of adjustment and testing, the master was standing at the wheel, getting a feel of the helm himself. He was making very small movements and watching the edge of the sail, the luff, to watch for any flutter. After a few minutes, he left the wheel to the helmsman and announced, "Sir, I think we've done it. She's holding at six points with not a bit o' gripe. You can't ask much more than that from a square sail rig."

Duncan smiled broadly. "If you're well satisfied with her sailing, I shall accept that she is ready, Mr. Ellis. I guess there was never much danger of Barbuda getting in our way. We've hardly been out of sight of St. Kitts and Nevis for the day. Let's head back and see how she does with a following wind."

"Aye, aye, sir," Cole responded, since he was the current duty officer even though they were all still on deck.

Cahill stood close to Duncan and said softly, "Sir, might I suggest we tack through the wind and bring her around, rather than just falling off the wind? It would give the crew a little more practice and would hardly make a difference in our return."

Duncan responded, "Good idea. Proceed. I shall be in my cabin for a while."

As he entered his cabin, he handed Stanley his jacket and sat down at his desk. He pulled out a piece of paper, trimmed a quill, and got out his bottle of ink. After thinking for a few minutes, he started sketching out what he hoped would become his report to the admiral on how they had tested the changes in the trim and her ability to approach the wind. He wanted to not only describe what they had done and why, but also give credit to the individuals who contributed significantly to the success.

After an hour of scribbling, crossing out, and scribbling some more, he decided he had written enough to serve as his outline for the full report. He sanded the paper, blew on it, and after testing that the ink was dry, slipped it into a drawer of his desk before walking back out onto the deck.

The first dog watch had just begun, and Strickland was now the watch officer. Cahill was still on deck and was talking to the master. They began moving away from the windward rail as he approached, but he motioned for them to stay and join him. Once he was close enough that he did not need to yell, he asked, "So, how does she do before the wind? Have we broken her by trying to fix her?"

Cahill responded, "She seems a bit changed, but not necessarily in a bad way. Her finest point of sail has shifted by a half a point or so further abeam, but all in all, she still prefers a wind on the quarter, sir."

Duncan nodded and said, "I can live with that. Has she lost any speed?"

This time Ellis responded, "The wind hasn't been strong enough to tell, sir. She still feels fast and nimble. She rides well without excessive pitch or roll and takes the waves without buckin' or crashin'. I'm well pleased with her in all respects, sir."

"A successful outing, then. Thank you, gentlemen."

It was dark when they ghosted back into Basseterre Bay and let go the anchor.

Chapter Eleven

Duncan stood at the front of the quarterdeck looking down into the waist of the ship, sipping coffee. The main deck was already becoming cluttered with barrels, crates, and nets, all full of supplies being brought up from the hold. At the side of the ship, several crewmembers were using a whip attached to the yard to lower some of the bulkiest items into the two longboats tied alongside. Duncan suspected the gun deck was also being filled, but he had not gone down to look. Cahill had things well in hand, and there was no reason for Duncan to get in the way.

He noticed a small skiff pulling in their direction from the docks and watched it glide across the calm water. They were lucky to be in such a protected area, with good weather and a smooth sea. Hauling heavy items around the ship could be both difficult and dangerous, and shifting so much weight above the hold would make them more susceptible to rolling over in a swell. It was the perfect weather and a fantastic location to attempt the shift to permanently adjust the trim.

The boat was definitely coming to *Enchanté* and as it approached, Midshipman Webb called out, "Ahoy, the boat!"

The single oarsman yelled back, "Message for Captain Joseph Duncan."

Webb glanced toward Duncan, who gave a short nod. Webb turned back to the rail and said, "Come alongside."

A ship's boy went over the side to retrieve the note from the boatman and Webb delivered it to Duncan, who placed his mug on the rail and then broke the wax seal on the letter and began reading. Webb stated, "The boatman says he was tasked to await a reply, sir."

Duncan nodded absently as he scanned the short message from Étienne Thibeault. It was a response to the note of inquiry he left before they sailed on their experiment with trimming the ship. Étienne stated that he was still in search of employment and would be available to meet Duncan at 2 o'clock that afternoon in a small coffee shop near the docks, if that would be acceptable.

"I'll scratch out a quick response in my cabin, Mr. Webb," Duncan said, as he started to walk off. After a couple of steps, he remembered his mug and went back to retrieve it before heading to his cabin. A few minutes later, he returned with his response and handed it to Webb with a coin. "Be careful of the seal. The wax is still warm, and give this to the boatman for his troubles."

"Aye, aye, sir," Webb responded, and soon the boatman was pulling back to shore after a quick doff of his hat to Duncan.

"Mr. Webb, please pass the word for my compliments to Lieutenant Gladstone and could he report aft to my cabin at his earliest convenience.," Duncan ordered, as he headed back down the ladder from the quarterdeck.

Within a few minutes, the commanding officer of the fifty marines aboard *Enchanté* entered the cabin and asked, "You called for me, sir?"

"Yes, Lieutenant. What do you know of Brimstone Hill Fortress?"

Lieutenant Gladstone considered the question. "Well, sir, it's on the northwestern side of the island, maybe about ten to twelve miles from here. It's pretty much impregnable, although it was surrendered to the French (that de Grass character that caused so much trouble) during the war with the American Colonies. They gave it back though, as part of the Treaty of Paris. I've heard it's been expanded since then and more guns have been placed. The Gibraltar of the West Indies, some call it, sir."

Duncan smiled and replied, "It seems you are aware of it. Have you ever visited?"

"Oh, no, sir. I've not been so lucky. I've just read about it and studied it. The Citadel is of the new polygonal system of fortification…"

Duncan interrupted him when he paused for a breath. "Would you be interested in taking a ride out tomorrow to have a look around with me?"

"Oh, yes, sir! I would be thrilled, sir!"

"Very well. I shall be going ashore later today, and I will make arrangements for horses. Let's plan on an early start - four bells in the morning watch."

"Aye, aye, sir! And thank you for thinking to let me accompany you, sir!"

After lunch, Duncan buckled on his sword and took his hat from Stanley before walking out into the blinding midday sun. Approaching the side, he spoke to Cahill, who was standing near the entry port, to see him off. "I should only be gone a few hours. How goes the shifting of weight in the hold?"

"We'll have plenty to keep us busy until your return, sir, to be sure. I intend to be in position to start removing things from the deck tomorrow and everything should be re-stowed and ready by the following midday. The master and I are in agreement as to the plan and are only wanting in the completion. It is taking longer than I would have liked, though, sir. I'm sorry to have our beautiful frigate looking like some common tradesman."

"If we can sail her into the wind and have all the guns available, it will have been worth the wait, Mr. Cahill. Carry on."

Duncan disappeared over the side to an accompaniment of boatswain's whistles and dropped lightly into the boat. He stopped on the thwart and looked at the boat crew before exclaiming, "Very admirable job of outfitting the crew, Jenkins. They look right proper and are a credit to the ship."

He noted several smiles and looks of appreciation from the crew as he made his way to the back and took his spot in the stern sheets. Jenkins responded, "Thankee, sir. The pusser done found us some nice togs among his slop stores that match each other main well."

As they pushed off and started pulling for shore, Duncan had the opportunity to look a little closer at the new "uniform" his boat crew was wearing. They each had loose white duck trousers, a blue and white checkered shirt, and a red handkerchief tied about their necks. On their heads were matching straw hats that had been tarred until they shined. Each hat had a wide red ribbon with "Enchanté" embroidered in white at the front. They were also each wearing almost-matching black pumps with shiny brass buckles.

It was a short ride across the harbor to the stone jetty, and Jenkins carefully brought the gig to a stop next to the stairs. Duncan stood up and said, "You may return to the ship. Please be back to pick me up in three hours. If I'm not here immediately, you may let the crew stretch their legs on the jetty, but they're not to wander into town, or take any drink."

He headed for the side and stepped onto the steps as Jenkins responded, "Aye, aye, sir. We'll be back for ye in three hours."

Duncan adjusted his sword and pulled his cuffs down to look more presentable, and started walking down the wharf towards the shore. When he reached Pall Mall Square, he turned east and walked along the street until he saw a shop with a small sign identifying it as "Liamuiga Coffee House". The directions from Étienne Thibeault had been very easy to follow so far. Duncan thought that identifying Étienne might be difficult, but as he approached, there was only one outdoor table, occupied by a single man - and that man looked both very proper and very French.

When he was still a few steps away, the man rose to his feet, and with a slight bow said, "Ah, Captain Duncan, I presume. I am Étienne Thibeault, at your service, sir." He spoke with a rather slight, but definite, French accent.

"It's a pleasure to meet you." Duncan took the seat opposite Étienne, and they both sat down.

"Thank you for accepting my invitation, Captain. I don't know if it was proper of me to offer, but I didn't know how else we might be able to meet. I was intrigued by your first message and the introduction from Lord Fairhurst. He was a particular friend of my previous employer and I'm honored that he should even remember me."

An hour and two cups of coffee later, Duncan was satisfied to give the Frenchman a try as his new cook. He actually rather liked the man and was surprised by his ease and grace. Clearly, he was used to being in gentle company and his descriptions concerning experience cooking aboard a ship and acquiring local ingredients and recipes in various locales made him seem very competent, but not boastful.

Duncan finished his coffee and leaned back. "We are agreed then? You will come aboard tomorrow and prepare an evening meal for my officers as a test. For this, I will pay for the ingredients you require and give you two weeks' wages. If it doesn't work out, we'll set you back ashore and both go about our ways. If it works out and the situation is acceptable to you, you will remain aboard as my cook for the wage we discussed."

"Yes, Captain," Étienne responded. "That is quite acceptable, and I look forward to pleasing you with a meal based on local fare and what is available to me on short notice."

"Excellent! Then, I shall bid you adieus until tomorrow evening. I shall not be aboard tomorrow, but as I said, the first lieutenant, my coxswain, and my valet will be there to help you settle in. Also, the purser will be available if you need additional supplies." As Duncan stood to leave, he asked, "Would you happen to know where I could acquire riding horses for hire?"

•   •   •

Cahill found Strickland and Cole talking on the quarterdeck and called out to them as he climbed the ladder. "Ah, there you are. I forgot to tell you earlier, the captain has invited us to a special supper this evening as a test of his new cook. I hope you're both available on such short notice."

Strickland smiled and responded, "I shall have to check my schedule, but I suppose I can make that work."

"A new cook? How did he happen upon a new cook here? He's barely been ashore. It isn't someone from the crew, is it?" Cole asked.

"No, not a crewman. As I understand it, the admiral recommended someone who is currently here in Basseterre. A Frenchman, by the name of Thibeault. He should be coming aboard sometime this morning," Cahill answered.

"A Frenchman? Why on earth would the captain want a French cook?" Cole sounded incredulous.

Cahill laughed. "Perhaps he has a hankering for frog legs and runny omelets."

Cole turned up his nose. "I hope that's not what will be served this evening. I think I'd rather take my chances with Stanley's cooking."

"Perhaps," Strickland interjected, "the captain would like to have some meals that remind him of growing up."

Cahill and Cole looked at Strickland, then at each other, and then back at Strickland before Cahill spoke for both of them. "Why would a French cook remind him of growing up? He's Scottish."

Strickland explained, "The captain's father is Scottish, and thus his name, but his mother is French. I would presume there was a strong French influence on their meals. Given his fluency in the French language, it seems likely the Gallic culture was not suppressed in his household."

Cole laughed and shook his head. "Captain Duncan doesn't speak a lick of French. He had me translating with the prisoners when we captured the convoy, and I can barely get my point across in French. It was rough going, I tell you."

Strickland smiled knowingly. "I assure you, he speaks French so well that no one would know he wasn't raised in Paris. It is not unheard of for people to pretend not to know their enemy's language, so prisoners might speak freely amongst themselves. It can provide an advantage. I suspect you were unwittingly helping the captain with his deception."

Cole just stood with his mouth open, remembering his struggles to converse with the prisoners.

"Hmm," Cahill said after a pause, "I guess quiet rivers do run deep. He had me convinced, as well. In any event, please help the cook get settled in and make sure Stanley doesn't throw him overboard or anything. I'm not sure he's going to like the idea. As soon as the men finish their breakfast, I'll be heading back to the hold to direct the re-stowing."

As there was very little to do on watch when in harbor, Midshipman O'Toole was the closest thing to an officer on deck when a strange boat came rowing towards *Enchanté*. There was one passenger sitting rather stiffly, surrounded by bags, boxes, crates, and chests. O'Toole called out in challenge, "Ahoy, the boat!"

The oarsman responded, "Captain's cook, come to join."

O'Toole had been warned to expect this newcomer, so he called back, "Come alongside." And then to a seaman nearby, "Carlson, rig a whip and help get the cook's dunnage aboard."

Carlson knuckled his head and responded, "Aye, aye, sir."

With no further ceremony, the new cook clambered up the side and worked out with Carlson what to send where before he headed towards the captain's cabin. O'Toole accompanied him to make sure he found his way and then left him there as he had been instructed.

About half an hour later, Jenkins walked into the captain's cabin. There was no sentry on duty since the captain was not aboard and Jenkins was on his way to visit Stanley. He stopped in surprise upon seeing a stranger in the cabin, but recovered quickly and said, "Well, ahoy there. You must be the captain's new cook. How do we call you then? Have you got a name?"

"I am Étienne Thibault. Yes, I am the cook. Who are you?"

"A-ten? What kind of name is that? I heard you was some sort of Frenchie."

"Étienne," Thibault repeated slowly and after seeing the puzzled look on Jenkins' face, he added, "You may call me Stephen, if you prefer."

Jenkins smiled, "Stephen? Yeah, that's a right proper name. Nice to meet you, Stephen, and welcome aboard."

Thibault returned the smile and shook the hand offered by Jenkins. "That will be easier on your English tongue and my French ears, but you still haven't told me who you are."

"Right! Sorry about that. I'm Timothy Jenkins, the captain's coxswain. Most folks call me Jenkins and I don't mind that, Timothy, or even Tim."

"Nice to meet you, Timothy."

"Where's Stanley? Are you getting settled?"

"I've not yet had the pleasure of meeting Mr. Stanley. The captain told me about him, as well as you, but you are the first I've met since I came aboard...not counting the midshipman who let me board, and a Mr. Carlson who helped me with my supplies. I've just been sorting things out and planning dinner, now that I've seen the dining coach."

"Well, that's odd," Jenkins exclaimed. "I would have thought he'd be around here. I'll go see if I can find him. Do you need anything or need to be pointed toward anywhere?"

"Thank you, no," Thibault responded. "I think I'm quite fine for the moment. I shall begin to prepare things and I should like to see the galley soon, but not just yet."

"Right then. I'll scare up Stanley and we'll be back to give you a hand." Jenkins left after saying this and then paused outside the door to consider where to look first.

There were only three places he would normally look for Stanley besides the captain's quarters. Normally, the most likely place would be on the gun deck talking or playing games with his friends. Given the current disorder on the ship and everyone working in the hold, this seemed unlikely. The second option would be the head, and he was not going to check there. By process of elimination, he headed for the galley and that was where he found Stanley sitting on a stool and chatting with the ship's cook.

"Hello, Jenkins," Stanley greeted him cheerfully as he walked in.

The cook, an old man with a stiff leg and eye patch, gave him a lopsided grin and nod of the head in greeting.

"Stanley, the captain's new cook has come aboard. I know you're probably upset to have another cook, but that's the captain's choice and you might do yourself a favor by helping him get settled and what not," Jenkins said.

Stanley looked surprised and said, "Upset? Why I'm tickled pink. I was just tellin' Harold, here, that aside from missing the chance to see him what when I was cookin', I'm so relieved to not have to do it no more. There's nothin' I despise quite as much as cookin' and what's sure is that I'm no good at it, neither. Better for the capt'n and better for me, it is."

"Oh. Why, I didn't know you felt that way. You've never let on that you didn't like to cook," Jenkins said.

"It don't signify to complain. When someone's got a duty, they're just to do it. I like being the captain's servant and doing other stuff for him. He calls me his 'valet' and I like that just fine. I just don't like all the cookin' and spices and such. I never much knew what to do with food other than eat it. I'm right glad he's found hisself a right proper cook."

Jenkins scratched his chin. "As I understand it, the dinner tonight is something of a test. If you want to have him stay aboard so you don't have to cook, maybe we better help him make sure the captain likes his dinner."

•   •   •

All of the ship's commissioned officers stood in the dining coach, chatting amicably and sipping punch. Stanley stood near the sideboard where the punch bowl was located. He scanned the level of punch in the glass goblets they each held to see if he should offer any refills. The door to the coach opened slightly and Jenkins nodded to Stanley through the opening before silently closing it.

Stanley moved swiftly to Duncan's side and spoke softly to him, "Sir, dinner is ready to be served."

"Ah, thank you, Stanley," Duncan replied before announcing more loudly, "Gentlemen, if you'd please take your seats, I believe it's time to sup."

As the officers moved to their seats, the door opened and Jenkins came in first to hold the door. He was followed by Thibeault carrying two large, covered serving dishes. Behind him was a parade of servants, each carrying one or more dishes which were all placed on the table, as directed by the cook. Several servants left after placing their dishes on the table and the remaining ones each took a position behind one of the seated guests. At that point, Thibeault lifted the covers from the two dishes he had been carrying and nodded to Duncan as he backed out the door, followed by Jenkins.

Enjoying the delightful aromas, Duncan scanned the table. "I will gladly cut the beef and venison, so please let me know if you would like some of each, or either." With that, the servants stepped forward to serve the other dishes, which included artichoke soup, a pigeon pie, a bowl of pelau, tuna with fennel and mint, mackerel in oyster sauce, spinach, various other vegetables in rich butter sauces, quiche aux champignons, and a tomato and goat cheese tart. In addition to all of this, there were two trays of fresh, hot white bread and large plates of chilled, salted butter.

Stanley and the other servants made sure everyone's wine glasses were kept filled and their plates were refilled with whatever was desired. There was little conversation at first as the diners focused on their food, but soon they were chatting and talking easily. Duncan smiled slightly to himself as he put the last bite of hot pigeon pie - prepared in the French style with asparagus, mushrooms, artichoke, truffles, and morels - in his mouth.

Cahill put down his fork and picked up his wineglass. "Sir, I must say you set an exceedingly fine table. The soup is divine, and the rest of the dishes are...absolute ambrosia."

"Thank you, Mr. Cahill," Duncan responded, as the servants began clearing the first course and Thibeault entered carrying a bowl of salad, followed by a servant carrying a plate of cheese.

The salad was of young mixed greens with a light citrus flavored vinaigrette dressing. Duncan was appreciating how well it cleansed his palette when the door opened and Thibeault led the parade of servants in placing the second course on the table. Not only was his new cook skilled at preparing food, he also seemed to have a nearly perfect sense of timing.

Once again, the table was covered, but not crowded, with various dishes including a very spicy ragout, roast chicken, a sweet potato and ricotta cheese tart, cucumbers in cream, asparagus, bacon, cinnamon pastry, thinly sliced dry sausage, apple tart, cauliflower, macaroni, and a tart made from some local fruit that Duncan could not identify.

Just trying a little of each left Duncan almost uncomfortably full, and several of the dishes were so enjoyable he would have liked to have eaten more. Everyone finished at about the same time and Duncan knew that it was likely the junior officers had been closely watching their seniors to make sure this was so. It was not so long ago that he was at the other end of the table. He was quite sure that they had not gone hungry, but had either eaten more than they really wanted, or more quickly than they would have liked, in order to match his timing.

He would have to remember to take his time in the future to make sure his guests did not feel rushed, but in any event, everyone looked happy and satisfied as the dishes were cleared and the tablecloth removed. Thibeault and a smaller number of servants entered and placed dessert on the highly polished table. There were walnuts, raisins, figs, almonds, sliced apples, pears, oranges, several cheeses, candied ginger, and some sweet cakes. Finally, the bottle of port wine was placed by the captain, and everyone but the seated guests and Stanley left the room.

Duncan poured himself a glass of port and passed the bottle around the table. Lieutenant Gladstone was the last to fill his glass and, as the junior officer, gave the toast to the King. Lieutenant Cole followed with the traditional Thursday toast of, "To a bloody war or a sickly season!"

"Sir, might I enquire as to how your trip to the fort went today?" Strickland asked.

"You certainly may enquire, and I'm happy to report that it was a very enjoyable adventure, although I must admit my backside is a bit tender from the ride. It seems I'm woefully out of practice on horseback. Perhaps Lieutenant Gladstone would like to recount more about Brimstone itself, as he is the expert in these matters."

"I'd be honored, sir," Gladstone began. "The fortress is most impressive and exceeded all expectations. Both the earthworks and the mounted cannon are awe-inspiring." He continued for a few minutes, giving a detailed description of the fortification, its armament, the men assigned, and a short history of the place. His excitement about the topic held the interest of the naval officers, who otherwise might not have cared to hear so much. He had the good sense to realize this, and he concluded his comments before anyone got bored with the topic.

"Now that everything is re-stowed, sir, and we're ready for sea, what are your plans?" Cahill asked.

Duncan emptied the bottle into his wineglass and motioned to Stanley to start another as he responded, "I'd like to have the crew inspect and tighten all the standing and running rigging tomorrow. Although I don't necessarily believe in the old superstition, there's no need to tempt fate or worry the crew. So, it's best to avoid starting a journey on a Friday if there's no pressing reason. We will leave with the tide on Saturday morning and still be back in plenty of time for the ball."

"Ah, yes, sir, about the ball…the four of us have gone in together to hire a carriage to take us over to St. John's. I had presumed you would be traveling on your own."

"Yes, thank you. The governor is providing a carriage for me," Duncan said.

"If the food is half as good as what we just enjoyed, it should be a wonderful evening, even if the ladies refuse to dance with lowly lieutenants," Cahill stated.

"It seems you would recommend I keep this new cook. What think the rest of you?"

Strickland said, "If you were not to keep him, sir, I should try to convince the wardroom to hire him. Although I doubt we could afford all the ingredients, I suspect he could make common rations taste better. His skill with spices is sublime."

Everyone looked towards Cole next. "I'm not used to such rich fare, sir. Until just a few weeks ago, a spit roasted rat was a special treat for me as a mid. I've never tasted such wonderful dishes as we shared this evening."

Gladstone made it unanimous by adding, "There were spices and foreign tastes a plenty, but enough I recognized to make me feel like a British officer, sir. I quite enjoyed it and thank you very much for the invitation."

"Well, that settles it, then. I shall keep Mr. Thibeault as my new cook and plan to spend extra time walking on deck to keep from getting too heavy."

Cole spoke hesitantly in the quiet moment that followed Duncan's announcement. "Sir? I've never been to a formal ball hosted by a dignitary like the governor. I'm not quite sure what to expect, or what is expected of me."

"You're expected to have fun, Mr. Cole," Duncan laughed. "There's likely to be some pomp and speeches, but on the whole, it will be a light dinner followed by dancing. As long as your uniform is clean and you act as a gentleman, little more will be asked of you. You may have the opportunity to talk to members of society and perhaps ask a lady to dance, if you like, but there's no need to actually do anything. On a small island like Antigua, many of the attendees are likely to be fellow members of the military."

"I'm hoping for plenty of plantation owners' daughters to be present, too," Cahill added.

"Oh, I'm sure you won't be disappointed on that account," Strickland interjected. "The West Indies have no shortage of beautiful women, and the governor's wife is normally quite careful to properly balance the guest list so everyone may find a dance partner."

Cole looked worried. "I don't know how to dance."

"Not to worry. There's still time to rectify that," Duncan said. "I can recommend an instructor in Falmouth, if you like. I made a few visits myself before we sailed. The favored dances change quite often, and my mother always recommended staying current with the styles. She made me promise years ago that I would seek instruction before each ball."

Cahill smiled. "Did she really, sir? My mother made a similar request, but luckily it wasn't so much a required promise as it was a suggestion. Still, I might do well to take a lesson, as well. Perhaps we can get a group rate."

"Oh, yes," Duncan laughed. "My father wasn't very concerned about such society matters. He spent much of his younger life fighting in the wilderness and wanted me to know how to take care of myself. However, my mother came from a very proper family, and she put great stock in the finer points of society and a classical education, including music, the arts, and languages. I'm sure I'm quite a disappointment to her."

"Surely, you're being unfair to yourself, sir," Strickland said. "I expect she will be quite proud of you when she hears of your exploits and promotion."

"I was a strain on her, to be sure. Although I enjoy listening, I have no real ear for music and no talent for playing. I've also absolutely no ability in anything approaching art, and aside from Latin and French, languages do not come naturally to me. She wanted me to learn Greek and Italian to be a proper gentleman, but I just wasn't able to pick them up. When I decided to join the navy, she cried for a full fortnight after my father gave me permission. She may not cry any more, but I don't think she'll celebrate when she hears the news."

The bottle of port was passed around again, and they continued to chat about various topics until Cole asked, "Sir, how are Lieutenants Miller and Williams doing? Have you heard anything about them?"

"Miller and Williams were shipmates of mine and Lieutenant Cole's on *Fidelity*," Duncan explained to the rest of the guests before answering. "Lieutenant Williams was gravely injured and lost his hand in our battle with the French, but I'm happy to report that he is recovering well. He's not so well that we should expect to see him at the ball, but I visit him quite often at the hospital and he is getting stronger every day. He intends to return to England as soon as he is well enough."

"As for Lieutenant Williams, sadly, that is another quite different situation. I visited him once in the hospital, but he is still so taken with a fever of the brain that he doesn't recognize anyone, and his body has become so weak he must be fed by the nurses. He clings to life, and I continue to hope for a recovery, but each day seems to make it less likely."

Duncan recalled the toast for the evening and felt a little guilty that his own promotion had not resulted from just his actions, but also from both a bloody war and a sickly season.

Luckily, Strickland quickly changed the topic and the mood by asking, "Sir, now that *Enchanté* is ready for sea, do you have any idea what the admiral has in mind for us?"

"I do not, but I hope it won't be long before we find out," Duncan responded, in a cheerful tone to try to shake off the previous thoughts. "Whatever is asked of us, I'm confident in the ship, the crew, and all of you."

Cahill raised his glass in a toast. "To *Enchanté* and our next adventure!"

"To *Enchanté*!" they all responded enthusiastically.

Chapter Twelve

The sail back from St. Kitts to Antigua was largely uneventful. In order to test the new trim of the ship and her performance sailing to windward, Duncan and the master plotted a longer route than necessary. First, they had sailed southeast, past Nevis, before turning northeast, toward Barbuda, then as close to the wind as they could on a weather side tack out into the Atlantic, before finally running west to English Harbour.

The strong, steady trade winds had hastened them along, and both ship and crew performed well. Duncan was pleased with the performance of *Enchanté* and the progress the crew was making. Even so, they had many things to work on. Most notably, they needed more gunnery practice. They had done a significant amount of dry fire drilling - repeatedly going through the steps of loading and firing, without actually firing the cannons. Most of the gun crews were getting more organized, but they were still much slower than Duncan would have liked. Using powder and firing the massive guns caused a lot of extra confusion, which slowed them even further.

They had spotted one strange sail while tacking out beyond Barbuda. At first, they thought it to be just another of the small local traders, or perhaps a fisherman, but it had altered course as soon as they were in sight. Unfortunately, they were unable to investigate further for a number of reasons. Technically, their orders prohibited them from actively engaging with the enemy if it could be avoided, since they were still testing and getting the ship combat ready. Practically, the unidentified sail was windward when spotted and controlled the weather gauge. Finally, it appeared to not be a square-rigged ship and therefore could probably sail closer to the wind and faster in that direction than *Enchanté*.

In the end, they had watched the strange sail remain just at the limits of visibility until they had turned back toward Antigua. Duncan was anxious for a time when his orders and his crew's abilities would allow him to seek out and engage the enemy. After all, that was why *Enchanté* existed, and how they would do their part to win this war.

They had anchored in an area very close to their previous location in English Harbour. Duncan had prepared a report of their cruise and the adjustments made to the trim, concluding the report with a statement that he was now confident *Enchanté* was ready in all respects for whatever service was required of her. The report had been delivered to the flagship by Midshipman Webb on Sunday afternoon, within an hour of the anchor splashing down.

Separately, he had also requested authorization for additional gunpowder for drill and practice. There had been no response to either, and now, five days later, Duncan and the other officers were preparing for the ball in the evening and not expecting further news until after that auspicious event.

Duncan was completing his daily review of reports and paperwork when the purser was announced. Duncan pushed the pile of papers aside and sat back in his chair. "Ah, Mr. Lloyd. Have you brought the ledgers for us to review?"

"Aye, sir. I have them right here." He patted the two leather-bound tomes.

"Before we start, I've a couple of requests. I'd like you to help my cook to become familiar with the local markets and assist him in laying in my personal stores. I'm also interested in using the 'special account' to acquire gunpowder we could use for practice in firing the cannons...beyond our standard allotment, that is. Are you aware of any sources?"

Lloyd scratched his chin and thought for a moment before responding, "Quantities of powder sufficient to fire cannons might be a challenge, sir, but I shall endeavor to find a source. I presume this needs to be coarse powder, sir?"

"Yes. I don't want to burst any barrels, so it should be slow burning, coarse powder. It won't be used in battle, so being less powerful than the standard issue would not cause concern."

"Aye, sir. I shall do my best."

"In my limited experience, Mr. Lloyd, you seldom disappoint. I am sanguine you will find something appropriate."

Lloyd smiled and replied with a nod of the head, "Thank you, sir."

"Let's get to those ledgers, then, shall we?"

•   •   •

At the appointed time, Duncan was rowed to the dock in his gig by Jenkins and found the governor's carriage waiting for him. The footman bowed as the officer approached and opened the door for him. He stepped up into the carriage and, as he was to travel alone, sat in the center of the seat.

The original plan had been for Admiral Fairhurst to also ride in the carriage with him. However, early in the afternoon, a note arrived for Duncan notifying him that circumstances had required the admiral to travel to St. John's earlier than planned. The footman lifted the step into the carriage, closed the door, and climbed atop. The coachman snapped his whip as soon as the footman was aboard, and they began their journey with the horses trotting comfortably.

The sun was low in the sky as they started. It glared in from the left, making Duncan uncomfortably warm. He thought about lowering a window to relieve the heat, but as it had not rained in several days, the road was quite dusty. So instead, he shifted as far as he could to the other side to avoid the sun shining directly on his dark uniform.

Soon they turned east along the shore road through Falmouth. Duncan was relieved to no longer have the sun beating down on him, even though the carriage remained stuffy and hot. Leaving Falmouth, they turned northeast and headed into a valley with steep hills to either side and dappled shade from trees along the road. Without the intense sun, it was almost comfortable in the carriage, and Duncan relaxed and watched the countryside pass by.

The road from Falmouth to St. John's wound its way across the center of the island. It mostly stayed in the valleys between the hills, but occasionally they would climb a hill and get some broken views of the sea. The sun continued to sink as they traveled, and the shadows became longer. After about 35 or 40 minutes, they were atop Clark's Hill, where there were glimpses of the sea on both sides of the carriage. Duncan took his watch out to check the time. He judged them to be about halfway to their destination, and it seemed they would be right on time.

The sun was just setting as they started back down out of the hills and into St. John's. The Government House had been burned during some unrest in 1710 and had not been rebuilt in the intervening 85 years. So, the governor lived in a private residence on a hill overlooking the bay. The carriage slowed slightly as the driver navigated the busy streets.

As they approached the house, Duncan shifted and stretched his legs. He checked his uniform and sword, preparing as best he could in the limited space. There was a line of carriages along the road waiting to deliver their passengers to the front door, but the driver ignored them and continued along beside them. Duncan sat as straight as he could and looked forward. From the corner of his eye, he could see faces in the carriages trying to get a glimpse of him.

He realized that this was part of the show and that the governor had not offered his chariot purely out of the kindness of his heart, but because it would reflect well on him to have Captain Joseph Duncan, the popular local hero, seen in a carriage bearing his livery. Perhaps, Duncan mused, he was being unkind to think so, but he suddenly felt like he had been used as a pawn.

As they approached the main entrance, the servants made way for them by directing other carriages to move. The carriage came to a stop, and the doorman hopped lightly to the ground, opened the door, and placed the step. Duncan tugged his sleeves down, shifted his sword, picked up his hat, and stepped out.

The loose stone crunched and shifted under his feet, and his stiff legs felt a little unsteady as he realized everyone was watching him. He put his hat on, took a deep (but hopefully inconspicuous) breath, and started towards the light-colored stone stairs that led to the main entrance of the mansion.

At the top of the stairs, a servant took his sword and hat, and he was greeted by the steward. "Good evening, sir. The Governor General has requested that I guide you directly to him. Right this way, please." Duncan was relieved that he was not going to be formally announced to the attendees, as was still the custom in some houses.

The ballroom glittered in the light of hundreds of candles in three massive chandeliers and dozens of candelabras along the walls. Many had large mirrors placed behind them to make the room seem even larger and brighter. The walls were cream colored with light blue and gold accents, and the intricate parquet floor had been waxed to a high gloss. The eloquently dressed crowd was little more than a blur to Duncan as the steward led him directly across the room.

As they approached an older couple and their teenage daughter standing by themselves near a door to the gardens, the steward turned to Duncan and announced, "His Excellency, Lord Lockerbie, Governor General of Antigua…and the Ladies Lockerbie." Then turning back to the governor, he added in a much less grand voice, "Captain Joseph Duncan, of the Royal Navy, M'Lord." Duty performed, he departed.

Duncan bowed. "I'm honored to meet you, your Excellency. Thank you for the invitation and for allowing me the use of your carriage."

"Yes, you are quite welcome, Captain. The evening is, after all, in honor of your outstanding victory over the French. It seemed the least I could do." The governor spoke with a warmth in his voice that Duncan had not expected. "In fact, considering we are in my house, I didn't really need the carriage." The governor actually smiled and Duncan smiled back, thinking that perhaps he had misjudged this man.

Before Duncan could think of anything to say, the governor continued. "Ah, where are my manners? This is my wife Philomena and our youngest daughter, Penelope."

Duncan bowed to each of them. "A pleasure to meet you, M'Ladies."

Lady Lockerbie smiled and nodded her head very slightly. "It's nice to make your acquaintance, Captain. Thank you for defending our little island."

The governor spoke again, "I hope it's not too much to ask of you, Captain, but I should be most grateful if you would be willing to take the first dance this evening with my wife. I turned my ankle earlier today, and it pains me to even stand. I cannot begin to imagine being able to dance on it, but it would be a scandal to not have the Lord and Lady of the House begin the dancing. Would you be so kind as to represent me?"

"It would be my honor and great pleasure, M'Lord."

Lady Lockerbie spoke up, "Had not Lord Lockerbie injured his ankle, we would have imposed on you to take the first dance with our daughter. It seems a shame she should have to miss out on account of his injury."

"I'm sorry I can only dance with one of you for the first dance. However, perhaps it would be acceptable for me to take the second dance with your lovely daughter," Duncan offered.

Lady Lockerbie and Penelope smiled broadly, and the governor chuckled softly. "If you're not careful, we will take up all your time, Captain, and you won't have an opportunity to dance with anyone of your choosing. If you are willing to give up the first two dances, I am much obliged to you."

"It will bring me great joy, and I assure you that there is no one else waiting to dance with me," Duncan said.

"I should relish a chance to hear about your exploits with the French. I've read the reports and heard from Admiral Fairhurst, of course, but to hear it in a firsthand account would be a true joy. Sadly, now I must continue to welcome guests. You'll have the seat of honor at dinner. Perhaps you would be willing then to tell me your tale."

"I look forward to it, M'Lord," Duncan said to the governor, and then turning to his wife and daughter, he added, "and to our dances to follow dinner, M'Ladies."

His audience with the governor ended, and he stepped a few feet away and began scanning the room for familiar faces. Admiral Fairhurst was standing with a small group of people across the room and beckoned him over.

The admiral was talking to a tall, slim gentleman with thinning, white hair, and a silver cane who stood with his back to Duncan as he approached. Beside the gentleman was a stocky gray-haired woman and a tall, thin young woman with light brown hair. The young woman's hair was tied in a chignon on the back of her head with one unruly strand hanging in a loose ringlet down her long, pale neck. Her light green dress had been made in the new, high-waisted, loose, and simple fashion that had not yet generally found its way to the West Indies.

As Duncan stepped beside the man to greet the admiral, he realized that he knew the couple and tried to hide his surprise.

"Captain Duncan, please allow me to introduce you to Admiral Huntington-Whiteley."

"Why there's no need to introduce us, Admiral Fairhurst, we know Captain Duncan from way back. It's nice to see you, and joy to you on your promotion, Captain."

"Oh, I was not aware that you were acquainted," Fairhurst said in surprise.

"We're neighbors of a sort. That is to say we are neighbors - and particular friends, I might add - of the captain's family. Why, our daughter's very best friend is the good captain's sister, Annabella. We've known Captain Duncan since before he was Midshipman Duncan."

"It's nice to see you, sir and ma'am," Duncan was finally able to interject, "I must admit to being quite surprised. I didn't know you were in the West Indies."

"So pleasant a surprise, is it not?" Mrs. Huntington-Whiteley said. "It will be lovely to tell your mother we were able to see you and let her know how healthy and sound you look. She does fret so over you, and news of your recent actions will make her worry even more when it arrives in England."

"Thank you, ma'am. I'm sure your report will...comfort her."

Admiral Huntington-Whiteley nodded towards his daughter. "You remember Lillian, I'm sure."

"I do recall Miss Huntington-Whiteley, but I must confess I would not have known her if she had not been with you. It has been some time since last I had the pleasure of seeing her."

"Nine years, Captain. I'm not surprised you wouldn't recognize me from the twelve-year-old you last saw," Lillian said.

"Nine years!" Admiral Huntington-Whiteley exclaimed. "Why, how can that be possible?"

"My dear," Mrs. Huntington-Whiteley said as she touched her husband's arm, "time does fly by. You will remember that Lillian was visiting my sister during the captain's last trip home, and before that she was away at school when he passed for lieutenant and left with Captain Vancouver."

"Nine years, you say. My, but I must be getting old. How many years then is it since I retired? On second thought, don't tell me. It would make me feel even older." The admiral laughed. "You two young people should have a dance and catch up. I'm sure Lillian has plenty of news from Annabella to relate."

A look of annoyance, directed at her father, flashed across Lillian's face, but she quickly recovered. She rolled her eyes and smiled at Duncan. Duncan returned the smile and said, "I would be honored if you would be willing to dance with me, miss. Unfortunately, I am previously engaged for the first two sets. Might I have the third with you?"

Lillian smiled again and responded, "I accept, Captain."

Admiral Fairhurst looked pleased. "I'm glad to have provided for this reunion of sorts instead of the introduction I had intended."

The group chatted for a few more minutes, though Lillian did not join in the conversation except to answer questions directed to her. Duncan learned that the two admirals had served together many years before when Huntington-Whiteley had commanded a ship of the line and Fairhurst had been his first lieutenant. Although it had been years since they had seen each other, there was clearly a shared respect and many fond memories.

Duncan spotted a group entering the room and said, "If you'll excuse me, gentlemen, and ladies, I see that my officers have arrived. I should like to introduce them to the governor so they may thank our host for the invitation."

The audience with the governor was very brief. He was pleasant and cordial but there was a line of guests starting to form to give their respects and the lieutenants were among the lowest ranking members present. In fact, there were very few other military officers below the rank of commander in attendance.

Cahill, Strickland, Cole, and Gladwell were happy to mingle on their own after meeting the governor, and Duncan left them to their own devices when he heard someone calling his name. He turned and replied, "Captain Zimmerman, nice to see you again, sir."

"A pleasure to see you as well. We've got *Fidelity* put back to rights after the knocking about she had, and what a fine ship and crew! I give credit to you and poor Captain Blackwell. She's a beautiful ship with a well-trained crew, to be sure."

"I'm very glad to hear it. I've many fond memories. I wasn't really aboard for very long, but then it's not the days we remember, but the events, isn't it?"

"Truer words have never been spoken, Captain Duncan. How go things with *Enchanté*?"

"She seems to be another well-built French ship, and I'm still getting to know her ways. As for the crew, they're still coming together, and I'm pleased with the progress. I'm looking forward to getting back out to sea."

"I'm sure that will come soon enough, though I'm anxious as well."

They talked for a while longer and then went their separate ways. Duncan worked his way around the room and talked to Captain Tankersley, Captain Larson, and several civilians he did not know, but who introduced themselves to him. He was having an enjoyable time when he heard a bell ringing. The crowd fell silent, and the butler announced, "Dinner will now be served. Please make your way to the tables."

The governor and his wife led the way and everyone else started shuffling towards the dining room. Duncan happened to be near the entrance, and as the governor limped past, he signaled for Duncan to follow. The dining room was huge and was set with two long tables running parallel to the length of the room. Still, there was not sufficient seating for everyone, and two adjacent rooms had also been cleared to hold tables. Duncan had the seat of honor next to the governor, as had been promised.

The Huntington-Whiteley party had been a good distance from the doors and as they made their way slowly with the rest of the attendees toward the dining room, Lillian asked, "Father, could you help me to understand something?"

"Anything within my power, my dear."

"That gentleman over there, whom I heard named as Captain Henry, wears his epaulet on a different side than Captain Duncan, and that charming Captain Tankersley has two epaulettes, while many of the captains have no epaulettes at all. Does not the Navy understand the meaning of the word 'uniform' when setting out how these captains dress themselves?"

Admiral Huntington-Whiteley chuckled, and responded, "Quite observant of you, my dear, but there are reasons, I assure you. To begin with, there is a change afoot. Just this year, new regulations have come into effect, and we find ourselves in the transition period where both are allowed. You are seeing the older style without epaulettes and the newer style with."

"So, it's a bit like the various dress fashions represented this evening," Lillian observed.

"Hmm…I suppose it is. Also, you may be surprised to hear that the man referred to as Captain Henry is really Commander

Henry, and he is called captain only out of courtesy, since he commands a sloop. However, as a commander…and until last year he would have been officially a master and commander, which used to be the full title but no longer is… he holds the rank of commander only so long as he commands a sloop. After that, if not made post, he'll revert to being a lieutenant and no longer have an epaulet at all…unless that has changed as well, perhaps commander is permanent now. It's so hard to keep track of these things."

"Made post?" Lillian interrupted his rambling. "Is that another rank?"

"Ah, well, that's what we say when a man is given the rank of captain, as opposed to just commanding a ship. Anyone who commands a ship is referred to as the captain, but only those who have been posted to the rank of captain are truly captains and therefore to distinguish them we sometimes say, 'post captain', although we would never use that as a title, as they are just called captain. When promoted, their name is 'posted' in the Gazette, you see."

"I believe I'm more confused now," Lillian said dryly. "You still haven't explained why some modern captains wear one epaulet and others two."

"Oh, as to that, you will remember that Captain Duncan has only just been promoted, while Captain Tankersley has held that rank for quite some time. In the new system, a captain with less than three years seniority wears a single epaulet on the right shoulder, while one with more than three years, like Captain Tankersley, wears two."

"That all makes perfect sense now. Thank you, Father."

"Sarcasm does not befit a lady," her mother scolded. Lillian gave her mother an impish smile and slight curtsy in response. "Oh, you'll be the death of me, Child."

"Oh Kat, don't be too hard on her. She reminds me so much of you when we were courting. A little sarcasm, when paired with intelligence and natural curiosity, can be quite attractive to the right sorts of men," the admiral interjected.

"Do you imply that you're the right sort of man, sir?" his wife retorted.

"Well, we've been married these eight and twenty years, so I certainly hope I am," the admiral responded brightly. Turning back to Lillian, he added, "I believe Commander Henry was a shipmate of Captain Duncan's aboard *Fidelity*. If I have the story correct, they were both lieutenants, with Henry being the senior. Then, Henry came back in a prize and was promoted to commander before Duncan returned with his little fleet of prizes and was made a captain."

"Was he?" Lillian said quietly, as she glanced around the crowd looking for Commander, or Captain, Henry.

Once everyone was seated, the governor stood, and again the crowd was silent - although it took a few moments for those seated in the other rooms to become aware of the situation. "Welcome, everyone, to this evening of celebration. Let us begin with a toast to our King." At this, everyone stood. Aboard ship, naval officers were exempt from standing for the royal toast, but on land, they stood like everyone else. "To His Royal Highness, George the Third, King of Great Britain and Ireland. Long may he reign!"

"To the King!" everyone responded, drank, and then sat back down.

The governor continued, "We are a nation of islands and as such we depend on our mighty navy, the wooden wall about our lands, and those with true hearts of oak who serve to protect us. This evening we remember those thousands lost in the great endeavor to keep us safe from the evil forces which would seek to overthrow our king and take away our freedom. And we celebrate a new hero in the battle against the French, our very own Captain Joseph Duncan, the victor at the Battle of Isla Mona!"

Duncan tried to hide his surprise and felt a sudden rush of embarrassment. He had not heard the battle called anything, and he was not sure capturing a convoy was really worthy of a name. However, the governor was still going on, "So, I welcome you all to celebrate this victory and the many more to follow. To Captain Duncan and the Royal Navy!"

With that, the governor sat down, and dinner was served.

Once Duncan had recovered from the embarrassment of the governor's speech, he enjoyed dinner and the lively conversation. He recounted the events of the convoy action - leaving out some of the gory details and making it sound a little less dangerous, out of respect for the mixed company. He was aware of other nearby conversations stopping, as everyone strained to listen.

After dinner, he escorted Lady Lockerbie to the dance floor. He was surprised, and unexpectedly annoyed, to see Lillian lining up with George Henry. Lady Lockerbie was an able, if not overly graceful dancer, and her daughter was less of each. The first set was about 25 minutes long. Lillian danced the second set with a marine major Duncan did not recognize, but whom he felt looked unreasonably dashing. That dance lasted for over half an hour.

Finally, when the second dance ended, Duncan made his way through the crowd to Lillian, just as the music began again.

"I really am completely surprised to see you here," Duncan said, as they started to dance. "I've received several letters from Anna, and she didn't mention you would be traveling to Antigua."

"It was a rather sudden decision. You might still get a notice, albeit too late to make a difference now. Father has been trying for some time to resolve some issues concerning land holdings on Tortola. His local partner passed away, and he had been working through a barrister to finalize things from England. When it didn't work out, he suddenly decided to sail over to deal with it in person. Mother was concerned about having him travel on his own. He really hasn't been without us since his injury and retirement from the Navy. So, we convinced him that we should all come. Things took longer than expected and the onset of hurricane season delayed our return. Father thought that coming to Antigua would give us the best chance of finding a ship home as soon as possible." She paused and then asked, "Do you count it as a good surprise?"

Duncan's reply was delayed as they traveled down the line of dancers before being reunited at the other end. "It is a most pleasant and welcome surprise, I assure you."

"At least to see my parents, but you didn't recognize me."

"I've already admitted to that, but it makes me no less happy to see you."

"I can't pretend to be shocked or bothered by it. I admit to being much changed. You, however, are much as I remember you. Although much older and weather-beaten. Anna warned me your face was turning to leather from the wind and sun, but still I was unprepared."

Duncan was shocked for a moment until he saw the mischievous sparkle in her eyes. She smiled broadly at him, and he laughed. "Your tongue is no less sharp than when last I saw you. May I change my answer about my surprise?"

"No, you may not. Disliking my wit is not the same as not being happy to see me," she replied in a false, arch tone.

"It is still enjoyable to see you. Listening to you might be otherwise."

She pretended to pout and then smiled again. "I'll admit that I'm happy to see you as well. Anna talks about you constantly and often reads me your letters - your short, infrequent letters, I should add on her behalf. You don't feel as much like a stranger as I had thought you might."

"Anna mentions you often, as well. I was still picturing the twelve-year-old I last saw, even though I know you are both grown women."

"So, you pictured me?" she asked.

"Well, I had little choice. The stories often concern things you'd done together, and I couldn't properly imagine her without having someone in the other role."

Again, the conversation was interrupted as they passed down the line. When they came back together, she changed the subject. "I took the first dance with your old shipmate, Commander Henry."

"Did you?" He pretended not to have noticed. "Is he a good dancer?"

"Not particularly. No, he is not. He also doesn't seem to like you very much. I saw you watching us. Might I infer that the feelings are mutual?"

"I should prefer to not speak ill of a fellow officer, but if pressed to do so, I would pick George."

Lillian laughed out loud, and Duncan was surprised by how good it made him feel. The banter and teasing receded for the remainder of the dance, and they instead talked openly and easily about a variety of topics. They continued together for the following dance, both enjoying the conversation and each other's company. The music ended and Lillian took his arm. "It's quite warm in here. Would you be willing to escort me for a walk in the gardens?"

"Gladly," he responded, and they walked out the open French doors. The relatively cool air and breeze were instantly refreshing, and they paused for a moment before walking slowly down the stairs and into the moonlit garden.

They spent a while wandering along the paths, made of crushed shell, which provided great contrast to the dark vegetation. Lillian paused as they approached a stone bench in front of several large rose bushes. She sat down and invited Duncan to join her.

"What do you miss when you're at sea?"

"I've never given it much thought. I've spent most of my time aboard a ship for so long that it just seems normal." Duncan pondered for a moment and then said, "Fresh bread. Even in port, the bread is usually stale and dry. We always had fresh bread every day when I was home. I miss that. Fresh, still warm from the oven. Yes, that's it. I miss bread. Now, every time we sail, I'll have to think about missing bread." He smiled at her.

"I didn't mean to cause trouble. I was just curious. Father tells stories of his times in the Navy and it all sounds so foreign and difficult. I should think I would miss many things. Our trip here was in comparative luxury and still I missed the simple pleasures of going for a walk in the morning before the dew has lifted and listening to the birds singing. Ships are full of strange noises and have very little room to be by oneself. Not to mention the smells."

"That's all true. I suppose I've just gotten used to it. Of course, I have a lot more room now than I ever have before. Still, you're right. Even as a captain, I'm never really able to be alone. Funny. I had forgotten all about birds singing in the morning. I used to love that."

"Well, let's change the subject before you get depressed."

"I don't mind," he said honestly. "I chose a life in the Navy, and it does have its redeeming qualities. There's nothing like the feeling of racing across the waves, like a stone skipping across a pond. And the places I've seen...it's only fair to give something up to be able to have something else you enjoy."

"You may write to me," Lillian stated matter-of-factly as she stood up.

"What?" Duncan asked.

"You may write to me...when you're at sea, I mean. I'm giving you my permission, as it might be improper for you to presume you could. My mother always said that she learned to say things to my father as soon as she thought of them because sometimes he would be called away by the Navy unexpectedly and she might not see him again for months. That happened when she waited to tell him she was with child. She decided to wait for a special moment and then a messenger came and he had to sail that night and I was born before he returned. So, will you?"

"Will I what?"

"Will you write to me?"

"Oh! Yes, of course."

"You don't have to if you don't want to."

"No…I mean I want to. Nothing would give me more pleasure."

"Not even me writing to you?"

"What?" Duncan was genuinely confused.

"It wouldn't give you more pleasure for me to write to you than you to write to me?"

"Erm, no, of course not. I mean, yes, it would give me even more pleasure for you to write to me."

"So, then me writing to you is nothing?"

"What?"

"You said nothing would give you more pleasure. So, is me writing to you 'nothing' since you've now said it would give you more pleasure?"

"What? Are you toying with me?"

"Yes, I am," she said as she started to walk away. Then she turned back to him, continuing to walk backwards toward the mansion, and smiled mischievously, "However, you may still write to me."

They were laughing as they walked back up the stairs and into the bright, hot ballroom. The music was just ending, and people were milling about preparing for the next dance. A civilian in perfectly tailored clothes came up to them and spoke to Lillian, "Excuse me, miss, but might I have the next dance with you?"

Lillian looked at Duncan and then back at the man. She frowned and replied, "I'm dreadfully sorry, but I've promised the next dance to Captain Duncan. Please forgive me."

He bowed. "I shouldn't want to keep you from the hero of the ball. A pleasure to meet you, Captain." He walked away and asked another lady nearby and this time, was successful.

"Shall we dance, then?" Duncan asked.

"If you don't mind, Captain."

Duncan laughed and offered his arm to escort her to the dance floor. "What would you have done if I had already promised the set to someone else?"

"I have no idea. Lady Lockerbie looks very tired, so I was hoping you were not otherwise engaged."

"You can call me Joseph, you know. We've known each other for years, even if it's been a while since we've seen each other."

"Yes, and that doesn't seem to matter so much anymore. However, you must call me Lily if I'm to call you Joseph."

They smiled at each other as the dance began.

It was a long dance, the longest of the evening, but Joseph and Lily did not notice and were disappointed when it ended. They were even more disappointed to learn that an announcement had been made while they were walking in the gardens that this was to be the last dance of the evening. They made their way back to Admiral and Mrs. Huntington-Whiteley, who were again, or perhaps still, standing with Admiral Fairhurst.

"Ah, there you two are. Did you have a nice evening, Daughter?"

"Yes, Father. I don't recall the last time I enjoyed a ball as much. The airs here in the West Indies are magical, just as you told me."

Admiral Fairhurst spoke to Duncan, "And how about you, Captain? Did you have an enjoyable evening?"

"Aye, M'Lord, I did," Duncan responded honestly.

"Well, don't expect a ball every time you sail or fight the French. Still, it was mighty sporting of you to dance with both Ladies Lockerbie."

"Speaking of being sporting, thank you, Lord Fairhurst, for spending so much of your evening with an old man and his wife. It makes me miss the Navy, so, to be here with all of you. But still, it was a most enjoyable evening remembering our times together at sail," Huntington-Whiteley said, with real feeling.

Fairhurst eyes lit up. "I've just had an idea. Captain Duncan says his new ship is ready. What if you were to take a short cruise with him and certify its readiness for me? You could sail on Monday morning and be back in the evening. You could even take the ladies with you if they would like to see what a warship is like."

"That would be most enjoyable, if the captain wouldn't mind."

"I'd be honored, sir."

"Kat? Lillian? What do you think?"

Lillian looked hopefully towards her mother, who answered, "Yes, I think that would be a good reminder, and just one day should be reasonably tolerable."

Fairhurst clapped his hands together and said, "Excellent! It's decided, then. We should pay our respects to the governor and leave before we're the last, and they start sweeping us out the door."

Chapter Thirteen

Saturday morning there was not a single cloud to mar the bright blue sky. There was a very soft breeze with occasional gusts, and as the sun rose higher in the sky, it became very warm and humid. Duncan had been up early despite his late return from the ball. He was filled with nervous energy and left the ship soon after breakfast to visit his friend, who was still in the hospital.

Duncan strode into the now familiar hall and headed towards Williams' bed, as he had on almost every day they had been in port. Williams was standing next to his bed and was fully dressed. Drawing near, Duncan said, "Rupert! Good morning to you. You look like you're ready to rejoin society. Are they finally kicking you out?"

Williams smiled and said, "Aye! I am being released, at long last. I was just gathering together my belongings and awaiting the doctor doing his morning rounds so I might pay my respects and thank him for pulling me through."

"Joy to you, my friend. Where are you off to, then?"

"My paperwork and release from the ship have all been completed and delivered here, so I suppose I'm off to St. John's to join one of my father's ships," Williams answered as he loaded things with his one hand into a trunk beside the bed. "The doctor warned against riding for several more weeks, so I shall look into hiring a coach, I suppose."

"You'll need to pay for a carriage both ways, most likely, even if you're only going one. If you wouldn't mind the company, I'd be happy to take the ride over with you and then come back on my own. I'll even split the cost." Duncan offered.

"Ah, you don't trust that I'm leaving and want to make sure, eh?"

"Yes, and besides, you owe me a dinner and there is a very expensive chop house in St. John's where we could settle the debt before you sneak off."

Williams laughed. "I would enjoy the company and I recall that I owe you both a dinner and a case of wine. At least I can buy the dinner today, and the wine will come in time."

"You may have lost a hand, but your memory is more clear than usual. To be honest, I had forgotten about the wine. How long do you expect before I'll see that?"

"My good sir, as we both know, wine gets better with age, so you should want to wait."

"I suspect the wine won't be any older or better, no matter how long I have to wait," Duncan said. "In any event, I'll take the dinner today."

While Williams waited for the doctor and finished his packing, Duncan left the hospital to hire a coach. Within an hour, he was back in a rather plain, but fairly comfortable, black carriage being drawn by two almost-matched gray horses. There was a driver, but no footman or additional servants, so Duncan opened the door and let himself out when it rolled to a stop in front of the hospital.

He found Williams speaking with a man he presumed to be the doctor, so he waited a polite distance away to let them talk in private. After they shook hands, the doctor walked away and Duncan approached. "Have you made bail, then?"

Williams smiled. Although he still looked rather thin and gaunt, his face had color again and his eyes were sparkling. "I have been released into your custody, sir."

"I never agreed to that. I'm just looking for a pleasant ride and a very nice, very large, and very expensive dinner."

"Ah, well, then, let's leave before they change their minds."

An orderly carried Williams' trunk and placed it on the back of the carriage. Duncan and Williams got in. Once they were settled, Duncan knocked on the side of the cabin and the driver snapped his whip and started the horses.

The ride to St. John's was a bit slower than his ride the night before, but the time went quickly as the two friends chatted and discussed the passing scenery. Duncan had been giving an account of the ball and as he was finishing, Williams interrupted, "Belay there, one moment. You mean to say you took three dances with the same young lady? Have you learned nothing from me?"

"I've learned plenty. Normally, I find that if I observe your behavior, I may do best by doing the opposite."

"But with all those ladies present, you spent the entire evening - aside from obligatory dances - with one lady. Have you never heard the saying about eggs and a single basket?"

"It was a very enjoyable evening, Rupert, and I quite enjoyed the company."

A sudden realization came to Williams, "And I suppose you're not planning to call upon this lady today while you're in town? I feel that I might be a convenient excuse for your visit."

Duncan smiled. "What a wonderful idea! I'm so glad you suggested it. Perhaps I will look in on her before I return. I suppose it would only be the courteous and expected course of action, given her family's connections to mine."

"I'm shocked, sir!" Williams feigned indignation. "To use a friend so ill? Appalling!" Then, after a short pause, "May I meet her?"

"Only if you promise to be on your best behavior...and you buy dinner first."

They spent almost two hours enjoying a large lunch and having many laughs together. Duncan was surprised and pleased to see how happy his friend was now that he was out of the hospital, eating real food, and about to start the next adventures in his life. He seemed genuinely excited to be going back to England to join in his father's business. They shared memories, argued about certain details of events they had experienced together, and talked about their futures and plans.

Duncan realized that he had not had anyone to talk to like this since just before the battle when he took command of *Fidelity*. He had been separated from his friends and all the other officers by becoming a captain. Even before he was awarded the actual rank, the gap had developed between them.

Williams was true to his word and paid for the meal with hardly any complaint. They walked back to the waiting carriage and Duncan gave the driver the address of the house the Huntington-Whiteleys were renting. It was not a long ride, and it was passed mostly in silence.

The wheels of the carriage made a grinding noise as they rolled through the crushed stone of the semi-circular driveway at the front of a well-kept, dark gray stone house. The carriage came to a halt and Duncan opened the door. He stepped down onto the drive and headed up the stairs to the front door with Williams close behind. The knocker was of blackened iron shaped like a pineapple with a ring hanging from it.

Duncan knocked, and the door opened to reveal a very dour-looking servant who asked, "May I help you?"

"Captain Joseph Duncan to see the admiral, if he is in."

The servant stepped back and motioned them in. "Please wait here." He closed the front door and disappeared through another door on the side of the entrance hallway he had left them in.

Williams glanced around appreciatively. "Nice place. I thought you said they were just in town until they're able to find passage."

"They are. They were able to rent this house, fully furnished, on a monthly basis. My understanding is that the owner has several homes throughout the islands and isn't on Antigua often," Duncan responded.

"Hmm...I suppose I shall have to find a place of my own back in London," Williams pondered. "I can't imagine living with my family again."

Duncan was about to make a snide joke when the side door opened and the servant reappeared to say, "The admiral will see you." He motioned them through the door.

They walked through the sitting room to a library beyond another door and found the admiral sitting in a large leather chair. He greeted them happily, "Captain Duncan! What a pleasant surprise!"

"Thank you, sir. I hope you don't mind the intrusion without warning. Please let me name to you my particular friend, Rupert Williams."

The admiral rose with some difficulty and offered his hand. "It is a pleasure to meet you, Mr. Williams. Any friend of the Duncan family is welcome in my home...even if I'm just renting it. Williams, you say? Are you the Williams I've heard about in stories of the convoy capture? You were wounded, I believe."

"Aye, sir. That would be me," Williams said, holding up his bandaged stump. "I'm honored you recognize my name."

"Bah! The very least I could do, given the sacrifice made by a hero. Captain Duncan spoke so highly of you at the ball that I almost feel that I know you. Ah, the ball, that reminds me, I'm sorry to report the ladies are not at home. I'm sure they would have liked to meet you...and to see the captain, of course."

"I'm just glad you were not out as well, Admiral," Duncan said. "We cannot be disappointed, as we had made no prior appointment."

"Have a seat, gentlemen. Perhaps if we spend some time talking, they will return," the admiral said, as he eased himself back into his chair.

They talked for several hours with topics ranging from updates on Duncan's family, other news from England, to the admiral's career (with only a brief mention of his injury and retirement), and how things had changed, or had not changed, in the Royal Navy. It was an enjoyable afternoon for all of them, and after finishing tea, Duncan said, "Thank you so much for a thoroughly entertaining afternoon, sir. Unfortunately, we must be going."

"Ah, but the ladies have not returned. Might you be convinced to stay for dinner? That way, you'd be sure to see them."

"That is quite kind of you to offer, sir. However, I must be getting back to my ship. I've been away longer than I had intended already."

"The needs of the service, yes, I remember those obligations," the admiral said. "We will be traveling to Falmouth tomorrow afternoon and spending the night at an inn. I can't recall the name…something to do with a bird, I think."

"The Brown Pelican?" Duncan offered.

"Yes! Yes, that is the very one. You are familiar with it?"

"Yes, sir. I stayed there for a few days while between ships."

"Very good. As I was saying, we're going to stay there tomorrow evening so that we do not have to travel early to join you for our cruise on Monday. May I impose on you to join us for dinner tomorrow evening? My wife and daughter are caught up in the eating styles of London, I'm afraid, and they take their main meal in the evening rather than at lunch like we navy men."

"I'd be very pleased to join you, sir," Duncan responded, while trying to ignore the smirk Williams was having a hard time hiding - if he was, in fact, trying.

"Oh, that is excellent news, and I should hope that it shall be enough to keep me out of trouble with the ladies when they hear that they missed you today."

Duncan and Williams climbed back into the carriage and started off towards the inn where Williams was going to stay. He was smiling and staring at Duncan. Finally, Duncan could not take it anymore and said, "What?"

Williams laughed. "I think you like this young lady even more than I had previously guessed. I've never seen you so polite and talkative. Trying to make a good impression on her father, eh?"

"You forget, sir, that the admiral is a close family friend. Why should I not be polite and enjoy his company?"

"Yes, of course, and you didn't look towards the door every time there was the slightest noise? Hoping the ladies, or perhaps, really, one particular lady, might be coming home?"

"You are incorrigible!" Duncan responded.

Williams sat back. After a few moments, he said in a more serious voice, "Still, the admiral does seem like a good man. I really wish I could have had the opportunity to meet your lady friend."

"I wish you had, too. I think you would like her," Duncan said.

Williams was not able to remain serious on such a topic for too long and added, "The apple does not fall far from the tree, so they say. However, it can at times roll downhill. Perhaps she's not too good for you after all."

•   •   •

By Sunday evening the glass had begun to drop and even in the shelter of the bay the wind was creating choppy waves. Clouds had grown to fill the sky, and as the sun approached the horizon, the sky to the east was dark and foreboding.

Cahill approached Duncan as he walked towards the entry port on his way to shore for the evening. "Sir, the Flag has signaled for all ships to place a second anchor and prepare for a blow."

Duncan looked up at the commissioning pennant whipping nervously in the growing wind and glanced from horizon to horizon before answering, "Carry on. Strike the top gallants and rig the pumps, as well. Better ready now than working in the rain. I'll be back later this evening, but if anything should go wrong, you're to send me a message at the Brown Pelican."

"Aye, aye, sir. You needn't worry about us. We'll take good care of *Enchanté* until your return. I happen to know she's quite well found in a storm."

Duncan smiled and gave a short nod as he disappeared over the side into his awaiting boat. The pull to shore was short but wet as the spindrift covered his boat cloak and dripped into the bottom of the boat. His original plan, since he was unsure of the time, had been to take a bum boat back. However, with the weather worsening, he preferred the idea of having his own gig and crew to count on.

They came alongside the dock and the front oarsman hooked a woven rope bumper to hold the boat tight. Duncan stood and said, "Jenkins, please return at four bells in the first watch. I shall meet you here."

"Aye, aye, sir," Jenkins responded. "I'll have the lads in their oilskins in case you're delayed, sir. We'll be here."

"Thank you." Duncan stepped onto the dock and started towards the inn.

It was not raining yet when he arrived at the inn, but it felt as if it would start at any moment. Duncan handed his cloak, hat, and sword to a servant and was shown to a private dining room off the main area. He found all three Huntington-Whiteleys assembled there waiting for him.

The food was excellent, but even if it had been horrible, Duncan would have enjoyed the dinner. Mrs. Huntington-Whiteley and Lillian had much more to relate about events in England, with plenty of stories involving Duncan's family. Everyone seemed completely at ease and the conversation and laughter flowed throughout the meal and for some time after the cloth had been removed from the table.

With just the four of them at such an informal gathering, the women remained at the table with the men sipping sweet wine and nibbling on candied ginger until Duncan finally felt compelled to break the spell of the magical evening and announce, "Sadly, it seems time that I return to my ship. Thank you so much for a truly enjoyable evening."

"We look forward to seeing your ship tomorrow, Captain," the admiral said. "Do you think this blow will continue and will it impact our plans?"

"The glass has been dropping steadily since this morning, sir. I'm not sanguine that it will be over by morning. As you know, the wind and tides are not within our control. We shall have to wait and see what the morning brings."

•   •   •

The morning brought even worse weather, with gusting winds and rain blowing almost horizontally in great sheets that left visibility of only a few hundred feet at times. Duncan was up before daybreak. After consulting the glass and noting the conditions in the gloomy gray darkness that persisted long after the sun must have risen, he resigned himself to the fact that there would be no cruise today.

He decided to go in person to deliver the news and found the three would-be passengers sitting quietly at their breakfast table.

Lillian spotted him first and looked hopeful as he approached the table. He frowned and said, "I'm terribly sorry. The weather will prohibit us from sailing today."

"Bah!" The admiral shrugged. "You said yourself we cannot control the weather. No need to look so glum. We can go tomorrow or the next day. We've nowhere else to be, and I'm sure Lord Fairhurst will allow us our little inspection when the weather clears."

Lillian's face lit up. "Father, do you really mean it? We can stay and wait out this horrid storm?"

"Well, I for one am not traveling back to St. John's in this weather," Mrs. Huntington-Whiteley interjected.

"So long as the captain would still allow us a cruise on a later date, I should see no problems. I shall scratch out a note to Lord Fairhurst directly to make a formal request," the admiral said.

Duncan could not help smiling, especially upon seeing Lillian's apparent pleasure. "I should be happy to have you aboard whenever it is possible, sir."

"Then, it's settled. Do sit down and join us. We haven't yet eaten. I shall delay the writing of my note that long."

Duncan accepted the invitation and, although he went back to the ship later in the morning, he returned and spent the evening and dinner with them. The admiral had sent his note to Lord Fairhurst and had received a quick, friendly, and obliging reply.

Tuesday morning, the storm showed no signs of lessening and Duncan again spent much of the day with the Huntington-Whiteleys taking meals with them and sitting in the inn's library - talking, reading, and occasionally playing chess or cards.

On Wednesday, the rain lessened, and the winds seemed to be weakening, but it was still unsafe to leave harbor. Duncan found that he was no longer disappointed to see bad weather and enjoyed another day relaxing and conversing at the inn. He stayed until late after dinner that evening, expecting they would be able to sail the next day and not wanting to miss a moment of time with Lillian. He was no longer trying to pretend to himself that he was there for any other reason. It was Lillian he thought of as he walked to the inn each morning and Lillian he immediately missed when he left in the evening.

To everyone's surprise, the weather was not appreciably better on Thursday morning, and Duncan joined them again at the inn. He was somewhat concerned that he might wear out his welcome, but they seemed genuine in their continued invitations. He did not think Lillian minded, but he was unsure if she was really pleased to have him there or just happy to have the distraction, considering they were essentially stranded at the inn with nothing to do. He did not dare to hope that she enjoyed his company as much as he enjoyed hers.

It was almost sundown on Friday before the storm finally decided to end and the glass began to rise. The sky was filled with brilliant shades of red, reflecting off the retreating clouds as the sun dipped below the horizon. Duncan had dinner at the inn but left earlier than had become his norm to ensure both he and the ship would be ready to start their delayed cruise the next morning. They had agreed on a time for one of the ship's barges to pick them up at the dock and transport them aboard. All was prepared.

A bosun's chair had been rigged to lift the guests from the barge to the deck. The admiral had protested to his family the night before and lost the argument. His stiff leg and the slippery, wet wood of the entrance were considered more heavily than his pride. Still, he sputtered and complained to himself as he was lowered onto the deck. Once he was extricated from the harness, he turned to Duncan.

"Welcome aboard, *Enchanté*, Admiral," Duncan said, as the bosun's chair was lowered over the side to retrieve the next passenger.

"Thank you, Captain," the admiral responded, as he straightened his clothes. "I'm appalled by having to be brought aboard like...cargo. I recall being a young captain seeing old men hauled aboard and feeling embarrassed for them. Now, I find myself the old man and I feel the embarrassment that much more."

"Sir, you honor us with your presence. We are all aware of your service to the Crown and the honorable nature of the injury that required the bosun's chair," Duncan said, loud enough to be sure those around him were reminded that this man in civilian clothes was to be treated with the dignity due an admiral retired by wounds received in service.

Mrs. Huntington-Whiteley was lifted aboard next, and her knuckles were white from her grip on the ropes. She sighed in relief as her feet touched the deck and fanned herself as Duncan welcomed her aboard. It was a moment before she trusted herself to respond, but soon the color was coming back to her face, and she was smiling while checking on her husband, who was still grousing.

Lillian's head rose above the deck to reveal a broad smile. She looked from side to side, taking in the view of the ship until her eyes met Duncan's. Her smile became even brighter. She glanced down and swung her feet nervously, as if she were on a swing, and continued looking around the ship as she was carefully lowered to the deck.

Once they were all safely aboard, Duncan briefly introduced them to the officers before guiding them to the quarterdeck. They stood at the front of the deck, holding onto the rail as the anchor was raised. Just before the anchor came free from the bottom, Duncan offered them seats on the flag locker where they would be able to see and hear what was happening without getting in the way as the ship made sail.

To Duncan's great relief, everything went smoothly and soon they were in the open sea with a strong wind and large swell.

Cahill and the master knew the planned course and at Duncan's nod, they gave the orders to put *Enchanté* on her best point of sail with the wind on her quarter and start to pile on all the canvas she could carry.

Lieutenant Cole came on deck leading three seamen carrying folding chairs and lengths of light rope. They placed the chairs on the deck slightly forward of the binnacle and attached them securely using the rope attached to ringbolts. "Thank you, Lieutenant," Duncan said, and then addressed his guests. "It might be more comfortable now to move to the chairs. We needed the deck clear to get underway, but now you'll have a better view from here."

Duncan offered his arm to Mrs. Huntington-Whiteley to steady her on the slanted deck and helped her to a chair. Lillian was helping steady her father while making it look as if he were escorting her.

The morning was spent cruising on various points of wind, showing the speed of the ship by reaching twelve knots and demonstrating turns, sail handling, and various evolutions. The admiral was clearly enjoying the experience and Lillian wore an almost constant smile and had many questions for Duncan. Her mother occasionally looked rather green, but maintained her composure.

•   •   •

Jenkins was sitting with his mess mates chewing on a tough piece of beef when Carlson asked him, "Why are you eating down here with us? Shouldn't you be up in the captain's cabin feasting on fancy French leftovers?"

"There ain't no leftovers to be had right now. Thibeault says that proper folk eat their dinner in the evening, so he just made what he calls 'light refreshment' for now." He smiled slyly and added, "Of course, that means there might be something for me later."

They continued eating and talking amongst themselves until someone at another table yelled, "Hoy, Jenkins! Who's this admiral, and why isn't he wearing no uniform?"

Jenkins noticed a silence fall across all the mess tables within earshot and swallowed before answering, "I hear tell he's retired from the Navy for some time, and he lives right close to the captain's parents back in England."

"Old family friend, eh?" someone else asked, then added, "Is he what they call a patron of the captain?"

"Wouldn't rightly know anything about that," Jenkins said. "Never laid eyes on the man afore today."

"I can tell you about the admiral, I can," came a voice.

"Who's that there? Keith, is that you soundin' off?" the first man yelled.

"Aye, it's me," Keith responded. "I knows the admiral from back a few years ago."

"Speak up then and tell yer tale."

Everyone's attention shifted to the old seaman, and he started, "Was back in '89. I was servin' on *Monmouth*. Little Black Ship, we called her, and she was a beautiful ship, too. Anyway, we sailed out of Portsmouth on one of them diplomatic missions and the admiral, well, he was the one what was going to do the talking. We was headed to the Kingdom of Naples, but we never made it.

"We sailed south with a couple of frigates as far as the Rock and then they stayed there and we passed on into the Mediterranean, sailing alone. Everything was going fine until one night when I was off watch, and I woke up to the worst racket and people yellin' 'Fire!'

"Somehow a fire had started down in the hold. The captain, he was a right tartar and wouldn't allow anyone to smoke on deck. I think someone snuck down there to have a pipe, but they never did figure out what started the fire.

"Anyway, the fire was burnin' and there was smoke everywhere. The officers were yellin' and sendin' us this way and that. Then the order comes to flood the magazine and so we did, but not soon enough because some of the powder that weren't wet yet must've caught fire and there was the biggest explosion I ever did see. Flames shot up into the sky and left a big hole right there through all the decks, but somehow the hull stayed together.

"The captain was killed right away and the first officer was mangled up something fierce and was hauled off screaming. He died later. We was in a bad way and the admiral, he got us organized again and told us we was going to save the ship 'cause we had nowhere else to go and nobody what was going to help us or find us.

"His leg was all busted up and nearly been blown off, but he tied a splint to it and just kept marchin' around givin' orders. We fought that fire all night, and in the morning when the sun finally came up you couldn't hardly recognize our little ship - but it was still afloat and though smokin', it was no longer on fire.

"It took us a week to get back to the Rock, and they took the admiral off with the other wounded - what was most of the crew that weren't dead already. He was taken bad with the fever by then, besides havin' his leg chewed up. They towed poor *Monmouth* back to England. Somehow, I was one of the lucky ones what didn't get hurt but for some scratches and little burns and I went back with her. I never saw the admiral since then until this very morning."

There was silence as Keith finished his story, and it held until the bell sounded to end their break. Everyone got up to go back to their duty stations and Jenkins walked over to talk more to Keith.

•   •   •

On the quarterdeck, Duncan was sitting in a fourth chair that had been brought up at a small table with his three guests. They had been enjoying some cold meats, fresh fruit, and pastries while drinking, what in Duncan's estimation, was a particularly fine white wine. The admiral spoke as the table was cleared away. "She's a lively little ship and very quick. It's been so long since I've been on a frigate, I'm not sure if I can say she is more lively or quicker than normal, but I do enjoy it!"

"As do I, Father," Lillian said. "The wind and the spray from the sea are exhilarating, is it not, Mother?"

"Yes, dear. Clearly you get your love of the sea from your father. As exhilarating as it may be, I should prefer to have my feet on solid ground. I find it quite troubling and hard to walk with the deck shifting about so."

"Perhaps you would be more comfortable in my cabin, ma'am," Duncan offered.

"Oh, no, no. I'm quite all right. I enjoy complaining sometimes, but Lillian is correct. It is quite lovely with the sun to warm us and the breeze to keep us cool. I should think there are blessed few days so nice for you at sea."

"Some days are better than others, to be sure, but on the whole, I must admit to liking more than I dislike," Duncan responded. "Especially here in the West Indies. You'd not know it from the last week, but bad weather is really not typical and seldom lasts long."

They spent the next several hours sailing along peacefully and talking. From time-to-time Lillian would take a stroll about the deck to stretch her legs and Duncan would accompany her. The admiral remained seated most of the time with his left leg held stiffly, but usually with a smile on his face. Cahill had a pleasant discussion with him during one of Lillian's walks, and his wife seemed content to sit quietly.

After pacing the deck for several minutes, Lillian and Duncan returned to the chairs, and the admiral stood and said, "Would it be inconvenient for you to give us a short tour, Captain? I really should move about before you need the bosun to lift me from this chair."

"Of course, sir. I would be happy to show you about. Would the ladies care to join us?"

Lillian helped her mother from her chair and said, "We'd be delighted! Wouldn't we, Mother?"

"Yes, actually," Mrs. Huntington-Whiteley said, "I would rather like to see more of the ship. The admiral often talked of various parts, places, and decks, and I've never quite gotten them straight in my mind."

They began the tour by going down the ladderway to the wardroom. Cahill acted as their host and guide, describing who had cabins there and how they ate together. From there they made their way forward, glancing down but not entering the hold before climbing the forward ladderway to the galley. Thibeault was there preparing dinner and Duncan introduced him.

Duncan was surprised when both ladies began speaking French, discussing the dinner plans with the cook. He must have let it show on his face because as they left, Mrs. Huntington-Whiteley said, "Surely you must not be surprised that I've learned a bit of French from your mother in all these years of her being my best friend?"

They did not enter the crew area on the gun deck, and the admiral explained to his wife and daughter that to do so would be inconsiderate since it was their home and the guests had not been invited. At the forward ladderway, they climbed to the forecastle and then descended to the upper deck, walking between the rows of cannons heading towards Duncan's cabin.

Lillian paused to look more closely at one of the cannons. "Father says that the real purpose of ships is to move cannons to where our enemies are hiding. They certainly look rather imposing. How are they used? In battle, I mean. How does one load them with the front-end right against the side of the ship?"

"Those ropes can be used to haul them back inboard," the admiral said.

"Would you be interested in a demonstration?" Duncan offered. "We don't have to fire the cannon, as they are quite loud and messy, but I could have the crew show you how we handle them and the steps they would take to fire them."

Lillian's face lit up, "That would be most wonderful, if it's not too much bother. I should really like to see."

"Mr. Chapman," Duncan called out.

"Aye, sir?" the Gunner responded.

"Select your best gun crew to demonstrate the firing sequence to our guests."

"Aye, aye, sir. Edwards! Assemble your gun crew and serve number seven."

Edwards and four other men came forward and positioned themselves around the cannon. Cahill looked to his captain, and Duncan said, "Proceed."

Cahill bellowed out, "Silence! Man the gun. Cast loose and provide."

The gun crew leaped into action, removing the extra breech ropes, gathering their tools, and hauling the gun inboard while Duncan narrated to his guests, "The gun only has to be hauled in before the first shot. When fired, it comes back on its own and is stopped by those large ropes around the cascabel - that nob at the rear of the cannon."

"Load cartridge!" Edwards ordered, and a powder monkey stepped forward and pretended to give something to the loader.

Duncan continued his explanation. "That young boy would give the loader a flannel bag filled with just the right amount of powder. He transports it from the magazine to the gun he serves in a leather passing box, which protects it from any stray flames or sparks which might ignite it. The loader places it in the cannon, along with a wad to keep it in place. And now you'll see the rammer push it and the gun captain make sure it's all the way in. If there are gaps, the cannon can burst when it is fired."

"Ram cartridge," Edwards said, while holding a wire into the touchhole, then pretending to feel the cartridge, he added, "Home!" Stepping back, he ordered, "Shot your gun."

"The loader would now place a ball in the barrel with another wad to keep it in place, and that would be rammed down. Then, they prime the touch hole using a quill filled with fine powder and get the gun in place to fire," Duncan explained slowly, as the steps were acted out by the crew.

"Prime," Edwards said, then, "Run out." He held the lanyard to the flintlock loosely until everyone was clear of the cannon. Then, pulled the string tight and held his fist in the air.

"Fire!" Cahill ordered, and Edwards gave the string a quick pull. The flint struck, and sparks flew. Mrs. Huntington-Whiteley jumped and put her hand to her mouth.

Edwards called out, "Stop your vent!" The crew hauled the gun back away from the side of the ship. "Sponge!"

"So, to remind you, they wouldn't actually need to haul it back in if it had been fired. They sponge it out with water to make sure there are no embers left to ignite the next charge and repeat the process. Every fourth shot, they clean the barrel with a worm to get out any debris that has collected, and every ten to twelve shots they cool the barrel with extra water," Duncan concluded.

"What is the meaning of stopping the vent?" Lillian asked. "I saw a man touch the cannon. Is that to see how hot it has become?"

"The hot gasses will erode the touchhole, if allowed to escape. So, one of the men covers the hole with a piece of leather to protect it," Duncan answered.

"It's still hard to imagine," Lillian said. "Could you fire one so I may truly understand?"

Duncan looked at the admiral, who looked at his daughter, and then said, "I suppose I am here to make sure the ship is ready, and the ship is nothing without her guns. Would you mind firing one, Captain? If you can spare the powder."

"Mr. Chapman. Have cartridges brought up and we shall time Edwards and his crew firing three times."

"Aye, Captain. Would you like to use regular issue powder or the training powder the pusser got, sir?"

"Training powder, if you have cartridges prepared," Duncan responded.

"I do, sir. The pusser got some blue flannel so we can keep 'em separate."

"Very well, then. Carry on and we shall watch from the quarterdeck. Mr. Cahill, please take charge of the operation and time the crew."

"Aye, aye, sir!"

The powder monkey had already returned with the first cartridge and stood behind the cannon to the left by the time the observers had positioned themselves on the deck above, so each had a good view. Lillian and her mother stood in front of the admiral and Duncan.

Strickland came up the stairs to the quarterdeck and offered cotton and beeswax to the group, which Duncan accepted. "Ah, thank you, Lieutenant. Ladies, I recommend you place this in your ears and also cover them."

Lillian protested, "But I should like to hear the cannons, sir."

The admiral took some and stuffed his ears while chuckling, "Oh, you will most definitely still be able to hear them, Daughter."

Cahill came to the bottom of the stairs and said, "Ready, sir."

Duncan waited until Lillian had grudgingly stuffed her ears and then said, "Proceed. Three rounds, timed."

The gun crew took their positions around the cannon, which was still all the way back and ready to load. Cahill said to them softly, "All right lads, the admiral and the ladies are watching and I'm going to be timing you from when you start until you swab after the third round, since you're starting empty and in-board." Then louder, he said, "On my mark…go!"

Immediately, the crew began the loading process and as soon as the gun was run out, they fired. There was a thunderous explosion and a plume of stinking smoke accompanied by a tongue of flame erupting from the side of the ship. The concussion took Lillian's breath away, and she was awed by the unexpected power. The cannon crashed back down on the deck and the crew was moving through the motions they had previously demonstrated with amazing speed and precision. Soon they were firing again, and even though she was ready for it, the second concussion took her breath and again they were reloading.

Immediately after the third discharge, Cahill ordered, "Cease firing." And as they removed the steaming sponge from the barrel, he said, "Time!" and looked at his watch.

Lillian could barely hear him over the ringing in her ears, and she realized she was laughing without being able to hear herself. From the corner of her eye, she saw her mother falling backwards, where Duncan caught her.

A few moments later, they were in the captain's cabin, and Mrs. Huntington-Whiteley was lying on the cushions of the transom bench with Lillian fanning her. The surgeon had been called but was not needed, as the patient had recovered from her fainting by the time he arrived. "I would recommend a snifter of brandy for the lady," he advised, before leaving.

Stanley quickly brought her a large glass of brandy and she sat up and said, "Now, don't make such a fuss over me. I've just had the breath sucked from my lungs. I'm quite all right now. I had no idea how loud the cannon would be. It felt like I was kicked by a mule each time it was fired."

"I'm so sorry, Mrs. Huntington-Whiteley…," Duncan began.

"Don't be silly, Captain," she interrupted him. "I was anxious to see the demonstration. In all the years I've been married to the admiral, I've never been so close to a cannon being fired. I'll admit, I don't care to do it again, but fainting aside, that was quite…amazing."

"I wish I had only had them fire once. Three was just too much."

"Bah! Three was just fine." Then, smiling at him, she joked, "Four might well have killed me, but three just gives me a good story to tell."

Duncan smiled back, relieved that she was feeling better. "Please don't tell my mother your story or I shall pay dearly the next time I hear from her."

"What was the time?" she asked, as she stood with Lillian's help.

The admiral answered, "Four minutes and thirty-eight seconds, Katherine! Quite credible, as the gun was not loaded at the start, so they had to fully load three times. Very credible, indeed."

"Sir, I must admit the gun crew you saw is the very best on the ship, and is not representative of all the guns," Duncan said.

"They may teach the others and set a proper example, Captain. Having even one crew capable of such a performance reflects well upon the entire ship. I shall definitely tell Admiral Fairhurst of this. However, I believe there is one important test remaining before I can say you are ready in all respects."

"Sir?" Duncan asked.

The admiral smiled. "Why, your cook of course! Shall we have dinner, now that my wife has ended her theatrics?"

•   •   •

The master stood watch and oversaw the long tacks back towards English Harbour while all the officers joined their captain and his guests for dinner. The meal impressed even those who had come to expect great things from Thibeault. The fare was lighter and less spicy than what had been served at the first test dinner, but the variety and excellence were even greater.

All three guests were clearly comfortable eating food beyond the standard British offerings, and even Lieutenant Cole was more adventurous this time. The conversation was a little awkward at first, but the officers soon realized that the admiral was a relaxed gentleman who was quick to laugh and share stories. Having ladies present was a novelty, but eventually the meal had the feeling of a pleasant family dinner.

Chapter Fourteen

The sun had fully set by the time *Enchanté* sailed silently back into English Harbour. They dropped anchor by the light of the third quarter moon. The three guests stood on the quarterdeck and watched the sails disappear within minutes. They all watched in silence at the end of a long and enjoyable day.

"I know he doesn't really need a report from an old man to know you're ready for sea, but I shall give Lord Fairhurst a very positive review, none-the-less," the admiral said softly. "Thank you for giving us this day, Captain. It brings back many memories and reminds me of the good times I had at sea. I had begun to dwell more on what I had lost rather than what I had done."

"Yes, Captain Duncan, thank you," his wife added. "You and your crew were gracious hosts, and I thoroughly enjoyed dinner and getting to know your fellow officers. You seem to be among good company and have little chance of starving so long as you keep your cook. Your mother will be happy to hear both."

Lillian gave Duncan a tired smile but did not say anything. He was pretty sure she had enjoyed the day as much as, if not more than, her father, but he was not sure she had enjoyed it more than he himself had. "You are most welcome and really, I feel I should thank you. This was my first opportunity to show off *Enchanté*, and for it to have involved such good friends makes it all the more special for me."

Cahill came up the ladderway, made his way to Duncan, and they shared a whispered conversation. Cahill nodded and headed back down the ladderway. Duncan noticed Lillian giving him a quizzical look, and he smiled at her. "Admiral, if you don't mind, a member of the crew would like to speak with you."

The admiral looked somewhat confused but said, "By all means, Captain."

Cahill came back up the ladderway, being followed by a nervous-looking seaman holding his hat in his hands and wringing it absentmindedly. Cahill stepped to the side. The seaman stopped in front of the admiral and knuckled his forehead before saying, "Sir...Admiral...Sir...I be Able Seaman Keith and you won't be remembering me, but I was aboard *Monmouth* with you, sir. I always said you saved my life and everyone else who came back alive had you to credit for it. So, sir, I just wanted to say thankee, sir, and God bless you...and your family, sir." He knuckled his head again and left the deck quickly.

The admiral did not trust himself to speak and just nodded with a glimmer of a tear in his eye. His wife stepped closer and put her hand on his shoulder. He took her other hand and gave it a gentle squeeze before he turned to Duncan and said, "We'll be spending the night in Falmouth before heading back to St. John's tomorrow. Would you be interested in joining us for breakfast at the inn so we may thank you properly for this wonderful trip aboard *Enchanté*?"

"I would be honored, sir."

•   •   •

The next morning, Duncan found the three sitting at a table in the dining room of the inn. "Good morning," he said brightly as he approached. "I'm sorry if I'm late and kept you waiting."

"Not at all, Captain," the admiral responded. "We've only just arrived, and I believe we are all, in fact, early."

"It is a lovely day. You should have good weather for your ride across the island."

"Indeed," Mrs. Huntington-Whitely said. "Lillian and I were just discussing the beautiful weather and wondering if you would be available to join us for a short promenade to see the shops and sights on this side of the island before we leave. We've been here nearly a week and yet all we saw was rain through the windows."

"I am at your disposal and would be delighted," Duncan said. "However, I must warn you that Falmouth is a much smaller town than St. John's, and the High Street is not nearly so…high."

The admiral spoke up. "I'm not as quick as I used to be. You needn't be slowed by me if you'd like to run up and down the street. I could stay here or wander on my own."

"Nonsense," his wife said, "you and I shall take our time and walk together while Lillian and the captain walk by themselves on their young legs. It's quite a public place and there could be nothing improper in that."

When they had finished breakfast, the admiral stood and said, "If you'll excuse me for a moment, I must retrieve my hat, and I seem to have forgotten my watch, as well." He patted his empty watch pocket and started walking slowly towards the stairs.

Just as he disappeared into the stairwell, Mrs. Huntington-Whiteley said, "Oh my, and I've forgotten my parasol. Lillian, would you be a dear and get it for me before your father locks the room?"

"Of course, Mum. I'll be right back," she responded, and quickly walked off.

Mrs. Huntington-Whiteley watched her go and then turned to Duncan with a stern look on her face. "Forgive the indiscretion, Captain, but as we haven't much time, I feel the need to be blunt. I want to make sure we understand one another. What are your intentions with my daughter?"

Duncan was taken aback. "Ma'am? I'm not sure the meaning of your question."

"Do you intend to offer her a promise of marriage?"

"Erm, ah, I hadn't really thought that far ahead, ma'am."

"Well, you need to - for her sake. In London, Lillian would already be well on her way to being considered a spinster. I was selfish and allowed her to be taken up with caring for the admiral when she should have been being seen in society. Luckily, in the country, it is not too late for her yet, but if she spends years waiting for you to return from sea because of a misunderstanding, it will certainly be too late."

Duncan was too stunned to respond, so, after glancing towards the stairs, Mrs. Huntington-Whiteley continued.

"I'm not trying to influence you either way, Captain. You're a nice young man and I love your mother dearly...but Lord knows I can speak from experience about the difficulties of being married to a Navy man. She's clearly taken with you, and I'd be a fool not to see that. I can't have her waiting around, hoping, if there's no reason for hope, sir."

"I should never like to cause her pain, or difficulty, ma'am, but this seems...of a sudden and I'm not prepared to answer."

"You, of all people, certainly know we're at war with the French. And who knows for how long this time? Time marches on and in troubled times, it goes all the faster. Just be clear with her, either way, before you are parted. It could happen at any time, and you well know that, as well. It's for you and her to decide what you want to do, but you must decide and be agreed on it either way." She sat back and straightened her dress. "There, I've said my piece and now I'll say no more."

"I shall give it thought and make clear my intentions to Lillian as soon as I am aware of them myself, ma'am. I give you my word."

Lillian and her father appeared at the bottom of the stairs, and Mrs. Huntington-Whiteley gave him a brief, tight smile and a curt nod of her head before turning to her husband and daughter. "Oh, good. You're back so soon. Let us go and enjoy the day."

A half an hour later, Lillian led Duncan out of the bright sunlight into the cool shade of a small shop. She picked up a wide-brimmed hat and placed it on her head. "What do you think?"

He looked at her and absentmindedly said, "It looks quite lovely."

Lillian frowned and put the hat back. "What did she say to you?"

"Who?"

"My mother, of course. You were white as a ghost when Father and I came back into the dining room, and you've barely said a word since." Lillian's voice had an edge of annoyance. "What did she say to you?"

Duncan's mind raced for a way to avoid this conversation, but when he looked into Lily's eyes, he abandoned all hope. He could face a French broadside, but he could not stand before that withering stare. "Ah, well, she asked about my intentions concerning you."

Lillian looked surprised and lowered her eyes. "Oh, I see. And what did you tell her?"

"I was taken by surprise. I told her that I was not yet clear myself and I promised to discuss it with you as soon as I knew what to say."

There was a short pause and then Lillian asked, "Have you had time to consider further?"

"I don't think it is fair to ask you to wait for me when I don't know how long the war will keep me away," Duncan began slowly.

"That relates to the answer, not the question. It would be up to me, not you, to weigh that factor when considering my answer. Unless *you* were not willing to wait for *me* until your return, which is something quite different."

"Oh, no, it's not that. I was really thinking of you."

Lillian said, "If it would make it easier for you, let me tell you that if you said that you enjoy my company, but you have no intention of making me a promise, I should be perfectly happy to continue as friends out for a walk and return to England without obligation. However, if you were to make me an offer of a promise to marry, I would accept - even understanding the uncertainty concerning when we might be able to wed."

Duncan smiled and said, "Would you marry me, Lillian, when I return to England?"

"Yes, I will!" she responded, then with a smile she added, "Since we're engaged, I should be completely honest with you. I lied when I said I'd be perfectly happy if you didn't ask and we went on as just friends. I would have been most upset and likely have left in tears."

"Yet another reason to be happy in my choice to ask you, then. We were able to avoid hysterics and public embarrassment."

"I certainly hope you are able to count better reasons than that," she responded archly. "You'll need to ask my father for permission, of course, but he'll agree to whatever I want."

"I'm beginning to think I might have more in common with the admiral than I thought."

Lillian smiled. "Who will get to tell your sister?"

"I would have to write to her. You could write to her, too. Or wait and surprise her when you are back in England. Which would you prefer?"

"I should very much like to surprise her, if you don't mind. She has no idea we've even seen each other. It could be so much fun."

"We've already established that I can't resist, so you may proceed with your scheme."

•　　•　　•

Lillian and Duncan had decided - or more accurately, Lillian had suggested and Duncan had agreed - that she would discuss the proposal with her father that evening after they had returned to St. Johns. Duncan would join them by midday on the following day and talk to the admiral himself. That would leave them the rest of the day to visit a goldsmith and see about an engagement ring, presuming they gained the admiral's approval. Lillian seemed confident in her plan, and Duncan had no reason for doubt.

The only slight alteration of the plan resulted from them not being able to keep the secret from Lillian's mother. However, once she was informed of the discussion, she became a willing and agreeable conspirator. After seeing them off in their carriage, Duncan headed back to his ship with an extra spring in his step and thinking it was just about the most beautiful day he could recall.

Even the ubiquitous piles of paperwork could not alter his happy disposition. There was more than usual to be done to address deficiencies and requisition replacement supplies from their recent cruises in order to be fully ready for sea. Duncan noted to himself yet again how lucky he was to have Cahill as his first lieutenant.

Strickland was turning out to be a very lucky addition to the crew, as well. His knowledge of how the larger system worked, along with the relationships and positive impressions formed while he was the flag lieutenant, had benefited *Enchanté* several times already.

Duncan felt that at the moment, everything in his life was going well, and he slept soundly in spite of being nervous about the coming day.

The next morning was another beautiful day in the West Indies. The sky was bright blue with small scudding clouds, and a stiff breeze kept the sun from feeling oppressively warm. Duncan ate breakfast alone in his cabin and then paced about the quarterdeck while drinking a second mug of coffee. A few hours later, he headed for shore in his gig and informed Jenkins that he was unsure of his return time and would signal from the shore when ready, or just hire a bum boat.

Duncan hired a carriage and made his way to the Huntington-Whiteley residence. The servant was expecting him and led him to the sitting room, where he found all three seated. Lillian jumped up and came to him as the admiral stood slowly and said, "Ah, Captain Duncan. I understand we have some business to discuss. Would you join me in the library?"

"Yes, sir," he responded as he looked at Lillian and raised his eyebrows in question. Her smile was enough for him to relax - at least a little - and he followed the admiral into the next room and closed the door.

The admiral lit his pipe and threw the match into the empty fireplace. He took a couple of deep puffs to ensure it was properly lit and then turned to Duncan with a broad, expectant smile.

"Sir, I find that I've fallen in love with your daughter, and I would like your permission to marry her," Duncan said, knowing it was not what he had intended or how he had hoped to sound.

The admiral chuckled and clapped Duncan on the shoulder. "Welcome to the family, Joseph. If you haven't already learned, you'll soon realize that it's easier to sail directly into the wind than go against the wishes of the ladies of this house. I've no reason to object and find it to be a good match...but really, my opinion wouldn't matter much if I disagreed."

Duncan was relieved, and felt the tension drain from his shoulders. "I have noticed, sir, that I do tend to defer to Lillian's wishes."

"Then you've already learned a lesson that took me a few difficult years. I suppose we should settle the details, such as the dowry."

"Sir, a dowry won't be necessary."

"Bah! Necessary or not, Lillian is my only daughter - only child, for that matter. I decided some time ago on 10,000 pounds for her dowry and it's in a special account. I'd also like to provide 1,000 pounds per annum in support."

"That is more than generous, and I must reiterate that I would not require either a dowry or any funds for support, sir."

"Oh, I understand, but it will all go to you someday, anyway. I've no heir and I'd like you both to be able to enjoy it while I'm still around to see you live in comfort. So, if that's acceptable, let us shake hands and make it official. I can have my attorney draft something later, but a handshake between fellow officers should be enough."

The admiral offered his hand and Duncan took it. "Thank you, sir. For your permission, for the support, and especially for entrusting me with Lillian."

The next hour was spent with champagne, laughter, and some tears as the four celebrated the news. It was decided, as suggested by the ladies, that there should be a dinner to celebrate the occasion. The dinner would be held on the following evening to allow time for proper preparation for such an important event. The deferral to the next day would also allow more time for Duncan and Lillian to visit a goldsmith.

Mrs. Huntington-Whiteley was of the opinion that the most well-respected smith on the island was located on the other side of St. Johns. Having no opinion of his own and heeding the advice from the admiral, Duncan accepted this as most likely true and helped Lillian into the carriage for the short ride.

Lillian was sitting next to him holding his hand and asked, "Have you thought about what kind of ring you will get me?"

"Ah, that's a trap, to be sure," he responded. "What kind of ring have you always dreamed of, my dear? That is exactly the sort I was thinking."

She smiled, squeezing his hand, and then said, "I should think a posy ring, with very small pearls set around some type of centerpiece…perhaps a gem of some sort. Do you think that would be acceptable?"

"I think that anything that keeps that smile on your face is worth whatever the smith demands."

"Be serious. I don't want to start our engagement with you resenting me for wanting a certain ring. I would still gladly marry you if you refused to buy one at all. The ring is only to remind me of you. It means nothing without you."

"I am being serious. Until yesterday, I had no notion of being married and had never considered what an engagement ring might look like. Today, I want desperately to marry you and want to get you whatever ring will bring you joy and make you happy when you see it and think of me. We're likely to have to spend a lot of time apart - months at a time, and I want the ring to remind you of me and bring only happy feelings."

She squeezed his hand again and laid her head on his shoulder. After a few moments, he said, "A diamond."

She raised her head and asked, "A diamond…what?"

"I think the center gem in the posy should be a diamond. I mean, unless you had something else in mind."

"A diamond would be lovely, but do you think they will have one?"

"Well, we shall see," Duncan said.

After they described the engagement ring to the smith, he took a piece of paper and sketched a design. He asked several questions confirming the size and placement of the components and measured Lillian's ring finger. He held up the sketch and asked, "So, is this what you have in mind? I presume you'll want this in gold and to have foil beneath the stone to add brilliance?"

Duncan looked at Lillian and she nodded enthusiastically. He turned back to the smith and answered, "Yes, that will do nicely. How soon can you have it ready?"

The smith scratched his head and stared into space for a moment before answering. "The pearls I have on hand, a nicely matched set for size and color. I can get a diamond. I know a man on Kitts what should have just what we need. To get the stone and complete the setting…a week from Wednesday."

The price was agreed, the delivery date accepted, and a down payment made. Lillian and Duncan left the shop hand in hand and climbed back into the carriage, sure that they were both the luckiest and the happiest couple in the world.

•　　•　　•

The morning after ordering the ring, Duncan was standing on the quarterdeck enjoying a cup of coffee. He had stayed up working later into the night than he normally would have, but the happy consequence was that he was all but caught up on paperwork. He was looking forward to a relaxing morning and then heading to St. Johns in the early afternoon to spend time with Lillian before their celebratory dinner.

He was daydreaming and staring in the general direction of the dockyards when Midshipman Hyde interrupted him, "Excuse me, sir. There's a signal from the flagship - our number and captain repair aboard, sir."

Duncan snapped back to reality and ordered, "Acknowledge the signal and call my boat crew." He started to walk away towards his cabin as Hyde responded in the affirmative. Suddenly, his relaxing morning was going to require a trip to see Admiral Lord Fairhurst. He had not shaved yet, and started quickly washing and shaving while Stanley assembled his uniform. Fifteen minutes later, he was climbing down the side of the ship into his gig.

Jenkins pushed off and the boat crew started rowing towards the flagship as soon as Duncan was seated. About a half an hour after the signal had been sent, Duncan was climbing through the entry port on *Glory* and being greeted by Tankersley. "Welcome aboard Captain Duncan. It's nice to see you again."

"Very nice to see you too, sir. Do you happen to know why I've been summoned?" Duncan responded cheerfully.

"I do, but it wouldn't be proper for me to say more than there's to be a meeting. The others were already aboard when you were called, so we better head right down to the admiral's cabin." Tankersley said this as he started guiding Duncan forward. When they reached the door to the cabin, they were announced and immediately invited in.

The admiral was seated at his table, rather than his desk. There were two other men sitting with him. Duncan recognized one as Mr. Hirschhorn, the advisor from the Foreign Office and the other was a marine major whom Duncan did not know but recognized from the ball. It was the same major who had danced with Lillian.

The major stood as they entered and the admiral said, "Thank you for coming quickly, Captain. You know Mr. Hirschhorn. This is Major Tisbit. Come and have a seat."

"A pleasure to meet you, sir," Tisbit said, and offered his hand.

Duncan shook Tisbit's hand and responded before sitting down, "Likewise, Major."

"Where to begin?" asked the admiral rhetorically. "First, let me explain that the major is acting on special orders from the admiralty in support of operations here in the West Indies. As such, he performs various duties related to a number of ongoing concerns and is not assigned to a ship, per se. He often helps Mr. Hirschhorn in matters relating to the Foreign Office. Perhaps you would like to take it from there, Mr. Hirschhorn?"

Hirschhorn steepled his fingers and looked directly at Duncan. "Yes. Since your capture of the French convoy and our discovery of the British cannons aboard, I have been making subtle inquiries with the goal of discovering how the situation came to be. It has recently come to my attention that two men who might have information helpful in this cause have moved from England to Nova Scotia - Halifax, to be more precise."

He glanced at the marine and then back to Duncan as he continued, "I cannot be in more places than one, but there are often many places that require my attention. Therefore, I have certain associates whom I trust implicitly to act on my behalf. Major Tisbit is one of those trusted gentlemen and I have asked him to go to Nova Scotia on my behalf to try to find and interview the two men in question."

"Speed, of course, is of the essence to minimize the risk of losing or misplacing these contacts. So, I have requested a fast ship from Lord Fairhurst, and he has granted me you and *Enchanté*. I must admit the irony of using one of the French ships for this mission does further recommend it as the best course of action," Hirschhorn concluded with a chuckle.

The admiral spoke next. "I have orders ready for you to depart with the tide. Tisbit will gather his dunnage and be aboard by then. Clearly, you outrank the major, but as your orders indicate, you are to support him in his mission to the best of your abilities. Anything related to sailing and the safety of the ship will be your sole responsibility, but I request that you consider any suggestions the major might make. He will be privy to certain information and aspects of the mission that may not be shared with you and the crew. He will not be assigned to the ship, or directly under your command, as he will travel on special orders. Do you understand?"

"Yes, My Lord," Duncan responded, while processing the information and quickly thinking through the inventory and status of stores for *Enchanté*, including how much of the crew might be on shore leave.

Tankersley said, "You have family in the area, Captain, do you not? Perhaps you'll have a chance to visit them while the major is busy ashore."

"Erm, yes, sir. My uncle, aunt, and several cousins live near Halifax."

"It is important to get the major to Halifax as quickly as possible, but once he's landed, there will be little for you and *Enchanté* to do beyond awaiting his return. Depending on what he learns, you may need to hurry back, or it might not matter how long you take. In any event, you can expect at least a week, perhaps two, of waiting at anchor," Hirschhorn offered.

The admiral spoke with an edge of annoyance in his voice. "I would like my ship and captain back without wasting any time, regardless of the nature of the information gathered." Then, in a more relaxed tone, he added, "However, if the mission will require prolonged time in port, I see no issue with Captain Duncan visiting his relatives and shall include a note to the port admiral requesting shore leave be approved, if requested."

"Thank you, My Lord," Duncan said. "My ship is ready to sail. However, several crewmen are ashore at this time."

"Then, perhaps you should return to your ship and take steps to recover them quickly. I expect you to sail with or without them. If they are not on board when the major is ready and the tide is flowing, we'll round them up and keep them safe until your return. Understood?" the admiral asked.

"Yes, My Lord. If you'll excuse me then, I shall return to *Enchanté*," Duncan said, as he stood up. Then, turning to Tisbit, he added, "I look forward to welcoming you aboard soon. Do you need a boat and crew?"

"Thank you, no, sir. Captain Tankersley has been kind enough to provide me with transportation. I shall be aboard in about two hours, I should think. I just need to gather my gear from the dockyard barracks," Tisbit responded.

Tankersley accompanied Duncan to the side, where his gig was waiting and said, "Godspeed Captain Duncan. Tisbit is a good man. Don't let his association with Hirschhorn taint him."

Duncan smiled and shook the huge man's hand. "Thank you, sir. I'll see you in a few weeks."

As soon as he was seated in his gig, he spoke to Jenkins, "Pull hard for *Enchanté*. We're heading to sea." Jenkins and the crew all smiled broadly and heaved on the oars.

Cahill was waiting by the entry port, wondering why Duncan had been called to the flagship. He had placed a small wager with Strickland that it was because confirmation of the captain's promotion had been received. Strickland was nearby, as well, waiting to see the outcome of the bet.

Duncan's head appeared above the rail. He stepped inboard, saluted the ship, and then bellowed, "Hoist the Blue Peter and fire a signal gun! Mr. Cahill, prepare the ship for sea. We sail with the tide…with a guest. How many of the crew are ashore?"

Cahill responded while noticing the smile on Strickland's face, "A few dozen, sir. I don't know the exact number, but I can check the roster. Who's the guest, sir?"

"A marine officer, Major Tisbit. He'll be on special orders, sailing as a supernumerary. Best see if Mr. Greene can throw together another cabin in the wardroom. If he can't, you'll all have to shift around to make room. I will have several notes shortly to be delivered ashore. Please send a midshipman to my cabin to retrieve them."

Just as Duncan finished giving directions, the signal broke out at the masthead and the signal gun boomed out on the forecastle.

Duncan had given his hastily scribbled notes to Midshipman Powell and was about to head back on deck when the marine sentry called out, "The master, sir!"

"Enter," Duncan said. "Ah, Mr. Ellis. I was just going to look for you."

"The first lieutenant informed me that we would be sailing on the tide, sir. That will be in full flow within a couple of hours. However, sir, he couldn't tell me where we were headin' and I was hoping you might know," the master joked.

Duncan smiled and responded, "Precisely why I was going to seek you out. Halifax is our destination, and speed is of the essence, as they say. In fact, they did say precisely that. We're to crack on as fast as we can without blowing the sticks out of her. Do you know any shortcuts?"

The master made a rasping noise by scratching his stubbly chin. "No, sir, I'm not aware of any shortcuts, but if it's a fast voyage you want, we've got the right ship and we're going in the right direction. Coming back, well, that's more of a challenge, but going north we'll have the currents and the wind both on our side."

"Please plan out a course, and I'll join you in the chart room in a few moments. I just want to check on the other preparations first," Duncan said.

There was a flurry of activity on deck, and several boats were approaching with returning crewmen. Some of the crew looked like they had been drinking heavily, in spite of the fact that it was not yet noon. Cahill approached Duncan and reported, "Including the ones I can make out in the boats, it seems we've got all but seventeen of the crew aboard. I expect more will still make it back, sir, but I'm not sanguine they'll all be here by the time the tide flows. Oh, and a marine just left the dockyard in a boat that appears to be pulling in this direction."

Duncan took a telescope from the rack and scanned for the boat from the dockyard. "Yes, that's Major Tisbit. Rig a whip to get his dunnage aboard."

"Already done, sir, and a crew is standing by. The carpenter has cobbled together another cabin, so we have a home for him. We can offer him a subscription to the wardroom stores if he'd like a share of our food. That would be polite, would it not? He won't have had time to make any arrangements on his own, and I'd hate to see him on common rations."

"Hmm. I hadn't considered that. As supernumerary, he'd have to pay for rations, too. Insult to injury, eh? It is quite kind of you to offer him a share of your stores, but you might run short with an extra mouth to feed. I'll dine him in as my guest a few nights a week to lessen the impact."

"Thank you, sir. That is most thoughtful and generous of you," Cahill said seriously and then added, "If you'd like any additional company, I would be happy to eat anything Thibeault might be preparing, sir."

Duncan laughed and said, "I suppose I should host a meal to introduce him to all of you. Although I have only barely met the man myself."

.   .   .

The master consulted his watch and then placed it back in his pocket. "Captain, the tide is running, and the wind is fair for an offing."

"Thank you, Mr. Ellis," Duncan said. He turned to the first lieutenant. "Weigh anchor and take us out, Mr. Cahill."

"Aye, sir," Cahill responded. "There are still three crewmen missing."

"Then they can try to explain when we return," Duncan said flatly. "Carry on, Mr. Cahill."

The capstan was turning quickly and the anchor being drawn in when Duncan noticed that several of the crew waiting for the order to release the sails were pointing astern and laughing. Before he had a chance to look back, Cole came up to him and said, "Uh…sir, it looks like some of the crew are still coming back."

Duncan turned to see a small boat with a single oarsman racing toward *Enchanté*, carrying three drunken sailors as passengers. They were all yelling and shouting. One had removed his shirt and was waving it for attention while balancing in the bow of the little boat. Duncan sighed and glanced toward the flagship, wondering who was watching. "Carry on. It looks like they'll just about make it."

Cahill started to smile, caught himself, and forced a frown instead. "Aye, aye, sir. Silence in the ship!"

A few minutes later, the call came from up front, "Anchor aweigh!"

"Let fall the topsails and sheet home!" Cahill called out.

The ship started to move forward with the wind just as the rowboat came alongside. A rope ladder was tossed over the side, and as *Enchanté* began to pick up speed, the three crewmen climbed over the railing and fell sprawled on the deck. The rowboat bobbed in the ship's wake, where the oarsman rested before heading back to shore.

"Welcome aboard," Cahill said sarcastically. Then, he turned to Duncan and said, "All present or accounted for, sir."

Chapter Fifteen

Once they rounded Antigua, the prevailing winds and currents would have allowed them to travel in a straight line to Halifax. However, the shortest distance between two points on a sphere, like the Earth, is not a straight line, but rather an arc that forms part of the great circle around the earth connecting the two points. The master laid out a series of course headings and distances that would keep them as close to the arc as they could sail while following a compass. This course would be the shortest distance, and given the winds and currents, should allow the fastest transit.

Aside from the potential impacts of weather, the enemy, and other unknowns, there would be very little for the crew to do, so Duncan planned to use the time for drill and gun practice. He had already mentioned this to Cahill, and he was sure that the first lieutenant would put together a detailed and well-considered schedule. With all the immediate needs addressed, Duncan was standing on the quarterdeck thinking about Lillian and wishing there had been a chance to say goodbye.

"Excuse me, sir," Tisbit said from the ladderway, with his head just appearing above the deck. "Might I come on deck?"

"Ah, please do, Major, and join me for a stroll along the rail, if you're so inclined," Duncan responded. "Are your accommodations adequate?"

"Quite! Thank you, sir. Your officers have been very kind in allowing me to purchase a share of the wardroom stores. I must say, they've already made me feel welcome. I don't always get such a pleasant reception aboard ships."

"Really? And why would that be? You don't seem terribly objectionable upon first impression," Duncan joked.

"I suppose it comes down to one of two things, or a combination of both. First, I'm not actually assigned to the ship and thus I am an outsider, never to be allowed to join the inner circles. Second, I'm a marine officer and, in general, we are not viewed the same, or particularly favorably, by many navy officers. It probably does not help either case that I technically outrank everyone else in the wardroom."

"Yes, I cannot recall ever meeting another marine major. Marine lieutenants are aboard every ship and sometimes a marine captain is to be found on larger vessels or in charge of barracks in port. Then, of course, there are many 'honorary' lieutenant-colonel titles given to naval captains to fatten their purses. But majors are a bit of an oddity, are they not?"

"Indeed, we are quite a rare breed, sir," Tisbit said. "To be frank, it serves my masters well for me to outrank all but the captain of a ship when I take passage, and marine major fits that requirement. I seldom catch rides on sloops, as then I would be considered equal to the commander, and that might cause problems."

"Do you imply there are politics in the establishment of rank?" Duncan's tone was sarcastic. "I'm shocked."

Tisbit laughed. "I'm sorry if I only implied politics play a part in that narrow role. What I surely meant to state unequivocally was that politics play a part in everything."

Cahill approached and said, "Excuse me, gentlemen." Then addressing Duncan, "Sir, there appears to be sail following us. It's difficult to be sure, as it seems to be staying just at the horizon."

Duncan raised an eyebrow. "How would someone pick up our scent this quickly? And why would they follow us?"

"No idea, sir. I've no reason to connect the two, but it puts me in mind of the strange sail we tried to run down on the way back from Kitts. We're in pretty much the same area of sea. Could it be a privateer watching?" Cahill theorized.

"Well, our orders are clear. We're going to Nova Scotia as fast as the wind will allow. If they want to follow us, they'll have to keep up," Duncan said.

•   •   •

Cahill entered the captain's cabin, removed his hat, and stood waiting. Duncan prompted him by saying, "What can I do for you, Lieutenant?"

"Sir, I have several disciplinary items to discuss at your convenience," Cahill answered.

Duncan frowned. "Matters concerning discipline are seldom convenient. Have a seat. We might as well get this over with."

Cahill sat down. "As you know, sir, we had several crewmen return drunk from leave. Given the somewhat sudden and unexpected departure, I would be inclined to look the other way, except in the more severe cases which resulted in the offenders not being able to perform their duties."

"I would tend to agree with you. We cannot ignore it if they could not perform their duties."

"Well, to begin with, sir, Mr. Hyde was among those returning in such a condition. He was also missing a shoe, but I don't know if that is a punishable offense, or just an indication of his state of intoxication."

Duncan sighed. "I presume you've already given him a good tongue lashing."

"Aye, sir. He is seemingly repentant, yet the crime deserves punishment, in my opinion."

"I agree. Masthead him for a day and let him think more about it while he misses a few meals. Nothing seems to get to a midshipman faster than an empty stomach. Assign him whatever additional duties you see fit, as well."

"Yes, sir. I have a few things in mind. There are then seven men who could not work upon their return, including the three clowns that made our departure into a spectacle."

"Those three were more visible, but the underlying crime was the same. Quiet drunks and loud drunks are equally useless," Duncan said. "Have them all stand together before me and I shall give them all the same punishment, unless you recommend otherwise."

"That is fine with me, sir. I agree with your assessment." Cahill paused and then said, "That brings us to the most serious and frankly rather confusing offense. A crewman, by the name of Pratt has been cited for dereliction of duty by Mr. Murray for failing to properly secure riggings, as ordered."

Duncan raised an eyebrow. "That is indeed serious, but I fail to see what is confusing."

"Well, sir, you are aware perhaps that we have two crewmen by the name of Pratt. One is an able seaman who served with me on *Swallow* and the other, the one in question here, is a young landsman in Lieutenant Strickland's division. Strickland is of the opinion that Mr. Murray mistook the landsman for the able seaman and ordered him to do something quite beyond his capabilities."

"You're standing on a slippery slope, Lieutenant. If he didn't know how to complete the task, he should have asked for help. We cannot undermine the bosun's authority by not supporting him in his complaint, if he feels it justified."

"Aye, sir. I understand. Strickland has told me that this Pratt has not settled in well and does not appear to have friends or a sea daddy to watch out for him. He is having a hard time adjusting to life aboard, and a flogging might turn him hard in the wrong ways. I know we can't excuse the offense, but perhaps Strickland could discuss it with Mr. Murray and see if they might agree to some mitigating circumstances."

"I have no objection to Lieutenant Strickland having a discussion with Mr. Murray, but I won't stand for any pressure or browbeating. Mr. Murray's decision will be considered final and that will be the end of it. Understood?"

"Aye, sir. I will ensure Lieutenant Strickland understands."

"Pratt has been listed in the books. You'll need to call him before me for judgement. Mr. Murray will know what to do if he is moved by Strickland. We'll witness punishment today for all these offenses."

•   •   •

The bosun's whistle sounded, and he called out, "All hands! All hands to witness punishment!" The crew crowded onto the deck and, after a few moments of rustling, quieted down, and looked at Duncan expectantly.

The straight lines of marines standing at attention with their muskets and Duncan's tone left no doubt as to the seriousness of the occasion. "Mr. Cahill. What offenses do you bring before me today?"

"Sir, seven members of the crew were found drunk and unable to perform their duties." Cahill listed the seven names, and the crewmen came forward into a line.

"Have any of you something to say on your behalf, or does anyone else speak for you?" Duncan asked. The accused shuffled nervously, but said nothing. "You shall all forfeit your daily grog for a period of one week, commencing today, and shall also be part of the deck cleaning crew each morning for the next week, regardless of your watch standing."

The group melted back into the crowd, disappointed to lose their grog and some sleep, but relieved the punishment was not worse.

Cahill called out, "Jonathan Pratt, Landsman, is accused of dereliction of duty and failure to follow the rightful orders of a superior!" Pratt came forward carrying a bright red bag containing the cat-of-nine-tails he had braided for his punishment, if found guilty.

"Do you or anyone have anything to say on your behalf before I pass judgement?" Duncan asked.

The bosun stepped forward and said, "Excuse me, sir. I am the one who accused Pratt and I have something to say on his behalf. Upon further reflection, sir, it seems to me that Pratt did not act in malice, but rather was ignorant of the correct way to perform his duty. Although ignorance can be no excuse, sir, if you would indulge me, I offer that perhaps in lieu of punishment, Pratt might be provided some form of additional guidance."

Duncan kept his expression blank. "What do you have in mind to suggest, Mr. Murray?"

"Sir, if willing shipmates who have the skills Pratt lacks could be found who would take upon them his proper training - say on the next make and mend day, perhaps that would answer well as a conclusion to this unfortunate incident and serve as a remedy to ensure it never happens, again."

"Hmmm. Well, first then, are there willing, able seamen who would accept this task and offer the training?"

"Aye, sir, I'll do it."

"And me, sir."

"If it be a third man you need, then I be him, sir."

"Very well. Would anyone else speak to the circumstances of this offense or the merits of the suggested resolution?" After a pause, he continued. "Jonathon Pratt, as you have been found lacking in the performance of your duties in regard to rope work, and as your shipmates have seen fit to offer you instruction, you shall spend not less than eight hours of the next make and mend day working with Able Seamen Carlson, Edwards, and Keith to improve your skills and learn your new trade. I hope you comprehend that your shipmates are demonstrating that you can count on them and that you need to learn your skills so that they may count on you. A ship is only as strong as its crew."

"Aye, sir. Thank you, sir."

"Mr. Cahill, please be so kind as to dismiss the crew and carry on."

Duncan went back down to his cabin, where Thibeault had his dinner prepared. "*Merci*, Étienne. I've invited the officers and our passenger, the marine major, to dinner tomorrow. I'd say you don't have to prepare anything extravagant, but I suspect you'd just take it as a challenge."

"Of course, sir," Thibeault responded. "If I might inquire, as I am still becoming familiar with life in the Royal Navy, when you say dinner, are you referring to the midday meal, such as this, or evening meal, sir?"

"Good point. I should be more clear about that as customs ashore change more rapidly than our traditions at sea. It will be a midday meal. The galley fire is usually extinguished after the midday meal to save on firewood. In general, I'll only ever have light meals in the evening, and if I invite anyone, it won't be an occasion, just an informal gathering. That might be different if we're dining in civilians. I shall endeavor to be more clear in the future."

"Thank you, sir. I have a spirit stove upon which I can prepare small meals for you in the evening, so not everything will need to be served cold."

"That sounds quite lovely. I'm sure we shall get used to each other and our habits soon."

Upon finishing his meal, Duncan wiped his mouth with a napkin and moved to his desk. What he *wanted* to do was start a letter to Lillian, but what he *should* do was ship-related work. He had never actually felt a desire, rather than an obligation, to write to anyone before. The realization startled him and for a moment he did nothing but think about Lillian. Finally, he picked up a quill and took the top report from his stack of waiting papers, concerned that if he did not work first, he might not want to bother at all.

Dinner with the officers began rather stiffly the next afternoon. Major Tisbit's presence had disturbed the balance of the group and left everyone unsure of how to act or what might be said without causing offense. For his part, Tisbit was somewhat reserved, likely owing to a feeling of being the outsider.

Luckily, they were an agreeable group of men and, since they had not been together long enough to be set in their ways, the conversation soon began to loosen. By the time the cloth was removed, and port wine made its rounds, the group was laughing and talking boisterously. Duncan was pleased. A happy ship started with happy leadership.

Tisbit demonstrated himself to be a willing and capable conversationist. He asked questions, engaged in discussions, and told several humorous stories of his adventures. Duncan appreciated his quick wit and dry sense of humor. Most of the group used sarcasm freely and Tisbit fit in perfectly. Cole was the exception - not for want of trying, but from lack of experience. He was usually the last one to laugh, taking longer to comprehend the true meaning of some comments, but he always got there, eventually.

•   •   •

The wind and weather held, and the first week was uneventful. The ship following them remained just on the edge of visibility. Sometimes it would be gone in the morning, only to reappear later in the day. Duncan wanted desperately to double back in the dark to try to surprise them to find out who they were and why they were there. However, his orders did not allow him the latitude for a such a time-wasting maneuver, and they sailed on with their shadow just out of reach.

Duncan had been invited for dinner in the wardroom one afternoon and accepted happily. It was an enjoyable group and although their cook was not as talented as Thibeault, there was still plenty of toothsome fare to go with the pleasant conversation.

Duncan had invited Tisbit to dinner for a few days, as he had agreed to do. Although it started as an obligation, he quickly formed a budding friendship with the marine. By the end of the week, he had given Tisbit a standing invitation to join him for light meals in the evenings - usually soup and cold meats or leftovers from dinner.

Many nights after their daily duties were completed, they got together to play cards, backgammon, or chess. Strickland and Cole turned out to be avid players of whist, so on a couple of evenings the four played until lights out was called throughout the ship. Duncan enjoyed the opportunity to talk to someone with whom he could converse more freely than he could with any member of the crew.

On the tenth evening after leaving Antigua, the sentry called out, "Major Tisbit, sir!" and Duncan invited him to enter.

Tisbit held up a board and cards and asked, "Would you be interested in a game of cribbage this evening? It seems Cole is busy and Strickland and I couldn't cajole Cahill into taking a hand of whist. In fact, he said he'd sooner walk the plank than have to play cards. Strange man."

"I believe I would be within my legal rights to offer him that choice, but perhaps that wouldn't be a very sporting start to the game," Duncan said. "Cribbage will be fine. Feel free to serve yourself a brandy or whatever you want. Stanley is up forward with the fiddlers and musical merriment. I'll join you in a moment."

"I cannot help but to have noticed that several nights you've been scribbling away on that growing missive. Either you are very dedicated to documenting everything that is occurring, or you have a sweetheart to whom you are writing. Am I correct? And if so, which is it?"

Duncan smiled as he sanded the page. "A lady. My fiancée, in point of fact. Not that it is any of your business."

"A fiancée? Well, there was nothing in your dossier about a fiancée or even any steady female associations."

"My dossier? Would you care to explain that comment, sir?"

"We can come back to that. I'm on the trail at the moment. I recall you spending an inordinate amount of time with a particular lady at the ball - one with whom I had a single dance. She was too thin for my taste, but definitely the prettiest face there that evening - and quite a lovely dancer. I recall her asking me if I knew you. I didn't, of course, at that point, and she didn't seem interested in my favorite topic - me."

"I'd like to know more about the dossier you mentioned," Duncan pressed.

"Hmm, she couldn't have been your fiancée, or someone would have been sure to mention it to me. You were the guest of honor, after all. But three dances? Not in a row, though. That would have been improper. You both disappeared for a couple of dances in between…Ah, I've got it! She is the lucky woman, and you are only recently engaged, perhaps as a result of that evening. That's it. I'm correct, aren't I?"

"Yes, fine. You're correct. Now tell me about the dossier."

"I believe she was the daughter of a retired admiral, a quite well-healed gentleman I've been led to believe."

"Did you read that in his dossier?"

"I haven't read his yet, but you can be sure I will when I next have the chance."

"Seriously, is all this talk of dossiers just to tweak me, or is there really a file about me?"

"Seriously? That's a lot to ask. However, I can see from your face that you mean it. Yes, there are files on everyone of importance. The Navy keeps some, of course, boring stuff, usually about this assignment or that action, et cetera, et cetera, blah, blah, blah. But, the Foreign Service, ah those are the juicy ones. I can't believe they missed your fiancée."

"I can't believe the Foreign Service keeps a file on me," Duncan said incredulously.

"I'm not sure they did before your action with the French convoy. I cannot really say either way, as I would never have had a reason to see it. Hirschhorn was in quite a tizzy to fill it up when you sailed back with your own fleet, though. Oh, I'd love to be the one to tell him about your fiancée. What was her name…Lillian something? A long name…the retired admiral with a limp…Huntington-Whiteley. Yes, that's it, isn't it?"

"Yes, that's her name. You seem to have a very good memory concerning people you've barely met," Duncan noted suspiciously.

"Occupational hazard. Quite bothersome at times. I can't forget people even when I desperately want to. Can I tell him? I feel I shouldn't without your permission as the information has come to me via our friendship, not professionally."

"I suppose he'll find out either way, so you might well be the one to tell him."

"Thank you! I so seldom get a chance to surprise that man. It's endlessly annoying, I assure you."

"What exactly do you do for him, or the Foreign Office? I'm not even clear exactly for whom you are doing whatever you do."

"Whatever needs be done. Technically, I'm working for the Foreign Office, but usually via Hirschhorn, at least of late. I deliver messages, gather information, negotiate deals, investigate matters, take…actions, when required. Like on this mission. I'll look for these two men and if I can find them, I'll convince them to share information with me."

"Seems like low odds to sneak up on someone in a scarlet tunic. I always pictured spies as civilians."

"Oh, you cut me deep to call me a spy!" Tisbit pretended offense. "I am merely a representative of the Crown in matters requiring discretion. Also, I don't wear my uniform when I'm working."

Duncan laughed, and they started their game of cribbage.

•   •   •

On the thirteenth day of their journey, the master closed his telescope and said, "There's Cornwallis Island. I can even make out Hangman's Beach. We should be at anchor in Halifax Harbor by later afternoon, sir."

"A fast passage, Mr. Ellis. My compliments," Duncan responded. "However, I believe it is more commonly referred to as McNabs Island now."

"Aye, you're correct, sir. I've an old chart and haven't caught up with the times. I should have called it Maugher Beach, as well, since that's its more formal name."

"A rose by any other name?" Cahill joked.

A pilot boat led them to an anchoring location. The anchor splashed down, and the sails disappeared. Tisbit was on deck in well-worn civilian attire. "Sir, I should like to disembark as soon as possible. I shall be at least a week before my return."

Duncan nodded. "Jenkins, prepare my gig and please deliver Major Tisbit ashore at whatever location he desires." Then to Tisbit, "Good luck and happy hunting, Major."

"Thank you, sir. I hope you enjoy your time visiting your family."

Duncan went over the harbor watch list with Cahill and authorized Thibeault and the purser to go ashore for supplies over the coming days. Cole agreed to stay on board to oversee the rewatering and other activities necessary to ensure *Enchanté* would be ready to sail again in a week. Cahill and Strickland were granted a few days of leave to see what trouble they could find ashore.

In the evening, Duncan updated his letter to Lillian and then locked it in his desk. He had considered mailing it from here and then starting a new one, but since he would likely be back on Antigua before any mail would arrive, he decided to wait and deliver it by hand. It was not an exciting letter and was really more of a journal describing the events of each day and how often he thought of her. He wanted to share this part of his life and help her to imagine what he was doing when away.

Stanley packed a bag for him, and by the time he put out the lanthorn to go to sleep, everything was prepared for his departure from the ship in the morning.

Duncan was happy to have his boat cloak as his gig made the short row from ship to shore through a cold breeze with a light, misty rain. Jenkins delivered him to a dock near the port admiral's office, and Duncan strode across the slick cobbles and entered the reception hall. A servant met him and took his wet cloak, hat, and bag. The fireplace in the waiting area contained a small fire and Duncan stood close to it, considering how thin his blood had already become from his brief time in the West Indies.

He only had to wait a few minutes before the servant returned and invited him to enter the port admiral's office. The admiral was an elderly man with a balding head and protruding stomach. He had a pair of spectacles perched near the end of his nose and looked over them as he said, "Come in, Captain Duncan. I understand from the letter you provided from Lord Fairhurst that you'll be here for a week or two and would like permission to leave your ship overnight to visit family."

"That is correct, sir. If agreeable, I should like to be gone for up to one week."

"I have no objections. I presume your officers will keep discipline on…" he glanced again at the papers in his hand, *"Enchanté* while you're away. I will not stand for any disturbances ashore."

"Aye, sir."

"Name of Duncan…is your family then, Lord Edgemond?"

"Aye, sir. The Earl is my uncle."

"Will you be staying at Edgemoor if we need to reach you?"

"I've not had the opportunity to warn them of my arrival, but I presume I will be allowed to stay there. Any messages for me can be delivered there, in any event, sir."

"Very well, my compliments to Lord Edgemond, if you please. Your leave is approved." He stamped the paperwork, scribbled a signature across it, and handed it to Duncan.

"Thank you, sir."

"I don't think the rain will last, but it is colder than usual, even for a late August morning. Have a safe journey and I expect you back in a sennight."

With his absence from the ship authorized, Duncan's next task was to procure transportation. He decided to hire a horse and ride, rather than take a carriage. He approached the hostler at one of the largest inns and asked, "Do you have any riding horses for hire?"

The man looked at him for a moment, taking in the naval uniform and shiny boots spattered with mud. "Yeah, I might. For how long and how far…Captain?"

"A week, and I'll be riding about fifteen miles out of town," Duncan responded.

"Hmm…a newish lookin' captain that wants to ride a horse fifteen miles. Any chance you're headin' to Edgemoor?"

Duncan was surprised at this guess, but did not see a reason to deny it. "Yes, that is my destination."

The man smiled broadly, "Then, you must be little Joseph Duncan, come home after all these years. We've been hearin' about your adventures in the Carib, and it was all over town last night what that your ship was here in port."

Duncan did not realize he was such a celebrity and, after allowing himself a moment of pride, he thought to hope that it wouldn't negatively impact Tisbit's chance of success to arrive on a ship of such notoriety.

"I've got a horse for you and maybe we could come to an agreement. The Earl has been lookin' for a horse for his new ward and I think I have just the pretty little mare that would suit nicely. She's too small for you, but I'll give her to you as a pack horse at no cost if you'll take her to Edgemoor for consideration. I'll even charge you half price for a more suitable riding horse for you, if you'll do the favor," the hostler offered.

"And if Lord Edgemond does not accept the mare?" Duncan asked.

"Then you bring her back with you or leave her there and I'll retrieve her…no cost. I only want a chance for her to be seen and considered."

Knowing how much his uncle loved horses, this seemed like both a plausible story and an acceptable course of action. Duncan was unaware of his uncle's new ward and was not in need of a discount, but he did not see any harm in proceeding.

In a few minutes, two grooms led horses out of the stables. The first was a large gray gelding fitted with a saddle and bridle. The second was a small chestnut brown mare with only a halter and lead. Both horses looked like fine animals to Duncan's eye. He would admit to not being an expert on horses, but he had learned enough to know what to look for, and these seemed perfectly acceptable.

By midmorning, the sun had burned off the cloud cover and Duncan was uncomfortably warm. He took off his cloak and eventually shed his uniform coat as well. One benefit of the recent rain was that the road was not dusty. Duncan took a deep breath, and the smells of the scrubby pines and late summer flowers gave him a sudden feeling of nostalgia. Continuing his journey further inland, the trees grew taller and straighter and soon he was in the comfortable shade of a mature forest.

Duncan's stomach was rumbling and his backside was sore from riding as he rounded a familiar bend in the road and got his first sight of Edgemoor in almost thirteen years. He stopped the horses in order to take in the view from the hilltop at the edge of the forest. Before him were the fields and orchards of the sprawling grounds. Perched majestically on the next hilltop was the manor house.

The center of the dark gray stone building was three stories tall, with a two-story wing flanking it on either side. The slate roofs were dark blue and looked almost black against the bright azure sky. To the left of the main building were the low stone stables, and to the right were several wooden barns and other outbuildings. There was a thick hedge outlining a crushed stone courtyard of light brown which matched the twelve-foot-wide drive that led from the road to the courtyard entrance in the hedges.

Some of the wooden buildings were unfamiliar to Duncan, and the stables had been made larger since he left, but the manor house looked exactly as he remembered it. He glanced further down the road and could just make out the cottage in the trees where he had lived with his parents and sister.

He realized he was smiling, but did not know if it was from the memories or the beautiful view of the place he still thought of as home. He clicked at the horse and nudged it forward with his heels, then stopped again to put his jacket back on. He wanted to look as presentable as possible for his surprise visit. Soon, he was off again with the horses at a trot.

Two stable hands met him in the courtyard and took charge of the horses. They led them towards the stables as Duncan walked up the stairs and banged the knocker a bit more loudly than he had intended, due to his excitement. The door opened immediately to reveal a dour-looking butler to whom Duncan said cheerfully, "Hello Hobbs!"

Duncan thoroughly enjoyed watching the sequence of emotions flit across the butler's face. First was confusion, then surprise, the briefest hint of a smile, and then the studied control, which depicted no emotion. "Master Joseph. My, how you have grown to a full man. I'm sorry I don't know what uniform you wear, or how to call you, sir."

"It's a captain's uniform, but Joseph will do fine. Is Lord Edgemond at home?"

"Please come in, Captain Duncan," he said, regaining his full formality. "I'm sorry to report that Lord Edgemond is out at the moment and isn't expected to return for several hours. However, Lady Edgemond is in the gardens. You may refresh yourself from your journey while I inform her of your presence."

"Thank you, Hobbs. Is there a chance I could get some water or lemonade? I'm quite parched from the ride."

"Of course, sir. I shall inform Mrs. Hobbs of your arrival, and she will send a parlor maid with some refreshments."

Hobbs had only just disappeared when Duncan heard a scream from deeper in the house, followed by the housekeeper bursting into the room and shouting, "Why, it is you! I'd hardly recognize you, but for the same mischievous eyes. My, how you've grown. A right fine-looking gentleman you turned out to be, Master Joseph."

"And you look exactly the same, Mrs. Hobbs. It's so nice to see you," Duncan replied.

"Oh bah, you shouldn't lie to my face. I'm older and fatter, but it's nice of you to pretend you don't notice. Oh, the countess will be so happy to see you. We had no idea you were coming. Why ever didn't you let us know, so we could be prepared?"

"Joseph is welcome at any time and need not warn us ahead of time." Lady Edgemond entered the room and gave Duncan a hug. Mrs. Hobbs stepped back and said nothing. "It is so wonderful to see you. How long do we have you for? Please don't tell me you cannot stay for a while."

"You have me for a week, if that's not too long. I shouldn't like to be an imposition. I would have alerted you, but I only arrived last night and decided to come straight here rather than sending a message ahead," Duncan answered.

"Only a week? Why, that's not nearly long enough," his aunt said. "We shall have to make the most of it. The earl is out with your cousin, hunting. They normally return in late afternoon." She turned to indicate a young woman standing near the door. "Allow me to introduce our ward, Miss Isabelle Rossignol."

Duncan had not noticed her, though she must have walked in with his aunt. She was very petite, with dark brown hair and even darker brown eyes. She appeared to be in her late teens and was strikingly beautiful. She curtsied slightly and gave a nervous smile. Duncan gave a slight bow of his head. "A pleasure to meet you, Miss Rossignol."

Lady Edgemond said in a soft voice, "Isabelle recently came from Montreal to live with us and doesn't speak very much English yet. Oh, but I've forgotten that you speak French, so that won't matter so much for you. We have your mother to thank for us getting to know Isabelle. Her family were friends of your mother's family. She lost her parents to influenza this spring and your mother wrote to ask if there was something we might do. Of course, we sent for her immediately."

Three maids entered with trays containing water, lemonade, tea, sweet biscuits, and several types of pastries. Lady Edgemond guided Duncan to a couch and called to Isabelle, "Come sit with us, my dear, and we'll hear all about Joseph's adventures before Lord Edgemond returns and takes him away from us."

Chapter Sixteen

Duncan was still in the sitting room with the ladies talking when the master of the house returned from his hunt. They heard the front door opening and Duncan could make out some muffled discussion followed by his uncle exclaiming, "What? Who? Where is he?" He flung the door open and strode across the room toward Duncan, who hurriedly got to his feet.

His uncle was older, but still looked very much as Duncan remembered him. "Good afternoon My Lord, I hope you don't mind the intrusion," Duncan said with a slight bow.

"Bah, what is this 'lord' nonsense?" the earl bellowed as he grabbed Duncan's hand and shook it vigorously. "I was your namesake and uncle before I was ever an earl. In this house, I shall always be Uncle to you. Joy to you on your promotion, Joseph! We've been reading about your exploits in the paper. Had no idea you'd be this far north, though!"

"Nor did I, Uncle. It was a sudden and unexpected trip. I shan't be long here, however, and will return to Antigua within a fortnight."

Duncan's oldest cousin had followed his father into the room. He had been a grown man already when Duncan had moved to England. He looked much the same, but with some gray hair about his temples and a much thicker waist. He smiled slightly and offered his hand to Duncan, "Hello, Joseph. It is a pleasant surprise to see you after all these years. It seems I can no longer call you Little Cousin Joey."

"It's good to see you, Edward," Duncan replied, as they exchanged a handshake. "You look well." He had never been close to Edward. Their age difference had been too great, and Duncan had still been a child when he left for England. He was surprised by the softness of his cousin's hand. His grip was firm, but clearly, he was not one to do any work that would make his hands rough.

The earl clapped his hands together. "We shall have to celebrate with a dinner. The prodigal son…well, godson, at least, has returned. We must kill the fatted calf and all that."

"Yes, Father," Edward said, "that would be most wonderful. I should be getting home. When would you like to have this dinner?"

"I don't suppose there is any chance we could do it tonight?" the earl looked hopefully at his wife.

"Certainly not!" she exclaimed. "Mrs. Hobbs would not have enough time to do justice to the occasion. Besides, by the time Edward rides home and alerts Sarah, why, she wouldn't have time to prepare herself. It just won't do. Tomorrow. Tomorrow, at the very earliest."

"That is quite true," Edward agreed. "Perhaps if it were winter and we could bring the sleigh across the lake, we might have time, but having to take the carriage around the lake this time of year, I'm afraid it would not be possible this evening."

"Then, tomorrow it is!" the Earl proclaimed.

"My apologies, Joseph," Edward said. "I really must be going. Mother, we shall come early tomorrow and bring the children, if that would be acceptable."

They said their goodbyes, and those remaining sat down. There were two sitting rooms at Edgemoor, and the party was in the smaller, less formal one. The room contained two couches, four chairs, and an upholstered bench arranged in front of the unlit fireplace. The fireplace surround was of very light gray stone with intricately carved wooden columns supporting a large mantle. Above the mantle was the family coat of arms carved from the same rich, reddish-brown wood.

Large tapestries hung on either side of the fireplace, from ceiling to floor. Elsewhere, the walls were set with deep wooden panels. The floor was covered with a brightly colored woolen carpet. The room was both elegant and cozy. It had always been one of Duncan's favorite rooms in the house and was the scene of many lovely memories.

"We have thirteen years of catching up to do in only a few days," his aunt was saying, as he focused on the conversation again. "It wouldn't be so hard, perhaps, if you wrote more often. I don't suppose I can feel too ill-treated, though. From what I understand, you seldom write to your mother, either."

Duncan knew from her tone and the twinkle in her eye that she was teasing him, but he did feel bad for not writing more often. He was about to apologize when his uncle saved him. "You can't expect him to fight the French while he's holding a quill."

They talked until dinner, trading news and stories about themselves, Duncan's parents and sister, his youngest cousin, Daniel, who had gone to India in search of adventure, and their other relatives and common friends. In some ways, it seemed to Duncan like he had not been away long because they fell so easily into conversation. At the same time, however, their lives also seemed worlds apart.

Dinner that first evening ended up as a continuation of the discussions over delicious food served in a single remove. It was an informal family meal with only the earl, the countess, Duncan, and Miss Rossignol present. The young lady was attentive and polite but had very little to add, and Duncan wondered how much she could understand. Even if she could understand, it must all be dreadfully boring to someone unrelated to the family and without any shared history.

The next morning, after breakfast, Duncan wandered into the library and, after perusing several volumes, selected a book to read. It was too nice a day to spend it indoors, so he walked out the rear of the house across the great flagstone patio. At the far end of the patio, was a low stone wall and stairs leading down the hill into the gardens.

He walked down the stairs and turned to the right to follow the perimeter path. He strolled along slowly, smelling the various flowers, and enjoying the scents that smelled to him like home. The trees had grown much larger, and some sections had been changed, but the gardens mostly matched his memories. Further along the oval path, he saw several honey bee skeps sitting in recesses within the outer wall. The busy insects were buzzing in and out and streaking across the garden.

When he got back to the stairs he had come down, he turned onto the path that led to the center of the garden. He passed a massive maple tree that he recalled climbing, and falling out of, as a child. The more rustic and natural landscaping changed to carefully trimmed hedges as he approached the circular pond at the very center of the garden.

He walked down another set of stairs onto the stone pavement surrounding the pond and looked at the dark, still water. He saw a dragonfly skimming along the surface. A frog jumped into the water with a croaking alarm and swam away. Close to the center, there was a partially submerged log with a line of small dark turtles sunning themselves.

Pink, yellow, and white flowers bloomed among the lily pads. Duncan smiled to himself as he was reminded of his own Lily. He went to a bench that was partially shaded by several large willow trees growing outside the hedge to sit down. For a while he just sat there, enjoying the peaceful scene and wishing he could share this moment with Lillian. With a deep sigh, he opened the book and began to read.

Several hours later, Duncan was still sitting there reading when he heard someone approaching. He noted his page and then closed the book. He turned to see his cousin, Heather, approaching with a herd of children. She smiled and waved to him, and he stood up, though they both waited until they were closer before speaking.

She walked directly to him and gave him a hug. "Look at you. I'd have hardly recognized you if Mother hadn't warned me what to expect." His cousin looked older but still had the same calm demeanor and soft voice that he remembered. "It is so wonderful for you to visit. I haven't seen you since my wedding day."

"We left while you were on your honeymoon. I think we would have moved earlier, but Mother and Father would not miss your wedding. You look stunning. Clearly, married life and motherhood agree with you."

Heather gave him a coy smile and said in a conspiratorial tone, "Some days, they do." Then, gathering the children, she added, "Children, this is your cousin, the great naval hero, Joseph - but you are to call him Captain Joseph. Joseph, these are my children. There should be five of them, but I've not counted recently. I'll not trouble you with their names because you won't remember them, anyway." Then to the children, "There, you've met him. Now, off you go and play, but don't leave the gardens. Anne, keep an eye on the little ones, especially John."

She watched them leave. The older boys bounded up the stairs with the youngest boy and girl scrambling to keep up. Following the rest, and herding them along, was the older girl, whom Duncan assumed was Anne.

After the children disappeared beyond the hedge, Heather turned back to Duncan. "I'm sorry to have interrupted your reading. May I sit with you for a while? I'm already too exhausted to go for a walk."

"Of course," Duncan said. "Please sit."

"What are you reading?" she asked, as she took the book from him. "*Candide, ou l'Optimisme*, by Voltair?" She made no attempt to make it sound French. She glanced inside the book and added, "Oh, the whole thing appears to be in French, not just the title." She handed it back. "Is it good?"

"I find it to be an interesting diversion. Actually, the best part was the irony of sitting here and realizing that Voltair is telling us that we must each cultivate our own garden. At least I think that is his main point. He's quite harsh on everyone and everything, but it is humorous in its own way."

"You always did like books. I never have - even ones in proper King's English. Have you met Miss Rossignol? I'm sure she would like to blather away with you in French. Only Father speaks it well enough to converse with her. Daniel was quite fluent, but we haven't seen or heard from him in years. He's married. Did you know that? He got married in India and none of us have ever even laid eyes on the woman. He hardly ever writes and when he does, it takes half a year for letters to arrive."

They talked for quite a long time until Anne came back carrying a small, screaming boy. Heather made her apologies, promised to see him at dinner, and left with the children. Duncan took two more laps around the garden and finished his book before heading back into the house.

Dinner was to be a formal affair that evening. Duncan had not brought any civilian attire that was suitable for the occasion. It occurred to him that he did not own any suitable civilian attire, so the oversight had not just been during packing. He had worn one of his best uniforms to meet the port admiral and had that with him, so that was what he decided to wear.

In addition to the attendees from the last evening were Edward and his wife, Sarah, and Heather, with her husband,

Wilfred Laddler. The meal was quite formal and the conversations somewhat muted. There were three removes and Duncan was beginning to fear the buttons might pop off his jacket when they finally finished.

Most of the food had come from the manor grounds, and Duncan was delighted by the freshness. Several of the made dishes, as well as the preparation of some of the meats, brought back such vivid memories that he almost thought himself a child again, only dreaming of being an adult.

In spite of the formal dinner, formality was dismissed when it was over. Rather than the men and women going into separate rooms, they all moved to the larger sitting room, which contained more places to sit than the one they had been in earlier. It also contained a harp and large pianoforte.

There was no singing or playing this evening, however. Instead, they sat and talked and shared stories. At times it was almost deafeningly loud with everyone talking at once. After a little more than an hour, Duncan noticed the young French girl speaking with his aunt. His aunt nodded and said something in return before Miss Rossignol quietly left the room. She looked sad and Duncan thought again how difficult it must be for her to have lost her family and now be here experiencing this loud gathering in a foreign language.

The multiple conversations eventually started to coalesce into a single discussion. The origin of this was Duncan beginning the story of how he fought the French convoy in response to a request from his uncle. Edward had started to listen, followed by his wife and Wilfred, until finally Heather realized no one was listening to her and she fell quiet as well.

Duncan told the story without the gore and ugliness that had really existed. He knew that to most people outside the military, the war was a distant thing they read about in the papers. Their sanitized view did not allow for the horrors and those were only felt when someone close to them died. Even then, death was such a normal part of life. Unless you were there to witness the event, did it matter that a musket ball smashed your brother's head instead of him dying of a fever? Most people could not comprehend the war, and Duncan had learned to tell the stories in ways they could understand.

He finished with a humorous account of his second meeting with Admiral Lord Fairhurst and his promotion (provisionally) to captain.

"My, but that is quite a tale to tell," the earl said, "and certainly, there is no doubt that your ascendency shall be made permanent. How could it not be?"

"Now that you're a captain, you should be taking a wife and starting a family. Shouldn't you?" Edward said, sounding like he had perhaps drunk a bit too much already this evening. "Maybe you could marry Miss Rossignol. Two birds with one stone, what?"

There was a sudden, awkward silence as everyone was shocked by the comment. Duncan could see his aunt's embarrassment. He recovered quickly and said, "Ah, but I've not had a chance to tell you. I'm already engaged."

Of course, this led to another story and disclosure of the lucky girl's name.

"Huntington-Whiteley? Is she the admiral's daughter then?" his aunt asked.

"Why, yes, she is," Duncan replied in surprise. "I was not aware that you knew the family."

"Your mother writes often about them, and always in a most favorable light. She must be thrilled with your engagement."

"I hope she will be, but it is such a recent happening, I've not had time to tell her," Duncan admitted.

"Well, then, we shall say and write nothing of it until we hear it from your mother. It wouldn't do for us to bear such news, and you can never count on the mail arriving in the same order it is sent," the countess stated.

Duncan was relieved that it was left in this manner. He did not want to try to explain that he had not written to tell his parents because he was letting Lillian surprise his sister with the news. He did not think this course of action would be approved by another mother.

"It seems to me," the earl said, "we should have another dinner to celebrate your engagement. How about in three nights hence?"

The details and timing of another great family gathering were decided, and the evening began to wind down. Edward and Sarah made their excuses, with Edward seemingly embarrassed by his gaff and Sarah clearly quite angry. They were spending the night at Edgemoor to defer the hour and half carriage ride until morning.

Heather and Wilfred lived in a cottage on the estate, not far from the manor house. They made their goodnights and headed home in the crisp night air. Duncan's aunt yawned and said goodnight as well. The two Joseph Duncans - uncle and nephew - were left alone. They moved to the earl's study, sipped brandy, and talked well into the night.

·　　·　　·

The next few days were the most relaxing Duncan could remember since joining the Navy. On the rare occasions that he had been on leave or had been between ships, there had always been something to do or the feeling that time was being wasted. Here at Edgemoor, he had no responsibilities, and nothing was expected of him.

He went riding each morning with his uncle and went on an afternoon hunt with Wilfred and Edward, who apologized sincerely for his drunken comment and was forgiven. Duncan barely knew Wilfred and had only vague memories of him. However, he found that he enjoyed his company…perhaps a bit more than Edward's.

Duncan also spent time reading in the garden and library. He wandered the grounds of the manor and visited Heather and Wilfred early one afternoon. He and his uncle spent much time together. Often, they chatted about happenings in the world, but other times, they just enjoyed each other's company while reading. Duncan had always known his uncle kept an extensive library and, unlike many gentlemen of the day, it was not just for show but indicated a genuine enjoyment of reading.

The second dinner party was as successful and filling as the first. However, this time they did not just retire to the sitting room for conversation, but instead were treated to singing and music by those with skill, and some without. There were games of whist and chess, as well, and everyone, including Miss Rossignol, stayed up until midnight.

The next morning, no one aside from the servants had risen for the day yet besides the earl and the captain. They had just finished eating and Duncan was drinking a cup of coffee while his uncle drank tea when the door to the breakfast room opened. The butler walked in and announced, "A Major Tisbit, requesting to see the captain, My Lord."

Lord Edgemond gave his nephew a quizzical look, to which he responded, "He is a friend and associate, Uncle. However, I was not expecting him."

"Best check into it, then. Duty may call. Quite early for a social visit."

"Thank you," Duncan said, as he stood up. "If you'll excuse me, then?"

Duncan walked into the sitting room to find Tisbit admiring a painting on the wall. "Greetings Jeremy! Or is it Major Tisbit? Are you here in a professional capacity to gather information, or are you here as my friend?"

Tisbit turned and smiled. "Might we agree that both can exist concurrently?"

"I'm beginning to believe I will always have to think in that manner where you are concerned. I didn't expect to see you here. Have you completed your tasks?"

"I don't know as where 'completed' is the correct term, but I have done what I can. I tracked down one of the men and he knew nothing of value. The other has already moved on and I've contacted an associate to continue the search. Having nothing else to do, I thought I'd drop by and check on you."

"Should we be on our way back to Antigua, then?" Duncan asked.

"There's no hurry," Tisbit assured him. "And I promised you at least a week with your family. My report will indicate that I judged it proper to wait two or three days to hear back from my associate before I was ready to depart. Presuming that's acceptable timing for you."

"A fictionalized report? What would Hirschhorn say?"

"Not a fiction as to the actions, but rather a creative interpretation of my intent and reasoning. As to Hirschhorn, he would say something to the effect of 'You've failed me again, Tisbit!' But he won't care in the least when I get back, as I've nothing of value to share with him."

"I'll send word to Cahill to be ready to sail in two days' time. I appreciate you allowing me time with my family…but I'm also somewhat anxious to get back to Lillian."

"Oh, yes! I had almost forgotten that I have that news to report. At least I won't return completely empty-handed."

"Will you be staying here until we depart?"

"If that's an invitation, I accept!" Tisbit responded enthusiastically. "Perhaps there is more still to add to your dossier."

·   ·   ·

Late the next afternoon, Tisbit and Duncan were walking back along the road towards Edgemoor Manor. They had been hunting rabbits with three of the earl's hounds. The dogs were loping along, generally with the men, although they sometimes darted in front and sometimes fell behind. The hunters had not been successful by any measurable criteria and were coming home empty-handed. However, they had enjoyed each other's company, and neither was disappointed with the outcome.

"So, you actually grew up here?" Tisbit said incredulously as he looked around. "How does a Scottish earl end up in the colonies, anyway?"

"That's a bit of a story, actually," Duncan said.

"Well, we've still got a bit of a walk, so let's have at it."

"My father and uncle moved to the colonies in 1756, just as the Seven Years' War started," Duncan began. "My father joined the Army and my uncle settled here. Well, actually on the other side of the lake, in the house where my cousin lives now."

"I think you've skipped something important," Tisbit interrupted. "I can understand your father coming, but why did the heir to an earldom come and why did his family allow it?"

"Oh, Uncle wasn't the heir at the time. They had an older brother. I'll get to that."

"Then I shall endeavor to hold my questions to the end. Please proceed."

"My uncle married a couple of years later and my grandfather, the Fifth Earl of Edgemond, did not approve of the match. That caused bad blood between my uncle and grandfather, but with the Atlantic Ocean between them, I understand it was mostly handled through strongly worded letters."

"My cousin, Edward, was born in…must have been 1760 because he's ten years older than I am. A couple of years later, my older uncle - his name was George - died without issue and Uncle Joseph became the heir to the earldom. Grandfather was still angry but was willing to put emotions aside for the family's sake and wanted my uncle to move back. My uncle was still angry, and he said he'd never move back to Scotland. So, he started building Edgemoor Manor as the new family home."

"Meanwhile, after the Seven Years War, my father decided to settle in the Massachusetts Bay Colony. He met my mum, and they got married. Three years later, I was born and that same year, my grandfather passed away, making my uncle the Sixth Earl of Edgemond.

"With the establishment of the Massachusetts Provincial Congress and the general unrest in the colonies, my parents decided to move here when my sister was born. We lived in the cottage - the same one my cousin, Heather, lives in now. I was five."

"May I ask questions now?" Tisbit asked when Duncan seemed to have finished.

Duncan laughed. "Of course. I haven't bored you enough?"

"It's actually all quite interesting. A family feud over a wife? Seems rather petty in the big picture, but I'm not of the quality and have not always understood such matters," Tisbit said. "So, here are my questions. First, what happened to the Edgemond ancestral lands in Scotland and why did your parents move to England?"

"Ah, those are related, actually. The family still owns the lands and manages them remotely via local agents. It's not just the original holdings in Scotland. The family owns various holdings throughout England and Wales, as well. The time to communicate between here and Great Britain made responses and decisions challenging, and after some significant issues, my uncle asked my father to move back closer to manage things on his behalf. I don't think my mother wanted to live in Scotland, so they ended up in England."

"It's so beautiful here. I can't even imagine a childhood spent on these lands," Tisbit said with real feeling.

"Where did you grow up?"

"London, and not the pretty parts," Tisbit responded. "That's a depressing story and we're almost back. I'll tell you another time if you really care."

"I'll hold you to that."

•   •   •

On the morning of their departure from Edgemoor, Duncan walked into his uncle's study, where the earl was seated at his large desk reviewing some papers. "You wanted to see me, sir?"

"Ah, yes, Joseph. Do come in and have a seat. I wanted a word alone before you leave."

Duncan moved to one of the three chairs in front of the desk and sat down. "It has to do with your upcoming marriage."

Duncan tilted his head in question, but didn't say anything. The earl continued, "I will be doubling your annual allowance, and you can plan on a wedding gift of 10,000 pounds to help you establish a proper home."

Duncan was surprised by his uncle's gift and had not expected an increase in his allowance. "Thank you, Uncle. That is quite kind and generous of you."

"The Duncan family provides for its own. We've a small family and for now, there's plenty to go around. Aside from you being my godson, your father has done the family, and me, a great service over the years by managing our affairs back in the Isles. It is the least I can do, and I shall make it clear to the next Earl of Edgemond that it would be my wish for your support to continue."

"Hopefully, that won't be a concern for many years."

The earl laughed. "I agree whole-heartedly and I've no plans of dying anytime soon. However, one can never be sure of these things, and it is best to be prepared. I hope you'll visit again sooner, or I might not last long enough."

Duncan smiled. "I shall certainly try to get back again sooner. I've had a wonderful time."

"I wish Daniel had been here to see you. Actually, I wish Daniel would just come home. I don't like the idea of him being on the other side of the world. I suppose we must each follow our hearts. I haven't much moral high ground on the subject, given my move here from Scotland when I was even younger. Perhaps he is a bit too much like me."

"I think you could say worse of someone, Uncle. Thank you so much for allowing me to stay, and for allowing me to have Major Tisbit here, as well. It's been a very pleasant respite from the war."

"Oh, you are most welcome here anytime. As long as I live, you should see this as your home. You may come at any time, stay as long as you want, and bring as many friends as you like. It would be particularly nice if you could visit with your wife after you are married. I might not otherwise get a chance to meet her."

"Thank you. I would love to show her Edgemoor and introduce her to the family. We shall have to see about the war and my duties. I've no idea when we'll be married or where I'll be sent afterwards. Speaking of my duties, we should probably be off soon. Thank you for the use of your carriage."

"It is a much more comfortable way to travel such a distance, and it's good exercise for the horses. Your aunt and I don't take the carriage out as often as we used to. I find I prefer to be close to home as I get older."

"What have you decided to do with the horses I brought from Halifax?"

"I'll keep them both. The mare is perfect for Isabelle, and I have to say, I quite like the gelding. I sent payment yesterday along with a wagon with a few things for you to take aboard ship with you. Just some trifles, really, to add to your comfort and table."

"Well, again, I say thank you, and now I must be off." Duncan stood. The earl stood as well, and they shook hands.

"Godspeed, Joseph. Take care of yourself."

There were more tears involved in his goodbyes with his aunt and Heather. Even Mrs. Hobbs was sniffling and found it hard to speak. Edward had said goodbye the previous afternoon and was not present for the final sendoff.

As the carriage pulled away and Duncan waved to the assembly, Tisbit commented, "They certainly seem to like you. There's no accounting for good taste, I suppose."

Duncan laughed and turned back from the window. "Oh, you're just upset that no one cried for you."

"Well, they're not my family...although I can't imagine my family shedding tears. I suppose you're right. I am a little jealous. Thank you for letting me stay and sharing your family with me."

"Did you learn anything to add to my file?" Duncan asked.

"Nothing I shall share with Hirschhorn, but perhaps a few things to remember myself."

The ride back to Halifax was uneventful. Tisbit went directly back to the ship while Duncan went to see the port admiral. The admiral was not available, and Duncan left a message with an assistant to thank him and inform him that they would be setting sail the next day, if the winds were favorable.

Cahill was waiting to greet Duncan as he was piped aboard and saluted the ship. "Welcome back, sir. I trust you had a good visit with your family."

"Quite lovely, thank you. The ship appears to be in one piece. Any problems?"

"None to speak of, sir. Some minor disciplinary issues - the normal, really. We received your message and are ready for sea with all crew aboard. The most exciting thing was trying to fit the wagonload of supplies aboard, sir."

Duncan raised an eyebrow, and Cahill took the hint and explained. "I'm sorry, sir. I had assumed you had sent it. The driver stated that it was being delivered for you ahead of your arrival."

"It was my uncle. How much and what did he send? I had expected it was just some foodstuffs for my personal stores."

"Well, the livestock is forward in the manger, which Mr. Greene had to expand to make room. There were two pigs, a goat, several geese, ducks, rabbits, and chickens. Oh, and a crate of quail, or perhaps it was two crates. The other foodstuffs were taken by Thibeault, except for some of the barrels and the bottles that wouldn't fit in your wine cabinet. They are in the spirit locker."

"Barrels? Barrels of what?"

"Birch beer, mead, and ale, I believe. I think the wine was all in bottles, but there may have been one rundlet. Somehow Thibeault and Stanley got everything else to fit in your storage locker, except the furniture and crates, of course. Those are in your cabin. We didn't think we should open them until your return."

"I suppose I should go take a look. I presume we can still sail and are not resting on the bottom?"

Cahill smiled. "We're still afloat, but it was a near-run thing."

In his cabin, Duncan found two small bookcases and three crates. The first crate contained three brass lamps with glass globes and chain gimbles to hang them. There were also several bottles of oil and some extra wicks. The other two crates contained books and a short note from his uncle that simply said, "No one else in the family likes to read, so you might as well have these."

The bookcases had doors of slatted wood that could be latched to keep the books from falling off the shelves. It actually looked like they could be closed and carried to the hold when clearing for action without having to remove the books. Duncan would have to ask the sailmaker to sew up some canvas covers to protect them.

Stanley had offered to place the books on the shelves, but Duncan was doing it himself so he could do a quick inventory of what was present and determine what he might want to read first. Stanley hovered nearby as Duncan kneeled on the deck. "So, what else came aboard besides all this, the farm, and all the drinks?"

"Oh, sir, some of the most lovely looking food. There are some dried sausages that Thibeault says are venison, and pickles of every sort. Then there were jars of jams and preserves, along with some pots of honey, a big crock of sauerkraut, and several small potted meats, sir."

Duncan shook his head and thought to himself that he'd have to be much better about writing to his aunt and uncle, starting with a long thank you note. His thoughts and book organization were interrupted by the marine sentry announcing Cahill.

"What is it, Mr. Cahill?" Duncan asked, as he stood up.

"I forgot to mention when you came aboard, sir, that there have been several reports by ships coming into port of a ship lurking or watching from the horizon. A sloop was dispatched to look into it but came back without being able to catch it or even get a good sighting. Do you think it's our shadow waiting for us?"

"Well, if it is, we won't be in quite such a hurry on the way back to Antigua. Perhaps we can introduce ourselves properly."

Chapter Seventeen

Duncan pulled an oilskin coat on over his jacket and left his cabin. He walked up the ladderway onto the quarterdeck. The sun had risen, but the dark, low clouds prevented it from being very bright yet. There was a slight drizzle of rain, and the steady wind had a chilling bite to it on this early September morning.

Cahill and the master walked to him immediately, and he greeted them. "Is everything ready?"

"Aye, sir," Cahill responded. "We've only to man the capstan and we can be off."

The master was blowing into his hands and rubbing them together vigorously. "None too soon, neither. I find that I'm too old for these waters and will be happy to be back in the sunny Carrib soon."

Duncan laughed and said, "Well, then let's be off before Mr. Ellis freezes to death."

The master smiled back. "Mighty thoughtful of you, Captain. Thankee kindly."

They sailed out of the bay and once they were in open water, turned to sail as close to south as they could. Visibility was limited, but Duncan had ordered extra lookouts to watch for their mysterious companion. There were other ships and boats in the area, but all seemed to be going about their normal business.

After about two hours, the rain stopped, but the wind was still cold, and the hazy conditions continued to limit visibility. Duncan was just about to head down to his cabin when a lookout called, "Sail ho! Two points off the stern to leeward."

Duncan turned to the nearest midshipman and ordered, "Mr. Webb, take a glass up to the crosstrees and see if the sail is following us."

"Aye, aye, sir!" The young man quickly selected a telescope from the rack and climbed onto the shrouds.

A few moments later, Webb slid down the backstay and landed softly on the deck. He straightened his uniform as he approached Duncan with his report. "I could only get glimpses of her, sir, but she appears to be following our course. It could be the same ship from before."

Duncan accepted the information with a thoughtful look on his face and then replied, "Thank you, Mr. Webb. Carry on." Then he added to Cahill, "I'll be in my quarters if you need me." Without further comment, he walked off the quarterdeck, down the starboard ladderway, and disappeared into his cabin.

After Duncan had left, Cahill looked at the master with a questioning glance. Ellis responded with a shrug of his shoulders and said, "I guess we're waiting. At least in this direction, we should have the wind on our side whenever we turn to meet her."

Cahill nodded slowly in response, looked back toward the mysterious follower, and said, "Aye. It seems she'll be there whenever we take our chance."

The next few days passed by without incident as *Enchanté* continued her journey south with the other ship following. Occasionally, the masts of the ship would be visible from the deck, but normally one had to be in the crosstrees to see her. Even from that height, she was seldom close enough to show her hull. There was no way to make out details or learn much more about why she lurked there.

On the third evening, after they left Nova Scotia, Duncan hosted a game of whist in his cabin. They had played enough to know that Tisbit and Cole were the superior players, so they kept things interesting by not allowing them to be partners. Based on a draw of cards, Duncan was Tisbit's partner on this evening, while Cole and Strickland formed the other team. Divided this way, they were very evenly matched.

Stanley quietly entered the cabin, placed two plates of cold meats, cheeses, and nuts on the side table, and stood waiting. They completed the hand and Tisbit announced, "Ha! We've made three points and taken the game, Captain. Unless I'm mistaken, we are now tied at two games each for the evening thus far."

Duncan nodded to Stanley and replied, "I believe you are correct. Shall we take a short break? Stanley can refill our drinks, and it appears he's brought some snacks."

They all stood and stretched. Cole moved to the side table and found a few pickles that interested him. Stanley moved quickly around the group, refilling glasses before leaving the cabin. After a few minutes, they made their way back to the table and took their seats. Cole said, "The deal falls to you, sir. Shall I shuffle?"

"Yes, please do," Duncan responded. "Would you mind if I mixed business with pleasure by asking some questions concerning the sail that follows us?"

Strickland answered first. "I enjoy my posting so much, sir, that I see my business as a form of pleasure, so I take no issue."

"I very likely have little to add to a conversation about ships and sailing, but I have no objection to the topic, sir," Tisbit said before taking a sip of his birch beer.

Cole finished shuffling and placed the deck in front of Duncan. "My father says that I should take every opportunity to learn my craft, sir, so I would welcome the discussion."

Duncan handed the deck to Strickland to cut and then began to deal the cards. "What are your thoughts on how we might draw close enough to engage with our shadow?"

Tisbit asked in return, "How do we know the ship is an enemy with whom we need to engage? Might it not also be a friendly or neutral vessel?"

Strickland answered Tisbit's questions, "A friendly vessel would be unlikely to keep such careful distance and there are precious few neutrals in this war. I suppose it is possible it's an American ship, but it seems most likely to be French. Perhaps not a national ship, but a letter of marque."

Cole added, "We're a long way off the American coast. Why would a Jonathan want to follow us? I agree there is every reason to expect it to be an enemy of some type, and the French are the old enemy."

Duncan finished dealing and laid the last card, a three of hearts, face up in the center of the table. "Hearts shall be trump. Perhaps I should not have used the word 'engage'. We would, of course, have to confirm the flag before engaging, but we must get close enough for identification since they seem intent on keeping their distance and following in our wake."

"Could we not turn and run with the wind towards them?" Tisbit asked.

Again, Strickland answered him, "We could, but if it's the ship that followed us north, I doubt we could win a footrace even with the wind on our best point."

"Why do you say that, sir?" Cole asked, sounding almost offended. "*Enchanté* is a fast ship and her bottom is still mostly clean."

"Aye, she's a fast ship, and we were driving her rather hard on the way to Nova Scotia. Yet, our shadow followed us easily.

Sometimes she'd be out of sight in the morning, but by noon sights she'd be back on her station. Clearly, she could match, if not exceed, our speed and we were often on our best point of sail."

Cole looked crestfallen. "I hadn't considered that, sir."

"Could we double back at night?" Tisbit offered. "In about a week, there'll be no moon. Could we not turn back in the darkness and close the distance without them knowing?"

"We should have to be very lucky," Strickland said as he trumped Tisbit's ace of diamonds. "Her position varies several points off our stern. Were we to turn back when she could not see us, then one might presume we could not see her. We would have to guess at her location."

"But surely we could get closer and have a chance to run her down," Tisbit persisted.

Strickland collected the trick and threw off by leading with a two of clubs. "Yes, but if she can outsail us with the wind, we'd have to be within cannon shot at sunrise to force her to yield or fight."

Duncan followed suit with a queen, and Cole added the ace before asking, "Could we not deliberately sail back beyond her to avoid her running with the wind?"

Tisbit frowned as he was forced to follow suit, allowing the trick to go to Cole. "I think I know the answer to that one. If she is brig-rigged, as we believe her to be, then there's every reason to think she could outrun us to windward just as easily. Am I correct, or have I revealed why my uniform is red instead of blue?"

"Quite correct," Strickland answered. "I should think we could rather easily lose her by changing course at night and sailing an unpredictable pattern for a few days. But to force an engagement? I don't see any option that doesn't depend upon luck."

They played on in silence for a few minutes until Strickland took the last trick by playing his remaining trump card. He smiled and exclaimed, "Ah, a grand slam! It seems we've taken the game in a single hand, Mr. Cole."

Tisbit slumped back in his chair and said, "Captain, I should like to change my vote. It seems that talking business distracts us more than our opponents."

Duncan smiled. "We've essentially just repeated the conversation I had with the master and first lieutenant this afternoon. You've corroborated our conclusions. Perhaps we can forego any further talk about the ship and have a chance to redeem ourselves in the next game. Thank you all for your input."

Not talking about it did not help Duncan to not think about it, and the evening ended seven games to four, in favor of Strickland and Cole. The two lieutenants thanked Duncan for his hospitality and left together. After they closed the door, Duncan said to Tisbit, "Would you care for brandy? I'm sorry I wasn't a better partner this evening."

"Yes, please. I think you probably owe me that. You were simply awful," Tisbit responded. "What do you plan to do about the shadow ship?" He seemed to be able to instantly switch between the role of respectful subordinate officer to relaxed friend. The sudden change made Duncan smile.

"I'm duty bound to at least try to engage with her," Duncan said, as he moved to the sidebar and poured them each a glass of brandy. "As it seems, luck must play a large role. I suppose I shall wait until I feel luck is on our side."

"I find luck to be a fickle friend. I prefer to make my own way."

"Aye, we'll see what the next few days bring us and what we can make of it." Duncan handed a glass to Tisbit and collapsed back into his chair. They did not bother to move to the comfortable leather chairs, sitting instead at the table.

"At least there is no need to hurry. She seems content to follow us to Hell and back - or at least to Nova Scotia and back."

"Yes, and I'd really like to know why." Duncan paused to take a sip of his drink. "Did you find Nova Scotia to be that bad?"

"Oh, no, not at all. Quite the contrary, really. I found it to be rather enjoyable, especially the diversions of my time at Edgemoor. You are very lucky to have lived there and your family is quite lovely. Except maybe Edward...he's fine, but I wouldn't necessarily choose to spend time with him."

"You didn't seem to mind spending time with Miss Rossignol," Duncan commented.

Tisbit studied his brandy and replied flatly, "I really have no idea of your meaning, sir. We were the outsiders from the family, so perhaps we found it easier to talk to one another. Besides, her difficulties with the English language were quite apparent and a gentleman could not sit by without offering some assistance."

"I hadn't known you spoke French so fluently. Your accent is a bit provincial, but you have a thorough command of the language."

"Know thy enemy, and all that. It is my job to speak French - and to have an ill-defined but acceptable accent. It allows me to avoid a connection to any particular area or questions about the particulars of the region."

Duncan was a bit surprised by the blunt comments. "I hadn't thought of it as a tool of your trade, but you make a good point. There are more layers to you than would seem from your rather brightly colored uniform."

Tisbit smiled broadly. "And that is another part of the illusion."

After several days of beautiful weather and consistent, even if largely contrary winds, a series of squalls struck the ship. There was nothing particularly dangerous about the storms, but they quickly reduced visibility and made the sea choppy and hard to read. The ship was buffeted and occasionally lurched one way or another.

Duncan stood on deck, watching another squall approach. The dark clouds blotted out the sun and the thick rain looked like a misty wall moving towards them. He watched, considered, and calculated. He made his decision and ordered, "Beat to quarters! Call all hands and clear for action!"

No one had been expecting the order, but everyone responded instantly. The marine drummer beat a strong staccato tune while the boson's pipes sounded their shrill commands. Men poured from the ladderways, and hundreds of bare feet pounded across the deck as everyone rushed to their stations. Ten minutes later, the ship had been transformed and was ready for battle. The cannons had been loaded and the wispy trails of smoke from the slow match drifted about in the wind.

The leading edge of the squall enveloped the bowsprit and, even from the quarterdeck, it became blurred by the torrential rain. The wall of rain moved down the deck towards Duncan. The sailors standing exposed on the deck were instantly drenched but none reacted. This was just part of being in the navy and at least the rain would wash some of the salt out of their clothes and make them a little more comfortable once they dried.

Duncan stood with his hands clasped behind his back and his legs braced against the erratic motions of the ship. The rain moved over him, and he felt it pounding on his hat. He waited a few more moments and then ordered, "Bring her about!"

The helmsmen spun the wheel and topmen raced up the shrouds as sails were adjusted and trimmed. On deck, men pulled and hauled ropes while fighting for traction on the slippery wooden planks. Soon *Enchanté* was heading back in the direction from which she had just come and was picking up speed as the wind filled her sails and the rain whipped against her.

The wind driving them was pushing the rain ahead of them, and they could not outrun the squall. Duncan was counting on that and hoping they would be obscured enough that the ship following them would not realize they had turned and were closing in on them.

For what seemed like an eternity but was in reality only slightly more than half an hour, they continued in this way. The rain pounded heavily, and the wind swirled and gusted about the deck. The gun crews were trying to shelter the slow match to keep it from being extinguished by the rain. Duncan wanted to look at his watch, but did not want to risk exposing it to the elements. The glass was turned and the bell struck, finally providing some definite indication of time having passed.

If the following ship had not altered course and had maintained its speed, they would be closing the initial twelve miles distance at a combined speed of something close to eighteen knots. Soon they would either see the ship or it would be likely they had sailed past it in the storm.

Cole suddenly yelled and pointed, "There, sir! Two points off the windward bow!"

Duncan, as well as everyone else on the quarterdeck, looked in that direction and, through a slight lessening of rain, he could make out the other ship. From the location, it seemed she must have altered course to head more directly into the wind. This made sense when Duncan considered it. The smaller ship would be trying to take the seas more directly to lessen the impacts of the storm and maintain what speed she could.

"Mr. Ellis, alter course to intercept." Duncan had no sooner given the command than he saw action on the other ship as she began to turn. "Belay that! Watch her and keep us closing, Mr. Ellis. It seems we've been spotted."

Just as Strickland had predicted, either both ships could see each other, or neither could see the other. The intensity of the rain and squall varied over the next few minutes, with the ships periodically being able to see almost clearly before being totally obscured. Ellis made course corrections each time they could see the other ship well enough to make out her location and rough heading.

Duncan considered the actions of their rival. Given their relative locations, points of sail, and the direction of the wind, he had anticipated his adversary to turn to leeward and run before the wind. However, the ship had instead turned to windward. This would ultimately bring them closer together.

He pictured the ships and wind in his mind and realized that it was a gamble by the other captain. If they could stay just out of range and cross *Enchanté's* bow, then they would eventually be able to point closer to the wind and pull away without allowing a broadside to bear. Everything now depended on the smallest details - and frustratingly, on luck.

Over the next hour, the rain lost its intensity and turned into a misty drizzle. The gusts of wind became less severe and less frequent. There was still a large swell, and the winds were far from consistent. These factors favored *Enchanté,* as she was the heavier vessel, and the more consistent visibility allowed the master to make smaller course adjustments in order to maintain as much speed as possible.

There was almost complete silence, except for the sounds of the wind, the sea being pushed into a wake, and the creaking of the ship's rigging. It was as if everyone were holding their breath and waiting to see what would happen next. Even the master spoke in hushed tones as he instructed the helmsmen.

Lieutenant Cole had taken a telescope up the mainmast and Duncan saw him climbing back down the shrouds. He was glad to see that Cole had begun the transition to acting like an officer and had the dignity to take the long way down rather than sliding down a backstay as he would have a few months earlier when still a midshipman.

Cole approached him, not seeming to even be out of breath from the climb. "Sir, I've gotten a good look at her, but there's not much to report. It's a large brig - very large, perhaps 500 tons, or more. She flies no ensign or colors. We're still more than a mile off, so obviously I can't see the crew well, but I can't make out any uniforms. I don't think she's a national ship, sir. I also would hazard a guess that she's not British. The cut of her sails and the rake of her masts looks...foreign, sir. Not necessarily French, though. I think she's probably privately owned, but by whom, I really can't say."

Duncan frowned. "Thank you, Mr. Cole. Your eyes and your observations are always sharp. I trust your views and appreciate your opinions. You may carry on and return to your duty station."

Ellis spoke from his position near the wheel, "She's adjusting course again, sir. This will tell. If she crosses our bow, she's all but gone from us."

Duncan gave the master a short nod of acknowledgment and then ordered, "Run up the colors! General signal to heave to and fire a warning gun across her bow!"

There was a quick flurry of activity as the crew in various locations complied with the orders. A few minutes later one of the chase guns barked out and the smoke was instantly whipped away by the wind. They were firing at extreme range in rough seas. He watched closely and saw the shot hit a wave and skip harmlessly past the other ship's stern. So much for a shot across the bow.

The other ship continued as if they had not noticed the shot or the signal, and it became clear that they would win this battle of positioning. Duncan maintained the pursuit for another two hours in the hope that the other ship might suddenly make a mistake or suffer some damage. The distance between the ships continued to increase. He recalled his father once telling him that hope was not a strategy and sighed to himself as he gave the order, "Put us back on course for Antigua, Mr. Ellis. Lieutenant Cahill, secure the ship from general quarters and put her back together until next time."

As if mocking him, the sun came out and shined brightly on the quarterdeck at that very moment. Duncan started to walk towards the ladderway to head toward his cabin and dry clothes. He realized his cabin and his clothes were not there at the moment and turned to continue pacing the deck instead. He would have to wait a while to allow the crew time to secure the guns, reconstruct his cabin, and carry his belongs up from the hold. At least the sun felt warm and reminded him of Antigua…and Lillian.

•   •   •

"Land ho!" came the call from the lookout. "Two points off the leeward bow."

"That'll be Barbuda, if I'm not mistaken, sir," the master stated.

"Congratulations on another demonstration of your navigational prowess, Mr. Ellis," Duncan responded.

This was the first land they had sighted since Bermuda and they were exactly where Ellis had predicted. If the winds held, they should be anchored in English Harbour by late afternoon or early evening at the latest.

There were no incidents, and the sun was just above the horizon as they got their first glimpse of the harbor and prepared to sail in. Stickland lowered a telescope and said, "Sir, *Glory* does not appear to be at anchor, and I see a strange third rate flying a commodore's pennant."

"That's odd." Duncan took a telescope from the rack to confirm what Strickland had said. "I wonder what would have caused the admiral to leave and how we ended up with some newcomer in charge…hmm…well, I guess it will be an eleven-gun salute then, Mr. Chapman. We'll save a little powder, anyway."

Mr. Chapman, the gunner, chuckled softly. "Aye, sir. Eleven it will be." He walked down the ladderway to prepare the signal guns for the salute.

Enchanté was directed to a new berth windward of the new third rate, whose name they could not make out. The anchor splashed down, the echoing of the saluting guns died out, and they went about setting things right for being back in port. Midshipman Webb was squinting through a telescope in the direction of the commodore's ship.

Duncan watched him for a moment and then asked, "Mr. Webb, are you sightseeing? Haven't you other duties to which you should attend?"

Webb jumped in surprise and lowered the glass. "Sorry, sir. It almost looks like a signal, but I can't make out the flags or even quite tell if they are there at all, sir. It seems like they might be blowing directly towards us."

"Aye, sir," Lieutenant Cole spoke up, pointing across the bay. "Look over there. *Charger* has just shaken out the repeat signal with our number and captain repair aboard."

"Ah, thank you both. Have my gig brought around and I'll dash down to my cabin for my sword. I guess I get to meet the new commodore posthaste."

A few minutes later, Duncan was rowed across the smooth water to the entry port of the new third rate, which was, in fact, the very old third rate, HMS *Fame*. When Duncan saw the name on the transom, he recalled that one of his previous commanders, George Vancouver, had served in *Fame* as a lieutenant during the Battle of the Saintes. That had been over thirteen years ago and the ship, despite the fresh paint, looked as old and tired as she probably was.

Duncan clambered up the side and was met on deck by a harried looking lieutenant who led him to the commodore's cabin. He was left standing there for several minutes before he was finally invited in with a gruff, "You can get in here, now!"

Duncan approached the desk and stood at attention. "Captain Joseph Duncan, of His Majesty's Ship *Enchanté,* reporting as ordered, sir."

"So nice of you to finally bring my ship back," the commodore said in a snide voice. "I am in desperate need of frigates, and I was sadly disappointed to find out that one had been sent on messenger duty with an acting captain in charge."

Duncan was not sure how to respond, so he chose to keep quiet. The commodore either did not notice or did not mind, and continued, "Out of respect for my predecessor, Admiral Lord Fairhurst, I will allow you to remain as her 'captain' until we receive word from Admiralty that your promotion has been denied. However, you'll remain anchored until then. I'll need the ship with a proper captain ready for sea as soon as word arrives."

"Aye, aye, sir," Duncan said, not knowing how else to respond.

"I really don't know what the admiral was thinking. The regulations are quite clear since last year that only those on the list of commanders can be advanced to the rank of captain. I have it from the very best authority that no exception will be made in your case. My understanding, and again this comes from good authority, is that even promotion to commander is not assured. The decision was expected to be handed down soon after I departed England and it is probably following close behind me. Personally, I have no objection to you being promoted to commander for your little 'action'. However, I think it only fair to point out that I have no sloop available for you, so your best future is likely to be finding employment somewhere as a lieutenant, or you'll be on the beach."

Again, Duncan was at a loss for words. Everything the commodore was saying could be true, despite the tactless manner in which it was being said.

"I should not expect an inexperienced officer, such as yourself, to understand the political workings of our government," the commodore added condescendingly. "You may return to *Enchanté*...what a horrid name for a King's ship...and await my next orders. I just wanted to get a look at you. I'm a bit disappointed after all I read in the papers. I thought you'd at least be taller. If I call you back again, be quicker next time. I don't like to be left waiting."

"Aye, aye, sir," Duncan said, and then forced himself to add in a civil tone, "Joy to you on your appointment, sir, and welcome to the West Indies. Good day, sir."

The commodore frowned even deeper and glared at Duncan as he turned and left. He crammed his hat on his head and took a deep breath after leaving the cabin. He went directly to the side and into his gig while trying hard not to explode. Jenkins sensed the mood and headed back to their ship without question or comment.

Cahill greeted him at the entry port and said, "Sir, the mail bag arrived while you were gone. I expected you to be longer with the flag and I took the liberty of distributing it. I hope you don't mind. You have several letters and documents in your cabin."

"Thank you," Duncan responded flatly as he walked to his cabin, seeing the world through a haze of anger, worry, and disappointment.

His mood was temporarily buoyed when he found a letter in Lillian's hand atop the pile of correspondence. He opened it quickly and began to read.

My Dear Fiancé,

I must begin with an apology for the brief nature of this communication. Please know that you are in my every thought and believe that I will write in more detail and in less hurried a hand than I do now. Time, however, is in short supply at the moment and I must be quick.

The events of the last fortnight have taken us from highest to lowest and back again. With such rapidity, I can barely catch my breath. I shall endeavor to describe the major events in something approaching their actual sequence and promise a more thorough and detailed description as soon as I am able. So that you will understand my need for expediency, I shall begin the story by informing you of the current situation.

We are packed, and it is but hours until the carriages shall take us to the docks so that we might begin our journey back to England.

Even to write it fills me with both the excitement of returning home and the dread of not being still here upon your return to this warmer island. Let me now try to summarize how this has come to be.

Two Mondays ago, we were prepared to receive you for dinner to celebrate our engagement, as we had planned and agreed. My concern was great when the anticipated hour approached, passed, and then receded. Each minute filled me with dread that something awful had happened to you or that you had changed your mind about our engagement. Despite the attempts of Mother and Father to console me, I was inconsolable.

Being more familiar with the workings of the military and guessing that it was duty to Country, not lack of duty to your fiancée, that prevented you from attending, Father wrote a note to Lord Fairhurst to enquire as to your whereabouts.

He need not have bothered that good gentleman, for no sooner had the messenger departed than one appeared with your note explaining everything and putting my heart at ease. My concern and worry were at once transformed to disappointment and understanding.

We were further put at ease when, upon the next afternoon, Father received a reply from Lord Fairhurst confirming that you had been sent to sea on an urgent matter. I was happy to learn your destination to be Halifax and hope you will be able to visit your uncle, aunt, and cousins *while there. I was devastated to hear that you would be gone several weeks or perhaps even months and feared that we might leave before your return. However, at that time, we had no definite plans, and I clung to the hope of being here whenever you might be able to return.*

Last Wednesday, I awoke with a start - remembering at once that it was the very day we had agreed to return together to the goldsmith to claim the engagement ring you had commissioned. Although I know now, I had no reason for concern. That morning my concerns were great that the ring might be thought abandoned and sold to another. I couldn't bear to think of not having it, and I convinced Father to go with me to the goldsmith to see if we might somehow acquire the ring, or at the very least make arrangements to keep it safe until your return.

You cannot imagine our surprise when the smith informed us that a gentleman had already retrieved the ring and fully settled the account! My heart leaped that you might have returned early but fell immediately as the smith confirmed that it was not you who retrieved it. His description of the gentleman having but one hand solved the mystery and left us in no doubt as to the identity of the gentleman as your good friend, Mr. Williams.

Knowing not what else to do and feeling now that the ring was at least in good hands and safe for the time being, we returned home to find the aforesaid worthy soul waiting patiently in our sitting room drinking tea with Mother.

He explained your request of him, congratulated us quite heartily for our happy news, and presented to me the ring and the note you had given him to accompany it. The ring is absolutely beautiful, and I find myself often staring at it and thinking of you. I would of course have preferred you to be here in person to give it me and place it on my finger (it fits perfectly by the bye) but since you could not be, your note and the loving thoughts expressed therein, filled my heart with joy.

I was so taken by the ring and captivated by your note that I missed a conversation between Mr. Williams and Father but finally coming out of my personal revelry I came to understand that Mr. Williams had offered us passage on one of his ships, or I should more accurately say one of his father's ships.

All was quickly agreed, the sailing date set, and we began packing almost at once. And so, I find myself at the end of the story and about to leave for England. I also find that my "short note" has taken almost three sheets of paper and my time is very short until we leave.

So, I must close and promise to write again soon and provide more details, but for now I am off. I miss you and I look forward to us being reunited in England and wed. I pray it will be soon but will wait patiently as long as needs be. I still have the joy of surprising your sister with our happy news and shall write to you about that, as well.

Yours Forever,

Lily

Duncan slumped down in his chair and looked again at the date of the letter. It had been written only a day short of a month ago. Lillian and her family must be almost to England by now. They might hear the news of his not being promoted before he received confirmation himself.

•   •   •

The next morning, he was sitting at his desk responding to correspondence and catching up on world events by reading old papers when Midshipman O'Toole was announced and entered the cabin carrying a wicker basket.

"Excuse me for interrupting, sir, but this just arrived from shore for you."

Duncan raised an eyebrow and said, "Thank you." O'Toole placed the basket on the desk and left the cabin.

The smell wafting up from the basket was wonderful and immediately recognizable. There was a note tucked into the side, which he took out to read. "Dear Joseph, I hope you now have something more to miss when at sea. Since I cannot be here to welcome you, know that I am thinking of you. Love, Lily." He pulled back the cloth and found two delicious-looking loaves of fresh white bread. Despite his worries and concerns, he smiled and felt a pricking of tears at the corner of his eyes.

"Stanley! Be so kind as to bring a plate, bread knife, and some fresh butter, would you?"

Chapter Eighteen

Duncan's anger had completely faded to worry by evening when he met Tisbit for dinner. They were seated by a table at a chop house on a hill overlooking the bay. Tisbit had left the ship almost as soon as they had anchored, and Duncan had not had the opportunity to speak to him since his interview with the commodore. He could not share the discussion with anyone else and he had sulked and worried about what would happen if the commodore was correct. What would Lillian think, and how embarrassing it would be after acting the part of captain for this long?

Tisbit was laughing by the time Duncan finished his description of the encounter. "He actually said that? He thought you'd be taller? Haha! What a pompous windbag!"

Duncan could not help but smile in spite of himself as he took a drink of wine. "I didn't even know his name then. He was wearing the sash and badge of a Knight Companion of the Most Honorable Order of the Bath, but I didn't know if he was a lord, and I wasn't sure how to address him." He put a sarcastic emphasis on the honors.

"I can think of several words to describe him, but 'lord' is not among them," Tisbit said, as their food was placed on the table.

"Does he always sit around wearing his sash, I wonder? From what I've heard, Sir Charles Elliott is only a 'sir' because he has influential family and friends with creative interpretations of military prowess. The commodore has never fought a significant action or accomplished much of note. He's likely jealous of you more than anything."

"But what if he's right? Everything he said makes sense."

Tisbit looked earnestly at his friend. "You simply cannot be serious. You're not actually worried about what he said, are you? First of all, the war is going horribly, and your action provided a bright spot for the government to play up in the papers to make it look better. Especially now that Spain has signed a peace treaty with France. We're alone in the war, without even a token ally. After publishing your exploits, they simply could not afford to let you go unrewarded or have the public think you've been slighted. You're a bloody hero, for goodness' sake!"

He paused and then added with an impish grin, "Even Sir Charles thinks they should make you taller. Besides, Lord Fairhurst simply does not make mistakes. Have faith, my friend. All will be set right soon enough."

"Was not the timing of the admiral's replacement rather odd?" Duncan asked.

"Oh, it was a bit earlier than anticipated, but he was expecting to end his tour soon. As you recall, that's how you ended up with Strickland. He was ready to go, and as I understand it, he sailed the day after Commodore Idiot, I mean Elliott, arrived to succeed him."

Duncan snorted and almost choked on a bite of fish. "You should be careful, Jeremy. I don't disagree with your assessment, but he is the commanding officer on station now."

"He's not my commanding officer, and Hirschhorn will protect me if it comes to that. The old bag has to be worth something, after all. Did I tell you he already knew about you and Miss Lillian? Sometimes I really hate that man…well, most times, really. Still, he absolutely despises Elliott, so I suspect he's itching for a chance to put him in his place."

"Does Hirschhorn really have that kind of power?"

Tisbit shrugged. "I wouldn't test him, and not many people worry me."

"Interesting. I guess I still have a lot to learn about this business of intrigue."

"If you need someone on your side, Hirschhorn is a good choice," Tisbit elaborated. "I just wouldn't suggest trusting him behind your back. He likes you and he respects Lord Fairhurst. He'll do what he can to support you. I'm sure of that."

The conversation turned to less weighty topics, and Duncan enjoyed the distraction from his worries. They finished the meal and had just stood to leave when Tisbit nodded towards the entrance and teased, "There's your good friend, George Henry."

Duncan looked in that direction and said, "How is it that you seem to know everything about me and my associations?"

Tisbit laughed and responded, "Occupational hazard. Still, it was nice of him to repeat that signal for you. I bet he dropped a few spots on Elliott's list of favorites from that."

Duncan looked at Tisbit and then back to Henry. "Again, you surprise me with your knowledge, and even more with your insight."

Tisbit smiled and winked before walking off on his own.

Duncan walked over to his old shipmate and said quietly, "Hello George. Thank you for the signal when we came back into port."

Commander Henry looked around quickly and then said, "You're welcome…sir. I know we were never friends, but we are fellow officers. Sometimes the enemy doesn't fly the French flag, if you know what I mean." Just then, the rest of his party walked in, and he added in a louder voice, "Have a good evening, sir. It was nice to see you."

Duncan nodded and left the restaurant, not knowing exactly what to think of anything at the moment.

The next few weeks were the longest and hardest for Duncan since his first days as a midshipman. On two occasions he was summoned to the flagship, only to be told that the commodore was suddenly too busy to see him. There were constant requests for reports and account summaries, and all the while *Enchanté* swung at her anchor cable with no hope of going to the open sea where she belonged.

Duncan watched wistfully as the other ships of the squadron came and went on various cruises and missions. He felt like a bystander in the war and in spite of what Tisbit said, he worried that this was only the prelude to even worse times if his commission was not confirmed.

In the darkest moments, he wondered if Lillian would still want to marry him. He could not see how he would go back to being a lieutenant. Most of the time he could convince himself that he would at least be promoted to commander. That would provide some salve for his wounded pride, and at least if he was without a ship, he could go back to England and be with Lillian. Then he would wonder if she would want him, and he would spiral through all the possibilities again.

He had never worried so much about the future, and it occurred to him that this was because he had never before felt that he had so much to lose. It seemed like there should be some type of consolation in the realization that he had been so lucky. However, he could not keep the feeling of being lucky with what he had without worrying more about losing it all.

The days had started to blur together, and it was a dreary Saturday morning approaching mid-October when he received a note from Ebenezer Hirschhorn inviting him to visit that afternoon. He scribbled a response, accepting the offer, and sent it off with Midshipman Hyde to be delivered.

Duncan was on deck gazing around the bay when he saw the commodore's pennant being lowered from *Fame's* masthead, followed by a new pennant breaking out and flowing in the strong breeze. It seemed that Commodore Sir Charles Elliott had received his promotion to Rear Admiral of the Blue. "Oh, happy day," Duncan said to himself before heading back to his cabin.

A few minutes later, Midshipman Powell came to Duncan's cabin and announced, "Sir, signal from the flag for captain to repair aboard. Also, sir, it appears the commodore is now an admiral. The pennants have been changed."

Despite his best efforts to keep his emotions in check, Duncan sighed. "Thank you. Call my boat crew and I'll be on deck in a few minutes."

On the off chance that the new admiral actually wanted to see him this time, he wore his best uniform and made sure everything was proper and ready. He would not give Elliott an easy way to find fault with his appearance or actions. There was no practical difference with their relationship caused by Elliott's promotion, but it might embolden him to further harass Duncan.

After being rowed across to *Fame* and climbing through the entry port, Duncan was left waiting, as had become the custom. However, this time he was finally met by the flag lieutenant who led him to the admiral's cabin. Even more surprisingly, he was invited to enter after only a few more minutes of waiting.

He approached the desk where Elliott was seated. "Captain Joseph Duncan, reporting as ordered, sir. Congratulations and joy to you on your promotion, sir."

Duncan stood silently at attention, awaiting a response. Elliott looked at him and frowned. After a moment, he tossed a packet of documents onto the desk and said flatly, "It seems your promotion has also been confirmed. Your commission and orders arrived by mail packet this morning. That's your copy. So, joy to you as well. That will be all."

Duncan froze for a moment, making sure he understood what he had just heard. Finally, he stammered, "Thank you, sir."

"Well, go ahead and take it then and get out of here. I'm very busy at the moment."

Duncan took the documents and tried as best he could to suppress a smile. "Thank you again, sir, and have a good day."

•   •   •

Duncan handed his dripping cloak and hat to a servant before another led him up the stairs. Hirschhorn was waiting for him on a covered porch that led to an open deck where the afternoon rain continued to pour down. There were two rattan chairs with fabric cushions arranged with a small table between them.

"Ah, Captain Duncan, welcome. Please have a seat and make yourself comfortable," Hirschhorn greeted him and motioned to a chair. They both sat down as three more servants deposited trays containing glasses, a pitcher of lemonade, cups, hot tea, assorted small pastries, and sweetmeats. One of the servants poured a cup of tea for the master of the house while Duncan chose a glass of lemonade.

"I find that tea tastes best on rainy days. I seldom drink it otherwise. I've been so long in the tropics, I suppose I've mostly lost my taste for hot drinks." The servants all departed and Hirschhorn continued, "Congratulations and joy to you on your promotion being confirmed - not that there was ever any real doubt of that transpiring."

"Thank you, sir. I must admit that I did not share your confidence and I'm relieved to have the confirmation in hand." Duncan wondered how the news had traveled so fast, but then recalled Hirschhorn's occupation. Had Hirschhorn already known when he sent the invitation? It was possible and made Duncan wonder who really controlled information on Antigua.

"You've been listening to so much nonsense from that blowhard, Elliott, I suppose. You would do best to completely disregard anything that man says. He is lacking in spine, character, and brains. He is really nothing more than a puppet for his benefactors. And they are little better than he, in the end."

Duncan suppressed a smile. Tisbit was certainly correct in regard to Hirschhorn's dislike of the commodore cum admiral. He responded carefully, "Thank you for the advice, sir."

"Did he try to convince you that the confirmation could not happen because you were not on the list of commanders?" Hirschhorn asked.

"Aye, sir. He did mention that."

"Of course he did. It was his benefactors who put forward such a silly objection. There was no way it could have stood on its own and Fairhurst is much too sly to not account for it to begin with. He simply submitted two acting commissions for you. The first, with which he didn't bother to supply you a copy, was to commander of some such sloop. I don't recall the name and it doesn't really matter. The second was as captain of *Enchanté*. Everyone with half a brain saw the advantage of promoting you to captain. True, there were some who felt they must follow the rules, but Fairhurst provided them with a way to ease their discomfort by seeing it as two successive promotions. Never play chess with that man. He is always many steps ahead of any adversary."

"What do you mean by saying they would see the advantage of my promotion?"

"Well, there are several aspects to that, as there are with most issues of consequence. First, your actions brought credit to the Navy, so a reward not only reflected well on the Navy as a whole but also served as an example of what was expected of those who would seek reward and promotion. Second, the war effort has provided little good news, and this was a welcome diversion from less happy things. Third, there is now another dependable and capable captain on the list to help to prosecute the war, which directly aids those in charge. Finally, and by no means the least important, the public would demand it, and the masses must at least occasionally be given what they want to keep them in line without the need for harsher measures."

Duncan suddenly did not feel quite as proud of the promotion and decided he would focus mostly on the first reason. "Thank you for explaining, sir."

"You're quite an anomaly, Captain. Certainly, you are aware of that. Are you not?"

"I am not, sir. In what manner am I anomalous?"

"Sea captains who are cultured and comfortable among polite society are almost invariably from a privileged background, and as leaders or fighters, are quite useless. Having relied on contacts and favoritism for their advancement, they do little to risk their status and even less to prosecute the war. On the other hand, captains willing and able to fight and lead are most often men of little imagination and even less grace, who are best left at sea to avoid embarrassment. To be sure, they do their job, sometimes well, sometimes brutally, but always they do their duty. In my not limited experience, most sea captains can be easily placed in one of those two categories. Some can function marginally in both worlds, but almost none are comfortable both in the hierarchy at sea and in society on land."

"And yet, here you are. You demonstrate initiative, take chances, and willingly fight. You're known throughout the fleet, at least on the lower decks, as 'Dervish Duncan' based on tales of your exploits using Indian tomahawks. Ah, I see from your expression, you were unaware of that, as well. Despite not needing it, you practically roll in prize money and men want to follow you - not just for the chance of prizes, but because you have that special something that makes you a leader, someone for whom men rally in battle. Yet, in spite of these characteristics, you effortlessly blend into the most formal settings and are completely comfortable among the 'quality'. And even those of the quality see something in you and consider your thoughts and opinions valuable.

"So, you see, you are an anomaly among your peers because you really have no peer. You represent the very best of both worlds."

"You are too kind, sir, and I dare say you think a bit too highly of me. I do my duty and I act as I think proper. Nothing more than that."

"It is that self-assured lack of pretense that makes it work. No matter. Whether you believe it or recognize it, you are an anomaly and you are very valuable to the Crown because of it." He held up his hand to stop any further protest and continued.

"The Foreign Service has need of trustworthy and capable men, such as yourself. So much the better that you have an active commission to place you in an operational area without raising suspicion. Very few among the Admiralty know our assets, and even fewer know our plans. Therefore, a bit of luck is sometimes needed to put the right person in the right place at the right time. Often we have to be opportunistic and make the best of where people end up."

"Am I to understand that I am somehow part of this effort now?"

"Indeed, you are. Fairhurst will make certain of it. You should allow for no consternation caused by Elliott - even with his unavoidable promotion to admiral. His past attempts to discredit you have come to nothing and his future attempts will not succeed. If anything, he will destroy himself if he persists in attacking you."

·   ·   ·

A few days later, Duncan had invited Tisbit to dinner aboard the ship. In spite of all the wonderful restaurants on Antigua, it was hard to find a better meal than one prepared by Thibeault. In addition to the good food, there was an extra level of privacy in Duncan's cabin.

"I suppose I should welcome you officially to the club and congratulate you," Tisbit said, after Duncan recounted his conversation with Hirschhorn. "Or perhaps I should offer my condolences. I'm never quite sure when he's involved."

Duncan laughed. "I'll accept both. I suspect there's a bit of each to be experienced."

"Did he give you the anomaly speech?"

Duncan was surprised for a moment by the question and then realized he needed to be less naïve in the future. "Yes. Did he use it on you as well?"

"Ha! No, of course not. Wouldn't apply to me. He told me that sometimes the Foreign Service needs men who are expendable and who will do whatever needs doing. Funny what can make a man feel special."

"We all serve the Crown to the best of our abilities, I suppose," Duncan mused.

"Aye. They promise your widow will be cared for, but keep you too busy to find a wife. Oh, but then you've found your way past that already, haven't you? Have you heard more from Miss Lillian? Is she safely back in England pining for you?"

"They should be there soon if they're not already. As for pining, I can only hope she at least still remembers me. I wish we'd had more time together," Duncan said.

"Bah! You two are so completed besotted with each other, it is blatantly obvious to anyone who observes you together. She more than remembers you, just like you continue pining for her and grousing about being without her. Snap out of it, man! You've got your commission confirmed, you've got things to do."

Duncan laughed. "What things do I have to do? The admiral seems no more likely to send me to sea than he was before my commission was confirmed. My poor ship will sit here until she's beached on a reef made from the crew's beef bones."

"Oh, there you go whining again. You'll have your chance soon. Just wait and be ready when it comes. I might be involved, and I need to know you're focused and ready. No room for luck - we make our destiny through our preparation and action."

"What's that supposed to mean?" Duncan asked.

"I've said more than I should have already. Just have some faith and let Hirschhorn do the worrying. I'm going to be gone for a while, so I won't see you, maybe for a few weeks. Don't let Elliott trick you into doing something stupid or falling into one of his traps."

"Okay. But perhaps you could be a bit more mysterious and obfuscate things further," Duncan joked.

"I'd like your word, please. You're not to do anything stupid, like I would, and you're to trust Hirschhorn - about this, not just in general. I'd never ask someone to swear to that."

"You have my word, Jeremy."

•   •   •

Although the routine and reality of the next few days were no different from the previous weeks, Duncan felt completely different. *Enchanté* remained moored in the same location and the daily tasks were the same, but knowing his commission had been confirmed allowed him to see it all in a new light. It was suboptimal to be stuck in port, but he was in command of a beautiful vessel with a well-trained crew.

Along with the endless paperwork and official correspondence, he found time each day to add to his latest letter to Lillian. He had dashed off a letter describing the events surrounding the receipt of his permanent commission - without mentioning his conversation with Hirschhorn - and posted it immediately. While he remained in port, he intended to mail a letter each week and most days he added a section describing his day, his mood, his thoughts, or a recounting of some particular event.

Tisbit had disappeared, as he had warned he would. Duncan did not know if he was still on the island, but he suspected that he had sailed somewhere on a mission for Hirschhorn. Without Tisbit being available, not only did Duncan not have anyone to talk with, but they were also short a player for their whist table. Without these diversions, Duncan spent his evenings reading and appreciating the books from his uncle.

When not attending his duties - which were greatly curtailed while at anchor - Duncan spent time most days either walking or riding around the island. Some days, he would do both. Since there was a passing rainstorm most afternoons, he would use that time for paperwork and still have plenty of time ashore.

By the fourth day after Tisbit's departure, Duncan had settled into a routine and was almost enjoying himself when he again received the order to visit the flagship. His mood was light, and he was unconcerned as he made his way across the bay and through the entry port. The flag lieutenant met him there and was accompanied by a marine captain. Duncan did not recognize him, but assumed he commanded the detachment aboard *Fame*. He also did not know why he was walking with them, but as he had not been introduced, he did not spend much time thinking about it.

There was no waiting at the entry port or at the admiral's cabin door, and Duncan was surprised by this new treatment. He reported to the admiral and awaited a response as he stood in front of the desk. Both the flag lieutenant and the captain of marines had entered the cabin and were standing nearby.

The admiral spoke almost immediately, "Captain Joseph Duncan, you stand accused of actions in violation of the Articles of War as established by the Lords Commissioners of the Admiralty. The specific crimes are more completely set forth in this writ of investigation dated today, the 15th day of October, in the year of our Lord 1795. Violations including, but not necessarily limited to, Articles Eight, Twelve, Twenty-four, and Thirty-three are alleged based on your own records, logs; and reports."

The admiral paused to hand a stunned and confused Duncan a set of papers. Then he continued, "Based on your previous good record I will accept your parole and allow you to remain aboard *HMS Enchanté* under house arrest pending an investigation of the allegations and potential court martial. You are not to leave the ship under any circumstances unless responding to my direct orders. Is that understood?"

Duncan had read the Articles aloud to the crew and heard them read by previous captains enough times to know what each article meant. Among the accusations were taking money or goods out of prizes, withdrawing or keeping back from a fight, embezzlement of stores, and behavior unbecoming an officer. He had no idea what the basis of these charges could possibly be.

As his shock gave way to anger, Duncan was about to protest his innocence and demand the charges be dropped immediately. Then, he recalled Tisbit's advice and struggled to control his emotions before responding coolly with his jaw clenched, "Aye, aye, sir. I understand, and accept parole."

Duncan could not tell if Elliott was surprised or disappointed by the response, but either way, he recovered quickly and said, "Well, as you've demonstrated some good character by not protesting, I think we can dispense with the normal marine officer guard during your house arrest. That will be all. Return to *Enchanté* under your own recognizance and don't leave her, or I shall have to reconsider my leniency in this matter."

Duncan stared beyond the admiral, not trusting himself to make eye contact, and said, "Thank you, sir." He then turned and walked silently out of the cabin and back to his gig. Duncan remained silent as they rowed back, but from the mood and quick glances of the boat crew, he suspected they had more than a vague idea of what had happened. Somehow word traveled faster below decks and among the crew than seemed reasonably possible.

Cahill read the indictment letter while Strickland looked over his shoulder. When he finished, he looked to Strickland to make sure he had also completed reading. Strickland nodded and Cahill placed the papers on the table where they all sat. "That is complete and utter nonsense, sir. Everything you've been accused of is a fabrication or deliberate misinterpretation of the facts."

Strickland leaned back in his chair and said, "I concur. Perhaps the point is not to convict you, but simply to smear your name, or even to invite a response that might be used against you."

Cahill responded, "You may very well be correct. The first step will be an investigation and if we presume the admiral will pick someone sympathetic to his interpretation of events, it is likely to end in a recommendation for court martial. However, at that point, the facts surely must become clear. I cannot believe that a conviction could be made. There must be more to this."

"Sir," Strickland said, "might we take each charge independently and discuss them? Perhaps we can divine a subplot in this manner."

Duncan picked up the papers. "We could do. The charge of behavior unbecoming is really a catchall that doesn't include any additional or specific allegations. Embezzlement of stores and taking goods out of prizes are really just alternate explanations for the difference between our audited powder stores, the original issue, and how much we have expended according to our logs and records. They don't really provide any evidence that both or either occurred. The completely separate issue is failure to engage the enemy, which is based on my failed attempt to come to grips with our shadow, which again relies on our own reports of the incident."

Cahill huffed. "We were all there, and we all witnessed the attempt to engage the shadow ship. Given your past record, who would believe you intentionally avoided a fight?"

"Yes," Strickland agreed, "that charge will not stand under scrutiny. The powder issue is easily explained by your private purchase of supplemental stores, which are well documented by both you and the purser. The practice is not unheard of, or even all that unusual. The plan there must be to confuse the issue and sow doubt."

"Well," Duncan said, "I suppose the best thing to do is trust the system, stay calm, and be completely honest. There is nothing for me to hide and no reason for me to worry. Justice will be served, and I will be exonerated."

Cahill nodded and smiled. "It worked for me, sir. You may borrow my sword, if you like."

•   •   •

The next morning, Duncan had accepted his confinement and was pacing the quarterdeck when he heard Cahill swear loudly from near the rail. He looked over in surprise as Cahill turned towards him and said, "Sorry, sir. There's a boat pulling this way. I would guess it is the investigator. It's Captain Milliken, sir."

Duncan's heart leaped to his throat, but he forced himself to be calm and thought again of Tisbit's warning and advice. He tried to smile. "Well, won't it be lovely to see him again?"

A few minutes later, Captain Milliken had climbed the side of the ship, announced himself as the official investigator, and asked Duncan for a conference in his cabin. Milliken declined the offer of any refreshment and, as soon as they were seated, he began.

"Captain Duncan, the charges against you are quite serious, and the evidence is quite curious. The case is built entirely on excerpts from your own logs, reports, and records, as well as those of various other commissioned and petty officers within your crew. It would seem that if you are convicted, you would almost literally be hoisted by your own petard."

"I have not had the opportunity to see the evidence, as of yet, Captain Milliken," Duncan stated. "I have only been provided with the charges against me, sir."

Milliken frowned. "Captain, allow me to be blunt. I do not know you well, but I do not think you are a fool and even less so a coward. To believe the evidence provided to me would be to believe you are both. The key word in my previous statement was 'excerpts'. I will share the evidence with you and ask that you and your crew allow me to see the records from which they were taken. By doing so, I hope to come to understand things more clearly. With your permission, I should like to use your cabin so that I might meet individually with each witness…beginning with you. Here is the list of what and who I should like to see."

He handed Duncan a long, smartly written list with two columns. The first had names and positions, and the second had documents associated with each witness. Duncan scanned down the list and said, "Of course, sir. We will cooperate fully, and I'll gladly provide you the use of my cabin."

"I must warn you that I intend to be completely thorough and will not rush. I do this for the sake of justice and out of a sense of duty. If we do not complete the endeavor today, I shall return for as many days as necessary until I am fully satisfied and prepared to complete my report."

"I understand, sir," Duncan acknowledged.

"Good," Milliken said. "Somewhat surprisingly, there is no mention in the case concerning your employment of a French cook." Duncan was not sure where this comment was going.

"Fortunately, that puts him outside of my purview, so there would be no conflict if he were to prepare a meal for me. I've heard he's quite a master in the galley. Might he be available?"

"Aye, sir. Would you like to discuss the menu with him directly?"

"I think I should, yes," Milliken decided. "You really shouldn't be involved - as the accused."

Milliken was true to his word concerning how thorough he would be. However, as all the documents and witnesses were close at hand, he was able to complete his work just as the sun was dipping below the horizon. He walked to the entry port with Duncan.

He paused just before stepping over the side and said, "It would be improper for me to share my conclusions before submitting my report to the admiral. However, it would also be improper for you to waste another moment being concerned about the charges." He smiled briefly and added, "Good day, sir," before disappearing down the side.

Duncan was fairly certain he understood the meaning of Milliken's parting words, but he had to wait another three agonizing days before the signal arrived, requiring his presence aboard the flagship. He dressed in his best uniform and boots, and the crew rowed quickly to deliver him.

He took it as a perversely good sign that he had to wait an exceedingly long time both on deck and again after being announced at the cabin door before being invited in. He presented himself and stood at attention. He kept his eyes focused on the transom windows behind the admiral, but could still see the dour expression on his face.

"I have received a final report from the investigator, and it concludes that there is insufficient evidence concerning the charges to recommend a court martial." The admiral almost spat the words, and Duncan suppressed a smile as he pictured Elliott choking on them. "You are released from house arrest and may return to your normal duties."

"Thank you, sir," Duncan said, as flatly as he could manage.

"However, in my view, finding insufficient evidence is not the same as being innocent. Watch yourself, Captain, because I will be watching you."

Duncan decided this was a good time for the trusted response. "Aye, aye, sir!"

With that, the meeting ended. Duncan wore a broad smile as he walked across the deck and climbed lightly into his waiting gig. Jenkins and the boat crew could not misinterpret his body language and facial expressions, and they all rowed back to *Enchanté* in good spirits.

Duncan dined in all the officers to celebrate that evening and slept in later than normal the next morning. He had just finished shaving when Midshipman Powell entered with a message from the quarterdeck, "Sir, the flag is signaling our number and captain repair aboard."

Oh, what now?! Duncan thought, but out loud he simply said, "Call for my gig and crew, I shall be right up."

Chapter Nineteen

"This is a bloody outrage! I will not stand for this!" Admiral Elliott screamed at Duncan, and it would seem, at the universe in general. His face was red and the veins in his neck were bulging to the point that Duncan was concerned he might actually explode. He was not sure he would mind, other than the mess it would likely make of his second-best uniform.

"Someone will answer for this! Heads will roll, I tell you! To be treated like this is unconscionable! I am the bloody commander-in-chief and deserve more respect!"

Duncan still was not sure exactly what the issue was that had reduced the admiral to this state. The man had been screaming and complaining since before Duncan had actually arrived. Everyone on deck could hear him, and he had only paused for a moment to bellow for Duncan to enter when he arrived.

"You!" he said, pointing his finger at Duncan. "Somehow you are behind this, and I will make you pay!"

Duncan decided it was time to try to calm the admiral down, if for no other reason than so he could find out what was going on. "Sir, I apologize, but I don't know what you mean. Might you please explain what has happened?"

"Oh, don't play dumb with me, Duncan. You know bloody well what I'm talking about."

"Sir, I assure you I do not. I have no idea why you've summoned me," Duncan said, in what he hoped was a soothing voice.

"This! This is why!" He shook a piece of paper in Duncan's face before throwing it on the desk in front of him.

Duncan took a chance and reached carefully for the paper. He scanned through it first and then took the time to read it very carefully. It was an order from the Lord Admirals informing Elliot that Duncan, *Enchanté,* and her entire crew were no longer assigned to the squadron, and that they would sail under their own sealed orders to which he would not be privy. It also required Elliott, the local dockyard, and all other Navy resources to provide any and all assistance requested.

The stunned look on Duncan's face seemed to finally snap the spell for the admiral, and he slumped into his chair and went on in a hoarse and much quieter voice, "How could they not only steal one of my ships, but refuse to tell me why?"

In that moment, Duncan almost felt sorry for the older man. His reaction had been ridiculous and totally out of proportion, but in truth, the order was quite a slap in the face. "I am truly sorry, sir. I had no notion of this and don't understand it myself."

"Your orders were sent by a separate courier and will be delivered to your ship. You may go, now," Elliott said in a broken and dejected voice. "I believe you didn't know. I apologize for my...outburst. You're a lucky man, Duncan. Some of us never get the opportunities you've already had in your short career."

Duncan struggled for how to respond and finally said, "Thank you, sir. I hope to prove myself worthy. Good luck and good day, sir." He left the cabin and went to his gig, still trying to make sense of what had happened and what the special orders could mean.

"Is everything okay, sir?" Jenkins asked him after he was seated in the stern sheets.

Duncan looked at his coxswain and responded, "Yes, I believe it is. Back to the ship and perhaps we'll know more, but I think we may be sailing soon."

Jenkins smiled broadly. "That would be fine, sir. To be sure, that would be just fine." More loudly, he called out, "Right then lads, push off, out oars…and stroke. Put your backs into it, you lubbers! The sea beckons us, she does."

As they approached *Enchanté*, Duncan noticed a strange boat with two oarsmen bobbing on the end of a line at the stern. The captain's gig bumped against the side of the ship, and Duncan timed his step from the boat and up the side.

Cahill was waiting for him at the entry port and greeted him immediately. "Welcome back, sir. A messenger arrived with this note for you." He handed Duncan a small, sealed paper. "And a special courier arrived - a lieutenant. He's waiting in the wardroom. He refused to let anyone else sign for his package, sir, and said he must wait for you. I wasn't sure where else to put him and didn't think I should leave him on deck."

Duncan responded, "Thank you, Mr. Cahill. Please have him sent to my cabin immediately. I shall receive him there."

The man entered the cabin after being invited and introduced himself. "I am Lieutenant William Albright, sir, special courier for the Admiralty. You are Captain Joseph Duncan, are you not?"

"Yes, Lieutenant, I am. Please have a seat. Might I offer you some refreshment?"

"Thank you, sir," the courier said as he sat. "Your first was kind enough to let me wait in the wardroom, and your other officers provided me with a drink. Sir, I have a consignment for which I will require your signature, if you wouldn't mind."

"Not at all," Duncan said, as the lieutenant opened a leather bag hanging across his chest and pulled out three pieces of parchment.

"There are duplicate copies indicating that I have delivered this package to you," he explained as he removed a leather-bound packet tied shut and sealed in black wax imprinted with the Admiralty seal. "I will sign that it was delivered to you, sealed, and you will countersign to the same effect and then take possession. One copy is for you, and I will be required to take the other two back to London, sir."

Duncan had never seen anything quite this formal, but then he had never received special Admiralty orders, either. "Did they really send you all this way just to deliver a packet of papers?"

"In this particular instance, yes, sir. Normally, I have several deliveries to make throughout a general area or along a route. This time, I was charged to deliver this one package to you and to return immediately."

"You do this a lot, then, do you?" Duncan asked. He was unfamiliar with this aspect of the Navy communication system and had never encountered a special courier before.

"All the time, sir. I'm always going somewhere or other. India twice, and that takes the better part of a year round trip."

"How very interesting," Duncan said, as he read the simple statements on the document, made a point of double checking the seal, and then signed all three copies. He handed them back to Albright.

"This one is for you, sir. If you'll excuse me, I should be off so I can see if I can catch the mail packet before she sails on the tide."

"Oh, by all means, Lieutenant. I don't wish to delay you. Godspeed."

The lieutenant bustled out of the cabin and Duncan picked up the package and turned it over in his hand. Laying it back on the desk, he reached into a drawer for a knife to cut it open. Then he paused and instead broke the seal on the message Cahill had given him and read the short note.

It was from Hirschhorn, requesting he visit that evening. One phrase in particular stood out to Duncan, "...now that you are free from the confines of your ship and overseer..." It seemed that Hirschhorn again knew what was happening before anyone else.

•   •   •

Later that day, Duncan was surprised to see Tisbit had also been invited to Hirschhorn's house. The two men were talking together in the library when Duncan was led in by a servant.

The host greeted him, "Ah, Captain, you are most welcome. Thank you for attending on such short notice. You recall Major Tisbit, I'm sure."

"Yes. Thank you for the invitation," Duncan responded, and then nodding to Tisbit, added, "A pleasure to see you, Major. I hope you have been well."

Hirschhorn answered for him, "The major has retrieved some potentially valuable information, which is why I asked you here. Let's have a seat and discuss things, shall we?"

They sat in large, overstuffed leather chairs around a low table upon which there were assorted drinks and food. Once they were settled in, and the servants had departed, Hirschhorn began.

"We have continued to seek an understanding of how the British cannons found their way onto the French national ships you intercepted. As the innocent possibilities seem more and more unlikely, we have been forced to act carefully so as to not alert the potential traitor, or traitors, involved and allow them to disappear or further obscure their tracks. To this end we have pursued several leads and possibilities. So far, none have borne fruit, but several have been eliminated, which makes those remaining even more potentially important."

Hirschhorn paused to sip his wine and then continued, "From the very beginning, one potential source of information has been known to us, but unavailable. The commodore aboard *La Tempête,* a man named Gervais De La Fountain, might know something or someone which would lead us closer to the ultimate answer. Often, you see, these things are discovered in many small steps, not in a sudden revelation.

"Major Tisbit has acquired what I believe to be credible information concerning the location of *La Tempête.* I intend to have you intercept and capture the ship, in the hope that Commodore de la Fountain is still aboard. We have no indication that he has left the ship and appeared anywhere else, so we believe he is still aboard. Major Tisbit will travel with you and handle any... *discussions* with the commodore, if he is recovered."

Hirschhorn switched to a questioning tone without pausing. "You have received and read your orders?"

"Aye, sir," Duncan responded.

"And the special clarification of the orders?"

"Aye, sir." Duncan had committed the exact text of the brief directive to memory.

"And you destroyed them?"

"Aye, sir. I burned them." Duncan had been somewhat nervous about this action. The special orders had explicitly required that he share the contents with no one, make no written copy, and destroy the original completely. In his experience, orders were carefully duplicated in the captain's log and ship's log in case there was any question later of what they contained. He recalled a previous interview with Admiral Fairhurst concerning *Fidelity's* orders, and he now understood the real question behind that inquiry.

"And did you eat the ashes?" Tisbit asked sarcastically. "Come on, Hirschhorn, he's not an idiot. Let's get back to the mission, shall we?"

Hirschhorn gave Tisbit a disapproving glare, but then continued, "Very well. We believe *La Tempête* is sheltering in Castara Bay on the Island of Tobago. How soon can you be ready to sail?"

"We can sail immediately, sir. We've had nowhere to go for quite some time and are fully prepared," Duncan responded, while he tried to recall what he knew of Tobago. It did not take him long because he knew little more than the fact that the French had captured it about 15 years ago and it was somewhere near the Spanish America mainland.

"I suppose that is one thing for which we can thank Admiral Elliott. He kept you close by for when I needed you," Hirschhorn said with a sly smile. "I've heard that he had a right proper fit when he found out about your release from his squadron. Oh, how I would have loved to have seen that."

Duncan was trying to forget the incident and found himself feeling somewhat embarrassed for the man. "He was certainly quite upset, which is understandable, I suppose."

"I suspect he was expecting something, or he wouldn't have been so reckless about trying to discredit you. Such an amateur job, that! His benefactors will be livid with what must have been a result of his own initiative. They are cloddish fools, but even they would have handled it much better. It wasn't really a bad idea, just very poorly executed. A wasted opportunity, and now it will put them on the back foot. They should learn to leave these things to the professionals."

"I must confess that I was surprised it ended so abruptly," Duncan said.

"Ah, well, another mistake by Elliott, you see? Captain Milliken is a man of very little imagination and no tolerance for failing in your duty. But in the end, he is a fair man and lives by a strict personal code. Elliott should have known that and picked someone he could bend to his way of thinking. Milliken was always going to be thorough and fair. The charges could not stand up to that type of scrutiny."

"Perhaps I've misjudged Captain Milliken," Duncan mused. "I had a less than favorable impression of him from my first encounter at Lieutenant Cahill's court martial."

"He can be brutal and unapologetic when determining if someone is worthy of wearing the King's coat, but there is very little malice in his judgement. He voted to acquit your lieutenant."

"He did?" Duncan asked in surprise.

"Yes, he did," Hirschhorn assured him. "As I understand it, his comments in deliberations even swayed Ribacoff and in the end, it was unanimous." He took an absent-minded sip of wine while he looked into space and pondered for a moment. "Hmm…Ribacoff, that useless nitwit would have been a better choice for your investigation."

Tisbit laughed. "Like I've told you, Captain, you should thank your lucky stars Hirschhorn is on our side."

Hirschhorn gave Tisbit another withering stare and said in a dangerous tone, "And so should you, Major." Then he smiled unexpectedly and stood up. "Come, let us go to dinner and we can discuss this more over brandy later. You may wait until tomorrow to sail. So, we have time for a meal."

After dinner, they retired to the library, and Hirschhorn produced a map and chart of Tobago. They discussed the mission and how it might be best to approach the island. Castara Bay was open to the west and surrounded on the east and south by hills that would hide a ship approaching from windward. However, it could be assumed that there would be lookouts on the hills, so a total surprise would be unlikely.

Finally, when there seemed to be little left to discuss, Hirschhorn said, "I shall leave the final decisions to you,

Captain. This is your area of expertise, not mine. You are to engage and capture *La Tempête*. How you accomplish that is for you and your crew to determine. You may take the chart with you. I have had a copy made."

"Thank you, sir," Duncan responded, as he started to roll the chart. "If you'll excuse me, I should be getting back to my ship to make final preparations."

"Of course. Happy hunting, Captain."

Tisbit and Duncan left together, and as they walked down the steep road towards the waterfront, Duncan asked, "When should we expect you to come aboard?"

"I have a few things to do since I just got back to the island. It might be rather late tonight before I have completed everything. What time are you thinking of sailing? There must be a tide or something you go by, isn't there?"

Duncan chuckled, "How long have you been a marine, and you still don't follow the tides?"

"They go up and down. When I need to know which is when, I ask someone smarter than me."

"I don't know about that. It seems you might be the smart one if you're making everyone else keep track of things for you," Duncan joked. "Five bells in the morning watch, which is half-past six if you're going by a pocket watch."

Tisbit pondered for a while and then decided, "I'd rather come aboard tonight if that wouldn't inconvenience you. It might be midnight or so, if that would be acceptable."

"As long as you don't expect me to wait up for you, I can let the duty officer know to expect you. Would you like me to send a boat for you? That late, you might have trouble finding one for hire."

"Good point, and I thank you. Yes, how about midnight at the dockyard landing?" Tisbit requested.

They parted ways a few minutes later, and Duncan headed back to the ship. Cahill was waiting at the entry port, as he often did when he hoped for news. After the standard greetings, Duncan looked at his expectant face and with a broad smile and a voice loud enough for everyone to hear, said, "Make final preparations for sea. We sail with the morning tide." Then, just to Cahill, he added, "Find the master and meet me in my cabin in twenty minutes."

Cahill and Ellis arrived together and took seats in front of Duncan's desk. Stanley provided them each with a glass a wine and then closed the door as he left.

The packet of orders had actually included two versions. The first was to be shared with the other officers and had been copied into the logbooks, as would normally be done. These orders essentially defined the entire Caribbean as a cruising ground and gave Duncan the discretion to sail *Enchanté* wherever he chose, with the goal of harassing the enemy on land or sea. Other than the broadly inclusive language and the fact that they were unassigned to any local squadron, there was nothing particularly unusual. Everyone else had accepted them as just good fortune and a reward for a captain who had been successful in a previous cruise.

Only Duncan had seen and read the other supplemental orders. That single page had simply stated that Duncan was to take direction from, and report his progress to, Hirschhorn. Most of the page had actually been about the importance of destroying the written copy of the order and sharing its contents with no one...along with mention of the severity of punishment that should be expected by anyone foolish enough to ignore the directives.

Duncan found the situation to be rather disconcerting. He had not expected to be interacting with the Foreign Service, nor had he anticipated having to keep secret orders from his crew. However, he had memorized the exact wording of the supplemental orders, so he was sure of what he could and could not share with others. With these restrictions in mind, he began the discussion with Cahill and Ellis.

"As you've both heard me mention, there was a ship that I left disabled and was unable to capture in the engagement between *Fidelity* and the French convoy. That ship was named *La Tempête,* and I have recently learned that there is a strong likelihood she can be found operating out of Tobago. I have unfinished business with *La Tempête,* and since our orders leave me discretion to determine our targets, we will sail for Tobago on the morning tide."

Cahill smiled wolfishly. "I've got a score to settle with them, too, sir."

There was a rasping noise as Ellis rubbed his stubbly chin and gazed into space for a moment. "Tobago...four or five days sail in good winds. Can't say as where I've ever been there before."

"Nor have I," Duncan responded. "I was able to acquire a chart. It should be reasonably accurate, although the soundings are from about twenty years ago when we still controlled it." Duncan handed the rolled map to Ellis.

"Thank you, sir. I'll see what else I might have in the chart room and check them against each other. Do you have a course in mind?"

"I shall defer to you to recommend the best course based on wind and currents, Mr. Ellis. I should not like to waste time, but there is no need to take unnecessary risks. I'd like to arrive in one piece and be ready to fight if we're lucky enough to find her there."

Cahill spoke up. "Aye, sir. We've been at anchor for quite a while. A few days at sea will give us some time to sharpen the crew. Do you mind if I schedule some time with the guns?"

"I would think you a rather shabby first officer if you didn't, Mr. Cahill," Duncan responded with an easy smile.

"Well then, sir. If there's nothing further, perhaps we should excuse ourselves and begin preparations for the offing." Cahill glanced at the master, who nodded his agreement.

"Just one more thing," Duncan said. This was the part he was dreading trying to explain. "It seems that Major Tisbit has considerable discretion in his orders, as well, and he has requested permission to sail with us. I have no objection and have agreed to allow him to come aboard later this evening."

"Oh, excellent!" Cahill exclaimed. "You'll have your fourth for whist, and I won't have to put up with pestering from Strickland and Cole."

Duncan laughed in relief and genuine humor. "Then perhaps you'd be so kind as to send a boat to pick him up at the dockyard at midnight."

"Quite happy, sir. He's a rather pleasant chap and is welcome in the wardroom anytime."

With that, the meeting ended and Duncan was left thinking he might yet survive his new association with spies and secrets.

Duncan did not intentionally wait up for Tisbit's arrival, but he was nonetheless awake when the marine came aboard. The possibility of engaging with *La Tempête* had brought back a flood of memories. So much had happened and so much had changed in the months since their first engagement. There were both good and bad memories and Duncan spent well into the morning hours lying awake, reliving them, and second guessing his actions. When sleep finally came, it was a fitful and dream-filled slumber where memories and dreams merged and changed until he could not tell one from the other.

His eyes felt gravelly, and his head was foggy when he got out of his hanging cot just before first light. He felt a little better after splashing water on his face and pulling on his uniform, but he was still unsettled from his dreams. It had not cooled off much overnight, and the air was heavy, sticky, and warm. The few lights that could be seen ashore were shrouded in a misty haze that left indistinct halos and a general glow without form or shape.

Despite his best efforts not to, Duncan yawned widely as he rubbed his forehead and resettled his hat. Stanley appeared on deck and offered a mug of steaming coffee. Duncan took the cup with muttered thanks. The rich, acrid smell started to dispel the fog in his head and the pain of burning his tongue on the hot liquid further helped him to focus and separate reality from the residual feelings of his dreams.

"Good morning, sir," Cahill said from where he stood near the binnacle with the master, Strickland, and Cole. "The tide will begin to flow in about an hour and we have a light, but fair wind for offing."

"Off for fame and glory, or perhaps an empty sea," Duncan mused. "Either way, I'll be happy to have the anchor raised."

There were nods, expressions of agreement, and smiles from everyone on the quarterdeck. The only thing better than coming into port after a long journey was leaving port to start a new adventure.

The master had suggested a course along the leeward side of Guadeloupe, Dominica, and Martinique before crossing between Martinique and St. Lucia northwest of Barbados. From there, they would work south towards Tobago and approach the island from the northeast on what should be their best point of sail if the prevailing winds cooperated. Duncan had approved, so this was the course they shaped as they sailed away from Antigua.

It began as an easy sail in generally good weather and on the morning of the third day, they confirmed their location by sighting Mount Pelée in the distance on the French island of Martinique. Duncan lowered his telescope and turned to the master, who was taking measurements with his sextant. "Another credible demonstration of your navigational prowess, Mr. Ellis. Congratulations."

The master lowered the sextant and smiled broadly, laughing in his normally cheerful manner, "Thank you, sir. However, this is the easy part. Once we pass St. Lucia, we'll be in the open sea for the final leg. I hope to at least find Tobago - and perhaps be so lucky as to approach from the right side."

"I have complete confidence," Duncan responded with a laugh.

The first lieutenant climbed onto the quarterdeck and approached the pair, smiling at their good-natured interaction. Duncan noticed him as he crossed the deck. "Ah, Mr. Cahill. Do you still intend to exercise the crew with the great guns this afternoon?"

"Aye, sir, with your permission," Cahill answered.

"Mr. Chapman has informed me that we still have some of that French powder available. What say you to some live fire to remind the men what it sounds like?"

"I think it a splendid idea, Captain."

"The purser has agreed to condemn the staves on a few beef barrels and, although he'll have to charge me for the iron hoops, I suggest we use them for a bit of target practice." Duncan added.

Cahill's face brightened with a thought. "Might we also draw them behind one of the launches and fire at a moving target, sir?"

"Wonderful idea, Mr. Cahill. Please make the necessary preparations and be sure to provide a sufficiently long rope for towing the barrels."

Word of the plan spread quickly throughout the ship. There was a general buzz of excitement as the crew looked forward to something more exciting than hauling the guns in and out while walking through the steps for firing and reloading. The carpenter asked for permission to modify the barrels to make better targets, and Duncan was glad to approve the request.

Staves were added to the ends of each barrel with scrap iron placed at the bottom and old pieces of canvas, painted with concentric circles, stretched between them at the top. The iron was intended to keep the barrels upright in the water. It did not work perfectly, but it added to the feeling that this was a special occasion.

By four bells in the afternoon watch, all was ready. *Enchanté* reduced sail and Midshipman Hyde led a crew in one of the longboats with its mast stepped to sail along a parallel course, with the first barrel target bobbing and weaving at the end of a long rope behind the boat.

Duncan addressed the crew before they started, "There is your target, men. A guinea to the first crew to hit it." There was a cheer and huzzah and he waited until the crew was quiet before adding, "And a flogging for any crew who hits my barge!" This was met with more cheers and laughter. "Mr. Cahill, you may begin with a rolling broadside from bow to stern."

"Aye, aye, sir!" Cahill responded, as the gun crews moved to their positions along the larboard side of the ship, where the wind would be in their faces and the smoke would blow back through the ship but away from the target.

Firing began a few moments later, and the party atmosphere continued. Most of the shots were close to the target, striking the waves in front or behind. A few even skipped directly over the barrel. It was not until the middle of the third rolling broadside that a cannon ball split the painted canvas and left shreds blowing in the wind. A huge cheer erupted, and there was a pause to congratulate the winning gun crew. Two shots later, there was a direct hit, and the barrel exploded into splinters.

It took a while for the crew of the launch to pull in the rope, attach a new barrel, and stream the line back out. The gun crews used the time to drink from the scuttlebutt and wipe the black soot from their faces. Once the new target was ready, the firing recommenced. The games continued, with additional breaks to replace the target, until late in the afternoon watch, when an errant shot severed the towline and the final target bobbed to a halt in the water.

Duncan called down, "Full broadside, Mr. Cahill! Don't let that barrel escape!"

A few seconds later, the ship shuddered and was pushed sideways by the tremendous combined power of the cannons. The thunder echoed away to silence and as the smoke cleared, there was no sign of the barrel.

·   ·   ·

The rains came during the night, as they passed between Martinique and St. Lucia. The wind shifted north enough to threaten turning St. Lucia into a dangerous lee shore. By morning, the wind had shifted back, and the early light of day confirmed that they had weathered the land. Still, the wind was unsteady, with gusts and frequent changes of direction.

"I canna guarantee bringing us to the right location off Tobago with these conditions, sir," the master explained to Duncan as they stood in the chart room. "With the wind so unsettled, it's difficult to judge our leeway. Dead reckoning leaves too much room for error. We'll find Tobago to be sure, but maybe from the wrong end."

Duncan let out a sigh as he stared at the chart spread before them and listened to the rain dripping from the deck above. "And you think we'd do better to sail easterly to Barbados, then?"

"Aye, sir. With a sighting of Mount Hillaby, I can fix our position and set a course for Tobago. We'll be sailing with the wind on a better point and there'll be little leeway to consider in tracking our course."

"And we lose a day," Cahill spoke from the other end of the table. "Perhaps two days in order to time our approach, so we arrive at first light."

"There's no arguing that, sir," the master conceded. "Will it be worse to be a day or two late, or to miss our planned approach course?"

Duncan had been absentmindedly twirling a set a brass dividers in his hand and he tossed them onto the chart table. "Neither matters if *La Tempête* isn't there. However, if she is there when we arrive, our odds of taking her increase dramatically if we are in proper position. Change course for Barbados."

"Aye, aye, sir," they both responded.

•   •   •

From a distance, Barbados looked like little more than a lumpy green line just above the horizon. Mount Hillaby was not very tall, but it stood out against the light blue sky well enough for the master to identify it and Horse Hill. He took careful measurements with his sextant and consulted the binnacle compass before making several calculations on his slate. He then repeated the process before turning to Duncan with a content look on his face.

Duncan had been watching him silently and now asked, "Well, Mr. Ellis, are you satisfied as to our position now?"

"Aye, sir. I'm quite satisfied," the master replied with a wide smile. "If you'll excuse me just a moment to consult a chart, I shall provide you with the heading you requested."

Duncan responded with a wave of his hand toward the chartroom. "Please don't keep us in suspense any longer than you need to."

Ellis was back on the quarterdeck a few minutes later and *Enchanté* was pointed towards her destination off the northeastern tip of Tobago.

After the couple of days of squalls and cloudy skies, the weather turned warmer and drier. The wind returned to its customary direction and strengthened to a strong breeze. They were forced to reduce sail in order to properly time their arrival. On the third morning after taking sightings off Barbados, everyone was on deck awaiting the outcome.

"Send the lookouts aloft," Duncan ordered, after consulting his watch. It was not yet light, but the sky behind them was starting to lighten.

The gun crews stood silently by the cannons. They were ready, as they were every morning, to face whatever might be revealed by the light. Duncan glanced toward Cahill and wondered if he was thinking about the morning when a convoy of French warships was surrounding his little *Swallow* when the sun rose. *La Tempête* had been there that day, and perhaps today would be a chance for retribution.

Slowly the sky lightened, and gray replaced black, starting from somewhere behind them and heading towards an unseen horizon in front. Duncan realized he was holding his breath, and he forced himself to exhale and relax his shoulders.

"Land ho!" came the call from above. "Three points off the larboard bow!"

A cheer erupted from the crew and Duncan clapped the master on the back, "Well done, Mr. Ellis!" Then, still smiling, he turned to Cahill and ordered, "Put on all the sail she can handle. We may not be able to hide from their lookouts, but we can keep them from having much time to react."

Chapter Twenty

Duncan paced along the quarterdeck rail as they grew closer to the island of Tobago. The sun had risen almost directly behind them, making it more difficult for anyone on land to spot them from a distance. However, they were close enough now to make out the texture of the trees and separate the white surf from the golden sands of the beaches. If there were lookouts on the hilltops, there was little chance the ship had not been sighted by now.

Cahill fell in step beside Duncan. "A near perfect landfall. I'm not sure how the master does it, sir. The last cast of the log was a quarter more than twelve knots. We'll pass the headland within an hour and be able to see into Castara Bay."

"And what do you suspect we'll see?" Duncan asked.

"I hope we'll see a willing adversary," Cahill responded with a wolfish smile. "However, I would settle for an unwilling one. I just want *La Tempête* to be there, sir."

"So do I, and soon we'll know. If she's there, we'll engage her whether she comes out or not. You've reviewed the charts, have you not?"

"Aye, sir. It's not much of a shelter and she wouldn't be able to draw very close to shore. There are no shore batteries we know of and not many opportunities to place them. If she won't fight willingly, we should be able to sail back and forth and blast away for as long as needed."

"Sail ho!" The call from the lookout interrupted their conversation, and they both stopped to look around.

"Where away?" Cahill yelled to the lookout through cupped hands.

There was a slight pause and then the answer came, "A half point off the weather bow…just clearing the point. It's a frigate still shaking out sail."

On the quarterdeck, the sails blocked the view directly in front of the ship, so they could not see anything from where they stood. With a quick look at each other, they started forward without speaking. Cahill fell into step behind Duncan as they walked along the narrow catwalk connecting the quarterdeck with the foredeck. They arrived at the bow to find the master and Strickland already there.

Strickland handed Duncan a telescope as he approached and greeted him, "Hello, Captain. It's definitely a large frigate."

Before he could raise the glass to his eye for a closer look, he saw a flash of light and a puff of smoke explode from the bow of the other ship. He heard the distant thud of a cannon a few seconds later as he focused the telescope…just in time to see French colors flutter out in the wind.

"Are they challenging us?" the master asked incredulously.

Duncan lowered the telescope and handed it to Cahill. "Yes, Mr. Ellis. I believe they are."

"The way they were sailing out, I thought they were running," Strickland commented.

"It appears they're just gaining some sea room and intend to engage us," Cahill responded, as he studied the ship through the telescope. "That's her, sir. I'd stake my life on it."

Cahill had simply confirmed what Duncan already knew. The ship was *La Tempête,* and she was going to be a willing foe.

"Mr. Chapman," Duncan called to the gunner. "Fire a signal gun. Let's accept their kind offer."

The officers had just arrived back on the quarterdeck when one of the long nine-pound chase guns barked out the reply.

La Tempête was sailing to the northwest with only light sail set, so she was moving slowly to allow *Enchanté* to catch up. However, the angle required *Enchanté* to turn and sail almost directly before the wind. On this point of sail, she was not as fast and even with all the sail set, they slowed to a little under ten knots. Duncan accepted this with an outward air of patience while inside, he seethed at the delay.

The master lowered his sextant and announced, "Single shotted and max elevation, we might just reach her now, sir."

"Thank you, Mr. Ellis. We will wait," Duncan said as calmly as he could manage. He had decided to have the guns double shotted and had debated adding grape, as well. This would have required them to get very close before firing their first salvo, so in the end, he compromised with himself and went with two solid round shot in each cannon. The powder load needed to match the shot, so he could not change now without having the charges drawn and replaced, which was a long and dangerous process.

There was an eerie silence throughout the ship as everyone waited for the chaos of the battle that was to come. Some spoke softly to their mates, some prayed silently, some looked about nervously, and some napped - or at least pretended to. Only the sound of the wind in the rigging and the rush of the water along the hull seemed indifferent to the tension.

Duncan practically jumped when a call came down from the lookout. "Sail ho! Three points off the stern and just clearing the land."

Everyone on the quarter deck spun around to look in almost the opposite direction from the ship they were pursuing. There had been no other ship in any of the bays they had passed, and they had begun to leave Tobago behind them.

Cole already had a telescope to his eye. "Just weathering Crown Point and rounding the southern tip of the island, sir. It's brig-rigged and looks familiar. I think it might be our mysterious companion from Nova Scotia."

Duncan tried to hide his surprise and took a telescope from the rack so he could look for himself while Cahill and Strickland did the same. After a few moments, Duncan lowered his glass and turned to Cahill, who was looking at him in anticipation. Cahill nodded his head and Duncan said, "I concur. That's the same brig. We need to engage *La Tempête* before she can close with us or we'll be caught between the two. We'll also have to avoid grappling or coming together during the fight so we can maintain our maneuverability."

"Aye, aye, sir," Cahill responded.

"Mr. Webb," Duncan addressed the midshipman standing nearby, "your task is to watch that brig and tell me anytime she changes course or makes any adjustments to sail. Understood?"

"Aye, aye, sir!"

Tisbit wandered over as everyone shifted their focus back to the first enemy, going back to their duty stations. When he was close enough to Duncan, he said in a quiet voice, "Two to one odds are still pretty good given your past record. You might even call it one and a half to one with a brig involved."

Duncan smiled and glanced around to make sure no one could overhear them. "*Fidelity* had the heaviest broadside of any ship in that engagement and a very well-trained crew. We're still coming together, and gun for gun *La Tempête* is more than a match for *Enchanté*. Our advantage is going to be rate of fire and hopefully accuracy, but we need to deal with the frigate quickly or things could get really interesting."

"Sir, the brig is putting on more sail," Webb announced from near the rail.

"*La Tempête* is turning a point toward the wind and bracing up her sails, sir," Cahill said at almost the same time.

Tisbit smiled broadly and said, "I like interesting."

Twenty minutes later, the duel began in earnest, with the two frigates firing nearly simultaneous broadsides at each other. Nerves, cold gun barrels, and distance combined, so although there was tremendous noise and smoke, neither ship suffered much damage from the first exchange. The French ship fired three consecutive broadsides before allowing the gun crews to fire at their own pace, which resulted in a seemingly random and continuous series of shots coming from up and down the side of the ship.

Duncan had instructed his officers to continue firing as quickly as the individual gun crews could reload after the first broadside. If this was to a slugging match, they would need to overcome the disadvantage in size and weight of iron by firing faster than the French. At first, it seemed to be working, and he could see rust and black ringed holes appearing in the enemy hull. But as the battle continued, the adversaries grew closer together, and the damage began to mount on both ships.

There were no fancy sailing maneuvers or complex strategies in this. It was purely a battle of attrition, with both sides locked in combat until the other was forced into submission. The master stood near the wheel and directed the helmsmen to make small adjustments to maintain the distance once the ships were within about 50 yards of each other.

Both ships continued in a roughly straight line, reaching with the wind on the weather side quarter., This situation would become another disadvantage for *Enchanté* as the battle dragged on. The wind would carry the acrid yellowish gray smoke from the cannons forward, and the British would sail into it. The lingering haze of smoke enveloping the ship stung the eyes and made breathing difficult.

Duncan paced the quarterdeck so as to present a more difficult target for sharpshooters in the French tops. Truth be told, he could not have stood still no matter how hard he tried. His gaze shifted constantly, trying to assess damage and losses on both ships and look for any potential advantage he could exploit.

The thunder of cannons, crashing of shot, and whizzing sound of wood splinters became a background chorus, only somewhat muted by the cotton and wax he had stuffed in his ears. He blinked hard to clear the smoke from his watery eyes and looked at the enemy ship across the short expanse of ocean. She was battered and pockmarked, but there was no major damage or sign of weakening. Her crew was slowing as they tired, but so was his.

A particularly loud crash and clang of metal brought his attention back to the deck of his own ship. The third cannon from the bow in the main battery was overturned and there was a gaping hole in the side of the ship where the gunport had previously been. Two crewmen were dead under the cannon, another was sprawled motionless nearby, and the rest of the gun crew were slowly getting up from the deck with stunned and confused expressions.

He looked back across at *La Tempête*, hoping to see some significant damage, but the ship sailed on with fire erupting from her cannons. Crewman swarmed to fix tattered sails and replace severed ropes, but the damage so far seemed superficial and would have little impact on her ability to continue the fight.

A section of the railing next to him exploded in a spray of splinters and Duncan reflexively raised his arm to protect his face. Something hit him in the stomach, and he was relieved to look down and realize it was just one of the tightly rolled hammocks used to provide a bit more protection on the quarterdeck. Several were lying about the deck now, after being blown from the netting that held them in place. He pulled a large splinter of wood from the sleeve of his uniform and was thankful it had not even broken his skin. Kicking a hammock roll out of his way, he continued his pacing.

As he stepped forward, he glanced towards the wheel and stopped at once in surprise and concern. The body of one of the helmsmen was in a crumpled pile, surrounded by a pool of blood. The other was holding the wheel with one arm while the other hung limply by his side with blood dripped from his fingers. The master was down on one knee, holding a bloody hand to his head.

Duncan moved to the wheel to help steady the ship and hold their course. Members of the afterguard swarmed around him, helping the injured and dragging the body away. Jenkins and a quartermaster's mate appeared and relieved Duncan from the wheel and he watched the master being supported by two crewmen, who carried him to where the surgeon was no doubt very busy on the orlop deck.

"Helms not answering, sir!" Jenkins yelled as he and the other man strained against the wheel without being able to move it. "Something has jammed the rudder or blocked the cable drum."

"Head down and see if the tiller can be moved," Duncan ordered. Something whizzed past his ear, and he flinched before starting to pace again. "Mr. Murray! You'll need to adjust the sails to keep our course."

"Aye, aye, sir!" the boatswain responded.

At that moment, there were not many things Duncan would consider to be lucky. However, the fact that they were sailing in a straight line parallel to the French ship was. Without being able to move the rudder, the ship could only be turned by adjustment of sails, which was a ponderous and difficult task. Keeping her on a straight line could be reasonably accomplished in consistent winds, but maneuvering in any meaningful way was out of the question.

Jenkins returned a few moments later, shaking his head. "Tiller won't budge, sir, even with four men on the tackle."

Duncan nodded in acknowledgement and realized Midshipman Webb was frantically trying to get his attention. "What is it, Mr. Webb?"

"Sir, the brig is changing course to cross our stern!" he said in a hoarse voice as he pointed back toward the other ship.

For a moment, the thunderous din of the battle faded in his perception as Duncan turned and looked out from the stern. The brig was cutting across the wind and would pass within a hundred yards of the undefended rear of his ship. The speed and relative positions were such that even with a fully functioning rudder, it would be impossible to avoid being raked. Without the use of the rudder, there was nothing they could do without the risk of losing control and putting *Enchanté* at the complete mercy of both attackers.

There was no reason to expect mercy, and he knew he would do the same. In fact, he had done something very similar to *La Tempête* in their first encounter. He had a thought to appreciate the irony of the situation and wonder if the hand of providence was merely adjusting the scales of justice.

He shook off the useless thoughts and focused back on everything happening around him. The enemy frigate sailed on, still firing, albeit at an ever-slowing rate. His crew was returning fire, still faster than the French, but also slowing down. All but the one overturned cannon were still in service aboard his ship. Although he could not be sure, it seemed that perhaps as many as three of the cannons facing them had fallen silent.

Duncan struggled to think of a plan or even a single action that might turn the tide in their favor. Nothing occurred to him, and he watched helplessly as the brig came in line with their stern and the gunports flew open. He continued to watch as he saw the fat, stubby barrels poke from the side and he thought of the captain and commodore aboard *La Tempête* watching *Fidelity* months before.

In his subconscious, something tickled at his mind. There was something odd about the cannons. They were too large for a brig of that size, and they did not protrude very far from the side. They were carronades and at least 32-pounders. The French had almost nothing like that in their armament - a few howitzers were the closest thing. But odd or not, at any moment they would fire, and it was likely Duncan would die or have to surrender the ship.

Then realization and relief washed over him as he saw British colors break free from the mast and flutter brilliantly in the wind. The brig sailed past and fired its heavy broadside into the stern of the French frigate. The rear of the enemy ship seemed to rise in the air from the combined impact as the eight heavy carronades unloaded their deadly iron to fly the length of *La Tempête,* carrying destruction and death with them.

Moments later, the battle ended as the French flag was lowered, and the guns fell silent. "Cease fire! Cease fire! They've stuck! Cease fire!" the officers yelled to the gun crews up and down the deck who had not yet noticed. Cahill's voice could be heard above the rest, ordering, "Reload, runout, and cease fire! Boat crews and boarding teams to the entry port. Bring the boats around."

Tisbit appeared next to Duncan, wiping black soot from his face with a white handkerchief. "I believe this is my part, Captain. May I accompany the boarders?"

"Yes, please do," Duncan replied, as relief flooded through him.

•   •   •

Less than half an hour later, a boat pulled back towards *Enchanté* with Tisbit, a French captain, and a man in civilian attire sitting on the benches. Duncan's cabin had not been reassembled yet, so he greeted them on the quarterdeck.

Tisbit said, "Captain Duncan, allow me to introduce Capitaine de Vaisseau Louis Archambeau, previously in command of *La Tempête*. The captain has given his parole, and I thought it best to remove him from his ship. Capitaine Archambeau, this is Captain Joseph Duncan of His Majesty's Ship *Enchanté*."

The French captain gave a slight bow of his head. Tisbit continued, "And this is Thaddeus Kincaid, who commands the British-owned, private brig, *Seraph*, which sails under a letter of marque and reprisal."

The man just named stepped forward and offered his hand to Duncan. "Pleasure to make your acquaintance, Captain. I hope you don't mind me joining the party without an invitation. Can't let you naval types have all the fun, can we?"

Almost two hours later, the two frigates were tied together, and the brig sailed along with them a few hundred yards away. The French prisoners had been secured aboard the prize while their officers had all given parole and moved to *Enchanté*. The rudder was still not working on *Enchanté*, but they had finally discovered the reason. Repairs were still being made, but Duncan had allowed some leniency, so most of the crew was effectively taking a break while watching the unusual work being performed to fix the rudder.

The master hobbled onto the quarterdeck with a hastily fabricated cane in his left hand and his right arm in a bright white sling. His hat was resting higher than usual atop his head as the bandages wrapped around his forehead prevented him from putting it on as usual.

"Good to see you up and about, Mr. Ellis," Duncan greeted him.

"It's quite good to be up and about, sir," Ellis responded with a chuckle.

They moved together to the rail and looked over. Jenkins and Carlson were hanging from ropes tied about their waists. Their legs were braced against the rudder, and they were using heavy iron crows to try to free the French cannonball wedged tightly in the pintle. They maneuvered and strained from different locations as they tried to find some leverage. Suddenly, the ball shifted, and Jenkins lost his grip on the crow. It flew out of his hand and splashed into the sea a few yards from the ship.

"Pusser's gonna charge you for that, Jenkins!" the master yelled. The assembled crew, watching the operation, erupted in laughter.

"I'll gladly pay for it to have the rudder back," Duncan said good-naturedly.

"Lost in service to the ship," Lloyd said from somewhere in the crowd. "There'll be no charge for that one."

The master laughed. "Why, you've even made the pusser happy, Jenkins."

Carlson continued working from his side and finally the misshapen cannon ball popped out, allowing the rudder to settle completely down on the pintle. The wheel was spun to both extremes, and the rudder moved freely. A cheer erupted from the crew, which was repeated as Jenkins and Carlson crawled back over the railing.

"Mr. Webb, signal *Seraph* that we no longer need a nursemaid to watch over us," Duncan said. Seeing the confusion on the midshipman's face, he amended the order, "Just spell out 'thank you'."

"Oh! Aye, aye, sir," Webb responded, as he moved to the flag locker.

"If the prize crew is ready, Mr. Cahill, please cut us loose and set course for Antigua," Duncan ordered.

•   •   •

Duncan sat with Tisbit on the porch of Hirschhorn's villa while they waited for their host to complete some other business in his study and join them. They both quietly sipped wine while staring out at the afternoon sunlight glittering off the calm waters of the bay.

In the distance, *Enchanté* sat comfortably at anchor while her crew and the dockyard workers continued repairs. Her sides and rails looked like a patchwork quilt with the new, unpainted, bright wood standing out from the weathered and painted sections. *La Tempête* looked similar, but there had been fewer repairs made and there was less activity aboard her, as she awaited her fate to be decided by the prize court.

It had been two days since they limped back into port following the slow sail back from Tobago. Although the weather and wind had been favorable, the extensive damage to the ships prevented them from really taking advantage of either. Three times they had paused in the journey for Duncan to read passages from Blackwell's book of prayers and commit friends and crewmates to the sea. Fourteen had been sent over the side and five more had been transported to the shore hospital when they arrived. Beyond those, there were still almost two dozen aboard ship on light or no duty, but expected to fully recover.

As they waited for Hirschhorn, Duncan was thinking about the letters he had received from Lily. One had been waiting for him in the post and the other arrived this morning. The first had been primarily written while Lily and her family were en route and had been sent as soon as they safely disembarked. The other had been hastily written by a clearly exhausted hand when they first arrived home. Lily had not yet spoken to Duncan's sister, Anna, to tell her the news of their engagement.

Hirschhorn walked onto the porch and was handed a glass of wine by a servant, who then left them alone. He walked to the railing and looked out before turning to them. "My apologies, gentlemen, for keeping you waiting this evening, as well as for not being able to meet with you sooner. I assure you, it is not for lack of wanting. The last few days have been a veritable flurry of activity. Had not some news only just arrived, I might not have been able to meet with you for a few more days. However, events have transpired so as to make our meeting a very top priority."

He did not seem to require or expect a response, and he kept talking in his usual manner. "I gather from your reports that aside from capturing *La Tempête*, you were actually on a bit of a wild goose chase. Commodore De La Fountain was actually killed in the original engagement with *Fidelity* some months ago...although, frankly, it seems even longer ago than it has truly been."

"It had always been possible that De La Fountain was dead, or even if alive, he might know nothing of value. Really, it was considered rather a longshot that anything of value could be found with *La Tempête*. Still, we had to investigate and follow the lead. That is the way this game is played. We must follow every lead and search each possibility until we find the truth. There was no winner this time, and the game goes on."

"Game? How can you call it a game when good men died?" Duncan spoke with some heat in his voice and real pain in his heart.

"Captain, though the stakes are high, it can still be a game. If you bet a penny, a thousand guineas, or a man's life - the act of wagering makes it a gamble, not the amount. You say that good men died in this action, and I agree completely. I didn't know them as you did, but I trust that they were good men who fell."

"If I were to refer to it as an important endeavor, or great service to the Crown, both of which are accurate, would they be any less dead...or any more good? I am sorry if my reference to a game offends your sensibilities, but death is a part of war. It is a part of life, for that matter. That there were good men who died doing their duty is part of the game we must all play to protect the kingdom and end this war. I sincerely wish it were not so, but it is so, no matter what we call it."

"And what of the *Seraph*?" Tisbit interjected. "I had the decided feeling that you are deeply involved with both her existence and her appearance at Tobago."

Hirschhorn smiled thinly and took a sip of wine before answering. "Yes, my little guardian angel. I, or I really should say the Foreign Service, had her built in America and pay her crew to support our efforts."

"I thought as much," Tisbit said, glancing at Duncan. He had shared his suspicions, but there had been no proof, and the crew would offer no hints.

"To be honest, I ordered her over a year ago with only the vague concern that I might need a ship easily at my disposal when Lord Fairhurst inevitably moved from his posting here. Fearing the next commander might not be so accommodating, I took actions to ensure I could still operate effectively. It seems to have been a fortuitous prognostication and the timing of her completion really could not have been better."

"Why did you have her following us when we went to Nova Scotia?" Duncan asked.

"Ah, yes. You almost upset my plans during that trip." Hirschhorn chuckled to himself and then continued, "I had been quite fortunate in finding a captain with prior naval experience. Kincaid was a lieutenant in the Royal Navy who lacked patronage and had certain difficulties with following rules and being patient while awaiting promotion. He was, however, an exceptional seaman. I was able to convince him to leave the service and take command of *Seraph* when she was ready to outfit. He assembled the crew, and I was not involved beyond providing the coin."

"How's that related to him following us?" Tisbit asked.

"Well, I really didn't know Kincaid or the crew. I also didn't know you at first, Captain," he added, looking at Duncan. "So, it occurred to me that I could kill two birds with one stone, as it were. I could have Kincaid try to follow you, and I could see how you might react. It started on your trip to St. Kitts. I already trusted you by the time you went to Nova Scotia, but I still wanted to see how good Kincaid could be. I was quite impressed with him, but I almost underestimated you."

"So, did he follow us to Tobago or was he already there watching *La Tempête*?" Duncan inquired.

"Neither, actually. There was no longer any benefit to having him try to shadow you. On the contrary, it was, if anything, a danger to my plans. I knew where you were headed and had *Seraph* sail to Tobago to meet you there...and stay out of sight until needed. Of course, I trusted you to get the job done, but thought a bit of insurance couldn't hurt."

Duncan thought about how close the battle had been and wondered if he would be having this conversation if *Seraph* had not been there. He chose not to say anything about that, and Hirschhorn quickly changed the topic, anyway. "So, enough about *Seraph* and *La Tempête*. I have news to share that has both positive and negative aspects, but overall will be quite pleasant for me to relate and for you to hear."

He glanced at Tisbit. "Well, it might not concern you much, Major, but I'm sure you'll be interested at the very least, and it seemed best to invite you, if for no more reason than dinner will be more celebratory with more present."

"Thank you for those kind thoughts," Tisbit said sarcastically.

Hirschhorn smiled widely and looked back at Duncan. "A bit of background first, if you'll indulge me before the news. Some time ago, we had a discussion about Admiral Elliott and his benefactors, and it occurs to me that you might not fully comprehend the nuances of our government and political systems. You are, of course, familiar with the concepts of patronage in the Navy, and I presume you understand that a similar system applies to the government and civil service."

"Yes," Duncan responded simply.

"Good. So, at the very highest levels of government, a similar system applies, and is in ways more simple and in others more complex. You see, the stakes are higher and there are really only two factions - those in power and those in opposition, who wish to be in power. The individuals in each group can be fluid or switch entirely based on who is prime minister and who aligns with whom to keep them in power or overthrow them."

Duncan found this vaguely disturbing, but so far he was not surprised by anything being said, so he was silent and listened.

"These divisions and alliances can spread throughout the upper ranks of the ministries and generally down as far as positions that are based on appointment and subject to change when change occurs at the top. So, whereas what we call a 'career civil servant' might be in a safe position once first appointed, higher-ranking positions must always consider pleasing those in power in order to remain employed."

"I think we both know that," Tisbit said in a bored drawl.

Hirschhorn frowned at him and then said, "Some of the divisions are so stark that the representatives will oppose anything promoted by those they see as the opposition. They can be quite blind to the ramifications or likely consequences and purely see opposition as the ends rather than the means. A wonderful example now impacts you directly, Captain Duncan."

"And what exactly has happened to me?" Duncan asked, with more than a little trepidation.

"The factions in opposition to those who support Admiral Fairhurst and my divisions of the Foreign Service took it upon themselves to try to overturn your special orders when they failed to prevent your promotion. They've taken action to supersede them."

"How is that good news?" Tisbit asked, while Duncan got a sinking feeling in his stomach as he realized that he was a minor pawn in some complex political game.

"Of course, their temporary success is not ideal, but their methods have been better than anything we would have dared to attempt at this time," Hirschhorn responded. "They've come up with a way to have the Crown directly supersede the orders and bypass the Admiralty Board."

Now Duncan was confused, "What? How would they do that?"

Hirschhorn smiled like he could barely contain his glee. "They've suggested that you be given special honors by the King. Once our factions realized what was happening, they moved to support and press the idea. You are being recalled to England to be knighted and made a baronet! What's more, once the momentum built with public support based on recounts of your actions with the French convoy, our side was able to maneuver further, based on your Scottish heritage. You're to be named a member of the Most Ancient and Most Noble Order of the Thistle!"

Hirschhorn actually started to laugh, rocking back and forth in his chair. "Isn't that absolutely wonderful? I have only just today received the royal decrees and your orders recalling you, in order to be received by His Majesty for the New Year's Honors."

Duncan was stunned, and even Tisbit seemed at a loss for words. Luckily, Hirschhorn never seemed to mind talking alone, and he carried on, "Of course, I can understand you might not look forward to returning afterwards to serve under Admiral Elliott, but even he will tread more carefully around you with these honors. You could wear your Saint Andrew badge-appendant from time to time, just to remind him." He laughed again, seemingly unaware of his guests' silence.

After a while, he controlled his laugher and spoke earnestly to Duncan, "This is a great honor, but nothing more than is truly deserved. I am only so overjoyed because it was made possible by those who would have hurt you if they could. The irony is just too delicious. Admiral Fairhurst was able to make arrangements for *Enchanté* to have her lines fully taken by the Naval Surveyors. I understand this process will take several weeks, but it will allow your crew to be kept together. So, there may even be time for you to marry a certain young lady. You might have to apply for a special license, but given your current fame and high standing in society, I hardly think that would be out of the question."

It all started to sink in and Tisbit reached over and clapped him on the shoulder, "Congratulations, sir!"

Duncan smiled and mumbled a thank you to both of them before Hirschhorn herded them to the dining room for a dinner to celebrate and say goodbye until his return from England.

Three hours later, Duncan and Tisbit walked slowly down the road, somewhat uncomfortably full from the meal.

"I truly am quite happy for you, Joseph." Tisbit spoke with uncharacteristic sincerity. "Despite how it happened and how Hirschhorn explained it, you really are very deserving of the honors and I'm proud to call you my friend."

"Thank you, Jeremy," Duncan responded, touched by the words and emotion. "I look forward to seeing you when I return."

"I plan to be here. I can't imagine Hirschhorn will ever let me out of his clutches."

"I never had a chance to thank you for warning me not to react to Elliott's false charges, too."

"The what?" Tisbit asked.

"Elliott investigating me over misuse of powder and all. If it hadn't been for your warning, I probably would have lost my temper and gotten into deeper trouble. You were right about just letting it play out."

"I didn't know anything about that. I was just giving you a general warning."

Duncan looked at him to see if he was joking, but Tisbit gave no sign of it being anything less than the truth. "Well, it was even better advice than you intended, then."

"My advice is probably best when accidental," Tisbit laughed. "But I'll give you some very specific and intentional advice before your sail. Get the special license and marry Lily while you're in England. There's no telling where this war will take us or what will happen tomorrow. Find happiness whenever you can. You two deserve each other."

Duncan smiled. "That sounds like very sound advice from a very good friend."

As the sun rose and *Enchanté* sailed away from Antigua the next morning, bound for England, it seemed to Duncan like he was truly heading home.

Epilogue

A blast of cold, damp wind made him hunch his shoulders and pull his neck deeper into his upturned collar. He squinted out at the dreary dockyard through the flurries of snow and let out a breath, which instantly condensed and was whipped away by the wind. He shuffled his feet to warm them and rubbed his hands together.

"We'll have a boat ready to take you ashore soon, sir," the first lieutenant informed him.

"Thank you."

A few minutes later, he stepped toward the entry port to leave. He turned and tried to pull the collar of his scarlet uniform a bit higher as he said, "Goodbye, Captain, thank you for the ride."

"My pleasure, Major. Enjoy your time in England," the officer replied.

A short time later, he stepped from the boat onto the jetty and pulled out his watch. It was too late to find a coach today, but he would be off early in the morning. He was not in time to celebrate the honors, but he still might make it to a friend's wedding. And then he could deliver his news that they would be spending some time together again, but not in the Caribbean.

END

About the Author

Photo credit: Keith Claytor

Kent Schwendy wants to live in a world where everyone has choices, where the half-million bees he keeps never sting, and where *The Elements of Style* are always utilized.

A military veteran trained as an engineer and urban planner, Kent balances his day job as a corporate executive with his passion for writing. He believes that everyone is the sum of their experiences and seeks to create fictional characters that feel as real as possible. As a natural storyteller, he loves to explore how different perceptions can impact interpretations of events.

He lives in Connecticut with his wife, two cats, and a turtle named Zip.

Note from Kent M. Schwendy

Word-of-mouth is crucial for any author to succeed. If you enjoyed *Sailing Toward the Tempest*, please leave a review online — anywhere you are able. Even if it's just a sentence or two. It would make all the difference and would be very much appreciated.

Thanks!
Kent M. Schwendy

We hope you enjoyed reading this title from:

BLACK ❀ ROSE
writing™

www.blackrosewriting.com

Subscribe to our mailing list – *The Rosevine* – and receive **FREE** books, daily
deals, and stay current with news about upcoming
releases and our hottest authors.
Scan the QR code below to sign up.

Already a subscriber? Please accept a sincere thank you for being a fan of
Black Rose Writing authors.

View other Black Rose Writing titles at
www.blackrosewriting.com/books and use promo code
PRINT to receive a **20% discount** when purchasing.

Printed in Dunstable, United Kingdom